SIX SUNS,
TEN PLANETS,
ONE WOMAN

Dear Addie,

Come fly with me!

Till

SIX SUNS, TEN PLANETS, ONE WOMAN

By Theodore E. D. Braun

ISBN 1-58500-579-7

ABOUT THE BOOK

Christina Vasa becomes a member of Spacefleet's Extended Life Brigade. Her mission is double: fight the Militia (a terrorist organization of misguided religious fanatics opposed to scientific advances in general and in particular to the genetic engineering that makes extended life possible), and explore the galaxy for possible colony planets and for intelligent life forms.

In her adventures in other worlds, Christina will face death several times, will be charged with capital crimes, and will take part in the discovery of new worlds on which millions of Earth people will establish cities and farms. She will discover rich new worlds of biology, too, worlds in which evolution has gone down different paths than it had taken on Earth. Some of these encounters will prove to be terrifying, even life-threatening: a deadly virus, fierce jellyfish-like creatures that hunt in packs, flying creatures that devour their victims' flesh within minutes... With her crew she will fight the vicious members of the Militia, although final victory seems out of reach. But why is she arrested on Mars on returning as a hero from a successful expedition against the Militia on Mesnos?

She will finally pass through a wormhole to reach the spiral arm on the far side of the galaxy. There, at last, she will encounter the Damosians, a civilization of intelligent beings descended from warm-blooded lizards. Will this encounter be peaceful or menacing? How will people of radically different cultures and languages be able to communicate? Will the dreaded Schadite Tactical Units succeed in destroying the great ship Constellation? If they return to Earth, how will the people there accept these extra-terrestrials?

To my daughter Jeanne Velonis,
without whose sage counsel this book would have been
even more imperfect.

CHRONOLOGY OF CHAPTERS

PROLOGUE: CURIOUS BEGINNINGS

"What are you up to, Christina?"

"Well, Sven, while the other kids have gone home for the holidays, and there's some peace and quiet here, I thought I'd do something that Mr. Larsson has been trying to get me to do for over a year."

"Let's see... He wants you to imagine what Caesar would have said if he had had the courage to cross the threshold to my room. 'Alea jacta est' or 'Who threw that jacket at me?' or something like that."

"Very funny. No, he's been wanting me to get into history and more or less recent geological events. The Big Freeze that began around 2100, for starters, and the events that led to the topping of the mountains, and the unexpected results on global climate that followed."

"What a way to spend a holiday! You're working on some boring and nutty history project. At least you're doing something, though. I wanted to go skiing, but there hasn't been enough snow here in Sweden for, oh, maybe 200 or 250 years."

"Well, there's always the South Pole. That seems to be about the only place where they go skiing. But mostly, Antarctica produces lamb and mutton and milk and beef. Or so it seems. Not to mention the mines.

"Anyway, this project isn't boring. I've dug out some archival electronic newspapers, I've arranged some of the headlines in order, and I've bundled them for Mr. Larsson, so he can see I've been doing something worth while. If you're good, I'll let you rummage through them."

"What do you mean, good?"

"Well, no lousy jokes. Be serious. Imagine you'll be getting yourself ready to become a cadet in Spacefleet Academy."

"You've got to be kidding! No star stuff for me! I'm going to be a lawyer, then maybe a politician. World President, maybe. Just think, some day you'll be able to say that you knew President Sven Svenson when he was 16."

"OK, it'll be great to brag like that, but Mr. World President,

xi

if you don't know your world history you'll be kicked out of office and find yourself on your rear in the street up there in the capital, right in the middle of Quito! So, if you promise to behave, I'll let you in on some of the secrets of the past."

"All right, I'll be on my best behavior."

Christina wasn't sure what Sven's best behavior was. Like the other orphans in the school, the ones totally bereft of family, like her for that matter, it had taken some time, over two years in fact, for this tall 16-year-old to come to grips with his new situation in life and to learn to get along with the other kids. Sven's way of dealing with difficulty was to make a joke out of everything. Christina was much younger when her entire family was wiped out by the Militia during a family reunion back in 2509, nine years ago, when she was a little girl of seven. She had been sullen and withdrawn for over a year, and if it had not been for Mrs. Larsson, her housemother then and now, she might have slipped into darkness. She hated the Militia with a burning passion, only slowly extinguishing it by degrees and by intervals. They had taken her family from her —her mother, her father, her sister, her cousins and her aunts and uncles and grandparents, everyone. She survived because she was going to the bathroom in the basement toilet! The explosion wiped out the house, the yard, everything. Somehow, the debris had not fallen on her. A wall or something must have kept it off her. The perpetrators were never caught, and it was never clear why the Militia chose the peace-loving Vasa family as its target. What had they ever done to deserve such treatment?

Her eyes darkened, her face grew somber. She'd not had this kind of thought lately. Nor had Sven ever seen this side of her. She was a serious, studious, but cheerful and generally happy 16-year-old. Gloom and Christina were polar opposites–the antipodes, as she liked to say.

"What's with you?" he asked. "All of a sudden, you're a different person."

"Sven, I'm sorry. I don't like to get gloomy, at least not in public. But with you I know it's not really in public. It's just that the thought of the horrible day when my family was totally destroyed hit me like a hammer. Maybe that's why I've tried to avoid thinking about the past, or looking into it."

"Do you want to talk about it? Or maybe we should just look at the stuff you put together for Mr. Larsson? Or, if you can't do that now, maybe do something fun, like virtual skiing? Oops—sorry. Didn't mean to be flippant."

"Actually, I'd rather not talk about that awful day now. And I'm kind of glad you've not lost your light-hearted touch. Let's take a look at the package."

"A virtual package. Virtual newspapers."

Capetown Times*, 2 January 2110.*

WORLD AUTHORITIES WORRY ABOUT UNEXPECTED FREEZE

According to scientists meeting here, the Earth might be in for a long deep freeze. While no one has yet found a cause, the Earth has been cooling down rapidly for a full decade, dropping $1°$ a year in average temperature after over a century of warming due to the Greenhouse Effect.

"The Greenhouse Effect? And wow! a degree a year!"

"That was what happened when too many pollutants in the atmosphere trapped the heated air, preventing it from escaping. It wasn't until the oceans really heated up until people took things seriously and tried to reverse the effect. Maybe they went too far, or maybe something else happened to cool things down, but it was scary: human life on Earth was threatened."

"I guess other forms of life, too."

The Buenos Aires Gazette*, 18 June 2199.*

GLACIERS ADVANCE IN EUROPE, ASIA, NORTH AMERICA AND GREENLAND, ANTARCTICA, AND TIERRA DEL FUEGO

Glaciers will invade mainland Argentina and Chile within five years, according to scientists meeting in Buenos Aires. The Big Chill looks like the worst ice age ever to hit Earth. A leading authority claims that

New Dehli News, *22 August 2200*

FUTURE ONE SPACE STATION BEGUN

Construction in outer space has begun on the orbiting space station called Future One. "This will take at least 15 years," said Natalie Juillet, chief space scientist of the Earth Scientific Mission in Grenoble. Dr. Juillet refused to speculate on the exact mission of the station, saying only that it is expected to be incredibly large, the size of a small town of some 10,000 inhabitants and that it will be in permanent stationary orbit about 1500 km above Earth.

The multidenominational Primitivist religious group has long opposed plans to erect such a station. "God does not want human beings to live in such a place," said Deacon Ibn-Youssef. "We will oppose

Le Monde, *8 November 2250*

ANTIMATTER WEAPON UNVEILED; WILL DEFEND EARTH AGAINST ALIENS, SAYS PRESIDENT

President Moineau disclosed today that Earth Scientific Mission has created a weapon intended to destroy any hostile alien invaders. The matter/antimatter device is intended to deter the apparent threat from an alien race gathering its forces near Jupiter, on the side of the planet hiding it from Earth observation posts.

"Antimatter weapons! Alien invasion forces! Are these grown-ups talking?" Sven couldn't help acting out a little scene of invading forces and brave Earth soldiers repelling them. "Zap!"

"Sven, be serious. Sure, it turned out to be a hoax brilliantly perpetrated by a group of bored Future One cosmonauts. But it looked real. Anyway, the antimatter gun is what was used to blast off the tops of the Himalayas at the level of the Tibetan Plateau, and later of virtually every mountain on Earth over half that altitude."

"You want me to be serious? OK, here I am, Textbook Sven, in my flat textbook voice. 'Geologists reasoned as early as the 1990s that the Himalaya Mountain range was driving Earth's climate, preventing warm and moist air from moving north into Eastern Siberia. A century later, scientists calculated that removing the tops of the Himalayas would restore the climate of the Earth to that prevailing about the year 2000. Unfortunately, political decisions overrode purely scientific ones, and as mountain top after mountain top evaporated, each small cause brought about unforeseen and immense effects. The Earth overheated, the ice caps melted all over the globe in less than a century, islands fell below sea level, coastal regions flooded. Much of the population fled to newly warmed areas of central Asia, North America, and Antarctica.'"

"Bravo! You learned your lesson so well! I'm proud of you. So we'll skip a few of these newspapers, the ones that talk about that stuff. But I think there's some info you don't have."

London Times, *7 June 2301*

ANTIMATTER GUNS DESTROY TWO HIMALAYA PEAKS; VAST AMOUNTS OF ENERGY RELEASED, SENT TO FUTURE ONE FOR STORAGE

The first two Himalaya peaks were destroyed in remote parts of Nepal yesterday, disappearing before the eyes of amazed onlookers. Dr. Hélène Cruche explained that antimatter beams reacted with the matter of the mountains, causing a reaction in which both matter and antimatter were converted to an enormous amount of energy. The energy has been sent to Future One, which will become a kind of huge battery. The same technology that has made the direction of movement of the released energy possible will be used in the future to help create the conditions necessary for life on Venus and Mars, according to Dr. Cruche.

"Holy jalapeña! That's hot news! No, seriously, I mean it, I didn't realize that that's where the energy needed to fuel Aphrodite and Ares came from, or is coming from."
"And that's not all. Look at this."

Tokyo Sun, *7 June 2401*

PRIMITIVIST MILITIA FORMED IN GREENLAND AS FIRST GALACTIC SPACE EXPLORATION BEGINS

In a daringly public and visucapsuled Sermon in the Valley, an anonymous organizer of a militant branch of the Primitivist religious group has established a Militia, whose charge it is to destroy the scientific advances of the past several centuries. The mystery leader, calling himself The Deacon, speaking outdoors to a gathering of thousands of followers, denounced as the work of Satan the three space stations currently in operation, Aphrodite near Venus, Future One near Earth, and Ares near Mars. He also denounced the launch of the space exploration and the planned creation of an Extended Life Brigade, volunteers whose lives will be extended by about 200 years thanks to a genetic procedure developed by Dr. Stanley Narb, who has carried out the initial experiment on himself. It is not clear what actions, if any, the Militia will undertake in their opposition to Earth Government policies.

"Well, what do you think Mr. Larsson will say when he sees this? Do you think he'll see a future Ensign Vasa in me? For that matter, do I have what it takes? I understand that the Space Fleet demands intelligence, initiative, endurance, and strength."

"He'll love this stuff! And, hey, you're smart, imaginative, persevering, and pretty tough. I think you can do anything you set out to do, except virtual skiing. I spied on you that day you tried it. Are you ever a loser at that!"

"You dirty rat! I was supposed to be doing my thing in complete and absolute privacy. How did you sneak in and spy on me? I ought to bop you one!"

"Actually, I'm quasi innocent in this. I happened to be around when–OK, I had sneaked in to the gym, but honest, it wasn't to spy on you. I wanted to get in an extra hour of virtual skiing on the sly, but then I heard the door open. I hid as best I could, almost in the open, but you didn't see me. But I saw you break your legs five times in a row! I almost couldn't control myself–you looked so downhearted, so beaten. You should have seen your face!"

"You know, when you run for World President, I'm going to reveal your two-faced, cheating, lying ways. I'll..."

A tall middle-aged woman came softly into the lounge, with a holiday cake for the kids–"her" kids–who had no home to go to, literally no family at all. "My goodness, it sounds like an argument! What's going on?"

"Oh, it's nothing, Mrs. Larsson. Chris was just showing me a surprise package of old media clips she's put together for Mr. Larsson, and we were just carrying on like idiots."

Christina glared at him. He knew how much she hated being called Chris or or any other nickname! And now he's blabbed her secret surprise to Mrs. Larsson! "Don't tell him about it, please!" she begged with a whiny tone of voice. "I'll let you see the package if you promise not to tell."

THE SERMON IN THE VALLEY
6 JUNE 2401

Brothers and Sisters, we are gathered here today to consider embarking on a new adventure, one that is fraught with danger and possible pain, even death; but an adventure in righteousness, which has the sanction of Almighty God! But before we decide whether to follow the straight and narrow path to glory, we should see what has brought us to this bifurcation, this parting of the ways.

As you know, our all-knowing government leaders, our *World*-Government leaders, a hundred years ago this very day, put into effect a decision they had made a decade earlier. God, in his almighty justice, had begun to punish the sinners of the earth by inflicting upon them a renewal of the cycle of ice ages. Already, from about 2100 onward, the glaciers began to reform and to cover the northern and even the southern areas of the Earth, going within a century deep into Canada, Scandinavia, Siberia, Alaska, and even beginning in Tierra del Fuego and Patagonia, not to mention the Falkland Islands. Ocean currents were changing; animal and plant life was abandoning the upper latitudes; temperatures dropped by a calamitous 5 degrees in a century. But still our secular leaders, and the leaders of our major religions, refused to see in this new plague a punishment for the godlessness of the world's nations. Instead, they got together and tried to sidestep Almighty God's plans by building the first of a projected five sinful space stations, above the azure sky of Earth. Future One they called it. Future One! It was blessed by an assemblage of the leaders of the 20 most populous religions! Blessed? No, rather cursed! What blasphemy! *(Blasphemy, yes! Tell it to them, Brother!)* And today the first manned exploration of the galaxy has been undertaken, with the goal of colonizing planets we have never seen, and of establishing contact with intelligent species that neither the Bible nor any other fundamental book of religion mentions.

You remember the events of that cruel ungodly day a century ago, in 2301, a day the history books tell us ushered in the greatest era in human history. *(Yes, we do, Brother!)* We have all been forced to learn those events that have cloaked the human race in ignominy ever since, as though we should be proud of them! The first massive destruction of God's creation ever attempted on such a scale, a scale, Brothers and Sisters, unimaginable! The first of the Himalayan peaks obliterated, with all but four elevations above 4,500 meters eventually destroyed! Were our glorious leaders satisfied with this profanation? *(No, Brother, no, they weren't!)* You're right, Brothers and Sisters, they were not! Individual nations chose to level every mountain at the 3,500 meter level! The Alps, the Pyrenees, the Rockies, the Olympics, the Andes, and others yet! Almighty God was disturbed by his creatures' iniquities, and he visited upon them a second flood! *(Praise be the power of the Lord!)* In less than 10 years, the progress of the glaciers was not only reversed, but almost every trace of ice had disappeared from Antarctica and Greenland! The waters rushed towards the skies, engulfing islands and coastal plains, burying in the briny deep the homes of literally two billion people! Did our secular leaders care? *(No!)* They did not! They called the catastrophe a mere error of calculation, and persuaded our forebears to believe that this small error could produce such a large effect.

We know the real consequences of this "miscalculation," Brothers and Sisters: deaths from drowning, financial ruin, mass displacements of populations, the creation of an even more powerful and more secular Earth government, a change in climate that no one had anticipated, not even the servants of God themselves. The tropics spread north and south, the temperate zones have by now reached the very poles! With a more watery Earth, there's more rain, very few of the beautiful deserts are left. The once frozen tundra of Antarctica, Alaska, Canada, Greenland, and Siberia are today fertile lands, while the jungle has moved out to the once peaceful cities and farmlands of the world! The geography of the Earth has been altered, forever! And once again, our so-called leaders have refused to see the light! But their sins go deeper still, and there seems to be no end to their iniquity and their abominations. *(Death to the killers! Death to the blasphemers!)*

I have discovered, Brothers and Sisters, that on that huge space craft that you and I helped pay for—yes! we helped pay for it by paying taxes and being good citizens! —on that space craft there are several people whose genetic structure has been altered, contrary to the will of God. Listen closely to what I say, for you will hear that after trying to play God in space they are now trying to replace him in time. Oh, the abomination! On that space craft there are people to whom the powers that be on this Earth have given an extension of life. No, not a year, not a decade, not fifty years, Brothers and Sisters, but a full two centuries, yea, 200 additional years or more, counting from the day of their evil operation! *(Monsters!)* Monsters, yes; and these monsters will go forth in the name of humanity, and will make contact with whatever alien civilizations God in his infinite wisdom might have put on another planet, far enough away so that the twain would never meet. What representatives of humanity! Monsters who live inordinately long lives and who have been rendered infertile by the very operation that extends their lives. *(Monsters!)*

Who will these creatures meet? Let us assume for a moment that there indeed are intelligent beings elsewhere. Would they be, like the children of Adam and Eve, nay, like Adam and Eve themselves, made in the image of the Lord? Or would they be slithering serpents, made in the image of Satan? If Almighty God had wanted us to meet such beings, he would have told us about them in his sacred texts. They must therefore be not his children, but the children of his eternal enemy. And those who seek them out can only be fools, unbelievers! In Psalms 13, the Prophet sings: "The fool says to himself, 'There is no God!' Their conduct is all corruption and perversity, not one does good!" And these are our leaders! Down with the infidels!

3

(Down with the infidels!)

That space craft–you've seen the images–has flown rapidly out of sight. It may be too late for us to alter anything about that one missive from hell, but we can do something about the future! We can prevent the training of future space explorers! *(We can!)* We can prevent the hybridization of our kind! *(We can!)* We can reverse the evil political system spawned by the godless servants of Satan, who would like nothing more than to introduce Satan's sons and daughters to the Earth, the better to pollute the air we breathe and the moral code to which we adhere! *(We can!)* And to prevent this from happening we must take up arms against them! *(We must!)* We must infiltrate their ranks and corrode them from within! *(From within!)* Yes, an injection of the pure blood of the followers of Almighty God's justice will act like a poison in the venomous veins of the evil ones! *(Justice! Justice!)* We must serve Almighty God and spread his sacred word throughout the Earth, and even into the space stations! Into Future One, into Aphrodite, into Ares! *(We must!)* We must wage a holy war against the ungodly! *(War! War!)*

Nor are we alone, Brothers and Sisters: concerned persons of other religions, who are no less servants of the living God than we, are at this moment meeting around the world! A council of Elders has been formed, and those churches that agree to a program of concerted action will form a Sacred Alliance to Reclaim the Truth! As representatives of the true believers among our Judeo-Christian faiths, we are in a position to do the work of the Lord and to become leaders in the fight against the forces of Satan! Brothers and Sisters, Sisters and Brothers, our choice is clear: not join the enemy OR fight them, but join the enemy TO fight them! *(Fight the forces of Satan!)* We must go underground, and we must be strong. Perhaps our struggle will take centuries, perhaps we who are now here will not be present when the Lord is vindicated, but we will prevail! *(We will! We will!)* Are you for God, or for Satan? *(God! God! God!)*

4

If you agree to join with us, Brothers and Sisters, rise and repeat after me: "I swear my solemn vow *(I swear my solemn vow)* to resist the godless enemy *(to resist the godless enemy)*, to fight for the justice of Almighty God *(to fight for the justice of Almighty God)*, to reverse the progress *(to reverse the progress)* of the infamous World Government *(of the infamous World Government)*; and to this end *(and to this end)* I pledge my honor *(I pledge my honor)*, my fortune *(my fortune)*, my very life *(my very life)*, so help me God! *(so help me God!)*"

APHRODITE

In all her 143 years, Christina had never seen anything quite as opulent as this. The great hall in the ancient space station Aphrodite was made as spiffy as can be, walls all agleam, the colorful World Government flag—a blue field with bright swatches of red, orange, and yellow—and bunting in evidence, some of the top brass of Space Fleet on hand, and of course the President of the World Government and a large delegation. No worry: although her mission was purely scientific, and normally a relatively small staff of scientists, security, and support personnel, with some families, lived and worked here, Aphrodite could actually support a population of over 10,000. Of course, without land only minimal hydroponic agriculture was possible, and it was pretty expensive to feed even a small population. But the project was worth it.

Christina was always amazed and, yes, thrilled, when she had some duty on Aphrodite or its identical twin, Ares. Aphrodite's mission was mind-boggling: make Venus livable! And Ares's mission was equally mind-boggling: make Mars livable! Although she was brilliant in galactic navigation and galactic astronomy, and had learned an enormous amount about computer technology and space ship drives (what else do you do during these long and essentially boring flights between space stations and a colonial planet?), she had only vague ideas about the biochemistry of Earth and the chemical and physical geography of Venus and Mars. But she did understand that tremendous progress had been made in cooling down Venus by destroying, over more than three centuries, its thermal cover. Once it became possible to grow plants there, scientists calculated that within a century colonization could begin! Where would the water come from, though? And is the soil really able to hold and to nourish roots?

The problem on Ares was the reverse: **create** a greenhouse effect, and somehow keep whatever atmosphere is created in place: the weaker gravity of Mars could cause problems. But in a way, Mars was the easier problem to solve, and already the first hardy volunteers were there, living on the planet. The mission of Ares was to monitor the progress of the greening of the planet, and to find ways to speed it up. Rivers and lakes and seas were already realities there, and Mars wore a green belt around its belly! The Martian equatorial zone was now about as warm as the Earth polar zones, or about what the Earth felt in its temperate zones back in 2100 or so. The colonists' farms made them self-sufficient, and their cities were growing. It was expected that the average temperatures would continue rising there.

"Don't you think this is stupendous, Boris? I mean, all the pomp aside, maybe we're here to celebrate some breakthrough like they had on Mars a few decades back, before you were born," she said, poking Lieutenant Smirnoff in the ribs.

"Okay, old girl, I take your point. Yes, there **is** something awesome in this. It makes you realize the majesty of God. Just think of it: we're not only flying (if that's the word) to distant stars and planets, but God has chosen us to make two lifeless planets livable, after more than four and a half billion years! We travel incredible distances in the infinity of Creation, and we learn the secrets of the universe. We reverse natural processes in macroworlds, and in the microworlds of the human genes we create wonders like you longies (if you'll pardon my using that term). Science and religion working together!" He was clearly excited by this thought, which coincided with his religious beliefs and his professional training.

"You know, I've always wondered about you. You have this kind of fundamentalist belief in the word of the Bible, but somehow you reconcile a mostly literal interpretation with a zeal for the work we do. The Primmies would do well to listen to you: maybe their fanatical Militia could act like loyal citizens. Just before we left Earth, the Deacon had struck again, destroying all the research on a new Constellation; they have to start from scratch."

Boris thought for a moment, then said, "Christina, the Militia has it all wrong, and some of the Primitivists do, too. I don't see any contradiction between the Scriptures and..."

His sentence was interrupted by the sound of music.

Everyone rose to their feet, including the entire crew (a thousand people, more or less) of Constellation, their space ship and the jewel of Space Fleet. The whole population of Aphrodite must have come out for this event, and a large delegation from Earth. The Governor of Aphrodite and her entourage entered amid general applause. Then came the President, accompanied by advisers and Captain Valence. Governor Kyo welcomed the crowd to the Space Station (which she reminded them was once called Future One), and proudly introduced her staff and the leaders of the various scientific and military units. The task of introducing the President fell to Captain Allegretto, who gave a little speech he could not possibly have written himself: he despised politics, didn't like politicians, and here he is singing the praises of President Selim. Boris's elbow found its mark, Christina's rib cage. They had a hard time keeping serious looks on their faces. Finally, the President spoke. "Now we'll find out what this is all about," she whispered, perhaps to herself.

We have asked you to come here today, on 6 June 2645, millions of kilometers from Earth, to what can only be described as one of the marvels of human ingenuity, to announce an event that might change the life all of us will have in the future. I'm speaking about ordinary people, people with an ordinary 125-year life expectancy. What our Extended Life Brigade will experience is science fiction to us. But I have news that I'm sure will thrill all of you. You know our mission here: I have no need to repeat it to this gathering. But here's the best kept secret of the century: we're almost 100 years ahead of schedule! Just 325 years ago today operations began on Aphrodite with a faith in the future that was unparalleled in the history of humankind: we projected a 500-year mission to convert Venus into a twin sister of Earth. It was anticipated that, if everything went well, by 2695 to 2720 plant life would be solidly established and growing–maybe even evolving–on the surface of Venus, and that by 2820 the first colonists would settle on the planet. Governor Kyo and I can report today that in each of five separate areas of 1,000,000 hectares plant life is established abundantly, and water is flowing plentifully. I don't dare claim that we have created Eden, but the gardens of Venus are now realities.

While it is still far too hot for long-term human occupation, we are confident that human life will be established on the surface by well before 2720, and at the present rate of progress, even before this century ends.

At that moment, as the huge throng rose to its feet in applause, a red bolt just missed the President and the Governor and struck down Captain Valence. A voice was heard over the speakers: "Thus God smites those who defile him!"

The Militia!

"Boris, I mean Lieutenant Smirnoff, get our squad together and arrange for the others to move quickly. We'll meet at the back door of the hall in 10 minutes."

"Yes, Commander!"

Pandemonium seemed to spread in the hall. The Governor and the President were whisked away to safety. As acting Captain, Christina sprang into action, checking on the condition of Valence, having the Station Security clear the hall and get the people to their posts and their living quarters, and in general taking charge of the situation, while Boris was getting the Constellation crew to begin sweeping the immediate area of the hall for the Militia. "How's the Captain?" she asked the presidential physician.

"Dead. He didn't have a chance. The shot was intended for the Governor or the President, though: the Militia's been aiming at the President for years, and they hold this station in abomination. I'm afraid they'll try to destroy it."

"We'll do our best to prevent that from happening. I'm going to join my crew who will try to root out the perpetrators. You and the officials should have a communicator to keep in touch with me; I'm on channel 5." She raced towards the back of the hall.

Boris was already there, with the squad: three quadrants and three triads of the most experienced people on the Constellation. No need to go into detail with them about what to do: they'd been through this more than once together.

"Cardeño, take your quadrant to the left, oh, and take Lewis's triad. Mahari's quadrant and Chou's triad, check down these corridors to the right. Lieutenant Smirnoff will lead you. Keep in touch every half hour. The rest of you, come with me."

———

Cardeño was an experienced leader. He knew how to keep his soldiers quiet while they worked on operations like this. He thrived on Christina's organization of the security operations on board. Small, self-reliant groups of three or four people, working as teams. A combination of clear chain of command with strong leaders and room for personal initiative on the part of every soldier. Everyone liked her style. She often came, unlike the other senior officers, to pop open a bottle of ale with them.She seemed to care about them. And was she ever smart! She seemed to be able to figure out what the enemy was doing even before they did themselves. How did she do it?

The seven men and women went through their well-drilled routines, room after room, corridor after corridor, with occasional repeat visits, "just in case," as the Commander liked to say. Nothing. Just empty spaces. Now they were working their way cautiously to a rendez-vous spot. Suddenly, they heard a sound in an adjacent room. Something knocked over, something small. Cardeño looked at Lewis; he jerked his head up and to the left, indicating the door. Lewis and her triad paused, then burst in. Empty! But they heard something. Just a pile of rags on the floor. "Carlita, look!The rags are moving!" What was it? Maybe a robotic weapon. Can't be too careful. It moved again. Lewis went towards it, getting to what she assumed was the back of the robot or whatever it was. Six guns were trained on it. With a sudden motion, Lewis lifted up the cloth. A kitten! It was terrified, the poor thing! "It's just a kit..." Lewis could not finish her sentence: a red bolt came out of a ventilation shaft, hitting her in the leg. The kitten was a lure, like bait on a hook to catch a fish! And we took the bait. What fools we are!

"Pépé and Xin-wan, take Carlita to the medics; she'll need help. When you get there, report to Commander Vasa. We're going after the sneaks."

———

Meanwhile, Boris went in the other direction with Mahari, Chou and their groups. They fanned out cautiously: this is the direction the bolts came from. working in twos, they examined every cranny, every room, every closet. A canny operator, Boris made sure that even large vents were checked. They doubled back to make random checks at already-cleared rooms and areas. Nothing.

"Well, crew, we'd better get back to the Commander. Let's go! I'm sure she can use our help."

———

Christina knew this Station like the back of her hand. It was configured exactly like Ares. Between the two Stations, she must have combed every nook ten times over. And she had a great sense of direction, as well as a photographic memory of places she'd been to.

"The perpetrators have been contained in this level," she told her squad. "This makes our task easier in one sense, but more dangerous in another: we don't have to worry about 20 stories of areas to look at, but we will be confronting cornered rats. It's hard to know what they'll do, and we don't even know how many of them there are. We'll have to be alert at all times. I sense danger ahead."

They performed their routine checks, then came upon a group of about 15 Militia men and women trying to find a way out of an exterior corridor. Outside, Venus and its now pale blue sky, with wisps of white and grey clouds. No time for that. "Drop your weapons, and surrender!" Christina ordered. They turned around, startled. One laser gun, another, a third fell to the floor. Then one Militia man opened up his vest. His torso was encircled with explosives. What was his game?

"One more step, longie, one more word, and we'll all be out there, maybe falling to Venus, maybe exploding into pieces as we go into space."

12

"Move away from that wall, or..."

"Or what? Or you'll shoot me and make sure your patsies get blown up with us?"

"Or I'll do what I can to prevent you from doing what you want to do. You others, come here, one by one, with your hands up in the air. Maria, Misha, get your soldiers to frisk them and secure them."

The Militia personnel who had thrown down the weapons stepped forward. A red bolt felled one. "Shot by one your own men!" cried Misha. You can't even trust each other!" Those were the last words he spoke: a red bolt found its mark.

Christina fired a blast not at the killer, but at the legs of the body bomber. He cried in pain, then said, "Julie, you know what to do!"

Julie worked fast. Just before Maria's bolt hit her, she fired at the bomber, igniting the bombs. The blast was terrifying. Christina managed to find a secured post, and held her breath. The vacuum of space almost instantaneously sucked out the Militia members, then all of her crew! She quickly pulled down her oxygen mask and called Boris. "Boris! I'm in sector 45. Hole in the outer wall. Everyone gone but me. Need help fast."

"We'll be there right away, Commander!"

Boris and his squad ran to the area. "There's a kind of anteroom between us and the Commander. Quick! Mahari! Fasten this rope to something secure in there. Then everyone get back here. I'll go in the room, use it as a kind of air lock."

"Still there, Christina?"

"Yeah, but I don't have much strength left. And I see Maria's wedged under a table. She needs help."

"One at a time."

While speaking, Boris closed the door tight, then tied the rope around his middle, keeping enough at the end for one person. He pulled down his oxygen supply. Then he opened the door to the outer corridor. He was hurtled forward, then snapped back, held in place by the rope. Through the pain he felt in his back and waist, he could see Christina a few paces away. He struggled to his feet, attached the rope around her waist, and pulled against the force on Nature herself, back into the anteroom. He closed the door. "Quick! Pull her outside! I'm going back for Maria!"

This time he was prepared for the force of the vacuum, and was able to get to Maria. Can't tell if she's alive. No time for her oxygen mask. Get her back to the room. Another struggle with Nature. He closed the door, pulled down Maria's oxygen mask, called out. Everything turned black.

———

Corporal Chou was a small man, with a wiry build, a broad sense of humor, and a fierce loyalty to the Security team. "Damn it all," he said, "somebody's going to pay for this! Those are our friends who have been killed and wounded. Lieutenant Smirnoff, with your permission, I'd like to go with my triad on a search mission. The killers can't have gotten too far: everything's locked down tight. We'll find a way to lure them out of hiding."

"Permission granted. Make sure you check back every half hour on Security Channel 2. Cardeño, your crew can help me get the Commander and Private Mwambi to the Medical Unit. Mahari, we'll need your quadrant for protection. I think they're after Commander Vasa and all the ELBs."

"Yes, sir," they answered in unison, and the grim party began to make its way toward the elevators. On the way, Boris called headquarters to let them know what had occurred.

Although Chou was full of anger at this time, his mind operated in a perfectly rational manner. Some called him reckless, but none called him rash. He knew he would expose himself to danger, to death, but there was no other way to smoke out those cowardly bastards. His plan was simple. He would enter rooms, alcoves, and closets alone, with Brown and Gillian just outside and with weapons drawn, offering himself as a target. He would rely on his agility to get out of the way if he saw them ready to fire; Brown and Gillian would rush in and do the rest.

In the sixth room, he thought he had heard a noise. Where was it? Must be behind that door. Closet? Bathroom? Better check it out. He moved in a crouch, silent as a cat about to

14

pounce on a mouse, then threw the door open. Nothing. Damn it to hell! Wait. Shower stall. What's that there? Down on the floor; creep slowly; grab that curtain. Now!

"Get up, you craven..." It was a dummy! I'm in trouble now. I know I heard a noise, so I know someone's in here. If they didn't know I was here before, they know now. Shouldn't've yelled. Brown, Gillian, a beer for each of you if you get me out of this. Still, I'd better check the linen closet. I'll open it up. Damn! Nothing! Uh, oh, I see in the mirror they've spotted me. Jig's up, Chou.

"Get out of there, Corporal, so we can kill you quick."

"You guys like to operate as sneaks, don't you? You knock off the Captain. How did you miss the President? Did you skip class the day they taught you to hold your hands still when you fire?"

"Very funny. Maybe you'll get a job as a stand-up comic in Hell. If you come out now, we'll kill you painlessly. If you make us risk our lives, you'll die by degrees."

"You also set up the cat trick, huh? Shot Sergeant Lewis, huh? You'll be sorry to learn that she's okay. And by the way, my count so far shows that you've lost everyone but you. Fifteen to six. Not good odds."

"So what? We missed the President, but we got that longie. Did you know he was a longie, your dear Captain Allegretto?"

So these **were** the killers of Captain Allegretto and the people who shot Sergeant Lewis. "Have you ever tried fighting fairly? You know, out in the open, equal opportunity killing? Come on in, one at a time. I'll wait until you see me, then I'll shoot. Just make sure your gun is set at Kill. I don't stun easily."

"Don't try to trick us, Stargazer. We've got a bomb ready to roll in the bathroom. It paralyzes you and puts you in tremendous pain. You feel yourself dying. I saw it used once in a demo with a captured longie. Great fun."

One of them saw, out the corner of her eye, someone running in from the hallway behind them. She turned to shoot, but too late. "Here's to you, Militia murderers!" It was Gillian. Two of them. Two bolts, both on target.

15

AFTERMATH

Sergeant Lewis was lying in the hospital bed. "Damn!" she said. When can I get up and walk again?"

The surgeon replied, "We had to rebuild your shin bone, recreate some ligaments, restore muscles, reestablish the nerves, repair the third-degree burns on the skin, and after two days of consciousness in a hospital bed you want to get up and move around?"

"Well, I'm a person of action. I've never been able to sit or lie still. Give me a break!"

"Okay. I'll tell you what. We'll begin physical therapy tomorrow. If you make good enough progress, you'll be able to continue your treatments on board Constellation, when she leaves. But that won't be for a while."

"Why? What's up?"

"For one thing, after Captain Allegretto's assassination, Commander Vasa and Private Mbwami suffered from oxygen privation. They've pretty well recovered by now."

"How long was I out? Must've been some time."

"Just a day. And we helped Nature along, so we could operate while Aphrodite was stabilized."

"Stabilized? What do you mean?"

———

"Someone find out what's causing this swaying! We can't bear too much of it, and it seems to be getting worse."

"Ms. Governor, we've just received word that part of the exterior wall has been blown out by the Militia. A kind of hara-kiri. Fifteen of them were sucked out into space. We lost five Constellation crew members."

"What can be done?"

"We've sent an emergency crew there to seal off the area on the inside. A space walk will be needed to recover Aphrodite's skin. Repair crew is at the ready; we're getting the alloy out there."

17

"This wobble can knock us out of orbit if we don't watch out. Get the engine crew to begin some countersteering maneuvers. I'll be there to join them after I've checked out security and taken a look at the casualties."

"Yes, ma'am. We'll get at it right away."

Governor Kyo found President Selim in the sick bay, making sure that everything possible was being done for the wounded. He was particularly interested in assuring the lives of the two prisoners, and in isolating them in secure facilities. When they were stronger, he wanted to attend the formal interrogation. This was, after all, his area of expertise. Before going into politics in a big way, he'd risen to number one spy in Space Security at the age of 30! He was a man of great intelligence and of proven courage (just as Captain Allegretto had said in introducing him).

"How do these people do it? This Constellation crew is something else. In less than an hour, they mopped up the bastards. It's a good thing they were able to capture a couple of them. I can't wait to get my hands on them!" he said to the Governor as she entered. "Did we lose anybody? And what's going on with the Station?"

"There's been extensive damage to the outer shell: a 7-meter hole ripped in the side. Twenty deaths in all, five of them ours. Lieutenant Smirnoff saved the lives of Commander Vasa and Private Mbwami, who couldn't have held out too much longer. Another crew member, Sergeant Lewis, was shot in the leg. We're trying to save it now."

"And the wobble?"

"I've got the engineers working on that on two fronts: first, find a way to fight the force of space, if we can determine a pattern of waves causing the wobble. I have a couple of superb mathematicians on it right now. Second, a repair crew is about to go outside and put on a temporary skin. With luck, that will be finished in eight to ten hours. Within a week we'll have it good as new."

"Congratulations to everyone involved, Magita."

An official handed the Governor a note. She read it quickly, then said, "I've been assured that the two oxygen-deprived people are stable. No loss of brain power. We're in luck there.

Commander Vasa has been here so often, I feel I've gotten to know her. She's an extraordinary person."

"You know she's in the ELB, don't you?"

"No, I didn't. She's never mentioned it. No one else has, either."

"Maybe she doesn't want to be gaped at as though she's a freak. There are ten or so ELBs on board Constellation now, but we'll increase that number. Given all the time they spend in space, we need a core of people who just don't age. Especially with our next mission, as soon as we can get things straightened out with this damn Militia business."

"May I ask what that mission is, or is this a secret?"

"Actually, you'll be part of that mission, in charge of it, in fact. We're planning on going further than we've ever tried to go before, to the far side of the galaxy."

"You mean, the other arm? But that means somehow going around the core, the black hole, the antimatter escaping. And the time! Not everyone's an ELB!"

"No, but we have found several wormholes that will allow us to travel at well beyond the speed of light. You techies really understand all of that stuff; I only know what I'm told. But it will be dangerous. We don't know if the crew can survive the pressures there. One of your tasks will be to find the right crew. We had expected Captain Allegretto to take charge. But now..."

His voice trailed off. He tried not to seem overly concerned about the death of this well-regarded officer, just as he always tried not to show how deeply he cared for everyone he got to know. Not your average politician, even less your average chief interrogator.

"Damn Militia!"

———

Blurry lights. Two ovals, no spheres, no ovals. Awfully bright. Stars? Let's see. Ah... what's holding me down? Where am I? Oh, I remember. Everything blacked out. Boris saved my life! Did he get to Maria? Where's Maria? She tried to say something. All that came out was "Mmmff. I, waaaan;" but that was enough to bring a nurse to her side.

"How are you? How do you feel?"

Big light brown glob. Gotta focus. Oh, it's a nurse. I'll tell her I'm okay, except for a pounding headache.

"Ahmokayhedpoudsnhurts" is what the nurse heard. Christina could see the two lights clearly now. She was in the sick bay. A nurse was at her side. She smiled, then drifted off to sleep, glad to be alive.

She and Maria were up and about the next day. "All tests negative." Strange way to say that you're in perfect shape. They went to see Carlita, just as the doctor was leaving her.

"How's the patient, doctor?"

"Given all the damage that's been done to her leg, I think our team was fortunate to save it. With enough rest and the right kind of rehabilitation, she'll be as good as new. But do you have proper facilities on Constellation for physical therapy? and a complete medical staff?"

"What kind of freighter service does he think we run?" thought Christina. "This sick bay looks like a field hospital compared to our facilities." Out loud, though, she said, "You wouldn't believe how advanced we are. And our staff! One name will tell all–Dr. Stanley Narb."

"Dr. Narb! The creator of the longies, er, I mean, the Extended-Life Brigade! He's here on Aphrodite?"

"The one and only. And yes, he's here. You want to meet him? How about lunch today?"

"I'd be honored, but please, don't go to any trouble."

"No trouble at all. Maria, would you make the arrangements? Lieutenant Smirnoff can handle the details. When you've done that give me a signal before you come in."

The surgeon went away, almost floating.

Christina went in to see Carlita, alone.

"Commander! Sorry I can't get up. They have my leg in this contraption. Tell them I can do my rehab on board."

"Gee, you don't even let us say hello, and you want to get up and move about! Well, the good news is that your rehab starts tomorrow. And the better news is that I won't let them keep you out of Constellation when we're ready to go. And now I have a surprise for you. Close your eyes!"

The wobble became a jerk at this moment, throwing Maria into the room and practically on her cousin's injured leg. "Carlita!" "Maria!" They began asking each other so many questions that they never got around to answering!

Christina left them chattering away. "What a pair," she mused. She had never had a cousin or a brother or a sister, or for that matter, mother or father or any relative at all. They were all killed by the Militia when Christina was just a few years old. She always wondered what it might be like to have a real family. She was brought up by various foster families and in boarding schools. A perfect candidate for the ELB, if you can make it to and through the Academy. They look for people who won't miss family life, especially because the process renders you sterile, so that you'll never have a family of your own. Maybe they sterilize you out of humanitarian concern, she didn't know, no one ever told her.

Well, now on to the only family she had: Constellation! Her heart grew heavy when she thought of Captain Allegretto. He had taken her under his wing, showed her the ropes, was like a father to her. But now... She wept softly and wondered who the new Captain would be. But she knew she would never meet anyone like him again.

———

The inside work was holding pretty well, pressure was restored to the damaged room. It still looked terrible in there. Christina saw traces of blood on the floor, and a little icon that somehow the crew had not seen. All trace of her five crew members was gone, except for this. Christina thought that Boris, who was fairly close to Misha, would appreciate receiving this. A tear fell down her cheek. "You're all heroes to me. We'll find out what we can, and I swear I'll do what I can to help wipe out this Militia. If I can't do it legally before my time runs out, I'll have to find other means." Other means? what other means? She had no idea.

Just then, another jerk! What's going on? Uh, oh! Is there a crack in that window? Better get out of here!

She made it out the door just in time: the lock had barely slipped into place when a loud crack and a roar of gushing air could be heard.

Outside, the unexpected jerk of the Station had made the spacewalking crew lose its grip on the wall piece, which smashed in the glass in the temporary wall. They saw a chair fly out, but no person. "We seem to be in luck. Hope they've closed the doors, Charlie!"

Spacewalk is not exactly the word to use for this work, which in reality is much more dangerous than it looks. These Space Stations spin at just the right velocity to create internal gravity, which of course also affects the immediate area. The problem is, they're up here on the station, far above the not-quite-breathable atmosphere of Venus, and those damn suits are heavy! Not to mention the materials, which are not weightless: they have Earth weight. The pulleys and other equipment are not there for window dressing, and the work is hard.

Still, this crew finished their task well ahead of the schedule they were given. Once they got the permanent replacement wall in place, they were able to remove the inside temps, and another crew fixed up the damaged rooms like new. More importantly, the wobbling could now be arrested, and Aphrodite resumed its normal slow and smooth spin.

———

Two days of unsuccessful interrogation. All the staff could get out of the two terrorists was their names–Ah Sun and Rhee Su-Kyum. Threats didn't work. Soft talk didn't work. President Selim grew impatient. He decided to take over the interrogation himself. In a surprise move, he had the scene shifted to a secured committee room, with comfortable chairs, soft drinks, a view of Venus or the stars, depending on the time of day. As a precaution, an invisible field kept the terrorists away from him. He told the guard to watch the proceedings on the TV set-up, but not to disturb them unless danger arose.

"So, Ms. Ah and Mr. Rhee," he began, "you came here as

part of a contingent set on destroying Aphrodite. Naturally, we'd like to know why you're so intent on doing this, and how you expected to get back to Earth. We discovered how you'd stowed away in Blue Girl's freighter, in what must have been intolerable circumstances. It's bad enough being in the cabin of one of those old tubs, let alone in the hold."

A trace of a smile crossed Rhee's mouth. Maybe he'd struck a responsive chord there.

"Let's see, at the rate that old crate moves, it must have taken at least a week to get here. Just enough time for the mesovita to wear off. You must have been groggy at first."

"When we came out in the cargo area, we were ready to get you and your workers in the Devil's vineyard. Too bad Steph missed you."

Ah, so he **was** the prime target, as he had thought.

"But it's just as well that he hit Allegretto. That's one less monster in the world."

Allegretto? How could they have known he was a longie? Even the other longies didn't know that. "So you weren't after the Governor, after all. Hmmm. We thought you were after her, because she had figured out how to accelerate the de-greenhousing of Venus."

Silence. Glares. I'll try another tack. Don't want my opening to close.

"Rumor on Earth has it that Deacon Ong has decided to go after the planets. Mesnos might be next, they say."

"Mesnos? Chicken feed."

"Quiet, Su-Kyum," said Ah Sun.

"Don't tell me you're after the Polaris Station. That would be suicide! But then, suicide seems to be your game. What brought your leader to kill himself?"

"We're a disciplined group of people, Mr. President. And principled. Our objective, as you must know, is to put an end to the ungodly activities of the World Government."

"What do you mean, Ms. Ah, by ungodly activities?"

"Attempts to reverse God's reign over Nature. First, the mountains: look what happened when you tried that."

"I don't know what you're taught in the Primitivist faith, but

23

maybe you've never heard it from our side. An approaching ice age about 2100 A.D. caused the various nationalist Earth governments to join together in effort to save life on the planet. This is what gave rise to the World Government. Our scientists studied many ways to warm the atmosphere, and after looking at countless alternatives, they could find only one solution to the destruction of life as we knew it: by cutting the Himalayas to about 4,500 meters (the altitude of the Tibetan Plain), the coming ice age would be aborted. In the end, this plan would have restored Earth's climate to what it had been around 2020, before the glaciation began."

"Lies! The other mountains were cut down, too. God wanted to punish humanity for its sins and abominations, the decline of morals. Plagues and diseases only sharpened medical responses."

"We understand that point of view, Ah Sun, and we allow people to express it. What we don't tolerate is violent terroristic action designed to take lives."

"To save souls," corrected Ah Sun.

"Well, you probably know that many individual countries, thinking of the possible benefits to them of doing something similar, decided to proceed not only there but throughout the entire globe, leaving just a few mountains over 3500 meters standing. This was a political decision, not a scientific one. The mountain-leveling was accomplished by about 2300; but minor flaws in planning and execution–they hadn't listened to the scientists, who warned of dire and unpredictable consequences– minor flaws caused a rapid rise in the sea level, while converting much of the temperate zones into subtropical regions, and the polar zones into temperate zones."

"The Devil's work, it was," snarled Rhee. "What a disaster! We warned them! All the coasts, all the islands, gone! In less than a century! The ice melted, more of it than any of you imagined."

"You're right about that: slight changes in the jet stream caused major climatic changes. The Earth no longer looked the same; it rapidly became a tropical planet, except for some temperate areas at the upper latitudes, above 50^0. Worse, population growth brought pressure on available space; we had to look elsewhere. Venus and Mars were obvious places to start, and then we undertook rapid expansion of colonization efforts. The discovery of a hyperspace worm hole around the central core of the galaxy will soon send us to the far reaches of the galaxy, thanks to the discovery of a way to extend lives to about 350 years." Maybe this will stir them up a bit.

"Monsters like Allegretto deserve to die!Vasa will go next! Then all of the longies!"

Suddenly, Ah Sun drew a small plastic satchel from her pocket and broke it open on Rhee Su-Kyum's arm. "You've said too much!" she shouted, rubbing herself with the same poison. They both fell to the floor, writhing horribly, then suddenly lay quiescent, their eyes open in a glassy stare, saliva dripping from the corners of their mouths, their bodies stiff.

"Guards! Take these bodies to be examined right away! We'll have to develop an antidote for whatever poison they have. Quick! We don't have a moment to lose!"

THE EXTENDED LIFE BRIGADE

"You know, being in a new place is pretty exciting, but is it ever dull getting there!"

"Boris, you should do something to improve your mind. The time would pass quickly, and you'd end up with a new skill or some new knowledge."

"Is that what you do in your spare time, Christina?"

"Yes. I've been working on navigation lately. It's a very complicated business, you know, much more complicated than when I was in Space Academy."

"I should think so: that was a lifetime ago. A lifetime for someone like me, I mean, 125 years. What's it like being forever 28?"

"That's almost word-for-word what we asked Captain Dupuis, Commander Largo and Dr. Narb when a group of us were being recruited for the ELB, back in 2530. I can almost see the scene again, like I'm reliving it."

"Tell me about it. It might improve my mind."

———

A dozen or so junior officers, about equally divided by sex, were ushered into a kind of seminar room, or board room. We were all freshly promoted or recently graduated from Space Academy; I was now a lieutenant senior grade. I had never found out why the Space Fleet officers had naval ranks while the non-coms had army ranks. It's not that the services all merged or anything like that. But here they were, ensigns, lieutenants j.g. and s.g., an unusually young captain and an equally young commander, both of whom seemed to be about 30 years old. The only non-military person there was a man dressed in a lab coat and who appeared to be 40 or 45, somewhat bulky or burly, who was figiting with some equipment. Hmm. Maybe it will be a show and tell, I thought.

"Please find a seat around the table. I'm Captain Margot Dupuis, and I'd like to welcome you to this information session on the Extended-Life Brigade.Commander Beatrice Strozzi and I are representatives of the ELB, and after Dr. Stanley Narb's presentation, you can ask us any questions you might want to about the Brigade, what the procedure to have your life extended is like, how we deal with remaining frozen as young people even though we're already over 100, or anything else that comes to your mind.

"A little bit of background, first, though. Right now, the Extended-Life Brigade provides, as many of you already know, the main crew on the interstellar exploration teams looking both for possible planets to colonize and for signs of past or especially current intelligent life in the galaxy. We expect, within the year, to begin by becoming acquainted with a new class of spaceships, the Constellation class, which will be able to travel great distances in about 1/10 of the time we can now go. Of course, a fraction of say 50 light-years distance can still be a lot of time, 5 years, each way. Constellations and the ELB will make this kind of space exploration possible well beyond the solar system.

"We are also principally in command of Ares and Aphrodite, and expect to be able to send people up to Future One soon. These space stations have important functions connected with rendering life on Mars and Venus possible.

"In addition, we expect to take the first colonists to a relatively nearby planet called Mesnos within a decade or two. Mesnos lies at about 20 light years from the sun, and has a gravity and an atmosphere fully compatible with human life. This will be a major new initiative for the Earth, on a par with the Mars and Venus projects.

"Finally, it's no secret that the Militia is out to get us. They will have a new foe to deal with: Earth Government has assigned the task of combatting them to the Extended Life Brigade in the first instance, under the control of Space Fleet, of course; and Space Fleet in this matter will be responsible directly to the Ministry of Security.

"Finally again, you probably all know that Dr. Narb first tried out his revolutionary procedure on himself after years of experimentation on animals. The ELB has been in existence for almost 130 years, and so far no one has suffered any negative consequences from the procedure, aside from what Dr. Narb will tell you. And yes, before you ask, we want you to see what it's like, and whether anyone here is interested in joining us. This is, simply put, a recruiting session. But we want to stress that the decision you come to must be yours and not ours, because the results are far-reaching and permanent: there's no turning back."

Dr. Narb had been looking at all of us with incredible intensity while Captain Dupuis was talking. I wondered what he was thinking. I have to admit that I shuddered with excitement on hearing his name. I never knew what he looked like before then; I wanted to know why we never saw pictures of him, the real reason or at least the official reason why. Gee, who would ever take him for a 170- or 180-year-old? We must have seemed like children to him! He was just as exciting to listen to as I could have anticipated, and in all my years of acquaintance with him since then he's always seemed to be the same person.

Stanley had a way of masking his enormous erudition and his record of extraordinary scientific experimentation in several fields (computer technology, genetics, even geology and astrophysics–he made great use of his extended life) behind words that even the non-technologically-oriented could easily understand. Even with this group of young officers, whose training was in engineering and the sciences, he spoke in simple terms with a minimum of jargon. His talk was amply illustrated. A gentle, warm, and humble atmosphere seemed to emanate from him. He inspired confidence and empathy.

He began his presentation virtually without an introduction.

"I'd like to show you in the next few minutes exactly what the life-extending procedure consists of and why it works. It might be interesting for you to know that around the year 2000 people first found the genes that determine the death of cells. You can see them on this true-color hologram of some chromosomes of laboratory mice. Let me zero in on one of these and enlarge it a bit. There. By manipulating this and many other similar genes, it became possible within a century to extend the lives of laboratory mice and rats by about 100%, that is, to double their life span. Further experiments were carried on in the course of the next two centuries or so, using other species, from

29

fish and reptiles to shrews and cats and dogs, and on to monkeys and apes. You see here holograms of some of these animals and their siblings. You'll notice that the animals not only look younger than their siblings, their behavior corresponds to that of animals the age they were at the time they underwent the procedure. *(Wow! this is incredible! I thought, and probably everyone else in the room was thinking the same thing.)* The immature animals remained immature, the elderly remained elderly, those in the middle stayed there. It appeared that the age these animals had at the time of the procedure is the age they would keep almost until death. We weren't sure this would apply to humans, but given the large number of species we had experimented with, it seemed like a reasonable assumption. If you look at Captain Dupuis, Commander Strozzi and me, you'll see that that's what happens with humans, too.

"We had noticed several side effects, differing with the species involved and the number and type of cells whose genes were manipulated. The early experiments on mice, for instance, caused a change in the color of the fur; the rats shrank by about 10% of body mass; the caiman you see went blind. Bit by bit, such side effects were eliminated, but life was still extended by only 100%; that seemed to be the upper limit. Experiments in the last century changed that. Life extension in the order of 150% to 200% has become routine in the laboratory; we estimate that every member of the ELB can expect to live to the ripe old age of 325 to 350 years. Side effects were reduced to only two. But they are important, and seem to be impossible to avoid.

"The first is that at the end of life all the experimental animals, without exception, have undergone a telescoped aging process. And, in every case, equating the average age of the experimental animal to that of a human being, we come up with the same result: the three of us, at the end of our lives, will almost certainly age and die within a year, becoming apparently two years older every week. This is still a great unknown for science, since of course no "longie" has as yet died of old age. At 175, I'm the oldest living member of the Brigade, and am most likely at the half point of my life span. You should also know that having one's life extended does not mean that everyone will live to the full extent of the extension: accidents, injuries, murder, disease–any of these can kill us just as thoroughly as it can kill you. You live longer, but you're not immortal. Still, the point I'd really want to make about this is that the psychological effects of rapid deteriorisation, especially after an exceptionally long life, is an unknown; it might well be devastating. We won't be able to begin gathering a significant amount of data on this phenomenon for another 200 years or so! It's obvious that if you don't want to take the risk of not being able to handle this change of life pattern, you should not consider entering the Brigade.

"The second side effect is one that has had an impact on every current member of the ELB, and will have an impact on every new member. While the procedure does not in any way affect the libido–it neither enhances nor diminishes it, whether we look at animal studies or at our colleagues–it does render 100% of the subjects we have examined sterile, unable to have children. Yes, this includes all the humans who have undergone the procedure, about 1000 in total. Here too, and perhaps even more importantly than with the aging problem, you'll have to give serious thought to this matter before coming to a decision.

"You'll also have to consider what it's like outliving all your non-ELB friends and acquaintances. And you'll have to put up with a much slower promotion time-scale. Nobody wants to have a Space Fleet composed of captains or admirals who have been in rank for 100 years or more!

"Finally, I can assure you that in no case so far among the 1000 or so humans who have undergone this procedure has there been any other side effect. Except for those who have died of wounds or injuries or illnesses, all our Brigade members who were 30 years old when they underwent the procedure are still 30 years old. It is true that some of you, if you choose to join our ranks, are likely to be killed in combat or in some accident related to your duty, which is almost always hazardous."

It was now Commander Strozzi's turn to speak. She was brief and to the point.

"You might be wondering why you in this room were chosen to attend this presentation. In general, we try to look for recruits who have no close relatives and who are not themselves married.

31

Unmarried, unattached orphans: that can describe everyone in this room, all fifteen of us. I see a lot of quizzical looks on your faces. The reason for this criterion is simple, when you get to think of it: if you choose to join the Brigade, your life will be extended by 200 years or so, to a total of 325 to 350 years overall, we think. Unattached orphans are most likely to be able to find happiness in the Brigade over the long haul. They won't see their siblings age and die while they themselves appear to be eternal 30-year-olds; they won't have regrets if their spouse and especially their children age and die before them. In a way, your family will become the ELB, an extended family at least.

"You might also be wondering why you were brought in here under a veil of secrecy. I'll answer that as one of the security officers of the Brigade. Quite frankly, we try to keep the identity of most of our members a secret, at least at the beginning (after all, if you still seem to be 25 or 30 after 50 years of service, everyone will be in on your little secret!), because of the increasingly dangerous activity of the Militia."

I felt a cold chill run up my spine at the very mention of the Militia, those religious vigilantes who had murdered my family some years before, wiping out every trace of close relatives that I had. Every year about this time I recreated the events of that day, 21 years ago, in 2509, when I was a little girl of seven. (I still do this.)

"The Militia seems to have unleashed its venom on the ELB in particular, and on Space Fleet, Future One, Ares and Aphrodite as well. It considers the very process of extending lives as anathema, and wants to eliminate everyone who has anything to do with it. This is why we have never permitted Dr. Narb to be photographed. We don't want to expose possible recruits to the Brigade to any more danger than they already face as officers in Space Fleet. And members of the ELB staff our space stations, and will be the principal members of our future planetary exploration missions, which are set to begin next year. Space stations, interplanetary exploration, that kind of thing also seems to be a target of the Militia: they want to take the term 'primitivist' literally, although it doesn't stop them from traveling, often illegally, to those very places they revile."

"Now you know why you were selected to be brought here, and you know why your visit has been covered with a shroud of secrecy. You've learned first hand something about the ELB and the process that has made Dr. Narb, Captain Dupuis and me members of this organization. We'll now open the floor to discussion. You can direct your questions to one of us in particular, or to all of us in general."

Wow! all of us were what's the term unattached orphans. I didn't know there were this many: not just a dozen potential recruits and the three speakers, but, over the years, 1000 people. I wonder if the others had to deal with a family destroyed by those bastards? The Militia! A bunch of cowards. A bomb at a family reunion. Randomly selected family, they claimed. But I bet they knew something about Uncle Gustavus and his connection with the development of the mission of Ares and Aphrodite. I only wish we had had an inkling of what was to happen, or that something had gone wrong. That's what I was thinking. I'm not sure what other people were thinking, but no one was speaking. Stanley broke the silence, repeating Commander Strozzi's invitation to us.

"Captain Dupuis, Commander Strozzi and I will field any questions you might have."

"Dr. Narb," asked a young man, "how do you do this procedure? I mean, we've seen holograms of chromosomes and genes that are blown up way over life-size, but you didn't say what your manipulation of them consists of, how many you have to work on, what the pain level is, how long the patient is out of commission."

"There are several questions wrapped up in that one, and I'll answer as many of them as I'm allowed to. You see, the procedure is kept under far tighter security than what you have seen here today. What we do is this: we take tissue samples from various parts of the body, some blood samples, too, and work on all of these until we know for sure that they, that is, the affected genes, have all been altered in the same way. We run about fifty tests to make sure that everything is perfect and corresponds to a model. This causes in the subject no more discomfort than the collection of other tissue and blood samples that you're familiar with. We replace these altered genes in their chromosomes, and inject them, in a serum, into a nerve in the little toe of your less-dominant foot, which requires a local anesthetic. You're up and walking around with no problem, maybe in a few cases a little limp for a day or so. If all goes well, as it does in 97.5% of the cases, we know within a month if you're in the ELB. The cases that don't work the first time have always worked the second time around. All. 100% success rate."

"Is this an irrevocable procedure? I know that Captain Dupuis seemed to indicate that it is, but suppose I undergo the procedure, and then decide after five years that I want to have kids, or that I don't want to live until 2850, what can I do?"

"Ensign Plath, that's a question that calls for brutal frankness. Captain Dupuis has indeed indicated that the procedure seems to be irrevocable. We have been unable to reverse the genetic alterations in any of our animal or human subjects. It's the reason why we don't want you to rush into the Brigade. We give you up to five years to make up your mind. If we don't hear from you in that time, we assume you don't want to join. It's enough time for you to make a reasoned decision. And if you can't make up your mind in that time-frame, in a real sense you will have made up your mind not to join, because you won't be allowed in after that."

"Suppose I've always wanted to be in the ELB and want to sign up right away. Can I do it?"

"Lieutenant Vasa, you'll have to wait at least a month. But this will be a month in which you'll be living, working, playing with people like us. You can speak with people who have been ELBers since the inception in 2401, and with relative newcomers, who have been in the Brigade for only 10 years or so. Just as we don't want people to take too long to decide, we also don't want people to make rash decisions to join."

"Captain, how can 1000 people do all these things? I mean, this is a huge mission!"

"Well, that's true, it is a huge mission, and 1000 people can't handle it all, at least not by themselves. We'll be working with, alongside of, and in some cases under the control of, ordinary people on some or all these missions. At the same time, we hope to be able to grow at a more dynamic rate than we have up to now. One thing we have on our side is time. With patience we should be able to cross the galaxy eventually. And as Commander Strozzi will tell you if you ask her, we're determined to wipe out the Militia if it takes us a hundred years or more!"

A somewhat timid man asked, "Commander, will you expand on that? Why should the main target of the Militia be the ones to seek them out?"

"Lieutenant Ambab, the reason is twofold. First, we have a greater motivation than anyone else to carry out this mission. The problem is really that we have to work hard at removing the subjectivity from our task, we have to try to deal with an emotional subject–you're out to kill me–with all the calm of an entomologist studying an ant colony. Second, even if it takes us a millenium to finish the job, we have time on our side. Each one of us will live, on average, about two and a half times as long as any Militia person. We'll have to perfect our networks, improve our methods, discover new ways of dealing with this movement, create new structures to make our efforts as effective as possible. It will take courage, imagination, determination, energy, and time. We have all of those qualities."

"How **DO** you deal with being perpetually 30 years old even though you're really over 100? And, this is addressed to Dr. Narb, how can you spend your life never being out in public?"

"It's wonderful being 30 every day of your life!" answered Commander Strozzi, with exuberance. "The problem you see, and that we feel, is that our non-ELB friends grow old and a few of them that we've known have already died; that will only get worse in the future. And that's hard, just as hard as having a friend killed in action or dying because of an accident or of some disease. I think the hardest things to deal with are that you seem to others to be much younger and much less experienced than you are (the slow promotion track doesn't help there!) and that some people seem to look on us as freaks of some sort. That, and the need to keep up with the times, to move forward with the centuries, not to be stuck back in the century and the events of our childhood and adolescence. You do have lots of time to become conversant in many fields of knowledge; and while I don't think anyone has come close to matching Dr. Narb's versatility, many of our colleagues have studied art, music and literature, physics, philosophy and psychology, mathematics, politics and sociology, to name a few subjects. My own interest is history: I'm studying the effect of the rise in sea level on the coastal communities around my ancestors' home town, Genoa. This is a corps of pretty bright people, serious, action-oriented, studious. And like everyone else, fun-loving. If that's enough of an answer, I'll let Dr. Narb answer the question you addressed specifically to him."

"I think that the first thing I'd say about my never going out in public is that you're operating under a false impression. Since almost nobody knows what Dr. Narb looks like, I'm free to go almost anywhere. It is true that I travel with one or more companions and have a false ID (government-approved, of course!). You've probably seen me a dozen times without ever noticing me. I've been everywhere any of you have been for the past ten years or more, and might even have been in your home towns. Anyone from Ulan Bator? Ah, yes! I was there 12 years ago, traveling then under the name of an old French poet, Stéphane Mallarmé. I gave a poetry reading!"

"I can't believe it! That was you? I was there!"

"What more can I say? There are pictures of Stéphane Mallarmé reading his poetry in Ulan Bator, but none of Stanley Narb, research surgeon of the Extended Life Brigade. And, by the way, this is a military secret. Really."

———

"The questions continued for almost an hour after that, Boris. Then we were shown to our temporary quarters, and had a little chance for recreation and socializing before dinner."

"How many of you recruits decided to go through with the procedure. You, of course, but how many others?"

"I think that eight of us became ELBers. My memory's a bit vague on that; it was, after all, almost 120 years ago!"

"My friend and lover, a lifetime older than me."

"Very funny. Didn't you know I'm really 28 years old?"

Just then the loud speakers announced that Constellation was nearing Ares. Boris and Christina stood up, and got ready to move to their posts. Boris couldn't suppress a smile as he said, "OK, I've improved my mind. I'll try reading a book in my spare time on Ares."

"I'm not sure you'll have very much free time there at the beginning. But at least you won't have to familiarize yourself with a brand-new situation. You'll recognize the station as though you've run into an old friend: it's an identical twin of Aphrodite."

CAUGHT!

"Boris, do you see anything out there?" she whispered. This planet has no moon, she thought. No moon, no light at night, clouds all the time. It's creepy.

"No, Christina. But I hear people–someone or something–breaking through the brush."

"People? More than one? How many?"

"Sounds like a patrol. Maybe five or six."

Crack! A branch of a méki bush, dry, low, brittle. "Damn it, Srethims, be quiet," said a hoarse voice in the dark. "We know they're around here somewhere. We need to get them before they get us."

Christina held her breath, as did Boris. Are we being set up? Are they trying to lure us out of hiding? Do they expect us to fall for that old trick?

Suddenly, from across the meadow, a shout rang out. "Get 'em now, the bastards! They're over there!" The quadrant rushed towards the trap.

What the hell is Cardeño doing? He'll blow our cover! He'll get us all caught! Boris and Christina took advantage of the noise and ducked down further under the wide méki that was covering them.

A bright light came on, then another, then the field was lit up like a ball park. Cardeño, realizing his error, compounded it by opening fire. A ray from his gun missed the Militia leader and struck the méki, just at the spot where Boris had been hiding. Cardeño's shot was answered by several blasts. Four more dead; that makes nine so far. A double squad went out into the light, there were 12, 15, 16 Primmies. How many more were still lurking in the hidden recesses of these woods?

"We still don't have the big cheeses. Look at this: three men and a woman, not one even a sergeant. Keep an eye on the area, Mezclan; they can't be far. We'll catch 'em at dawn."

"What should we do with the carcasses, Deacon?"

"Leave them alone. The wolks'll swoop down and eat them. I can smell them coming already, even if we can't hear their wings."

Mezclan admired this kind of thinking. After all, these are infidels, or moderns, which amounts to the same thing. They don't deserve any better. They wouldn't want to be buried like proper human beings anyway. Still, the wolks were fierce. They began with the eyes, then the throat; after that, he couldn't bear to look any more. If any of the quadrant's alive, the wolks will take care of that in a hurry.

The Deacon and most of the crew left. Boris and Christina could hear another guard element behind them, in the forest. In front of them, the lights out again, everything was dark. But, God, the stench! The horrible sound of flesh being torn apart! The cries and the in-fighting of these disgusting flying lizards pierced the still of the night. The cloud cover chose this moment to break up a bit, and the dim light of the stars let the pair see the chilling sight of the carnage. Their crew members! Their comrades!

Suddenly, it was all over. The incredible silence of this strange world rolled in like fog.

———

Christina woke with a start. The first light of the Mesnosian dawn cast a grey pallor all around them. Boris was asleep; she gently shook him, then covered up his mouth with her hand just as he was about to utter some sound. "Shh. Let's take a look at where we are and see if we can get out of here."

Before them, gleaming bones caught the light of the first sun rising. Little mouse-like carnivores were finishing up the job the wolks had started. Probably what they call stots. Above, bad news. The clouds were all gone for the first time in almost a month. The sky, blue, white and orange, prom ised a very hot summer day, especially when the second sun would rise above the far horizon. Worse, the thin foliage of the mékis couldn't hide them for long. They'd have to move fast.

Boris looked around, then looked at Christina. He seemed to know what she was thinking. "I think there's one of those cellar units, or maybe a mine shaft, near here," he whispered. "Look.

40

The map shows a hidden entrance under a méki next to an abandoned hangar."

"Yeah, but the hangar's on the other side of the field. We'd be crazy to try to get there. They must have a hundred people around here."

Just then she caught sight of a quietly moving figure about 20 paces away. She yanked at Boris, and they both ducked. It was the leader of a small patrol, a triad. Her two soldiers were close behind. They looked into the brush and then out at the pile of bones and bloody fatigues. "Nobody around here," the leader was saying. "Too bad, there's a price on their heads. Ten credits apiece."

At this point Boris leaped up. "Sister and Brothers, take this!" he shouted. He fired at the leader, then at the others. They all fell, dead as rocks from Venus.

"Boris, what are you doing? They'll be sure to find us now! Let's get out of here."

"The triad will be found by their friends, maybe the Deacon. While they're occupied with them, we'll be able to sidle away, over towards the entrance."

A crazy idea, she thought, but what the hell? And there's nothing we can do about it now. So they crept slowly to the right, zigzagging a bit to stay under whatever cover the mékis could give them in the sunrise. Bush by bush, rock by rock, they were now just a few meters from where the map indicated a hidden entrance. Steady... don't let a branch get in your way, don't make any noise. Finally, the méki next to the now fallen-down hangar.

They waited until the bodies of the guard were discovered. Shouting, 10, 20, 30 Militia emerged from who knows where? From the edge of the forest, maybe. Commands were given, search parties began fanning out. Boris and Christina dug through an inch of soil until they felt a metal door. They lifted it up just enough to slip in, let it down slowly, and went down the ladder to the floor of what seemed to be an old tunnel. No light, but their flashlights revealed a concrete tunnel barely a meter high stretching out to the right and the left, slanting downward. To their right, it went under the open field and ended at another door; to the left, it led towards the long-abandoned underground factories built on Mesnos over 100 years ago. Protection from the wolks and the stots. The wolks live in caves high in the mountains nearby, the stots build nests at the top of tall dead trees. What a deadly one-two punch! But they never come underground. Maybe it's too cool for them here.

They went left, towards the factories, where perhaps they'd find some food and maybe a functioning radio.

A tunnel led to the right. Dead-end, according to Boris's map: it looked like an unfinished way out, or maybe it was intended to be opened up into another plant.

"What did they make here, Christina?"

"Some of the factories processed food, others wove cloth out of the fibrous under-bark of the méki. See if your map directs us to one of the luminescent caves that were the living quarters of the earliest settlers."

"Were those the settlers who became Primitivists? ... Ah! if we turn right here, we should come to a passage leading to one of those chambers."

"No, ordinary Primitivists never came here, but some Militia types landed just ahead of us. They seem to want to wipe out every vestige of civilization. Judging from the ruins of New Terra we saw, they must have killed thousands of people. Maybe there are a few colonials still alive. Mesnos was slated for full-fledged colonization until the Primmies, or rather, the Militia, came to put an end to that. By the way, it was not smart killing that triad. If there was already a price on our heads, what must it be like now?"

"I didn't kill them, just stunned them. They should start stirring in an hour or so. I don't like killing people."

"You're just the opposite of the Deacon. How can a person be high up in a church hierarchy and want to kill anyone who doesn't agree with him?"

"The Primitivists don't all act like that, you know. It's just their Militias. The Deacon must be a leader of a Militia cell."

"Well, they certainly all seem to take after me, Militia or not. I'm a nonbeliever, not just an infidel. Anathema. Get her in your sight and shoot: that's the kind of person I am to them."

42

"Look, a bit of light ahead."

"Let's be quiet and inconspicuous. Douse our lights."

They moved slowly towards the glimmering phosphorescent bluish light that seemed to come from behind a partly-opened door. Christina reached the door, then dropped down. "Cover me," she whispered, as she pushed the door open just enough to slip through. She looked around: no sign of life, but this was indeed an old factory. "It looks clear," she said to Boris; "looks like a food-processing plant. There might be something to eat in those cupboards."

Boris entered the chamber, closing the door behind him. The chamber was a natural cave, with a small stream of water running along one side. "I can use a drink," he said, and rushed towards the stream. Christina grabbed him with her unexpectedly strong arm and held him tight in her grip. He was surprised at the power she had–physical as well as mental and moral strength.

"Careful. We'd better test it first," said Christina. Boris was an impetuous guy. Sometimes his instincts worked, sometimes not. His plan to divert the Primitivists was an instinctive gem. But she remembered when he managed to get them in an ambush. They almost didn't make it out alive. And then, on Ares, when they almost ate the poisoned food.

"Okay, you win. I know what you're thinking. Ares, right? Maybe there's something wrong here, too." He scooped up a cupful of water and dropped in a small tablet. Some new kind of testing device. "What does it mean if the water turns green?"

"Remember the light's sort of blue here. That must mean the outdoor-light color of the water with this tablet in it is really yellowish. That means it's safe."

"See? You didn't have to stop me. I could have drunk that water without a worry in the world."

"Better safe than sorry."

They sat down at an old work table and had a long drink of the cool water, which had a sweet taste to it, sort of like flat unflavored soda pop. Or just plain sugar water. Christina found some tins of food, some kind of fish. That should help them get through the day: they hadn't eaten for 24 hours, and that was just some crackers. They could even wash off their faces here. Could they wash off that blue color? Nah, that was the luminescence.

"Anyone ever tell you you'd look real cute as a blue-blood, Boris?"

"I **am** a blue-blood. Aristocratic roots. Left-hand branch of Catherine the Great's family. Rumor has it some French guy named Diderot sired one of my ancestors, who became an enlightened serf-owner."

"Hey, that goes back hundreds of years. Eighteenth century, right? Gee, maybe some of our forebears knew each other. I'm named after my umpteenth great-grandmother, who was the Queen of Sweden, but gave up the throne to study physics, mathematics, and philosophy."

"Brains run in your family, eh? You cold and logical Swedes. We Russians always act without thinking."

"Cut out the stereotypes, will you? By now your genes, like mine, have been enriched by those of countless other people. We're really sixty-fourth breeds, or something!"

"Nevertheless, you've got to admit that in our cases the stereotypes work pretty well."

"Can't argue about that, I suppose. And now, the logical Swedish part of my brain tells me that we've got to figure out where to go from here, and what next to do."

"Well, we have two major options, I guess. One is to find our transmat site right away; the other is to hide out for a day or so, then look for it. I suppose you'd prefer the second option. 'Better safe than sorry.'"

"You know, I almost feel like making a run for our transmat site, just to be ornery. Or maybe to act like you."

"Believe it or not, I'd rather lie low a bit, maybe explore these factories, see where we are. I did take reconnoitering at the Academy, you know."

"Does your map cover this area?"

"No, it ends just inside the door. How's your sense of direction? Without a map, mine's terrible."

"Yeah, I know: you can't find your way out of a room that has only one door. You may not know that I've got a good memory for places I've seen and for the turns I've made. I bet I could duplicate your map right now."

"Okay, bet's on."

Christina picked up a pebble and scratched their route out on the floor. There was the méki they had been hiding under, the zigzag path they took to the old tunnel entrance, the position of the hangar outside, the tunnels they followed, the passageways they saw, the rooms, the spot where they were. Boris checked her sketch against his map. It was amazing! Where did she learn to do that? Is it instinctual, for that matter, or is it something you can be taught? This woman never stopped astonishing Boris.

"So if we went through one of those doors, and the halls turned out to be a maze, you'd be able to find your way back here? Did your umpteenth great-grandmother have this skill, too? Is that what made Sweden such a powerful country back in our blue-blood days?"

"No, just something I learned to do over the years. I'm a self-taught woman."

They reached the end of the chamber, which bent down and arched slightly to the left. The rock looked scarred in front of the right-hand door, as though it had been chiseled, but looked pretty natural around the left-hand door.

"My guess is that through the chiseled doorway we'll find the living quarters, and at least one exit to the outside. They would probably have kept the workshops closer to the interior. God, I wonder how many survivors there are. How many did the Primmies kill? And how did the Primmies get here?"

Boris thought for a moment. "I read somewhere that they've managed to infiltrate even the Space Fleet. Maybe they stole a Space Fleet ship, or maybe they bought or rented a freighter. With warp drive, we're only what? six months from Earth? It's hard to say because we didn't come here directly."

"Well, let's take a look in what I think are the living quarters. But we'd better go in carefully and quietly, in case there's an opening to the outside."

Once again, Boris covered for her as she pushed open the door. Not much luminescent material here. Their eyes adjusted to the dark a bit, then they turned on their flashlights. A big lodge-like room, with what were clearly bedrooms off to one side and a kitchen to the other, bending back parallel to the big chamber they just left.

"You're right again, Lieutenant! Over there, near the kitchen area, is what I suppose is the exit you believe is here. Should I open the door, or do you think it's too dangerous?"

"We don't know what's outside, and in any case the main sun must be up high. I'd rather wait a few hours, till twilight at least, before giving it a try. Let's see what's behind the other door first."

"You know what I'd really like to do?" he asked, looking at her somewhat hungrily.

"Yeah, but no, not now. If we do stay here in the living quarters, I think it would be best to get some sleep, so we'll be fresh for the evening foray."

"I feel pretty well rested. I'll tell you what. You take a nap, and I'll go see what's through the other door. I'll wake you up in, say, an hour. Unless I get lost."

"Let me see if I get the hint .You have no sense of direction, and since I say no to sex right now you want to go about exploring. Then I get worried, come out and spend a day or so looking for you while you're turning around in circles. How can I spare the anguish? Have sex, or go with you, and the hell with the nap. Right?"

"I didn't know I was so transparent. Now it's my turn to guess. We go exploring together."

"That's right, Lieutenant Smirnoff. But first, I've got to find a loo."

A few minutes later, the two officers went through the first place that the first colonists from Earth had ever built. Mesnos, where it all began. Well, almost. There were the two Space Stations, Aphrodite and Ares, before. But this was the first world found that already had a well-defined biota and could support human life. The wolks and the stots were fierce predators, but there were few other predatory species. Mesnos, within half a century, could already boast several towns and two cities above ground. Plans were made for further colonization. Then the Primmies came and changed all that literally overnight. New Terra was razed, maybe 10,000 people killed, the whole population! That city was just outside the cavern where they

46

were now standing. Sandstone Village was the next town up the coast. Is that the next target?

Through the door, the same blue light. Looks like a textile plant. Primitive machines, but when Christina tried a loom, it creaked into action, and the dust on it covered up some thread that could still be woven. When did she learn how to weave with this kind of machine? A hundred twenty five years ago? Before she became a longie, that's for sure.

Boris was chuckling. "You look so, so, so *domestic*," he said, with an ironic grin. "The truth is, I can't imagine you in a kitchen, but here you are, weaving cloth. Can you make me a new tunic? Mine's ripped and torn."

"Very funny. But you know, fishing and farming and weaving and hunting seems always to be the way societies begin. They had to start from scratch."

"Well, not quite from scratch. These people did have a lot of technological help."

Boris opened a door to another room, glowing with the now-familiar blue light. "This must have been a living room, Christina. There are doors leading from it, maybe to an interior room. Hey! Take a gander at this!"

Christina followed him in. A light flashed in her eyes. "What on Earth...!" Rough hands grabbed her from behind. She fought, broke loose, called out, "Boris! Give me a hand!"

Someone seized her arm. A little defensive maneuvre sent him spiraling upwards, then arching down. Bam! Right on his back, then on his head. Unconscious. But Christina couldn't see this. Another man took her by the shoulders. A hard blow backwards to his balls had him doubling over in pain. She spun around, crashing her clenched hands on the back of his head just as her left knee met his jaw. The impact must have been awful: blood spurted, probably from his mouth and nose. He fell in a heap to the floor.

"Boris!" cried Christina.

She was tackled from behind, fell over forward. A heavy weight fell across her back, another across her legs. "Get off me, you bastards!" But two other men quickly bound her hands and her feet. "Tie her up tight: she's a demon. She knocked out two

47

heavyweights!"

Then a familiar but hated voice could be heard. "Good work, Brother Boris. We have our prey. The trial will begin after dinner. The execution will take place in the morning."

DEATH ON MESNOS

"The prosecutor may begin by stating the charges against the defendant."

"Your Honor, the defendant, Commander Christina Vasa, stands accused of the following crimes: causing, or being otherwise responsible for, the death of 76 members of the Primitivist Militias in the course of the past 125 years;..."

The assembly, which must have included all of the Militia on Mesnos, reacted to this list of crimes in the way she imagined they would if the Deacon were preaching, like those people did in the Sermon in the Valley that she had seen so many times: with each accusation, and at other moments in the trial, they interrupted the proceedings with exclamations of agreement, with expressions of anger, and with other remarks. In this case, they cried out as though with one voice, "Kill her! Kill her!"

"...of having led numerous raids against the Brothers and Sisters of the Militias (*We were there! Yes, she did!*); of opposing the spread of the doctrine of the Primitivist faith, since she is a nonbeliever, yes, the worst form of infidel (*Death to the infidel! Death!*); of having willingly consented to the immoral operation which has expanded her life span by at least 200 years while keeping her suspended at her apparent age of 28 (*Monster! Abomination!*); and of committing these crimes on Earth, on Aphrodite and on Ares, and on Mesnos."

"Where are the accusers, Brother Prosecutor?"

"I am the principal accuser, having accompanied the defendant on several of her raids, on Aphrodite, Ares and Mesnos, and learned of other crimes from herself and from official documents. Sister Myrna has known her in the past, and is ready to testify against her, as am I." (*Lay it out, Sister!*)

"What evidence do you present?"

"Your Honor, I..."

"What a sham! You have already made a judgment against me, you are using as prosecutor a man who claimed for ten years to be my friend, who himself has killed countless Militia members, who..."

"Silence! Prosecutor Smirnoff is not on trial. We will not tolerate further outbursts from the defendant! Sergeant of the Guards, be ready to silence her."

"Yes, your Honor."

"...and who is at best a slimy turncoat, a traitor who might well decide, some day, to betray you, Deacon!" (*Silence, Monster!*)

"Sergeant!"

"Ow! Let go of my hair! Take that! Ah! Ooooh!"

"One more outburst, and we'll cut your tongue out. Sergeant, fasten her to her seat. I want two guards holding her down."

"Yes, your Honor. You two, come here. Any funny business, and ...you heard the Deacon."

"Yes, sir."

Christina's green eyes narrowed as she stared at Boris. She struggled against the cords, but the rough hemp cut into her wrists with each movement she made. She shrugged, hoping to get the two soldiers' iron grips off her shoulders, but in vain. She glared defiantly at the Deacon, sitting on a platform in his dark ceremonial robe.

How could Boris have done this to her? Worse, how could she not have noticed anything about him? He did, after all, kill some Primmies, but he would probably claim that it was in self defense. They didn't seem to know he was a double agent, a mole. A creature living in the filthy underground, not being quite in one camp or the other. And she didn't notice anything, either. Hah! a clue anyone could have missed: he never called them Primmies, they were always Primitivists to him. Still, he never seemed offended when she called them Primmies.

"...and this very weapon was used just yesterday to kill at least one quadrant."

"All four members?"

"Yes, your Honor."

"Does this weapon have a stun setting?"

"Yes, your Honor."

"Was it set at stun?"

"No, your Honor, it was set at maximum power: kill." (*Death!*)

50

Christina, as the gun was entered in evidence, became aware of the evidence that Boris was presenting. Basically, it's her rank and her uniform that will provide all the evidence these people need to justify their pre-drawn decision. "Wonder what form of execution I'll be given. Wonder if it's worth even trying to answer these charges," she thought. "Better concentrate on what's being said, and where I am."

"I repeat, does the defendant wish to make an opening statement?"

"Yes, I do, but not if I'm tied up and these palookas are digging their hands into my shoulders."

"Sergeant, place two more guards on her, stand facing her so she cannot lunge forward, and have the guards remove the bonds."

"Yes, sir."

"My defense," she said, in her clear and powerful voice, "can only be the facts. First of all, it is true that I have killed some Militia men and women, but I have never fired a bolt first: I was always defending my life or that of my comrades, including Lieutenant Smirnoff, whose life I saved on at least five occasions in this manner. Second, I have never opposed the spread of the Primitivist faith, or any faith, my own lack of religious beliefs notwithstanding. (*Lies! Lies!*) What I have opposed, and what I will always oppose as long as I live, if I survive this ordeal, will be groups like yours that set themselves up as counter-governments, and conduct kangaroo courts like this one." (*Her tongue! Her tongue!*)

"Be careful, Commander, I am not a patient man."

"In the third place, there is nothing illegal about becoming what you refer to as a longie. This procedure has been authorized by law, and can be performed only under certain very carefully defined conditions, and by licensed practitioners. I am proud to have been chosen as a member of the Extended-Life Brigade." (*Death to the monster!*) Christina looked defiantly around the room, at the Primmies assembled there, maybe 100 or more; then taking in every detail of this large natural chamber, transformed from textile mill to assembly hall. The blue light cast an eerie purplish glow on the heated faces of the audience and the jury, burning as they were with hate. She glared at Boris, who deflected his gaze from hers, and then at the Deacon.

"The testimony will now begin."

Myrna took the stand first, and testified that she had been present on Ares when Christina killed two Militia women who had jumped her. She fought furiously, "like a man," (*Monster!*) then drew her gun and blasted them without warning. On cross-examination, Christina, acting as her own defense counsel, was able to establish that the women attacked her without any provocation, that they had pulled knives on her and had stabbed her several times, and that she killed them in self defense. To Myrna's unwilling testimony she added: "This is the kind of struggle I have had in every case mentioned here: I was never the aggressor." She then indicated that she had no more questions to ask.

Christina wondered how Boris would interrogate himself publicly, without appearing to be ridiculous. "Where were you, Lieutenant Smirnoff, when on Aphrodite the defendant claims to have saved your life during a Militia attack five years ago?" "I was standing beside Commander Vasa, who at that time was not only my commanding officer but also my friend and my lover." "Is it true that she saved you from being poisoned on Ares, and you're now betraying her? Is that gratitude?" "It's true, and I'm the lowest of snakes." Could he carry it off? Oh, damn, look at this: it's more dignified than that. I should have guessed.

"Your Honor, since I cannot act simultaneously as prosecutor and witness, I request permission to suspend my functions as prosecutor until my testimony is complete. I have prepared a list of questions a deputy prosecutor might ask."

"Permission granted. Sister Myrna, you will act in Brother Boris's stead."

"Lieutenant Smirnoff, is it true that you served as a subordinate to the defendant in the Space Fleet?"

"Yes, it is."

"Is it true that in order not to reveal your identity as a spy for the Militia you had received prior permission from the High Synod to act as a regular member of Space Fleet, like our other Brothers and Sisters on this dangerous assignment, and that the

Synod knew that your official duties might include killing or wounding our comrades?"

"That is true; and I would like to point out that our esteemed Deacon was present at that meeting. He can verify the facts."

"Is this true, your Honor?"

"It is true. Unfortunately, we must make sacrifices to reach the final goal, which is the extermination of the World Government (*Yes! Yes!*) and the reestablishment of the rule of God (*Of God! of God!*). We are all sworn to make whatever sacrifice we must."

"Is it true, Brother Boris, that the Life-Extension operation, although sanctioned by the laws of the illegitimate government, is contrary to the law of God?"

"Our High Synod and our Governing Bishops have never once wavered from their belief in this doctrine. The Holy Scriptures do not sanction such a deviance from the life Almighty God has granted us." (*Monster!*)

"Is it true that the Space Fleet, being an arm of the illegitimate government, is waging war against the Militia? And is it not true that therefore no act of aggression against the Militia can be construed as self-defense, even if the Militia personnel take preemptive action?"

"Both statements are true."

"That is all, your Honor."

"Do you wish to cross-examine the witness, Commander?"

Christina stood up and looked straight at Boris, who squirmed slightly. Almost as though he felt she was looking deep into his soul. "Boris, we served together for almost ten years. Very closely together. After hours, we were often even closer, in private quarters. Was this part of your Militia service?"

"I object, you Honor, and I refuse to answer such a question, which is irrelevant to the point."

"Overruled. Our Brotherhood has sworn to tell the truth, all the truth. Answer the question."

"We became very close; we were lovers; I felt great affection for you. But I never once forgot my mission, and I learned much. It was thanks to our intimate relations that I was able to procure a map of Mesnos, which allowed the Militia to land here. I did

53

not know that New Terra had been destroyed by an earthquake and that the citizens, or most of them, had fled to Sandstone in the north, or had established a new New Terra a few kilometers to the south. But I did know that Space Fleet would follow the Militia unit here, since I arranged for a leak in their security system to lure your forces here. I also destroyed our communicators, which means that we have lost all contact with Constellation."

Christina was relieved to learn that the Mesnosians were still all alive. But what an actor this man must be! She had no idea! Their friends, all dead, because she didn't see through him! And yet, in retrospect, how could she have missed the signs? No time to consider that now; back to the cross-examination.

"You therefore admit that you committed treason against your own people, even murdering some? Your own people: it doesn't matter whether you think of yourself as a Space Fleet Lieutenant or as a Militia man, because in both cases you're a traitor! (*A traitor, no!*)"

"Your question is rhetorical, Commander. It would be improper to reply."

"Do you not acknowledge that the World Government began its operations against the Militia only after the Militia had attacked a score of sites and killed over 500 people? And that this is not the comportment of an aggressor organization, but a legitimate act of self-defense?" (*Lies! Lies!*)

"While it is true that the Militia attacked first, it is also true that the World Government refused to halt its illegal operations, and thus provoked the Militia with a virtual declaration of war. In this sense, the World Government has been the aggressor for generations, and the Militia has been defending itself. Sometimes self-defense must take the form of preemptive strikes." (*He tells the truth!*)

"According to this twisted reasoning, aggression is self-defense, terrorism is legal, and self-defense is aggression. It is hard to speak reason to a mind-set that refuses reason. No further questions."

"The defendant will now take the stand, closely guarded. Commander Vasa, do you wish to question yourself, or would you prefer to have a surrogate appointed?"

"No. I have already replied to the trumped-up and misrepresented charges against me." (*She lies! She lies!*).

"Prosecutor, do you wish to cross-examine the defendant?"

Come on, Boris, get after me. Ask me about the battle at the waterfall in Assam, when you blew up a cargo train full of Primmies, or the time on Ares when you killed the Deacon's predecessor. Come on.

"I do, your Honor. Commander Vasa, you claim that in the 76 murders you are charged with, you were never the aggressor. And yet you were a member of the aggressor force, the World Government Space Fleet, were you not? And your mission was to seek and destroy the enemy, the 'Primmies,' as you called them?"

"The Space Fleet was then and continues now to operate against the Militia in a defensive manner. When we are given orders to seek out its members, we are never told to destroy them. We aim to capture them, and to rehabilitate them. (*Liar! Liar!*) Furthermore, Lieutenant, you know this is the truth."

Boris chose not to reply.

"No further questions, your Honor."

"Take the prisoner to her cell. And let the jury debate the case in the adjacent chamber. And remember, Commander, any attempt to escape or fight will result in a slow and painful death."

Christina glared at the old manipulator, then turned to her guards and said, "I am at your disposal."

———

"Has the jury reached a decision?"

"We have, your Honor. Concerning the charge of murder, we find the defendant not guilty of murder in six of the cases (the two on Ares and the four here on Mesnos), not guilty of first-degree murder in the other 70, since she did not plan in advance to kill them; but we find her guilty of manslaughter in those cases, since she acted as a paid killer for the World Government, and in any case could have used less than lethal force."

Christina, caught by surprise by the not-guilty verdicts, was smitten by the manslaughter verdicts. The brief smile that had flashed across her face faded. Boris was looking at her, expressionless.

"Concerning the charge of leading raids against the Militia, we believe that she was behaving in a manner proper for a soldier in a time of war, and find her innocent."

"Concerning the charge of her being an infidel and a non-believer, she has admitted to this, and is guilty. There is no proof that she has opposed the Primitivist religion in particular, and we find her not guilty of that charge."

The crowd had been strangely quiet up to now. Perhaps the Deacon had instructed them to behave themselves, who knows? But suddenly they stood up and shouted, "*Death to the infidel!*" almost as if they had rehearsed their line.

"Finally, the defendant has admitted to having undergone the operation extending her life unnaturally, and is therefore guilty as charged." (*Death to the Monster!*)

"Thank you, Brothers and Sisters of the jury. Commander Vasa, please rise. I sentence you to 20 years in prison for each of the 70 counts of manslaughter; the sentences are to be served consecutively."

You don't have to have mastered macroquantum mathematics to calculate that 1400 years far exceeds even my lifetime, thought Christina; anyway she had only 175 years or so left to live. Unless she died first, she added, with a rueful form of gallows humor. The Primmies caught on to the math, too, and were on their feet cheering. The Deacon silenced them, and then continued issuing the sentences.

"For the crime of atheism, our divine law has but one sentence: death!" (*Death to the infidel! Death to the infidel!*) Christina stole a glance at Boris; he appeared to twitch a little, unless she was imagining things, but soon recovered his passivity.

"And for the crime of wilfully undergoing the unnatural operation, our law has but one sentence: death!" (*Death to the Monster!*)

"I will suspend the death sentences if the defendant chooses to embrace the Primitivist religion before the firing squad executes her in the morning. Do you have anything to say?"

"I wish to appeal this so-called trial."

"There is no appeal to a deaconate trial in a time of war. Guards! Take her away, and make sure she does not escape. Your lives are at stake."

———

Damn blue glow! How can you think when that's surrounding you? How can I slip past the guards? If I can just get past them, I'll find my way out that door Boris and I saw this morning. Boris! The bastard. Yeah, he told the truth, but not all of it. You'd almost think he was an angel. And what twisted reasoning! How could anybody believe that? Well, **they** did, that's what counts. And I die at dawn. I'll die, when there's still so much to do! when I have so many things stored in my brain! so many things I have to let other people in on! The Deacon, that hateful slug! How smug is the slug!

She chuckled softly at her little pun, when she heard a light thud outside the door. The door opened a crack. Boris!

"Get out of here, you son of a bitch!"

"Shh! I'm here to free you. Listen. I know you can't believe me, but I have just a few minutes before my task is finished. I had to go through with the sham trial in order to be able to come here and take care of my next-to-last mission, which is to get you back to the Constellation."

"You bastard! You just want to get me killed more horribly. I'm prepared to be zapped, but not to be tortured to death."

"Christina, please listen," he whispered to this bundle of hate tied up on a bed. "Let me cut the ropes. We have a unique situation tonight: all the Militia force is gathered here, in a few rooms, 165 of them. Either they will be alive tomorrow morning, or you will. It's your choice."

"Why are you doing this?"

"Not every Primmie, as you call us, supports the Militia. Most of us want peace, a quiet place to live, to practice our religion. We don't agree with your notion of extended life, of colonization as a means of dealing with the population pressures

57

on Earth. Maybe a planet of our own is the answer. Anyway, we're looking for a peaceful way out. And I have to get you out while there's time."

"What about you?"

"If I manage to get free, I have some ID that will allow me to become a Mesnosian. No time for sentimentality," he added, tears welling in his reddened eyes. "You know the way to that side door. Go!"

"Boris!" she sobbed. Then, seeing he was resolute, she gave him a final kiss on his cheek, and slipped out the door.

The maze of the tunnels was child's play to her, and she soon was out in the dark world outside. The stars were shining brightly overhead in the moonless sky. She had just reached the transmat site a few hundred meters away, at the edge of the woods, when she heard a mighty explosion. Turning around, she saw the old hangar blown apart, and a fireball consuming the tunnels.

"Boris!"

MESNOS IN THE SUNLIGHT

Calm down, Christina. Sit down here, catch your breath. And don't go up to Constellation until you stop blubbering. Stop that shuddering. Think about something else, get outside of yourself. Fix your mind on things that happened, as though you were not part of it. Remember that somehow you escaped. Look over there, at the fiery ruins of the hangar, think about the people burning in the tunnels below, people who didn't escape, who weren't given a chance to go free. Sure, they're fanatics and they tried to kill you, but according to what they perceived of as the law, and probably honestly. Maybe they died of asphyxiation, or of the force of the explosives, before the terrible heat descended on them.

And Boris! Was he able to make his escape? Where could he have gone to, if he did get out some secret doorway marked on his map? Who will he be now, what name will he use, if he's alive? If. There's no chance he escaped, he's a complete loss when it comes to finding his way out of a room. He's dead. How could he have done all of that? He must have had nerves of steel. And a conscience of steel, too, or maybe a lack of conscience: he killed so many of his own friends, or at least led them into ambushes. And then those Militia people, who like us thought he was on their side. Whose side was he on? Is there something about the blind faith of the Primmies that leads them to this, that allows them to justify their most heinous acts, their betrayals, in the name of their god? I wonder what it's like to have that belief, I mean the faith of these people, like Boris, who believe but who disdain the extremists in their midst. Maybe someday I'll find out. Hell, I've got about 200 years to discover things like that. But I doubt I'll ever understand, I mean **feel** what it's like to be a member of the Militia. What fanatics!

Boris, Boris, why did you do it? But in truth, you're a hero! You've saved the colonists on Mesnos, who will learn about your bravery, but will never know the pleasure of your presence. You'll occupy a special place in my memories, until the day I die.

Okay, Christina, you're almost back to normal. Dry those eyes. Take another look around, then summon the transmat. You've got a report to make, and our job here on Mesnos can now begin. Time now to pay attention to the settlers, the scientific crew, the supplies. Some further exploration of the planet. Maybe a chance to relax and get hold of yourself.

—

"Commander Christina Vasa reporting..."

"Omygod, Captain, what's happened to you? You've got to get to sick bay. We lost contact with you; I can see why: you don't have your communicator. We were about to go down after you and the expeditionary force, because you were gone for just over the 25-day limit you had set for us. Are the others waiting to come up? What's it like down there?"

Christina tried to answer the barrage of questions, then made her preliminary oral report to the Command Staff on Constellation, in the absence of Captain Stone, who was ailing in sick bay. She came close to breaking down again under the emotional strain of reporting the events of this month on Mesnos. Based on her report, a preliminary expedition was sent to the new site of New Terra, and another one was dispatched to Sandstone. They were to meet with the mayors and with the planet's governor. Supplies, information, news of family on Earth and the Space Stations, and over a thousand new settler families, each with its own new housing module, were all to be sent down as expeditiously as possible. About half the settlers were planning to go to each city.

Christina was sent to sick bay, where the medical staff gave her the usual examination, and then she took a long shower and washed her disgustingly filthy hair. Sometime later, she asked to see Captain Stone.

"Didn't they tell you?" asked Dr. Della Città.

"Tell me what, Giovanna?"

"Captain Stone had a stroke while you were gone. It was a massive stroke that paralyzed him totally. We did our best, but

I'm afraid... He's dead."

"Oh, no! I don't know how much more I can take. My entire expeditionary force, my friends, Boris... Now this... It's too much."

Christina lay down on a cot and wept, sobbing convulsively. Doctor Della Città gave her a tranquilizing shot from her medical gun, and soon Christina fell into a deep sleep. When she awoke, Commander Constantinos was with Giovanna at her bedside. "Homer! Giovanna! What happened? Where am I? Oh..." The memory of her return to Constellation, the questions, the report, the grim news, the overwhelming weight of being the lone survivor, thoughts of her friends, of her escape from death. She shuddered. "Do you feel better? Have you actually rested?"

"I feel restored physically, but so sad. I can't believe all that's happened in such a short time. At least, the settlers will have somewhere to go, and can become part of living communities. I was afraid for a while that New Terra was completely destroyed by the Militia, along with an entire population."

"Christina," said Homer, "I know, we all know that you've been through a lot. And I know that most of the news you've had to tell us and that you've learned from us has been bad. But we do have some good news to report: the new settlers are about to disembark, but they want to see you first, to thank you for what you've done for them.

"What I've done?"

"It's only been a couple of days since you returned, ..."

"A couple of days? I've been out for a couple of days?"

"Yes, and everyone on board, and probably everyone on Mesnos knows about your adventures and how you saved the planet from the Militia. The settlers also know about Lieutenant Smirnoff's vital role in making their safe landing possible."

"What a shame they can't thank Boris in person for his courageous act. He literally gave up his life for them. And what a shame they can't thank the Captain for what he did for them. He got us through meteor showers, a wild electrical storm in–literally–the middle of nowhere, and had to reroute our trajectory. They're both gone, now."

"They **have** come to thank the Captain. You."

"What?"

"Captain Stone had in his possession authorization to name you his deputy, which he was going to do after your expedition. The Staff has named you, for the duration of this mission, its Captain. We will request a permanent promotion when we return to Headquarters, in the name of Captain Stone."

Christina looked first at Homer, then at Giovanna, then back again. They looked dead serious, despite their warm smiles; this can't be a prank. I know the Captain intended to recommend me for a promotion, but he must have kept this news as a secret. She felt a warm surge, gulped, tried to hide her emotions behind a steely, expressionless face, but her charade lasted at best a few seconds. She smiled. Her eyes were brightened by teardrops of pride and gratitude.

"I... I... I have to get dressed and meet the settlers. We have so much to do! And what do I say? I've never been a Captain before!"

———

6 June 2650

A day for reflection. The destruction of the Himalayas and the Sermon in the Valley, both celebrated as holidays by different people. Tomorrow we leave. This second month on Mesnos is doubly blessed: it's been both peaceful and sunny.

I've now seen the cities and met the original settlers, by now full-fledged Mesnosians. The first Mesnosian children are already beginning to grow up. Our new immigrants are delighted with what they see, have great plans for the future. Each town has a fully-operational hospital, schools, all the social institutions needed for our kind of government. I feel good about their future. Still, I wonder about our enterprise: the colonization of compatible planets where there is no intelligent life. At least we're not driving off any natives. And there will have to be contact with Earth, dependence on Earth, at least until the population is large enough and its economy stable enough to allow for the establishment of a university. I wonder about how we, or rather how the Mesnosians will treat this planet, their home.

Evolution works in mysterious ways. Take Earth and Mesnos as examples. And Paracelsus 2 or any of the other planets with some life, or with a past history of life, that I've been on. In some ways, they all seem to have started creating life from a similar base: pools of water, the right organic compounds, some electrical storms or maybe a seismic event or a meteorite to provide a burst of energy, and voilà! life! Algae, bacteria, something we call primitive, but which is almost beyond understanding. They're still one-celled things, but they must be infinitely more complex than the organic compounds they sprang from. A few tens or hundreds of millions of years, once oxygen is plentiful in the atmosphere that these creatures have brought into existence, these remarkable beings give way to inconceivably more complex creatures. I've examined some of these so-called primitive one-celled plants and animals. How beautifully organized they are inside, and how different one species is from the other! And in every one of these beginnings on every planet and with every form of life, there must have been different initial conditions, a different environment, a different set of chance happenings, that makes them all (despite their similarities) unique. What was it Dr. Smith, my biology professor, used to say? "If life on Earth were to revert to some previous age, and it all took off again from there, everything would be different, and the human race would not have evolved." It would have taken so little for us not to be here as it is. Maybe on some other planets we'll meet some of our other possible selves, evolved so differently. There must be intelligent life somewhere.

It was on Calaban that I encountered those odd sulfur-based life forms. Some were about the size of crabs, and seemed to be on top of the food chain. Others looked like yellowish jellyfish, only living on land. Thousands of them in every little colony. They appeared to be scavengers, but were the favorite dish of those crabs. At the bottom of the line, there must have been something akin to plankton, themselves maybe feeding on the microscopic life forms that gave rise to the entire biota. Plants?

Animals? What were these things? Under analysis, we found something akin to DNA, but with a structure unlike anything we'd ever encountered before, although the basic elements were similar. Could that have happened on Earth? A crushing blow from a passing meteor of just the right size and at just the right time, and there might have been a sulfur-based life form (or maybe silicon-based, or nitrogen-based), or maybe there wouldn't have been any life on Earth at all. Maybe Earth would have evolved like Venus, before Aphrodite, a hostile environment for life as we know it. Or maybe life would have evolved differently, somehow. We never returned there, in any case, to Calaban. It appeared to be incompatible with our life systems.

On Mesnos, life has evolved to the level of something like lions or wolves. There is something like our plant life, the mékis being an example, and there are animals, warm-blooded like the stots and cold-blooded like the wolks. There's a food chain. But there are no flowering plants, nothing that looks like insects, no crustaceans. I don't know what fills their niche in the food chain, or what the evolutionary history of these creatures is. Our settlers have introduced Earth crops and some domesticated animals. They're trying to add Earth to Mesnos. So far they've succeeded, but you never know what will happen in the long run. A slight new element, an insect, for instance, might produce an effect truly unimaginable, like the introduction, back in the nineteenth and twentieth centuries, of rabbits to Australia or muskrats to the Netherlands, or so many species of flora and fauna to Hawaii. How un-Newtonian! No proportion to the reactions, which were not equal and opposite! Here, stots and wolks are in decline, but that means that some other animal populations are exploding. Where will it end? And it's nice seeing the live oaks and the red maples that have been planted here, and grass and corn, but how will this affect the native flora? What will happen when the Earth plants and animals get into the wild, mix in with, even mate with, the native biota, begin new lines of evolution? There's a close relationship between the DNA strands of the native life and ours, after all. I guess we have a right to do this. Colonization is commonplace in every life system. Ants colonize new territory, so do beavers. Humans have been doing it for millennia. But this is our first colonized planet.

The Mesnosians even began to make a historical museum out of the old factory area. I had been surprised by the primitive textile machines in the mine shafts, but it turns out that these machines are not really what the settlers used to weave clothing: they were trying to recreate some little bit of humanity's past here on this distant and alien world, even a past they've never known, to keep alive the memory our humanity's long rise to dominance on our home planet, even while they're adapting to life on this alien new world.

Mesnos can be nice, even beautiful, when the monsoon-like rains stop. I encountered a month of rain, and now a month of blue skies with two suns shining down on me. There are mountains and valleys, oceans and lakes, deserts and swamps. Different creatures, all of them exotic but the people have given them names like Earth animals. Loons. Baboons. Teals. Seals. They don't look anything like those animals, but they do occupy similar niches in the life of the planet. They'll have to adapt to people, who hunt some, eat many, and have domesticated yet others for food. The two suns—the large one up high and bright, the other, smaller one staying close to the horizon and distant— are extraordinary, now that I've been able to relax a bit here and enjoy the place. The golden sunsets of the main sun, on the western horizon, over the ocean, with the waves breaking in on the shore, while the other, smaller, sun drops a few degrees down to disappear from the horizon an hour or so later! The moonless nights full of stars in constellations so different from those we're familiar with! The weird calls of the creatures in the mékis and the oaks and maples, the strange smells in a world without flowers, the rough touch of the skin of the crocs (that seem to be neither animal nor vegetable, but a bit of both)! How different Nature is, and yet how similar! Clouds, blue skies, rivers! The ocean, the volcanic-sand beaches! This planet might become a tourist attraction for the super-rich. I almost dread the thought of what could happen if that came about.

The two suns are actually a binary star system, that the inhabitants call Castor and Pollux, rotating around each other.

Mesnos rotates around Castor. And although it has no moon, the gravitational pull of Pollux, along with that of Castor, provide enough energy for tidal action, and probably for at least some of the seismic activity we've noticed here, and that destroyed the first New Terra. Another tourist attraction: how many people have experienced the density of the stars here, and two suns to boot?

I've never seen cities that were more modern, clean and neat. The housing modules brought from Earth, the new houses built of local stone or of bricks made from a rich clay, the well-designed transportation systems. I expect that, given 200 or 300 years, this planet will have millions of people as the colonists pour in, and that it will be tremendously prosperous. Lots of metals buried underground, and lots of opportunities for people who are willing to leave everything and everyone behind, even if not quite forever. They remind me of those brave settlers on Earth who travelled to unknown places for whatever purposes, political, religious, economic, social, and established new homelands for themselves. Even in recent times, the settlers in the Gobi, on Greenland, in Antarctica are heroes in my book. So are the Mesnosians.

I hope they don't destroy the natural beauty of the waterfalls, the mountains, the lakes, the beaches. There's a waterfall of over 1000 meters near Sandstone, actually an underground river or a spring bursting out of the mountain and splashing down on the ground a full kilometer below with a roar you have to hear to believe and with a mist that fills you with awe. Impressive, spectacular, especially when seen from a certain angle that produces a gorgeous rainbow.

And there's another whole continent to explore! Why not make Pacifica a preserve, as Atlantica continues to be converted into a new Earth? What a unique opportunity! We could have done this with Antarctica, but instead we've settled it. Mines, farms, fishing villages. It's no more exotic than the fertile Gobi Plain! But here! Well, the inhabitants will have to decide what to do. And they have plenty of time before the population begins to outgrow the land.

Will I be around to see any of that, assuming I'm on some

future mission to Mesnos? Two hundred years sounds like a long time, but yet, when you think of the future, so many interesting things will happen beyond that span of time. I remember Stanley Narb, my friend Dr. Stanley Narb, telling me that in a way the procedure he was about to use on me could be a blessing or a bane, or maybe both at the same time. Two hundred years! It sounded like such a long time then, when I was only 28. But now! How right you were, Stanley! I've already felt the pain of a long life, and I've already felt the great pleasure it can bring. What happened to you, Stanley? Where did you disappear to? Are you still alive? If I looked for you and found you, would I have the courage to ask you to do the unthinkable, to add another 200, even 500 years to my life? And would you do it if you could?

We on Constellation have our own tasks to perform, new worlds to discover, new frontiers. There were rumors of really long-distance explorations, transgalactic explorations, when we were back at Headquarters on Earth. I don't think Constellation-type craft can do the trick. On the other hand, modifications would not take too much time or resources to install. But who would go? The ELB, of course; but ordinary people, with ordinary life spans, would they volunteer?

The Extended Life Brigade. Stanley Narb's dream! He had the initial experiments performed on himself. There must be hundreds of us around now, all owing two centuries of life to him. A two-fold debt: he worked out the procedure, involving changes in the structure of certain genes; and he performed all the procedures personally. I must find that man, if only to let him know how grateful we all are. The discovery of new worlds might not have been possible without him.

If we do discover new habitable worlds at the far reaches of the galaxy, or even beyond, this might be for the settlers (or even the explorers) the end of contact with Earth, that far out. They might get there, but would they be able to return? What dangers lurk in those uncharted regions? And if we decide to risk traveling through worm holes, how do we know where they end up, or whether we can get back through them? Who would be willing to settle that far away? We can get to Mesnos in a few months, but how long would it take to reach the other end of the galaxy? Maybe the Primmies would be willing to take the risk? Not a bad idea, after all. I like Boris's idea, a planet just for the Primitivists (not the Militia–that's another story altogether). There they could be what they want to be, without interference, without contact with Earth if that's what they want. A world of their own, on the other side of the galaxy. But would they submit to the use of technology like this to transport them to their paradise? Sure, they don't really seem to be opposed to most technology. They function normally in our world, travel around like us, dress like us. Their primitivism is in their thoughts and in the way they worship, I guess. I'll make a point of recommending this to the authorities when I get back home. Maybe even insert it in my report. Boris would be happy if he knew his idea might receive an audience.

It's getting dark, I hear Giovanna calling. A last look at the sunset, a last breath of this astonishingly fresh air. Time to return to reality.

———

"Thank you very much for your kindness and hospitality, Governor. The crew and I all have enjoyed our days of working and relaxing here on Mesnos. Those of us who can will return someday. I wouldn't be surprised if some of the crew decide to settle in Mesnos when they retire! But you know how little we control our schedules in our active life in Space Fleet."

"Once again, Captain, on behalf of everyone here on Mesnos, I would like to thank you for all you and your crew have done for us. We are in the process of erecting a memorial to the valiant soldiers who gave their lives so that ours would be saved. If only there had been another way... I imagine that Paradise will always be an elusive dream for us human beings. Elusive, but worth seeking. Enough philosophizing. Farewell, Christina my friend, and bon voyage!"

"Au revoir, Charles. Until we meet again!"

In small groups, the crew transmatted up to Constellation. Within an hour, Christina was to give her first command as

Captain (however temporary that captaincy might be). She had never been in command of a large craft before, or responsible for so many people. She just hoped the flight home would be smooth and without incident. But she thought she was ready for most emergencies now. It just seemed so strange to be sitting there giving the commands. This might be the first time, but she felt confident that it wouldn't be the last.

PARACELSUS:TERROR IN THE DEEP

Captain's Log for 6 June 2720

For reasons that will be clear later in this entry, I was physically unable to make a report during this first trip, and have been psychologically unable to do so for some time. I am grateful to Space Fleet Command to have allowed me these many years before making my official entry.

It's a long trip, even in a ship that can go ten times the speed of light. It's taken us, once again, five years to reach Paracelsus, which has been transformed in the last 200 years. Only two centuries! When we first came here, it was a hot and dry planet, mostly a desert, but with an atmosphere and oceans and great stores of fresh water in huge aquifers: a planet that was not comfortable, but was inhabitable by humans. We found a large island in the middle of an ocean, surrounded by at least 1000 km of water on every side. Here we planted some trees, set up a few buildings, and dug some wells. When we came back, it was with over 200 prisoners, Militia people who had been particularly vicious. They were set down in what had become a fairly green island. Nevertheless, they had to build a community from scratch. A hard life was in store for them. And, given the sea creatures we had found ten or eleven years earlier, we knew that they would have no chance for escape.

On the other hand, it could have been worse for them. Their new and final home was a prison without walls and without guards. The place was theirs to make what they wanted it to be. No weapons, of course; and no contact with Earth except for the rare visits when more prisoners would be brought. What they didn't know was that they would never have the chance to raise families there. Acting on orders from the Earth government, early in the course of the five years it took to reach Paracelsus 2, all the prisoners were sterilized, without their knowing it, through a combination of low-level radiation and certain pharmaceuticals delivered in their food. This practice was continued right up to the last group of prisoners, the last of the Militia.

We dropped off those first prisoners back in the 2700s, after putting down enough buildings to handle twice their number. There was a year's supply of food, and two years' supply of seeds. There were ample supplies of water accessible through the wells we had dug on our first setting foot on the island.

Then we revisited the planet's one huge continent, or perhaps it would be more accurate to say its two continents joined by a kind of isthmus. This is where the settlers, the colonists, moved to on subsequent trips, and it's a booming place today. Forests, actual rainfall now, and abundant wildlife brought in from Venus (that is, Earth animals that had adapted to the warmer conditions on Venus) and Mesnos. Farms, cities, schools and all the institutions of modern life and culture. Rivers and lakes. But out in the oceans, there's still a menace that sends chills up my spine when I think about it. Paracelsus 2 (we like to use the number because in another star system we had discovered a planet that seemed livable but that in the end began to spew forth toxic fumes from an excess of seismic activity) was also the scene of another direct and personal encounter I had with death up in the mountains. The sea and the mountains, a terrifying experience for me. All during that first trip. Not a good beginning for a long friendship.

———

"Captain," said Commander Constantinos, "this island has all that's needed to support and sustain human life, but our first exploration makes it look pretty bleak. No trees or other big plants. The oceans harbor life, seemingly a huge number of different life forms. We haven't had a chance to look into that, though: we'll need our experimental surface craft and our submarine."

"While you haven't been looking at the sea, we have been looking from above at something very promising, Homer, a continent about 1500 km to the west. Plenty of underground water there, too, just like here, according to our sensors. We'll tell you more about it when we get together, but we decided not to touch down there yet: it's probably better to do just one thing at a time, and a continent will take a good deal of time to explore, even in a cursory manner. We'll go back there later. This planet has possibilities. Have you seen any interesting plant or animal life at all down there?"

"There are grasses, ferns, moss, and such things, but not like what's on Earth or on Mesnos. There is a strange kind of animal life here, with many species: small ten-legged scurrying things of various colors. Incredibly, they seem to have bony skeletons and a thick skin, not exoskeletons and chitin like insects. They seem to be amphibians, but are in the size range of insects, and from what we've been able to see, have found a niche similar to the one insects have carved for themselves on Earth. We have a few samples of the fauna and flora if you think we should study them."

"If I think...! Of course, you'll have to bring them up! More miracles of life, other paths of evolution! Have you seen anything else on land? And what about that life you mentioned seeing in the ocean?"

"We haven't found any fish or fish-like things yet. There are soft-shelled or maybe it's soft-skinned creatures that look something like lobsters but also with bony skeletons, there are clam-like animals, and jellyfish-like swimmers washed up on shore: these are the most numerous. There must be a lot of life out there. But you won't believe what we discovered yesterday. "

"Try me. I've been to lots of places, seen lots of things."

"Try this for size. We saw near the horizon, in the seas, something that looks like a monster."

"What do you mean, a monster? Monsters belong in fairy tales or in myths and legends, not in a scientist's report."

"See, I told you you wouldn't believe me. Captain, we're talking something that's huge, maybe 30 or 40 meters across, swimming out there. I can assure you it's frighteningly large. We've captured it on visudisk, and it looks just as eerie on our scanners as it did out there in its element. The scanners are too small to allow us to get any detail, though. Maybe we can enhance the quality of the images and see something on the visuscreens on Constellation."

"Imagine that! A monster, a sea-monster at that! Pardon my skepticism, Homer, I find it hard to swallow."

"Captain, if it's as big as we think, it could swallow us!"

"No doubt about it: we'd better investigate that, and whatever else might be lurking in the sea, before we explore the continent. We'll be in transporter range in a few minutes. You can come up here for a day or so and let us take a look at your pictures, examine the life forms you've collected, and then we'll fly the sea crafts down to the surface. This sounds intriguing."

———

"Jama, what can you tell us about these scurrying creatures?"

"There are scavengers there, as well as vegetarians, and carnivore hunters. The couple of hundred samples Homer and his crew collected really cover a lot of ground. They all have fairly primitive brains, more like ganglions than brains, good eyesight (of course, the hunters are exceptional in that), and good hearing. Only one group of these animals seems to want to live in a colony. And they're hunters. The hunted seem to depend on speed and an uncanny ability to bury themselves in dirt in no time flat. The hunters don't seem to work alone, ever."

"Cooperative hunters, even at insect-size level. That's a new one. Maybe they move fast because of the heat here. It's a hot planet, somewhat hotter than Earth, about like Venus, I think. I imagine that they don't have any capacity to regulate body temperatures."

"Actually, they are both hot-blooded and cold-blooded."

"You mean, some are one way and some are the other?"

"No, I mean that they're all cold-blooded in the sense that they turn off their heat regulation systems when the temperature ranges between 25 and 37 degrees. Below or above those parameters, their warm-blooded mechanism kicks in. We've not exposed them to too-harsh temperatures, but they can take temperatures as low as 10 and as high as 45."

"Amazing. When we know what they need to live, maybe we can make a little terrarium for them."

"Or a paracelsarium."

"OK. A paracelsarium it will be. On another topic, are preparations made for the boats? When can we send down a larger party for that exploration? Have you chosen your staff? Have they been trained in using the equipment? Sorry about these questions; they're required by the manual."

"Everything's ready, Captain. We can leave in the morning."

"Good. We'll get everyone down, in rotations of about 100 people at a time. We'll try to combine some rest and recreation with the work we're charged with doing."

———

"Janus, as chief of security, you must make sure that no one gets out in the water to swim, or even dips a hand in it, until we're sure it's safe. All indications are that on this planet the oceans are warm and are teeming with life. Strange, on land it seems that living things are at a pretty primitive point of evolution. Anyhow, we can't take chances in the water. Everyone instructed and otherwise ready and properly equipped?"

"Yes, Captain. The submarine crew, all five of them, know that they must not provoke any of the creatures here. Their instructions are to try to evade pursuers, to stun them if force is needed, and to kill only in the last instance. I've spoken to the ten persons who will accompany me on the Wavehopper. They also know what to do, and what not to do."

"While your units are on mission, Janus, we'll be looking for a place to sink wells here on the island. We should have plenty of drinking water when you come back."

"Captain, so far we have not seen any evidence of serious atmospheric disturbances. There are clouds, there are winds, but there haven't been any storms. It looks pretty safe out there. Even the waves are moderate. How far out should we go? Do we dare venture much beyond the sight of land? And what about taking a dip?"

"For starters, I want you to be conservative. No swimming; I know that will disappoint some people, especially with the warm salt water and the hot sun, but we can't take chances with so many unknowns. Stay pretty close to shore. Make sure you keep within radio contact of the shore party; if you lose direct contact, get right on to the Constellation radio signals. And also make sure that Wavehopper and Deep Crawler are in constant touch. Remember, what had seemed to be a huge monster was actually a pod of something, like medusas, but swimming together as though with a purpose. On Earth, some of these things are poisonous. They might be very dangerous here."

"Aye, aye, Captain!" said Janus, putting on a sailor's cap that he produced from apparently nowhere. Another of his magic tricks. Christina smiled. It's a good thing his classical training is defective, or he'd slip on a mask with two faces, like the old Roman god whose name he bears.

The two crews got in a longboat and went out to where their craft were awaiting them in a kind of protected harbor. A bunch of jellyfish looked at them through their eerie ring of eyes. The on-shore party watched as they finally went away.

———

"Sentra, how has the photography been going?" asked Pharsilla, the commander of Deep Crawler.

"It's been a real treat, Lieutenant. It's amazing that we've not seen anything that looks like a fish yet. Lots of those jellyfish-like things, nautiluses, conchs, things that look like squid but with ten tentacles and two longer arms. We've been able to take pictures of floating islands of plants of all colors. Look at the one up there: red and yellow flowers, green stems and leafy-looking structures."

"Beautiful. Flowers swimming in the ocean, none on land. The Captain was right, though, some of these creatures look downright unfriendly. I wouldn't dare send anyone out in these infested waters. The sea is crowded, like some places on Earth and Venus where life is too abundant! I've never experienced an ocean so stocked with living things. Look at that ugly thing!"

"Lieutenant, these jellyfish-like things scare me. They have eyes making a kind of circle on their back; 16 eyes. And they seem to swim in groups. I've noticed that they hunt with incredible efficiency. Even those squids, that seem so fast, can't outswim them; they're sort of hemmed in by 20 or so jellyfish, which corral them and then move in for the kill. They're hunting machines. Even three of them seem to be enough to close in for the kill. Strange. You never see them hunt alone, or for that matter in pairs, even if their prey is smaller than they are. It's as though they get more intelligent when there are more of them."

"Yes, and the larger and the smaller species all seem to work in groups. Those creatures that made up what looked like a monster must all be over a meter across, with legs at least two meters long."

"Speak of the devil, just ahead of us, there's a welcoming committee."

"Olney, get in touch with Wavehopper right away. We'd better warn them about this. If these things are as organized as their smaller cousins, we might be in for something."

"Deep Crawler to Wavehopper. Warning. A school of those giant jellyfish, about 20 meters down, is approaching us. Be on the alert. From what we've seen of the other jellyfish, they can be persistent and deadly hunters. Over."

"Wavehopper to Deep Crawler. Warning received. We have our lasers readied and set at stun. We have observed smaller jellies at work: they're terrifyingly efficient hunters. Keep us informed of your progress. We're all glad we were not allowed to go for a swim. Over."

"Hermione, is that you? Pharsilla here. Listen, get your crew inside. Tell Janus, I mean tell Commander Skyhawk, that it might not be a bad idea to turn Wavehopper around. The school is huge, a circle at least 100 meters across and about two or three creatures deep. I'll leave the channels open, but we've all got to get ready for action here. They're sizing us up, and I think they're coming after us. They're beginning to break their circle and form all around us. It looks serious."

"Commander Skyhawk here," said Janus. I'm calling in the crew right away. Let us know if you need support of any sort."

Suddenly, on what seemed to be a signal from one of the jellyfish, the attack came, simultaneously from all sides. They were caught in a tangle of tentacles, with huge gaping maws and vicious teeth trying to cut into Deep Crawler's walls. The sub lurched sharply to one side, then another.

"They're working in harmony with each other!"

"They've grabbed the periscope! They've trying to pull it off!"

"Our orders are to try everything before using lethal force. Olney! Try a rapid deep dive! Sentra, a quick electric shock on the surface of the ship! That should loosen their grip."

The submarine dived suddenly to about 50 meters at the moment the shock loosened the grip of the jellies. They recoiled, as if caught by surprise.

"The evasive tactic seems to have worked, Lieutenant! No, wait, they've regrouped and they're coming after us!"

"Plunge deeper! Get down to 100, even 150 meters."

"They're following us this deep, Commander! Should I try 200 meters?"

"200 meters, and spin to starboard, then cut back sharply to port. OK. Up and down patterns now! ... We can't shake them!"

"Some of them have caught up with us."

"Head for the surface, or rather to 10 meters."

Standard evasive tactics did not seem to work. The shocks had less of an effect after the initial jolt; can they adjust that fast? Whatever Pharsilla tried, their pursuers kept coming. Even the amazing speed of this craft was no obstacle to the surging herd. It took some time, but finally, they caught up to Deep Crawler, and once again they attacked in formation and got her in their grasp.

"Stun the jellies holding on to us!"

"Stunning them doesn't seem to be enough! We may need more force."

"First level shock!"

"That seems to have gotten them off the ship, but they've got plenty of replacements."

In fact, they doubled the number of attackers, and began to pull the ship in different directions. Can they think? A frightening thought. And just look at those maws!

"Lethal force!"

One after another, the beasts loosened their grip, then floated lifeless towards the surface. After five attacks–was the number significant?–the survivors let out what sounded like a collective scream, and headed up to the surface.

"Commander, we're free down here. Had to kill a great number of them, 50 or more. Be careful: they're on their way up. They're vicious and seem to have a high degree of intelligence. Head back to shore! They might capsize you!"

"We've already turned around, Pharsilla. Follow after us. Kill any that pursue us. We hope we c..."

"Commander! Commander!"

The creatures had struck. Their tentacles had grasped the Wavehopper's railings. They were trying to pull the craft down, under water! The ship rocked fore and aft, and port to starboard at the same time.

"A soft approach didn't work undersea. We'll go straight for force here," shouted Janus over the strange piercing shrieks of the jellyfish. The crew wasted no time in firing.

A red ray from the cabin struck one, then another, a third. From below decks, more rays struck more jellies. The herd was attacked from behind by Deep Crawler. But the jellies attacked a second, a third, a fourth time. A hundred corpses were floating nearby.

Suddenly, Giorgina cried out in a crazed voice, "The bastards! They want direct contact, do they? Let me at them! They'll get what they want!" Saying this, she suddenly bolted out the door, firing at a jelly that was attacking the radio mast. It screamed, let off a puff of putrid pus-like blood, then loosed its grip, dead. A wave created by the action of the battle splashed over Giorgina. She aimed at another Jelly, shouting, "Take that, you bastard!" Then another.

Meanwhile Janus called out as loud as he could, "Sergeant! Giorgina! Come back inside! That's an order!" Too late! A fifth assault of the jellies turned the ship around, throwing Giorgina in the water. From Deep Crawler and from Wavehopper deadly rays finally freed the craft. But Giorgina!

"Pharsilla! Try to get to her. One of those things is about to try to swallow her whole!"

As Lieutenant Hermione spoke, Giorgina stopped struggling.

Through the transparent maw of the jelly her legs could be seen descending into the digestive system of the monster. Its serrated teeth ripped into the young woman's thighs. "Kill it! Giorgina's already dead! Don't let it eat her!"

The full power of the ray blasted the giant jellyfish apart. A deft manoeuvre allowed Deep Crawler to recover the bloodied remains of their crewmate. The herd, greatly diminished in size, swam away, leaving in all some 150 of their companions behind.

Janus remarked, "You would almost think they had real intelligence, at least as much as wolves or lions have."

The two ships returned to port, with their sad cargo. Giorgina's lifeless and mutilated body was wrapped in a heavy cloth. The first skirmish against a local life form. The first human death on Paracelsus. Would it be the last?

Wavehopper limped back, with some serious damage. Several crewmembers were injured by being thrown around the cabin during the violent battle with the giant jellyfish, but no injury was serious. Except for one. Deep Crawler's damage was slight. The crew was all safe.

Subsequent reconnaissance by Deep Crawler indicated that schools of these creatures roamed the seas all around the island. Interestingly, they now kept their distance from the submarine. Do they have enough intelligence to transmit their fear of the craft to other schools? They must have a method of communication, given the way they hunt. Are these intelligent or near-intelligent life forms?

Jama's team of experts verified that even a group of three can hunt successfully, but that they are helpless as individuals or as pairs. She concluded that they seem to have a kind of collective brain power, linked by psychic or telepathic forces that will have to be studied in the future.

Smaller versions of the jellies had a brain-like structure just behind the eyes, with huge portions of the brains running down four "seams" in their bodies, to a ring of neurons that ran around the edge of the bodies. Somehow the shape of the nerves seemed to have something to do with their ability to communicate with each other, and with other pods. That, and the fact that the large ones must have a brain the size of a dolphin's.

With these creatures surrounding the island, no future prisoner could conceivably escape. No guards would be needed to keep watch in this grim place.

PARACELSUS: THE LAND

Captain's Log for 6 June 2720 (continued)

Exploration of the double continent revealed two important facts: first, the large jellyfish apparently did not infest these waters (they probably don't get out to the deep water, because there's no prey out there); and second, the desert conditions were not uniform, as we had feared. There were pockets of what looked like fern-trees, fruit growing on something akin to banana plants, and even, in some swampy inland areas, primitive trees. In places there were large colonies of the scurrying creatures, some of them as large as salamanders. They came in all varieties and shapes and colors. Jama's team of botanists and zoologists were assembling a mass of information. Geologists and soil experts found the land to be fertile, capable of supporting Earth-type plants. There were huge aquifers throughout the entire continent, the parts we surveyed carefully and the parts we surveyed by distant sensors.

In several well-defined areas, we dug wells, planted trees and flowers, set insects loose, found a way to grow crop plants. The idea was to see, on a return trip in a decade or more, if the planet could become to some extent terran, and if these plants and insects could survive here on their own. But even more importantly, we wanted to plant trees and grasses in part to help retain water and bring about wetter conditions. If enough water were retained in the atmosphere, rainfall might result. Our mathematics experts assured us that their figures showed that we could change the climate of Paracelsus in just a couple of decades.

One day, I joined an expedition up a mountainside covered with lichens and dry moss. Springs and small rivulets provided water that was astonishingly cool, as though it came from deep inside. And it was potable. Tree ferns surrounded by grasses abounded around these springs, and great colonies of scurriers could be seen.

"Not exactly Paradise," I remember saying to Jama, "but a

lot nicer than that island. How about some coconut palms here? And some orchids?"

"Have you just named this spot, Christina? Not Exactly Paradise. Apt. And it looks like we could easily plant palms and flowers."

"Planting trees and flowers are definitely in the plans if we came upon a compatible planet."

I think it was about this time that we heard a distant rumble. "Thunder? You mean it rains here?"

"Well, we are on the windward side of the mountain. Maybe there's a rainy season of a week or two! It's hard to believe a rainy season here could last longer than that."

The rumble grew louder, and closer. "I don't like the sound of that, Jama," I said. "If I didn't know better, I'd almost think it was an earthquake."

"Or a paracelsuquake."

"A para.." As I was about to speak, the rumble was replaced by a loud crack, as if the mountain was being rent apart. We looked up towards the source of the noise, and saw that we were caught in an unexpected avalanche of stone. Tons of rock were bounding down the mountain, coming at us at what seemed like the speed of sound. No time to think! We threw ourselves behind boulders, in gullies, wherever we could find a place to hide. I tried to warn the party below us; they had already taken cover.

The landslide passed directly over us with a roar that has to be experienced to be believed. Pebbles, rocks, boulders crashing onto the rocky soil, onto the dirt, into each other. I am told it was over just as quickly as it had arisen. There were a few injuries, no broken bones, though. With a single exception. Me. Much of what happened there and subsequently I learned only a long time afterwards.

———

Everyone got up, brushed themselves off. People were dazed. A little bruise here, a gash caused by a sharp rock there. What luck! Cave-like indentations in the land, big boulders to hide behind, the big rocks bounding out away from the mountainside for the most part. Fortunately the rockfall was not a real avalanche, although some piles of stone were pushed a good 50 to 100 meters downhill, forming mounds of rubble. It was odd: once the dust settled, if you didn't know there had just been a rockfall, you wouldn't realize that the scenery had changed.

Jama called out the names of her staff. They were all there, present and accounted for.

"Commander, have you seen the Captain?" asked Henri. "Everyone's here except her."

"Captain! Captain Vasa! Christina!"

Dead silence.

"Omygod, she was right next to me! There's no one here, nothing."

"Do you think she could have been knocked out by a falling rock, or swept down the mountainside?"

"No chance! She was crouching down behind a stone right here." Jama's voice drifted off and slowed down as she realized that Christina's stone was no longer there. "The stone, a big yellowish-red stone. Where is it? Could it have..." Jama did not finish her sentence. Instead, she called down to the group below.

"Pedro! Monika! Is the Captain down there?"

At once the entire squad, those above and those below, scrambled to look among the rubble. Pedro called out, "I think this is her hat! And here are her binoculars!"

Painstakingly, stone by stone, they broke up the stone stack. Beneath every rock, nothing!

Another mound. Another futile search. Jama decided to call Constellation.

"Salini, this is Jama. Listen, we've just experienced a flash landslide, maybe caused by an earthquake. It was over in a minute. The crew is all here and accounted for, able to carry on despite some injuries, but we think the Captain is buried beneath tons of rock. Get a medical crew and some fresh bodies down here to help us dig through the piles of stone. Alert the medical group. Quick!"

"Jama," replied Salini from on board, "a crew will be down in a couple of minutes. Set your homing device in a safe place for 10 or 12 people and some equipment."

Just then, a cry rang out from below. They had found Christina! She lay prone, unconscious and immobile beneath a huge boulder. By some stroke of luck, her head seemed not to have been hit by the stones that must have been flying all around her. But one big one was resting on her legs, another on her back. It was not a scene anyone had wanted to see. The ground was stained with blood. Her face was gaunt. It looked grim and gruesome. We soon learned that it was even worse than it looked. But she was breathing! She was alive!

"Quick! contact Constellation! Tell them we need a machine to lift up the rock. The Captain's bleeding badly, maybe she's dying! Hurry!"

No sooner said than done. The emergency crew came within a minute with the necessary equipment.

Janus came down with the emergency crew and took charge of the operation. He placed a machine about ten meters up the hill from where Christina lay, a small derrick with an extensible neck that he had stretched out over the immobile body. "Quick, put the hoisting irons down there. Careful! Good. Are they on solidly? Now turn on the power, half strength. That's it. Lift it up slowly, slowly. Good!"

While Janus was giving orders, workers put a kind of metallic ring around the bottom of the huge rock that covered Christina's back, and up around the sides to the top. At Janus's commands, the stone was lifted by magnetic force projected from directly above Christina, then moved slowly to the side and set down a few meters away. The procedure had to be repeated for the smaller stone that had broken her legs.

"My god! look at that! It looks like every rib has been broken. Probably pierced her lungs and injured just about every organ in her body."

The sight of bones sticking up through blood-covered flesh and right through clothing is never pretty. It gets downright ugly when you see that condition in a person you admire, respect, and well, love. Would she survive, could she survive, and would she ever recover? And if so, in what condition?

Bernardo, the chief surgeon, who had come down with the

emergency crew, contacted Constellation. "Salini, Janus here. Jama, Pedro and I will accompany the Captain. Beam us directly to the sick bay. It looks terrible. It looks hopeless."

Bernardo's words took away any sense of belief that Christina would survive. Still, there were concerns for her safety.

"Is she in any condition to be transmatted? Can she withstand the pressures?"

"If we don't get her up there she'll surely die. This is no time to reason. Transport us now!"

The familiar blur of snowy light engulfed the small party of four. They disappeared from view, only to emerge kilometers above, in the sick bay. With great care, Christina was lifted onto a gurney. The medical team got to work. There were no smiles in the operating room.

Once her clothing was removed and the blood washed away, what the medics saw was frightening: both femurs and the right tibia broken, the right patella shattered. The left humerus and the right radius broken. All the ribs. Organs visible through torn flesh. The worst was the spine. The problem was where to begin. They decided to protect the spinal cord as much as possible, work next on the organs, and then take care of the fractures. They were estimating their work in days, not hours.

———

When I came to, I felt tremendous pain from my shoulders and arms down to my waist. And I had a mammoth headache. My eyes slowly focussed. I saw Bernardo. I said something to him, then went back to sleep. Or rather, since I had slipped out of a comatose state, it would be more accurate to say that I fell asleep. I was under medication, but there were moments of semi-consciousness when I could hear them talking. It didn't sound good, but I could not concentrate for more than a few minutes before drifting off into a feverish sleep again.

My legs and arms were broken, and literally every rib. With our medical equipment, these things can be repaired quickly, and you can get back on the job in about a month. Well, longer when it's a matter of all those things. I kept slipping in and out of consciousness and a deep drug-induced sleep, for months. My organs were repaired during this time: lungs, kidneys, spleen, liver. The boulder had done its job very well. The medics had done theirs superbly.

Finally, I woke up to a real consciousness.

"Hey, my headache's gone. My arms feel normal, more or less. No tubes, no contraptions holding me down. Why can't I get up? I can't seem to move."

"Captain, what a great recovery you've made so far! And how great it is to speak with you!"

"Bernardo, what's happened?"

He told me about the avalanche, filled in some details about the operations that went on, bit by bit, over a three month period, and that had put me all back together again, except...

"Except for what?"

"Your spine. It was crushed, smashed down, with ten vertebrae broken. And your spinal cord was severed in two places."

I could feel my heart sink as he spoke. "Spinal cord severed in two places?"

"Yes, right below the shoulder blades, and in the small of the back. We've been able to reattach the upper tear. All signs point to a complete recovery, in a week or so if it's not already taken place. You woke up as we were about to run a test to see its condition."

"Run it. Please. But what about the lower tear?"

"Captain, we tried to have your nerve tissue grow on tissue taken from frogs, which usually works. But it didn't work the first time. Or the second. Or the third. Then we tried experimental rat nerves. The results were also negative."

"You're telling me that I'll be crippled for life."

"I was trying not to say that. But honestly, unless we can find a way to put your spinal cord together, you might never walk again. We can hope that techniques back on Earth will work for you; they seem to be coming up with miracle cures every year. Still, in these operations time is usually of the essence; and a five-year journey is not exactly rapid. Unless someone can think of something, the prognosis is not bright."

"Bernardo, please run that test you wanted to do, then see if I can sit up well enough to eat: I'm famished! Then I'd like to have a couple of people in here to talk about this, and to see how our mission is going. Janus, Jama, and you. And tell them that as crazy as it might sound, I'm more hopeful than you are."

———

On the third day, now that I was able to sit up in a motorized wheelchair, I was allowed to leave the sick bay for an hour or two. I had never really imagined myself as being other than I was. After all, I'd been 28 for almost 200 years! But I also could not imagine myself crippled for the rest of my life, another 100 years. I kept telling myself, "I'll beat this, I'll beat this somehow." The question was how. I called together the flight deck crew. They let me know that Jama and Janus were splitting the duties of the command, that the explorations were going on and being continued successfully, and that they had no reason to doubt that this planet, now largely a desert, could in a relatively short time become quite habitable.

Everyone marveled at my recovery, which in fact is a triumph of Earth medicine and the skill of Bernardo and his team of surgeons and nurses. I was eager to get back to work to the extent I could, but I was more determined than ever to make them talk about my final injury and try to think of ways to reattach my nerves. "Nothing," I said over and over again, "can be too crazy. If you have an idea, suggest it."

Salini, ever the techie, offered an idea of creating a virtual spinal cord on the computer and somehow attaching it to my spinal cord above and below the cut, where it would function, as long as I was wearing a computer, like a real spinal cord. "It may be far out," he said, "but it's worth a try."

"Do you really think such a device can be created?"

"We've got the resources, and if I'm allowed the time to work on it, it might pan out."

Most people thought the idea was on the wild side, but maybe it would work, after all.

"I was speaking with Hermione about this the other day,

Captain," said Jama. "She had an idea that we should maybe try out some of the nerve tissue from some of these scurrying things, and see if that might work. I've gotten a kind of feeble reaction so far, about the same as with frog tissue: not enough to actually do the job, but enough of a reaction to suggest that this might be a solution. Still, there's got to be a bigger reaction."

Pharsilla had a sudden inspiration: "Why not use them both at once? You could weave the frog and the scurry nerve cells together, and see if that works."

"I'll get to work on it as soon as the meeting is over. It's a long shot, but so is everything else that's been suggested so far. But this gives me a second idea. Suppose we do manage to get some kind of reaction with some animal nerve tissue, do you think Salini's machine, if it works at all, could boost the transmission rate?"

"You mean, use them together? A kind of two- or three-pronged approach? Frog tissue, scurry tissue, virtual spinal cord?" I was so desperate for good news that this was beginning to sound hopeful to me. "If you're willing to do this, let's give it a try!'

Bernardo had an objection, though, a serious objection. Ever since a series of transplants of alien organs went awry on Mesnos, it's been strictly against policy to mix alien and human body parts. And, if that's the law, Bernardo did not want to break it. I was crushed. Still, I had the experiments begun, and right after the meeting I began scrutinizing the laws and the regulations.

It was discouraging. The law was written in an obscure manner that seemed to say what Bernardo had told us. Space Fleet regulations permitted experiments of this sort to be conducted, and put in the hands of the commanding officer of any craft or space station to right "authorize any procedure permitted by law when in his or her judgment conditions so warrant." That meant that I could authorize this multiple approach if it turned out to be legal. I had to go back to the law. Obscure, but brief.

"The nature of alien systems being incompatible with those of human beings, surgeons and medical experts should not mix human and alien body parts. Experiments may be performed, however."

What on Earth did that mean? I put the question to Janus, who asked for a couple of hours to meditate on it.

"Christina, I have an answer for you. On the one hand, Space Fleet regulations and Earth law agree that experimentation is OK, and Space Fleet authorizes you to order any procedure that's legal. The stumbling block is the wording, 'should not mix human and alien body parts.'

"First of all, we could argue that 'should' is not the same thing as 'must' or 'shall,' both of which would strictly forbid this kind of procedure."

"Come on, that's a terrible justification in and of itself. A grammatical rule would make this legal?! You've got to be kidding! And you've got to do better."

"I disagree with what you're saying: the law turns on little things like that. If it didn't, we wouldn't have need of more than a handful of lawyers. But that's only part of my argument, let's say one panel of a diptych."

"OK, what's the other panel?"

"Human and alien body parts should not mix. Suppose we could use Hermione's idea to produce a strand of nerve tissue that consists of frog and scurry nerve cells, with only the frog cells attached to the human cells? Whatever the spirit of the law might be, this would fall within the scope of the word of the law."

"You mean it would be perfectly legal?"

"Did I ever tell you I was lawyer before I entered Space Fleet?"

"It's on your record. That's why I wanted to consult you about this point. OK, I'm convinced."

"I forgot to tell you that one of Jama's experiments was by accident just like that, scurry tissue and frog tissue intertwined, and it worked. The power of the cells was not just doubled, but increased tenfold. And the cells began to forge together."

"Tremendous news! Now it will be up to you to convince Bernardo. And everyone who contributed to this experimental procedure, if it works, will go down in history as geniuses. And

Salini's computer, if he can figure out what to do and how to do it, can serve as a bridge while the spinal cord is repairing itself."

My only concern, and I'm sort of ashamed to say this, was that I might get to be as frenetic as the scurry who would contribute part of its nervous system to me. I had complete confidence in the team. And Salini's computer was as thin and about as small as a shoehorn: it could have been implanted in me!

A couple of months after the operation, which was known only to about a dozen people including the medical staff, I went in my wheelchair to the transmat room, and came down right at the spot of my injury. I was touched to tears by what I saw there: On the large stone that had crushed me almost to death was engraved:

STONE THAT ALMOST KILLED THE BEST COMMANDER IN SPACE FLEET, CAPTAIN CHRISTINA VASA, 13 DECEMBER 2720

The crew was finishing up its work on the continent, and we were all eager to get home.

"I've come to see how you're doing," I told them, "and I see I have a debt of gratitude to some great people. But I couldn't leave Paracelsus without paying a visit to my nemesis."

Everyone gathered around. They had so much to tell me, things they'd discovered, the excitement of the expedition. They still seemed sad, though, when they looked my way. I could read what they were thinking but were afraid to say out loud.

"Everybody! Give me some breathing room, please. Remember, I'm old and feeble, I'm already 218 years old, going on 219."

They backed away, giving me some space. I told them, "Now it's time for me to make a speech." I pulled out some papers I had stuffed in my pocket, and pretended to be about to read what was sure to be a 30-minute harangue.

Then I got up from the wheelchair, walked over to Jama and Salini and Bernardo, and said, "Hail to the heroes!"

MARS, 2799

"Don't forget to pick me up in three weeks. If my homing device doesn't work, check the transmat station I'll set up shortly after I arrive."

"I still don't see why you're going to Mars for your vacation, Christina. Sure, people can live there, but it's still pretty cold. They've got snow in the winters, and even at the equator it seldom reaches 35^0; elsewhere, it's even colder. I oughtta know, I was born there. Human beings weren't made to endure summers that seldom reach 30^0, which is the case in Canaan, where you're headed. Sure, it's on the equator, but it's an island."

"Well, Mustapha, that may be, but I've only been on Mars for a day or so at a time, and that was a long time ago, when I had duty on Ares off and on. Travel the solar system, visit the satellites, but why not Venus and Mars, too? Life's too short to let opportunities to stretch the mind go by. And besides, thanks to Ares and its continuing work, the temperatures are rising year after year."

Not only that, but time was running out for her, too. If she didn't manage to find Stanley Narb, her days might soon be numbered. Let's see, maybe 325 or at most 350 total years, or till sometime around 2825 or 2850. Can Stanley do something for her? Will he? He can, or should be able to, since he's somehow extended his own life by a few extra centuries. Will he is another story, given his trial, his imprisonment, his spectacular escape, his desperate flight to Mars. For that matter, maybe he can't do anything, since he's living with the Ancient-Day Primitivists, who don't even allow electricity. They sure picked the right place for their exile colony. Pre-industrial technologies, a whole way of approaching life that seems so distant and alien from what we in Space Fleet are used to. Is this really the good old days? It's just like the Middle Ages all over again.

Mustapha cut into her musings. "I don't think I've ever seen you in civvies. You don't look very stylish with those heavy clothes. They're so old-fashioned."

"Mustapha, I'm going to spend three weeks among the

Ancient-Day Primitivists. Do you think I'd blend in wearing the latest Earth fashions? And besides, I have to dress for the terrible cold you claim I'll face. Thank heavens for the translation device that Colombina showed me how to make. If it works right, I should be able to speak the way I usually do, only the ADPs will pick it up as their lingo. So if I'm lucky, I'll look something like them and sound like them, too."

"What's the point? Aren't these the same people as the Militia?"

"Hey, don't make the mistake I once did. The Militia are violent terrorist thugs who claim to be acting in the name of the Primitivists; the Primitivists are a kind of modified religious group, or rather a sort of umbrella group for a whole spectrum of fundamentalist religions; the Ancient-Day Primitivists are like the Primmies, except that they've chosen a pre-industrial life style. Just think of it as three weeks of bivouac, or indoor camping, along with a chance to see how people actually lived about 1500 years ago. It'll be like time travel!"

"Are you sure about all that? I heard that the Primmies were all in cahoots with the Militia."

"Listen, Bub, I didn't spend five years with Boris Smirnoff without learning some distinctions. He was a Primitivist, but believe me, he was no Militiaman."

"Okay, I yield to superior knowledge. I've found a nice spot for you to materialize. It looks like a kind of square, and it seems to be almost deserted, so you shouldn't be observed. It's right in the middle of the big ADP town. Or, if you'd prefer, I can set you down outside the town gates. They must shut down the town at night, just like they did in the old adventure books I used to read as a kid."

"That they do. Maybe it would be safer to set me down inside. The town square, you say?"

"Well, a town or a city, I can't tell which. Looks pretty big, but not a metropolis. Take a look at the screen. See? Horses and buggies and carts. No aircars, no street lights, no electricity at all. Can't imagine how they live."

"Maybe they read a lot, gather around a fire at night and tell stories, make their own music, entertain themselves. And work hard and almost constantly. No machines to do the hard work. Ah, three weeks in Nature!"

"Okay, grab your bags, everything's ready. See you in three weeks! Constellation will be at your beck and call."

"So long, Mustapha! Too bad I can't send you a post card!" Then, the tingling sensation, the momentary lapse of consciousness, and materialization in this obscure corner of Mars, far from the bustling world the planet had become in just one or two centuries. Time to get her bearings.

A large city square. A church with a tall steeple on one side, flanked by large houses; facing the church, a large public building, probably the Town Hall, also flanked by houses, probably apartments; on one of the other sides, a huge covered market place, at this moment totally deserted; facing this, more public buildings. Probably administrative offices, police, whatever. In the middle, a permanent platform, seems to be made of wood. Good place for the transmat station, maybe. All I have to do is slip this device underneath, just out of sight. Something's on the platform, hard to see from here. First, put this in; good. Now, let's see what's making that noise.

Actually, it sounds like someone moaning. It's a person standing in stocks, a prisoner. A woman.

"Hello, my name is Christina. I'm a tourist. It looks like you're in trouble with the law. What's your name?"

"My name is Madeline. I'm a widow, I live alone at the edge of the city. They think I'm a witch. I have another day of punishment here, then they'll let me go. Unless they decide to burn me at the stake."

"A witch? I didn't think there were such things."

"Quiet, Christina the Tourist, don't let the authorities hear you. It's blasphemy, you know, and you might be punished like me. I wasn't always old and wrinkled and poor; they didn't always think I'm a witch, a doer of evil, a slave to Satan. They think I consort with the dead, with ghosts who wander in search of their bodies. But there are no ghosts, and I am not a slave to Satan. But you must go. Do not let them find you here talking to me. If they think you are trying to set me free, you will be put in

95

jail."

"Well, I'll take my chances on that. But tell me about yourself, how you came to be thought of as a witch."

"Once I was the wife of a rich merchant, Peter the Draper. In those days they respected me. But since he died in a terrible accident, and especially since my children left Canaan and ceased belonging to the Ancient-Day Primitivist religion, I have been shunned. People stopped coming to the store. I grew poor as I grew old. I had to sell my house, it was just behind the Public Building, but no one would buy it at a fair price. I took what I could, and went to live outside the walls. I eat herbs and roots, because I have no money to buy food. If it were not for Dr. Lebenstein, I would long since have died."

"Madeline, your story is terrible. How can you live with these people?"

"Quiet, Christina the Tourist, don't let the authorities hear you. You will not want to suffer my fate. I live with these people because they are my people. Someday they will know they have made a mistake. I will be restored to my community. But now you must go. At dark, I will be moved to the jail. If they find you speaking with me, you will be jailed, too."

"Would I be burned at the stake, too?"

"If you are convicted of being a witch, and if you were to live here, perhaps. But you are a tourist; you would just be deported."

"Suppose I set you free, what would happen to you? Where could you go?"

"Quiet, Christina the Tourist. Don't let the authorities hear you. You might return to your home, but I live here, I would be found, and I would die."

"It doesn't seem fair, Madeline. The authorities sound cruel."

Christina thought she heard something at this time, but because dusk was upon them she couldn't see very well. Was that a person ducking behind the platform? Was it a government spy, gathering evidence against Madeline? Yes, there seemed to be a shadowy figure lurking there. Seemed. She wasn't sure if she was seeing or hearing things. It was all so eerie.

"Can I do anything to help you, Madeline?"

"You are kind to think of me. If you see Dr. Lebenstein, the pharmacist, tell him about me. Perhaps he will be able to help me."

"How can I find him? I am a stranger here, as you know."

"You go past the church, on the right side of the church, and follow the road you will be on. Up you will go, Christina, through the woods to the top of the hill. There you will see a big stone house. That is the pharmacy. They will take you in for the night. Beware the robbers on the way; it's a long road. Farewell, Christina the Tourist. May we meet again."

"I sure hope to see you soon, Madeline, and in better circumstances. I will tell Dr. Lebenstein about your fate. Farewell."

That noise again, like someone moving in the shadows. Is it my imagination? Do I see someone moving through the deserted marketplace? Hmm. I'd better keep my guard up. Well, here's the church. Right side. Follow the road up the hill. Wonder how far it is.

The road went straight into a now rapidly darkening wood, then twisted up a steep rocky incline. Above, the faint light of Phobos and Deimos could be seen. By early morning Ares will loom on the horizon. Ares. People have often asked me what it's doing now. What I tell them is that its main function is to maintain the density of the atmosphere, so that the planet's relatively weak gravitational pull (only about 0.39 that of Earth) will not permit the air to escape, as happened about three billion years ago. I don't tell them that it's also at work producing the energy needed to keep the world alive. With little seismic activity, Mars creates virtually no internal heat. Thanks to Ares, underground water is created, then heated, and tapped for energy. Even the ADP use this energy source, although they apparently don't know it's man-made and not natural.

The low gravity makes it pretty easy for someone not born here, and even those who **were** born here and keep fit, to carry something like this duffel bag that must weigh 20 or 25 kilos on Earth. Mustapha's right, these clothes are old-fashioned and heavy, but I'm glad I have them on, on this chilly evening.

Tamarack, oak, pine. Some underbrush I can't make out in this gathering darkness. What's that noise? A squirrel. "Look out for robbers," Madeline said. Can't be too careful, must stay alert. Dr. Stanley Lebenstein, the pharmacist, lives in a deserted part of Canaan's area, up the hill from town; I bet it's a good three kilometer walk. Lebenstein; pharmacist. Not bad. It seems to have fooled a whole lot of people.

Not many people want to move to Mars. The gravity and the climate. Maybe that's why the Earth Government set aside these three or four reservations here, including Canaan: one way to attract settlers, which in the long run should relieve population pressures on Earth. This one for the ADP. Another for rehabilitated prisoners. A third for descendants of people who had lived in Arctic lands, when there still were such things on Earth, and who for some reason have never been able to adapt to our tropical heat and humidity. I can't remember what the fourth was, or if there even was a fourth. But I do know that for most settlers, those who come to live on the main continent instead of these island reservations, it's either a call to adventure, or a means of escaping poverty (they get free land, I think, and a lot of help getting set up, just like the Mesnosians did), or both.

Ah, there's a light ahead. Strange. It's not flickering like a candle or a lantern. Electricity? Here? If so, it has to be my Stanley. How will I greet him? "Dr. Livingstone, I presume?" No, that pun on his alias is just too corny. "A ghost of times past?" Or, maybe... "Ouch!"

A heavy club fell on Christina's back, fortunately right on her duffel bag. She staggered, then fell to the ground, quickly rolled over, and saw a man coming after her with a pummel of some sort. She evaded his blow, then got up and got rid of her duffel. He swung again, but hit her with a glancing blow to the arm. She struck a blow to his stomach, which made him stagger backwards for a couple of steps. When he recovered, he came after her again, but this time she sidestepped and, grabbing his arm, she tossed him over her shoulder. In this gravitational field he felt pretty light, although on Earth he would have weighed 100 kilos at least. He grunted this time, the first sound he'd emitted in this entire struggle.

"Give up while you're ahead," she heard herself saying. His only response was to mumble something she couldn't make out, spring to his feet, and lunge at her. He appeared to be in such a rage that he couldn't think. She moved quickly out of his path, then smashed him on the back of the neck as he flew past her. At this he stumbled forward and turned around; she smacked him straight in the jaw. He collapsed, unconscious. She dragged him to a tree with the thought of tying him to it. A robber? Do enough people come here to make it worth while for a thief? A guard? Same question. But this guy's a sad excuse for a guard, if that's what he is. Maybe Stanley will let me in on the secret.

The house was only a hundred meters away. She saw the door open, a flood of yellow light stream out from inside. Then a young man emerged, looked out into the dark, and finally spotted her and the hulk next to her. He came rushing down, accompanied by a very large dog that growled. "Quiet, Caesar," he said. He introduced himself as Det Stisreg, the assistant pharmacist.

"My name is Christina Vasa. I've come to see Dr. Lebenstein. He's a friend of mine from Earth. But I should tell you that I was attacked by this somewhat incompetent thug."

"Ah, we've been expecting you. This is not a very nice first impression of the Canaan Pharmacy, I'm afraid. Hmm. You seem to have handled that man without any trouble. I'll take him to a safe place for the night."

"Expecting me?"

As his only answer, Det picked up the man, tossing him easily onto his shoulder, while Christina picked up her bag. They went up to the house and entered.

"Please sit down, Ms. Vasa. Dr. Lebenstein has spoken to me of you. I'll tell him you're here; as I've said, he's been expecting you. Meanwhile, I'll ask my wife to keep you company. Numamba, we have a visitor, a distinguished visitor!"

Before Christina could object to this way of being identified, a tall young woman, with long black hair and dark eyes, came in. Neither she nor Det was dressed like the people in town. They wore comfortable Earth clothes, what most of the Martians she had met in her earlier visits to the planet wore.

"Numamba, this is Captain Christina Vasa. I'll take Caesar along to the cell with this guy. I want to see who would have dared to attack Captain Vasa. She's done something to knock him out for this long."

"Be careful, Det, he may be faking it."

"I'll have the fiercest dog in Canaan with me, don't worry."

Saying this, he disappeared into a hallway. Numamba greeted Christina with evident pleasure, although she seemed to be concerned over her husband's safety. Caesar's growls and gnars reassured her.

"It's a terrible introduction to the pharmacy and to Canaan. We'll do our best to make you comfortable. Let's get over to the fireplace and brush off your clothes. Are you hurt? We've got excellent medical facilities here, as you might imagine, since you've come to meet an old friend with great medical skills."

"Oddly enough, I didn't get hurt in the scuffle. Maybe it has something to do with the gravity here."

"Yes, well, I understand what you mean, and you're right. We have an Earth gravity center down below, so we're always in perfect shape relative to the Martian natives. It pays to keep in training. And since you've just come down from Constellation, you must be in tune with Earth's gravity, too."

"How does everyone know who I am, where I've been, and when I was supposed to get here, and why I've come? It's spooky. It was supposed to be a secret. And by the way, please call me Christina."

"Okay, Christina. I think it might be best to let Dr. Lebenstein tell you about that. Stanley has spoken often about you, you'd almost think he was a proud father! How did you find him here? That was just as big a secret."

Christina's answer never left her mouth. A bulky man who seemed to be about 40 or 45 rushed into the room, exclaiming "Captain Vasa, I presume?" There were shouts of glee and joy, hugs, tons of questions, a barrage of information, fine sherry, noise and happiness. Det returned in the midst of the scene, saying that he recognized the assaulter and had locked him in the shelter for the night, where he'd be safe from the wild dogs and the strong winds that blow when the sun goes down and temperatures drop. They'd question him in the morning. "You must have really given him a wallop, he's still out cold," Det observed.

"Our hand has never lost its skill," Christina answered, with a laugh. "One of the things we learn at Space Academy is self defense. In this case it was easy: an element of surprise, a quick hard blow to the back of the head, where it meets the neck, then a knock-out punch. It's all a question of physics."

"We've just finished preparing dinner, and if you want, we can sit down to a meal and talk then. You can celebrate Liberation Day with us. It's the day my escape and all that were erased from the record, my conviction overturned, and my name cleared. I chose nevertheless to retain my new identity. I am a bit worried, though, Christina. I know you're resourceful, I know you're smart, I know that the computer aboard Constellation is powerful. I know all that. But if you could sniff me out, so could other people, and some of them are a worry: as you know, I'm not popular with the Militia."

"But the ADPs don't do business with them, do they?"

Numamba answered for Stanley. "They don't, but they have adopted an open port policy: they don't inspect travel documents, and the Militia have visited this reservation more than once, recruiting. Unsuccessfully, let me add. But they have come up here, and the odd chance that someone will recognize Stanley has us worried a bit. But more of that later. Christina, let me show you to our guest room. We'll have the table set in a quarter of an hour. Any plans for tomorrow?"

"I'd like to visit the city, find out something about life here in Canaan. And, to be honest, I have some personal business to discuss with Stanley."

"Personal business? I can't imagine what you mean," said Stanley Narb, with a wink. "I'm just a simple pharmacist, working with herbs to cure people of diseases."

"I got directions here from Madeline the Draper, who's in the stocks. She spoke warmly of you, as a person who doesn't believe in witches and who might help her out. She's in pretty desperate straights. She thinks they might burn her at the stake."

"Nobody's burned at the stake here. But I'll go to town in the morning. With a little luck, we'll be able to spring Madeline from jail. Maybe it's time we brought her here for good. Numamba, Det, you and I can talk about that over dinner. You'll come along with me in the morning, and I'll show you around town. But for now, freshen up, get yourself settled in. After dinner, maybe you'd like to see our little operation?"

"My appetite is whetted. I'm as hungry for knowledge as I am for food."

"Hmm. Some things never change, do they? I think you said something like that almost 270 years ago."

CANAAN

The sun, smaller and less brilliant on Mars than on Earth, was shining through the window. Christina rubbed her eyes, yawned, stretched, looked around. It felt strangely like Earth here. Much stronger gravitational pull than she had experienced on the way up from the city of Canaan. Why did they name the island and the city by the same name? How can you ever know where you are? Better get a shower, then go downstairs. Gosh, I found out a lot of stuff last night.

The Liberation Day meal was a monster. Ostrich and yams and vegetables and oranges and ice cream. I didn't think they had ice cream in the Middle Ages, but they probably didn't eat ostrich then, either. Besides, Stanley is not an ADP. And the wine was excellent. I'll have to tell Mustapha that the climate here is good for something!

———

"Stanley, I heard that you were captured one day when you were completely off guard some time after performing one or two illegal procedures, one of them on yourself. You were brought to trial, found guilty of the crime of illegal genetic manipulation, and sentenced to two consecutive life terms in prison in Mesnos."

"So far, your Constellation computer has it right."

"It was not the computer who told me that: I found that out on returning from a tour of duty exploring the relatively near-by parts of the galaxy for suitable planets and for signs of intelligent life. Funny how many planets seem to support life, and how little of that seems to have evolved an intelligence similar to ours. Not to mention all the planets where intelligent life–and maybe life in general–has died out. I landed on Venus for a new tour of duty, and eventually got caught up with the news of the previous six or seven years. While I has there, word came about your escape and evasion, your disappearance really. That's when I began to have the computer make some discreet inquiries."

"Discreet? How can a computer be discreet? Everyone knows a computer can't keep a secret. Someone always finds a way in."

"It's obvious that you've not met Constellation's computer. It gave me some leads, then I had it erase from its memory every trace of them, so that if someone should try to catch me at this, they'd have no information. It seems everyone on Earth suspected I'd be looking for you. I was being watched. I had to commit the data I picked up to memory, for fear of having it intercepted."

"My trial was over almost before it had started. Open and shut case, I was caught, so to speak, red-handed, just after a new unauthorized procedure. On Det. For some reason, they didn't prosecute him; good luck for us all."

"Actually, Stanley's covering up for me," said Det. "We had agreed that I would plead innocent, claiming that he had tricked me into the procedure. It was an outrageous and very obvious lie, but they bought into it: they wanted to demonize him, I guess."

"I was sent to Mesnos during its dismal season, with not the best of welcoming parties waiting for me, and with a bare 10 m^2 to live in. One window, an interior court, no way out. Sentenced for two consecutive life terms, one for working on Det, one for working on myself."

"Is it also true you added about 500 years to your life that time?"

"Yes, and that's what Det has, and Numamba now, too. What about you? You want an extension on your extended life? I can assure you it's safe to do it here."

"You know that's one of the things that brought me here. The other was to find you, and to see you again. You've not changed an iota."

"Anyway, after a year or two of that kind of jail you get the feeling that 500 or more years of it won't be a lot of fun. Imagine: two books a week. One hour of exercise a day. Under guard all the time. Some people think that prisons are paradise, but I can tell you I'd rather be free. Freedom, it's worth risking your life for. So I had to find a way out. I thought of constructing a series of silicon chips. There's lots of silicon on Mesnos, it's everywhere. It wasn't easy without proper equipment, but when you've got lots of time and nothing to do, you'd be surprised what you can accomplish."

"What did your chips do?"

"All sorts of things. Most of them were unifunctional, because I had to make them crude, given my equipment: forks and knives. One of them could read any code on the doors and open them silently, then lock them with a new code."

"The point of that being?"

"Come on, now! you can't guess? To slow down my pursuers. Let me tell you, it worked! Another chip could divert attention from me, make people look away, so they actually couldn't see me. I became the invisible man! That really helped me out of more than one jam, and probably made my escape seem so sensational. Other chips functioned together as a small computer, with voice commands but no monitor. That really exercised my memory! I had to steal some clothes (I eventually was able to make restitution for it). Then I had the good fortune to meet an old friend of yours, fellow by the name of Alexander Romanov."

"Alexander Romanov? I don't think I ever met anyone by that name."

"OK, that was his new Mesnosian identity."

"Don't tell me! Boris? Boris Smirnoff? You met him on Mesnos? He escaped that bombing of the tunnels when he destroyed the nest of Militia there?"

"The very guy, and yes, obviously he did. He told me about knowing you, and about being sure that you'd escape because of some incredible memory for places. Seems you never make a mistake about knowing where you are when you set your mind to it."

"He's alive!"

"Well, he was alive. Remember that he's not one of us, and that was 150 years ago. But he lived long, and claimed that you somehow showed him that the Primitivist religion was not for him. In fact, he helped us get set up here. He had become an interplanetary, interstellar land speculator, and had a lot of contacts who had no idea of his background. He got us in here as pharmacists, Det and me. He brought Numamba here a few years later; he'd met her on his travels, on Aphrodite, I think."

"Aphrodite! I was there with Boris. He saved my life! Stanley, you're bringing back too many painful memories."

"Would you want to change the subject?"

"No. For one thing, the memories are also warm, some of them. And in truth I'd keep coming back to Boris and you. I think that if I ever was in love with anyone, it was Boris. I've never gotten over his being a double agent, though, and it's made me wary, very wary, of emotional attachments."

"Boris was not a double agent with me. He procured me a new, apparently official identity, as Dr. Stanley Lebenstein, pharmacist. I let my hair grow, grew an ample mustache and beard, added a few pounds, and presto! Dr. Lebenstein was created, like a phoenix, from the ashes of Stanley Narb. Of course I also had to learn what was a new area of science for me. I traveled with Boris, or rather Alexander, and thought of settling here on Mars, on a reserve where the government couldn't get me. The problem was getting in, getting set up with the best equipment. That's where Boris stepped in. He knew the place, knew they needed sources of heat and power, and told them that if they'd let me live here in peace, and if they'd let me set up a secret laboratory here, I'd be able to take care of their needs."

"So how do you manage to provide them and yourselves with the heat and energy you and they need?"

"Patience, my dear, you've always been so curious. Boris also had contacts with people on Ares, not the same ones who were there when you were on duty in the station. New folks, civilians as well as military. He arranged a deal with them: I'd be able to tap into their power if they could find new places to get the antimatter guns to operate. That's where some of these caves into which the water filters have come from: we've been creating energy for Mars from chunks of Mars converted to energy on Ares; we use some of that energy for us and for Canaan, and we have access to Aretian computer space to boot. And it's not only legal, we have documents to prove it."

"Ah, so that's how you've gotten to know my life history, where I was and where I was going. That's how you could be expecting my arrival. Ares to Constellation to Canaan. You're wickeder that I thought!"

"Well, I don't know about that. Have some Madeira, m'dear, and pick up your story about how you found me here. When you left off, the computer was being discreet, I think."

"I learned that you had vanished into thin air on Mesnos, and were presumed to be in hiding there. An intensive search was under way. I was convinced there was more to the story than that, but I had to wait some years (OK, about a century) before an opportunity presented itself to continue. That was when, on Ares, I overheard a conversation about someone who was finding places for the few tons of matter needed every so often to maintain the station's energy supply. Nothing more, but it was a place to start, since apparently the people I overheard had never met you and had no clue as to who this mysterious person might be."

"Why did that make you think of Stanley?" asked Numamba.

"Think of it this way: here's a mystery guy doing high-tech stuff who even the officials don't know. Must be somebody in hiding, if not on the lam. He seems to have been in on a big deal involving highly technological stuff, and he appears to have been doing it for a very long time. Points to an ELB type. Who do I know who could fit this description?"

"So you guessed it was me. Then what?"

"Bit by bit, as I went here and there, my trusty computer found out some information, made some guesses, hit it right sometimes, wrong others, but after five decades of detective work it added up to a vacation in Canaan for yours truly. There is, of course, no trace of this, and I have left no hard evidence. I can't imagine that anyone else has had the time or the purpose or the resources to track you down. Now, you did leave out one interesting detail: how did you get your record cleared?"

"Numamba was a big help with that. She went over the trial data, volumes of minutia, and discovered that I had been convicted of a capital crime with only circumstantial evidence, which is not allowed. So she appealed, and we won."

"Were you retried on less serious charges?"

"By the time she appealed the case, just about everyone involved had died. Besides, given the tie-up with Ares, it was probably easier for the Court to drop the charges, so as not to reveal an embarrassing secret of the ADP. After all, they're not supposed to participate in this level of technological development."

"A secret? You mean it's not common knowledge? Among the ADP, I mean."

"The Bishop knows, and the Mayor. That's the great secret of their offices, one they vow never to reveal," explained Numamba.

"Now that we know why we're all here at this time," Narb added, "I should let you know, Christina, that Det and Numamba have been trained in everything I do, so that in case something happens to me either one of them can carry on my work. We've also made arrangements with the Bishop's office and the Mayor's office that the Pharmacy will continue to be off-limits to investigations in my absence or in case of my death."

"Your death! Don't tell me you're that close!"

"Oh, come on, no, I've got hundreds of good years left in me. But I'm not sure if after a couple of these procedures that we can guarantee stability; and we have only ourselves to experiment on."

———

That's about what Christina could recall, along with jokes and bantering. Oh, yes, they would see the Bishop, and try to win the freedom of Madeline the Draper, who could live with them if she chose to do so. Then perhaps they'd meet the Mayor. Christina also learned a lot about the pharmacology of certain plants, enhanced by chemicals and genetic experiments. It seemed as though Stanley had taken his new profession seriously. When do they open their shop, and when do they practice their trade? And when do we go to town? She hoped to find out about that at breakfast.

Christina had let the trio of Canaanites into a top secret bit of information about the mission of Ares, and why it had used up so much of the energy provided by Space One: to gradually regularize the irregular orbit of Mars, which once had a huge gap in its perihelion and aphelion. This has been stabilized at about 5%, quite an improvement over the 20% that nature had provided, and allows Martians to have a more predictable seasonal climate variation. Furthermore, Ares has established a Martian year exactly double that of Earth, which of course has closed the gap between the sidereal period (formerly 687 days) and the synodic period (formerly 780 days). Both of these projects now require only relatively low amounts of energy for maintenance, and might be able to operate without Ares in the future. Given the fact that the Martian day is almost identical in length to the Earth day, only a few calendar adjustments were needed to bring the months in tune (on Mars, they count each half-year as a year, to keep in line with Earth years). But the seasons are twice as long here. It makes sense to live as close to the equator as possible!

"Dynamite!" Det had exclaimed on hearing about the new mission of Ares. "So that's why you guys have been mucking around up there for so long! And it's been done so gradually that people have hardly noticed it."

———

At breakfast, she learned that they have pharmacy hours here in the Mansion twice a week, and they have an office adjacent to the market place, open for business on the two market days. They'll be going in for business in an hour.

Her attacker was identified as an ADP neophyte who has all the zeal of a new convert. His goal was to prevent any Canaanite from dealing with these non-believers; and because of the way Christina was dressed, he took her for a Canaanite, and he attacked her. They learned his name (Flotnal Semaj), warned him to stay away from the Pharmacy's market place office and the Mansion, which he agreed to do. He did not want to meet Christina, however, not wanting to be humiliated again by speaking with the woman who had knocked him out, but he did apologize to her, via Det. He was on his way home now, with a headache (soon to be cured by one of Dr. Lebenstein's herbal remedies), a sore chin, and a full belly.

After breakfast, Det stayed behind to work on a project, while Christina joined Stanley and Numamba. Numamba would open the shop, take care of consultations, and keep the business going, while Stanley and Christina would visit the Bishop and bring Madeline back either to the Mansion or to her house, and then go back to meet the Mayor and take a quick tour of the town.

———

"And so, your Grace, we would like to take Madeline in, if she desires. In this manner, she would pose less of a threat to the people. We have plenty of work for her to do at the Mansion."

"I am happy to comply with your wishes, Doctor. Valet!"

A youth entered the room. "You called for me, your Grace?"

"Yes. Have Madeline the Draper brought to me here, at once."

"Your Grace, that's not possible."

"What?" bellowed the prelate. "Why isn't it possible?"

"Madeline died in her cell last night. She had been weakened by her exposure in the stocks, and passed away with an apparent stroke. The coroner is performing an autopsy at present."

Christina looked crushed, and she was shocked. "Dead! She was so sad, and so helpful. She was afraid she'd be burned at the stake today, instead of being freed. I was hoping to speak with her again."

"This is most unfortunate, Miss Vasa. We have never had a prisoner die on us in over 100 years. I'll set up a meeting with the Mayor and the Lieutenant of Police to review the procedures. We want to punish blasphemers, not kill them. We've abolished the penalty of burning at the stake, but the people still think that's an option. Maybe the unfortunate Madeline was literally scared to death. We will have a public ceremony to pray for her soul. Valet, try to have the Mayor and the Lieutenant come here as soon as he is free."

"Yes, your Grace." And the young man left.

"We would also like to report an attack on Ms. Vasa by Flotnal Semaj, who I believe is a neophyte."

"He's a burly fellow. Were you hurt, Ms. Vasa?"

"No, your Grace. I was lucky."

"I will have him reprimanded and ordered to stay away from you. It would help if you attired yourself like your friends, so that zealots like Flotnal can't mistake you for one of us."

"You and Numamba are about the same size, Christina. She'll surely lend you some of her clothes while you're with us."

"I hope the rest of your visit will not be marred by this kind of occurrence, Ms. Vasa. An attack and a death. I am embarrassed for my nation and my city. I hope you can forgive us."

"I much appreciate your kindness, your Grace. You are clearly not at fault for what has happened, and there is nothing to forgive. I do have a request that might sound odd to you, which is to speak with one of your theologians about your religious and social beliefs."

"Theologians! We have none! Our religion and our customs are simple. We do not entertain metaphysical speculation. Our religion teaches us simply to adore God, to obey the law of God as written in our Scriptures, to obey the civil law of Canaan and of Mars, and to be just. Our social practices include what Dr. Lebenstein calls a pre-industrial life style, a communitarian spirit, and shunning of those of us who blaspheme. We are open to the outside world, and indeed are considering beginning a tourist industry here. It appears that many of your Earth citizens would welcome an opportunity to spend a few weeks in a retreat center here, where they can recover their spiritual values in peace and quiet. I think that is about all there is to say about us. Please feel free to wander about the island and the city at will."

"Thank you again for your kindness, your Grace. I hope to see you again before I leave."

"That will be my pleasure, Miss Vasa. And Doctor, be assured that we will investigate both the death of Madeline and the attack of Flotnal. Good-bye, my friend. May the peace of God descend upon you."

"Good-bye, your Grace. And thank you."

———

Before heading off to the Mansion, Christina checked to see if her transmat station device was still in place. It was not. That damn Flotnal! Stanley and Christina had no trouble finding him, and when confronted by his conqueror, he flinched; and without being asked, reached into a pocket and handed her the device, saying, "I think you dropped this in the square." Dropped it! The thief! Christina controlled her temper and thanked her assailant, with irony so thick you could cut it, for returning her little toy. Flotnal mumbled something and turned to hasten away, but walked right into the arms of a large ecclesiastical guard who had been seeking him out.

An extremely deep voice said, in a menacing manner, "I think the Bishop wants to speak to you." Flotnal fainted.

"I don't think he'll be bothering you again, Miss." Then he picked up the inert figure, and bowed to Stanley, saying, "Good day, Doctor." All three of them smiled. They checked in at the market place office, where Numamba had a couple of clients, one of whom had just bought some medicinal herbs and had to be told exactly how to use them, and at what dosage. Christina was able to secure her device, then they all closed up shop and went home for lunch.

Two days later, Madeline was buried in a sparsely-attended ceremony. The adjutant Bishop officiated at the last rites. Oddly, Flotnal was there, too. Was he spying on them? Unlikely, because he didn't seem to be too awfully bright, but you can never tell.

Christina spent parts of days watching the people make candles, spin and card wool, make furniture, do all the mundane things that are done in communities that refuse post-industrial technologies. She'd seen this in a few places on Earth, and in one little corner of Mesnos, but usually in living museums, and not on this scale.

One of the joys of Canaan was the seaside, a fishing port and a swimming beach located not too far from the market place, in the opposite direction from the Mansion. The island did not

112

have a deep-water port, although one was scheduled to be constructed once the breakwater now being installed was completed. It was extremely animated there, with the fisherfolk and the gentry mixing in together, the colorful sailboats the fishermen used, the neat stretches of sand, the clear blue water. She could recognize the fish and seafood, since all the animals came originally from Earth. Still, some of them had mutated in just a couple of centuries.

She had gotten used to seeing the two pale moons overhead, one going three or four times as fast as the other, and Ares slowly crossing the sky farther out. She had gotten used to the salty air, the crisp breezes coming in from the ocean, the smells and sounds of a busy port. She had also learned that these people were not "primitive" in the sense of being unable to speak or think coherently; they were just ignorant of the ways of the modern world. And she had learned that these people, for all the simplicity they preach, were not innocent: robbers and other criminals abounded in proportions apparently similar to those on Earth, elsewhere on Mars, and on Mesnos. Their lives, too, seemed less calm than she had imagined they would be, the more she saw these people working, running about to do their daily tasks.

This part of Mars, this entire little island–the windward side as well as this leeward side–had its share of beauty. She most appreciated the open spaces, the smell of the pine woods and the sea. "I'll be back here," she said to Stanley and Numamba and Det, "as soon as I get back to this part of the solar system. My next tour of duty will take me between Venus and Aphrodite for the better part of five years."

It will be hard to leave these wonderful friends, she thought, glowing in the knowledge that her life had been further extended. Another 500 years! I can breathe again, she chuckled.

Their farewell was tender but full of hope for the future. "Till we meet again!"

MURDER ON MARS

This is Cameroon Bynnar with a late-breaking story. Channel 77 has just learned that a prominent scientist has been assassinated at the capital city of Mars, Eris, as he was to board a shuttle taking him to an Earth-bound space cruiser. Dr. Stanley Narb, creator of the genetic procedure that has made the Extended Life Brigade a reality, and who is largely credited with founding the ELB, was felled by a red laser blast at about 5 p.m. local time.

Dr. Narb, subject of a bitter legal battle over a century ago, when he was accused and convicted of performing two illegal procedures–one on himself and another on his assistant–was sentenced to two successive life terms in a dreary prison on Mesnos. After ten years in jail, he managed to escape without being detected. Somehow he was able to change the coding on the locks of all the doors he went through, slowing down his pursuers. The most incredible aspect of the story, though, is that in a mysterious manner he was totally undetected, even though his escape was made in broad daylight and he had to pass through the crowded streets of Sandstone. How he managed this feat, wearing prison clothing, is an unsolved mystery.

Then he somehow managed to escape from Mesnos, in the midst of a massive manhunt. Years later he emerged under an alias, Dr. Stanley Lebenstein, as a pharmacist in the Ancient-Day Primitivist reservation of Canaan, on an equatorial island on Mars. He claimed to be an herbal pharmacologist serving this pre-industrial religious sect. The Government chose not to press charges against him, and in fact a later review of the case proved that there were no grounds for a capital charge to have been made in the first place. The mystery man was cleared of all charges.

I have just been notified that Earth Government spokesperson Rannug Lhashi has issued a statement on this assassination. We'll switch to Quito where we will hear the entire text.

"The Government deplores this act of violence on a peace-loving scientist who has brought much to our people. Dr. Narb will long be remembered as the creator of the Extended-Life Brigade, without whom our space exploration program, in its early days, would never have been possible. We will do everything in our power to find his assassin and bring him to justice."

Ms. Lhashi has refused further comment except to say that a more complete statement would soon follow. She did not take any questions.

Dr. Narb was in appearance 40 or 45 years of age but in fact was much older; indeed, he was born about 450 years ago. He was the first person to undergo his own procedure for extending life genetically, an operation he has performed on some 2000 persons, of whom half are still alive.

Now we have a live report from Mars. Because of the distance and transmission involved, we cannot have live questions from Earth answered by our correspondents on Mars.

"Morbey Scott here. The scene was pure pandemonium when the red bolt from a military-type gun struck and killed Dr. Stanley Narb as he was climbing aboard the shuttle which you can see just behind me. We can reconstruct the scene as follows.

"About 100 passengers were waiting in line when the attack came. Behind the customs barrier a small crowd of friends and relatives were waving. People were jubilant. As Dr. Narb began to climb up the ramp, a red bolt struck him in the back of the head. He fell to the ground, about 3 meters below, already dead. A tall, burly gunman shouted 'Death to the infidels!' and fought his way through the crowd, running into a machine shop where he disappeared. It is not known at this time whether or not he was able to leave the grounds of the spaceport or of the adjacent seaport.

"In the ensuing panic following the murder and the apparent escape of the gunman, the emergency medical team had difficulty reaching the stricken victim. The alleged murder weapon has been found near the door of the machine shop, and the assailant has been identified as Flotnal Semaj by persons who know him;

116

you can see his picture on the split screen. Police ask anyone with information on the whereabouts of this suspect to contact them im-mediately. Semaj might have another weapon with him. He is described as a strong man with a violent temper, and is considered dangerous.

"Eye witnesses are at present being interrogated by the police. Many here have declared this murder to be an act of cowardice–as noted, Narb was killed from behind, and probably did not see his assailant. Until more is known about the presumed assailant, it will not be profitable to speculate on motives, but unofficial reports indicate that he is a member of the Ancient-Day Primitivists, and might have met Dr. Narb, who is also known as Dr. Lebenstein, in Canaan. We will update our report as soon as more information is available.

"This is Morbey Scott, returning you to Cameroon Bynnar on Earth."

———

"Numamba! Come here! Listen to this!"

Numamba had seldom seen Det so stirred up. Didn't he know she was busy with a customer?

"Remember to take one capsule with breakfast and one with dinner for five days until all the capsules are gone. Come and see us here or at the Market Place shop if you have any of the possible side effects we've seen over the years–headache, rash, queasy stomach."

"Thank you very much, Dr. Stisreg."

"What is so important, Det?"

"Stanley has been assassinated!"

"What? I don't believe you! This is not something to joke about."

"This is no joke, Numamba. He's just been killed, and by that creep who assaulted Christina five years ago."

"Who? Flotnal Semaj?"

"Yes, that guy. We'll have to close shop here and head off to Eris."

"We can't do that. We have our customers to take care of.

117

And there's Caesar."

"Numamba, you go then, I'll stay here."

"It will be better if you show up there, Det. People know you better than me. Do hurry. And offer a reward."

———

"Mr. Mayor, I must get to Eris as quickly as possible. Dr. Lebenstein has been assassinated. I would appreciate your having me brought to the islet so I can access our speedship."

"Dr. Lebenstein assassinated? Is it possible?"

"I just saw the broadcast. My wife will keep the pharmacy open. It would be kind of you to send a guard to the Mansion to protect her. I suspect the Militia is behind this. The alleged assassin is someone I have reason to think is one of them, an old 'friend' of yours, Flotnal Semaj."

"Flotnal? We just released him–again–a week ago, and exiled him. Of course, Dr. Stisreg, I'll have a contingent go right up the hill. And I'll have the City skiff waiting for you in five minutes."

"Thank you, Mr. Mayor. Numamba knows what to do in this kind of emergency. She's already notified the authorities on Ares, and she will keep you informed of any developments. But in the meanwhile, please let the Bishop know what the situation is. We will have many things to talk about when I return."

———

"And now this breaking story from Morbey Scott in Eris, the Martian capital."

"The assassin has been positively identified as Flotnal Semaj, a habitual petty thief and minor criminal in Canaan City and in other communities on the Ancient-Day Primitivist reservation. Finger-prints on the recovered murder weapon and iris-scopes taken from a picture of the murder scene point in his direction. Eris is entirely sealed off. Unless Semaj has been able to leave the Port Peninsula, where the shuttle stop is located,

118

police officials expect that he will be apprehended in a few hours.

"Speculation as to his motives abound. Some believe that he was a dissatisfied customer of the pharmacy that Dr. Lebenstein, also known as Dr. Narb, ran. Others offer more probable suggestions, linking the assassination to some form of political or religious action, since the assassin cried out, 'Death to the infidels!' at the scene of the crime. It is known that Semaj is a devout ADP and that Dr. Narb is a non-believer. But the ADP are a tolerant sect, and have never been known to favor violence. It is also known that Semaj assaulted a friend of Dr. Narb's, Captain Christina Vasa of Space Fleet, when she visited him about five years ago; Semaj spent over a month in jail and in the pillory on that occasion. Nevertheless, where could he have procured such a modern weapon? Surely not in Canaan, since the ADP do not use modern weapons. Nor is it likely that he could have procured the weapon legally anywhere on Mars, because he is a hardened criminal whose record is well known. It is believed that he has confederates in this crime.

"You see here the SDD-47, a military weapon, that Semaj is alleged to have used in the attack on Narb from behind. This powerful weapon can aim at any part of a person whose fingerprints or irisscopes are programmed into it. Is it possible that Semaj has an accomplice in the military? Is this a random act of terrorism? If so, Semaj might belong to one of the few remaining cells of the Militia, one of which is believed to operate here in Eris.

"In any case, given the importance Dr. Narb has had in the development of the ELB, the Government has put all its resources into solving this murder and apprehending the criminal. The police are now combing the area carefully. None of us here at the spaceport is permitted to leave; we'll just have to sit and wait. We will report any new developments as they arise."

"We have just received word that Dr. Det Stisreg is on his way to Eris. Dr. Stisreg, you might recall, received an extended-life procedure in the case that sent Dr. Narb to prison on Mesnos. Court records indicated that Dr. Stisreg was an

119

unwitting patient, and that Dr. Narb extended his life against his will. Nevertheless, Dr. Stisreg became an assistant and then a partner of Dr. Narb in the Canaan Pharmacy. It has never been clear why these men and Dr. Stisreg's wife, Dr. Numamba Stisreg, chose to live in a society of pre-industrial Primitivists, given their training and their experience. We are sending a crew to Canaan and the Mansion to see if we can find an answer to this puzzle.

"And now, back to our regular programming. This is Morbey Scott reporting from Eris."

———

I've got to find a way out of this place. Too bad I dropped my gun. All I have is a handgun, not as powerful and not as accurate. At least I got him, the founder of the ELB, the infidel, the blasphemer. He won't be able to lead other people into a life of sin and error. And if I'm caught, I'll be a martyr, praised and honored by all right-thinking people, the main body of the Primitivists, the ADP, and the 10 or 15 of us still active in the Militia. Maybe the Militia will be reborn! What's that noise? Can't see anything. Maybe just a small animal, or the heater. I'll slip in behind this machine. Careful, Flotnal, don't touch anything. Stay away from the machinery. You don't want to become sausage.

When night comes I'll slip into the water outside and get to the seaport. From there I'll get up the hill to our hideaway. We'll have to decide what to do next, where to go. A light! Do they know I'm here?

"Su-Kyum, you and your crew check every nook and cranny of this place. The three of us will go out and take a look at the periphery, just in case he was able to slip out."

"OK, Guy, we'll start at this corner here."

They can't know for sure I'm here. This giant motor will keep me out of view; it's a place they surely won't be smart enough to look in. Gotta keep quiet. They're coming close. Try not to breathe too loud.

"Any way a big guy like that could squeeze into this shuttle

120

engine? It looks like even I couldn't make it in. I'll give it a try."

Stay calm. Don't move. I'm hidden from them by this big block of the engine. Never did understand these things. Good, the dope is turning around; he's going out. Cops are so dumb. Makes you wonder how they ever catch anybody.

"No way he could have gotten in there, and if he had somehow been able to, we would have seen him right away. There's no room in there for a rat."

"OK, Su-Kyum, you and Evita check out that office over there. Yma and I will cover the rest rooms."

So far, so good. In this season, the sun will set in an hour or two. By 8 or 9 o'clock I'll be able to get out via the sewage pipe. Not hard to get into that from this area: there's a big drain over near the wall. The idiots! It's almost too easy.

———

"Guy, we have the place surrounded. We know he's in the engine. Why didn't you let me just nab him?"

"Two reasons, Su-Kyum. First, I figured he'd not be too dangerous if he thought we didn't see him. But suppose you made a move on him? You'd be dead now. We'll get him sooner or later, without risking anyone's life. When he makes his move, he'll think we're not on to him, and he'll get away. Our orders are to let him escape, but to alert everyone as to where he is, and where he's going. This guy's not too bright. He'll lead us straight to his pals. That's when we move in."

"Won't you come into my parlor, said the spider to the fly, that sort of thing? A kind of running trap?"

"Exactly. You know, I hate to admit it, but some of those guys in headquarters are smart."

"I never thought I'd live to see the day when you would say something like that."

"Well, let's make sure we have every door and every window covered. And Su-Kyum, I think we should cover the waterside, too. The big bosses didn't think of that. We little guys have to do some of their thinking for them."

"OK, Guy, I'll take care of that myself."

"And tell everyone to let him go, but to tail him and notify HQ and us of what's going on."

"Understood, Mr. Spider."

———

Good. It's dark out. I'll slip into the water quietly, and they won't even notice. First, get out of this damn engine area. Ah! stretch those legs and arms. Now, slip over to the grating. It lifts up just as easily today as yesterday when I cased the hangar. Down the steps, lower the grate back into place. Not too far, I think. Yeah, there's the sea! Another grate to remove. Unh! This is harder that I expected. Can't make noise, though. It's just a bit rusted. Clear that out with my knife. Good! Easy as pie! Too bad I won't see their faces when they find me gone! Now into the water. Deep breath, then down. Swim alongside the hangar area until we're beyond the fence, then turn toward Pier 22. Come up for air just a few times, then finish up on the surface. Did it! The perfect escape!

———

"Guy. Su-Kyum here. He's just slipped in the water, probably from some drain. He seems to be following the building's edge, underwater... He's come up for air again, just beyond the fence... He's popped up again, seems to be heading over towards Pier 22... Yeah, he's swimming on the surface now. Better alert those guys, get there yourself. I'll keep the old eyes on him."

The old eyes. These binoculars let you see at night almost as if it were broad daylight. They're the new eyes I'm keeping on him.

"Guy. He's about 20 meters from the far end of the pier. My guess is he'll try to do that underwater... There he is, climbing up the ladder. Time for your crew to start tailing him."

———

Let's get out of the wet clothes now. Don't want to leave a trail of water. Good. Nice to be in these dry things Orteipid left for me, just where he said they'd be. Dump the wet clothes in the trash can. No one around, but keep to the shadows. OK, now it's in the open. Walk as though you be-long here, head up, sure gait. If anyone's around, just say hello. Little banter, maybe. Sports. Then go on. Here's someone. "Hi there, mate. Nice night, isn't it?"

"Just takin' a little walk, are you? Well it's a nice night for it. Too bad about that Narb guy, or Lebenstein, whatever his name is. You hear anything new?"

"Nothin' new, same old stuff. Better get home and check the news. See you 'round."

"S'long Cap'n."

Whew, I didn't expect that. And I don't know what's been said about this. Should have asked him. Well, here I am. Cross the Embarcadero, up Pike Street, up the hill. Always seems odd, here. A few blocks away there's always a crowd. Here, even now it's deserted. Turn right here. Good. The key's in my pocket. Up the stairs.

"Hey, guys, I made it!"

"Flotnal's back, Deacon."

"Good. Everything's going according to plan. You've done well, Brother Flotnal. Did anyone follow you?"

Brother Flotnal! I'm in, at last! The Deacon has called me Brother Flotnal!

"No Deacon, I got out without being seen. Those guys were so dumb, they couldn't see me in that engine part!"

"Brother Orteipid is a very careful planner; we can count on him. And now, Brothers and Sisters, we have to make our get-away. We can't risk staying here in Eris. When we reach Freia we can celebrate. Celebrate the revival of the Militia. We fifteen will be the foundation of the New Militia! But no time for that now. I have three aircars ready just outside the back door. You know who to travel with, five to a vehicle, and you know the separate routes we'll take, and where we'll meet. Check your weapons. Everyone ready? Let's go."

"Glad you could join us, Su-Kyum, we needed your talents. We left some people out front. Let's see if my hunch is right."

"Well, you were right about the water route of escape, Guy. You think those aircars are theirs?"

"Shh. Back in the shadows, everyone. When they're in their cars, go for them. Blast out the engines. We want 'em alive if we can get 'em alive."

Twelve men and three women came out silently from the door they were watching. They looked around, then climbed into the new aircars. Just as the last door closed, mammoth green bolts came from the shadows. The front ends of the vehicles melted! Red bolts streamed out from the passenger compartments in the direction of the green blasts. These were answered with other red bolts. The volleys continued for five minutes. Then, a silence that was finally broken by Guy's whispered question.

"Su-Kyum, did they get anyone?"

"Monti's dead. Marisa and Torrent are wounded."

"We have you surrounded. Open the doors and come out, one by one. Remove your outer jackets and throw down your weapons."

The second aircar's door opened. A red bolt just missed Guy. Su-Kyum's blast hit home.

"Aarrgh!"

"They got the Deacon!"

Bolts rang out in all directions, as the remaining Militia members struck back blindly and in fury. But in vain. One by one, the half-dozen still alive came out of the cars, removed their jackets, threw down their guns. The reinforcements arrived. The Deacon and his lieutenant, Orteipid, were dead. Of the survivors, only one was not wounded: Flotnal!

The Eris Six were quickly brought to trial. Proud to the end, they defended their acts of terrorism as the will of God. They repeated their charges that Stanley Narb was the instrument of Satan, that the ELB were agents of Satan, and that the human race would be punished for their sins. The investigators also determined that these were the last of the Militia. After 400 years this once-dreaded terrorist group has finally been exterminated.

"Captain Christina Vasa, a member of the Extended Life Brigade and one of Dr. Narb's friends, was to be your next victim, Flotnal. Why?"

"She's been our biggest enemy for 250 years. Her sinful and unnaturally long life has allowed her to pursue the Militia with a single-minded purpose for almost her entire career in Space Fleet. Space Fleet, another abomination of God! She went to see him five years ago to get an illegal further extension of her life, so as to pursue us to the last person. We were going to get her as soon as she returns. She'll sneer at us, now, the unbeliever!"

"What do you mean by this remark, Flotnal? And what proof do you have?"

"I heard them talking. After she k.o.'d me, I woke up in a kind of cell nearby to where they were. Their voices were clear as bells. I pretended to still be out when Det Stisreg checked on me. I heard them partying, then Lebenstein said that Det and Numamba had the operation, and he did, too. And Vasa asked to get it, too, and they all agreed she would. Maybe she should go to prison with us."

"What you're saying sounds preposterous, but we'll check it out. Meanwhile, you guys don't have a prayer. Pun intended. But if you do pray, ask God to let you be sent off to Mesnos rather than Paracelsus 2."

———

"The jury having found you guilty of the crimes of terrorism, murder, wanton destruction of property, theft, conspiracy, perjury, and lesser crimes, I find it necessary to sentence each you in perpetuity to prison on Paracelsus 2. Your crimes are dastardly and cowardly. You have taken lives and property without concern for the victims and for society. Do you have anything to say before the sentence is executed? We recognize Mr. Flotnal Semaj as spokesperson."

"All the so-called victims, for over 400 years, deserved what they got. They were all heretics, infidels, unbelievers. The will of God has been heard, and will be heard again. This might be the end of us, but it is not the end of the Militia. The Militia will rise, like a phoenix, from our ashes! Death to the unbelievers! And death to Christina Vasa, out there in the audience, who was illegally operated on by Dr. Lebenstein! Death to her and to all the enemies of the Justice of God!"

CHRISTINA ON TRIAL

"In view of Flotnal's public accusation, we will have to pursue a full investigation of the files of Narb. What Flotnal said struck a chord with me. I went back to examine the documents he had on him. Most of it was of no real importance. But his wrist computer had a short file that was a kind of log. Most entries just gave dates and the name of some remedy or such thing, or some coding I can't yet understand. But this one entry read: '2799.3.7.CV.500.' Nothing else. It didn't make sense then. Now it does."

"What do you mean, Lieutenant Onapac? I looks like a registration number for an aircar. Have you checked that out?"

"Yes, sir, that was my first thought, but there's no such number in use on Mars or on Earth."

"Well, what about Mesnos? Narb spent some time there, we know, after his escape from prison. And did you run down communication codes?"

"My staff and I did everything you can think of. But it took that numbskull Flotnal to open up my eyes."

"I'm not into numbskulls, Onapac, and my eyes are still closed. Give me a hint."

"Don't you see, Inspector? It gives a date, then a cryptic notation. I figure it was a kind of memo or note that Narb wrote to himself. I can't figure out most of them, as I said, but I'm sure that this one shows that CV–Christina Vasa– had her life extended by 500 years on 7 March 2799."

"By God, you're on to something! You might be right! And you're also right about the thorough investigation. What we need first is a search warrant for the Mansion in Canaan. If Narb did that operation, he had to do it there, which means that they must have very sophisticated equipment in Canaan, of all places. Herbal pharmacologists! What a cover! But what's their game?"

"Can't tell yet, but I've already alerted the Chief Justice that a warrant might be requested."

"Good, Onapac. Besides you, who are our best people for this job? We need investigators and computer people."

"We have top-flight investigators in Guy Stevens and Su-Kyum Dhen, who led Flotnal into a trap and drew out the Deacon and his cohorts. A good pair on the computer might be J. D. Snodgrass and J. C. Suedama."

"Good thinking. Experience and intelligence and daring. Take four or five tough guards, too. That Stisreg couple might be covering up something. But we'll deal with that later. Unless they cause trouble, don't let them think we're on to anything involving them personally. When can you leave?"

"If we can get the search warrant, in about an hour. We'll be in Canaan in another couple of hours at the most. We can cut another hour or more if you authorize us to use the teleporting system on the big Rapid Transport Craft."

"Round up your crew. I'll have the warrant waiting for you at the RTC at the spaceport. Keep me informed. You know my home code."

"Any hour, chief?"

"Any hour. I might grumble and mutter, but I can't hurt anyone as far away as you'll be."

———

I never realized how beautiful Eris can look at night. The harbor lights reflecting in the ocean, the lights in the streets, the illuminated store windows, the aircars. You can see the hills rising and falling, facing the sea. The lights are fast disappearing, growing dim, hidden by the clouds. I better let my people know exactly what our plan will be. Joan and Jacqueline have to know exactly what to look for. The warrant is broad, gives us the authority to search everywhere on the premises, both in the house and on the grounds. The Chief really knows how to get that kind of thing from the Judge. And I never thought he'd let us use this RTC. What a way to fly!

"OK, everyone, now it's time to get down to work. Here's the plan. We show them the warrant, we get in, we begin to look in every room. Ground floor first, then their shop, then the basement, then upstairs. Keep the Stisregs in one room, the living room or the kitchen. Don't hurt them unless they threaten you. We have to make it clear that suspicion has fallen on Narb, not them.

"As soon as we find their technological gear, JD and JC will get to work on it. One of the guards should be with them, maybe Torrent. We'll have to keep someone at the door, too, let's say Tanya, and someone in the shop, Marisa. Remember, we're after information we suspect Narb has hidden, perhaps in a computer. He might have an illegal lab set-up, too. But in any case, we're not after the Stisregs, got it?

"OK, time to get to the teleport."

———

"What's Caesar acting up about, Det?"

"I don't know. All of a sudden he's begun to growl and gnash his teeth. Look: he's gone towards the door."

"Maybe it's a patient. Or a burglar. Or maybe even some kind of Militia sympathizer, although I thought they were all rounded up. Word from Ares has it that Christina got the last ones on Mesnos, and even found a small cell of three or four of them on Aphrodite. I'm worried."

"Steady, Caesar. Stay. Good fellow. I'll take a look outside."

"Careful, Det. Check it out on the scanner."

"OK. Nothing there. Hmm. Wait! Look at this!"

"What is it, Det?"

"Numamba, Those ten people have teleported down from that craft overhead. That seems to be all. They're coming up the hill!"

Caesar's growling began again. On the scanner, three people were soon at the door; the others stayed behind in the shadows, but could be seen in the infrared. The big knocker was swung three times. Det opened the door a crack.

"Hello! We're looking for the Canaan Pharmacy."

"You're in the right place. Do you need an herbal remedy for airsickness?" asked Det.

"No, but we need information. I'm Lieutenant Mot Onapac from the Investigative Division of Mars Police. We have a warrant to search the premises."

Numamba, with a vicious-looking Caesar at her side, said, "Let me see your IDs and the warrant." After checking them, she added, "It all looks in order, Det. Come in, Lieutenant, you and your team are welcome here. I'd ask you only to have that craft hover higher, out of sight and hearing of the people in town. They find this kind of thing very disturbing. They're not used to the noise, the vibrations, the way all this looks. Remember, this is a reservation of the Ancient-Day Primitivists."

"We're aware of that, Dr. Stisreg. JD, have the craft return to base, but keep it on radio alert."

"Yes, sir."

"Would you like some camomile tea or some lemonade?"

"Actually, if you don't mind, I want my people to search your house and the premises. And I'd like both of you to stay in one place. I'll be recording this conversation for possible future use. We're here to investigate some leads we have that seem to implicate the late Dr. Narb in some illegal activity involving Captain Christina Vasa of Space Fleet. I believe you know her?"

"Why, yes, she was one of Stanley's–Dr. Narb's–old friends. She's become one of our friends, too. We expect to see her when she returns from her current mission."

"Her current mission? Where is she?"

"We're not sure. She set off on the trail of the last members of the Militia in the space stations and the colony planets, Venus, Mesnos, Paracelsus 2, maybe even Mars; but that's public knowledge. She doesn't reveal secret information of that sort."

"When did you meet her? I know she met Dr. Narb way back around 2530 or so, when she became a longie, excuse me, a member of ELB. When you say 'old friend' you really mean it."

"We met her five years ago when she came here on vacation. She'd somehow been able to trace Dr. Narb here, despite his alias as Dr. Lebenstein, and his change of profession from genetic surgeon to herbal pharmacologist."

"Vacation? She didn't come here for, uh, shall we say, uh, something else?"

"Something else?" asked Numamba. "Yes, she came here to study the ADP lifestyle, which seems to intrigue her. You know, living as she does, totally surrounded by modern technologies, she's very curious about these people. Their belief system, their way of life, how they cope with conditions here, how they organize their society, their slow and relaxed pace. She's in a unique position to compare lots of cultures. Sandstone and the rebuilt New Terra, on Mesnos, are so different, she says. Sandstone must be a bustling capital, something like Quito, while New Terra is a slower-paced provincial city. And they're just a few kilometers apart! But she claims that she can't find anything like the ADP anywhere she's been, not even on Earth."

"You're no stranger to Earth, are you, Dr. Stisreg?"

"Det and I were both born there. But it's a big place, and we've been here for a while."

"A while, indeed. We know that your husband was tricked into undergoing Dr. Narb's procedure, some 150 or 160 years ago, so that he's an extended lifer. But our records indicate that you've been here for some 125 years at least, and you don't look a day over 30."

"Some people age more gracefully than others, Lieutenant."

"Don't play games with me, Dr. Stisreg. I'm not asking for that kind of information, I'm just stating a fact."

"I'll take it as a compliment, then. But what kind of information are you looking for?"

"Let me put it to you this way. Dr. Narb is known to have traveled wearing a sophisticated and extremely powerful wrist computer of a type we don't have. Where did he get it? Either he has a supplier who has been able to hide a potentially hot seller from the entire solar system and beyond. Or he manufactured it here. Maybe you know something about that."

Sy-Kyum Dhen burst in excitedy shouting, "Lieutenant Onapac! Excuse me for this intrusion. I have to speak to you right away!"

"Excuse me, Doctors," said Onapac, drawing Su-Kyum to a corner of the room.

"What is it? I'm about to get important information from them. I don't want to let them think."

"This is big stuff, believe me; it's really important information. We've found what looks like a small operating room hidden in the infirmary, and a pretty large laboratory. There's a huge computer there that seems to have a permanent link to Ares. JD and JC are beginning to study the programs and try to find out their functions."

Numamba looked at the men speaking, then turned towards her husband and whispered, "Det, they'll eventually stumble on everything we have. They must have found the laboratory and the computer. They'll soon come across the Earth-gravity Center."

Onapac rejoined them at just this moment. "Earth-gravity Center?"

"Yes, that's what she said. But first, Lieutenant, I'd like to know what kind of information you have that made you think that Dr. Narb and Captain Vasa were engaged somehow in illegal activity? This is a pharmacy, and we do sell drugs, all legal drugs, mostly herbs that we grow ourselves."

"You know that's not what we're after. Dr. Narb had on him certain documents that point to an illegal life-extending procedure that took place during the time that Captain Vasa was here, and she was the subject of the procedure. That is very clear, and it's clearly incriminating."

"But Christina is already an extended lifer. What could he possibly do? He did it all, as you say, in 2530."

"He could add years to her life. Let's say, 500 years."

"And if he could, what makes you think he did that here? In Canaan?"

"That's what we want to find out. Dhen, dig for whatever you can!"

"Lieutenant," said Det, "have your computer experts stop where they are. They're dealing with state secrets. We'll fill you in on the details."

"You heard him, Su-Kyum, have them stop. And close the door when you go out. Send in Guy. Torrent will stay here with us."

———

"Except for Mars, Lieutenant Wan, we've now cleared the human-inhabited portion of the galaxy of the Militia. Do you think we should celebrate when we get to Eris?"

"Captain, how many do you think would be on Mars? Of all the places to live, Mars seems to be the least popular. There are even more people lined up to go to Paracelsus 2 than anywhere else, and a lot of them are Martians. Mars is such an unlikely place for terrorists. Maybe what we should celebrate is being in a place where you don't have to worry about those people."

"It is true that Mars has a climate problem, as the Admiral might say. But I think the real reason so many people don't want to come or to stay on Mars is the gravity problem. Mars has somewhat less attraction for people after a while."

"Pun duly recorded. Still, it's kind of fun being able to jump so far and run so fast you almost fly, don't you think?"

"It's fun for the first few weeks or months, but after a bit your body adapts to the relative lack of gravity, and then the realization hits you that if you went back on Earth, or traveled to Ares or any other place with Earth-like gravity, you'd feel as though a 25-kilo weight were on your back all the time. Your muscles just wouldn't be up to it. Everywhere else we've established colonies, we're pretty close to Earth gravity. But you're right: you've never been here, and it will be great fun when we materialize. Ready to teleport?"

"Transmat's all set."

"Let's go, then!"

As usual, the space travelers checked in at the reception area of the spaceport. Wan Xi-wun and Christina saw the pictures showing the Eris Six being marched onto the ramp prior to teleporting to a craft taking them to Paracelsus 2, and the huge headlines that seemed to scream at them: **"THE END OF THE MILITIA!"** Was it true? A moment of jubilation! But then, another headline shocked them both: **"BODY OF STANLEY NARB SENT BACK TO CANAAN."** Was Stanley dead? What happened?

Christina saw several members of the Mars Police approach her. She was about to ask for some information on Stanley's death, some details at least, when Lieutenant Onapac said to her, "Captain Vasa, I regret to inform you that you are under arrest for having secretly undergone an illegal life-extending procedure. I must warn you that anything you say will be used against you; our conversation is being recorded. If you have no statement to make at this time, you may contact your lawyer or agent."

How could they have learned about that? If I'm found guilty, it will mean exile and maybe solitary confinement on Mesnos or Paracelsus 2.

"Xi-wun, please get in touch with Judith Dreyfus. She's a lawyer I met last year. Here's her card. Will we be at Headquarters, Lieutenant Onapac?"

"Yes, Captain Vasa. We'll be there in a few minutes. Inspector Ongg is waiting for you."

———

"Inspector Ongg, I know that you understand the gravity of the situation. Otherwise, you would have opened up the publicity channels on this case. I tried to explain to Lieutenant Onapac that the materials his computer people came upon are in fact highly classified state secrets. Virtually no one on Mars knows about the existence of that computer and the hook-up to Ares. Virtually no one realizes how fragile the conditions of life are on this planet, and how crucial it is to maintain the two links, and their back-ups, to the anti-matter capacity of Ares. We've artificially rectified the orbit, making it almost a perfect circle, which has helped make the seasons more uniform. We've increased the gravitational pull slightly, but more importantly, we're trying to assure that the atmosphere is held in place."

Det was getting agitated. Numamba gave him one of those calm-down-you'll-have-a-fit looks that never failed to have its desired effect.

"Our operation in Canaan has made this possible," Det continued, controlling his anger a bit better. "I don't think it would be a good idea to get people worried about the future here. Imagine what would happen if all this got out. Panic, pandemonium. People would all want to flee."

"Dr. Stisreg, I understand what you're saying. But I also understand that we have uncovered a crime here. Our organization exists to uncover crimes and bring criminals to justice. More than once a case has caused a stir. Everything always gets back to normal after a short outburst. Your scenario is sheer nonsense; nobody's going to flee from Mars in fear of losing the atmosphere. In any case, letting it be known that Captain Vasa came here for an illegal procedure will not reveal any state secrets. What it will do is allow people to see that Dr. Narb's original conviction was probably justified, and that he even managed to corrupt a model Space Fleet officer."

"There is another dimension," added Numamba. "This activity allegedly took place in Canaan. It's quite probable, no, it's inevitable, that if this matter becomes public knowledge, the people there will eventually find out about the existence of the computer on their island, and sooner or later they will destroy it. What then?"

"If you'll pardon my cynicism, Ma'am, that sounds like another improbable scenario, like your husband's. So what if they find out? Why would that make them react the way you claim?"

"You've never lived among these people. Their leaders are bright, although innocent of industrial technologies, they're even urbane and well educated. But the people, for the most part, are very unsophisticated, and they believe that at least in their little reservation what they call the natural way of life exists in its purest form. I would be afraid to serve them if they suspected that we have such technological capabilities."

"You could have the Bishop break the news to them, gently. They'd listen to him, and they'd get used to you guys having some modern equipment in the Mansion. After all, they do understand that you don't seem to age, and some of them must know how to count up the years you've been there."

"We most certainly don't control the Bishop any more than we control the Mayor."

"When are they coming here to Eris?"

"They've already arrived. They've been conferring with our lawyers for the last several hours. They have an appointment with the Governor just about now. I understand the Chief Justice might be in the meeting, too."

Inspector Ongg heaved a sigh of resignation. "Typical. Have the Police do all the work, then keep them in the dark, and don't invite them in to an important decision-making meeting."

———

The Bishop was stunning in a bright green robe trimmed with gold, the crown-like white velvet hat on his head, and the staff of episcopal authority in his hand. At his side stood the Mayor, like the Bishop in early old age, white hair, scintillating eyes. He was dressed in a simple black velvet suit, or rather extremely dark green, wearing the gold chain and carrying the mace that symbolizes his civil authority. An earnest young woman, their attorney, stood to the right of the Mayor, dressed in ordinary business clothes.

The Governor, in full ceremonial dress, accompanied by the Chief Justice, clad in the long black robe of his office, moved forward to greet them. This was a state visit, and official protocol required nothing less than this level of ritual. A nod from the Governor, and the guards withdrew, closing the doors, and providing these five people with absolute security.

"Your Excellency, Mr. Mayor, Ms. Dreyfus, please be seated."

"Thank you, Mr. Governor."

They sat down in velvet chairs around a highly polished mahogany table.

"We understand that you have come here to plead the case of Captain Vasa," said the Chief Justice, addressing the two elderly men. "You know that the crime she is alleged to have committed is a major felony that can be punished by life in prison on a far-distant exile planet."

"It is not for Captain Vasa that we have come, Your Honor, although she has become a friend, a seeker after the truth, a person who wants to understand our way of life even if she cannot share it with us," replied the Mayor. "Of course, we are concerned about her. But we have come in the name of our people. We do not wish to cause panic and anger among them. Our intention is to protect them from the revelations that

Lieutenant Onapac and the Inspector wish to make public in a Court of Justice."

"To keep silent in these matters would perhaps be a mockery of that Justice which you honor. A trial would expose nothing but facts."

"May I ask what the charges are, exactly, and what Captain Vasa and the Drs. Stisreg have admitted?"

"The charges are that Dr. Narb performed an illegal life-extending procedure on Captain Vasa; we have clear evidence of that. We will also try to prove that he performed a similar operation on Dr. Numamba Stisreg: since she was born 150 to 200 years ago, but appears to be only 30 years of age, there is no other explanation possible. Captain Vasa has refused to cooperate: she has not answered any of our charges, and speaks only through Ms. Dreyfus."

"Ms. Dreyfus has shown us a copy of the search warrant that the Mars Police used. Here it is. Is this a faithful and true copy? Is every word on it accurate? Are the signatures and the titles authentic?"

What is this old Mayor up to? He's got to know that I signed that warrant at the Inspector's request. Better get on with the charade. The Chief Justice was puzzled by the simple question, and his confusion showed on his face. "This is indeed the document that I signed, authorizing the search of the property called the Mansion, which is owned by the Stisregs and serves as their pharmacological laboratory and pharmacy."

"Where," pursued the Mayor, "is the Mansion located?"

"Why, Mr. Mayor, you know that better than I do. It is located about two and a half kilometers from your office."

"The Mayor looked at his lawyer, then at the Bishop, then back at the Governor and the Chief Justice."

"Mr. Governor, where is my office located?"

The Chief Justice suddenly frowned. Damn it, how could I have made such a mistake? I hope the Governor will be able to answer his questions, this one and the whole line of reasoning that this is based on.

"Your office, the last time I saw it, is located in the Town Square in Canaan City."

"And Canaan City? Where is it located?"

"I don't see where you're headed. Canaan City is the capital and port of entry of Canaan."

"Ms. Dreyfus has prepared some copies of a document that you perhaps have not had need to read; but we have a formal reading of the entire document on Founding Day every year at Summer Solstice. This is a solemn occasion. The Bishop conducts a special outdoor service in the Square, accompanied by a procession of ministers and choirs of children and adults. This religious ceremony is followed by a re-enactment of our Founding Families' disembarkation on the public beach. At that point, and in that place, the entire document is read. Would you be so kind as to listen to Ms. Dreyfus read a few relevant sentences of this document to you?"

"This appears to be your Charter."

"That is correct, Mr. Governor. Please read, Ms. Dreyfus."

The Government of Earth grants to the religious group known as the Ancient-Day Primitivists, exclusive rights to a certain island located on the equator of Mars, at a longitude of 102^0 West of Eris, to be known hereafter as Canaan. This island shall be held by the Ancient-Day Primitivist religious group as a Reservation exempt from unwanted intrusion by any source, including the Earth Government and any Mars Government that might be in future duly established.

"Thank you, Ms. Dreyfus. Gentlemen, I believe the statute states in clear language that the sovereignty of Canaan is fully guaranteed."

"That is correct," replied the Governor. "But I don't see what that has to do with the case."

"If you will pardon my interruption, Mr. Governor," said the Chief Justice, "the Mayor seems to be suggesting that the search warrant I signed is not binding, is in fact illegal, because the authority of Mars Government does not exist on Canaan."

"You have understood my intention perfectly. Ms. Dreyfus has, furthermore, drawn up a list of antecedents, in which similar actions in reservations on Mars have been voided for the same reasons."

"But this involves a series of crimes. We have reason to believe that Dr. Narb has performed a minimum of two such operations, and possibly more. These are serious state crimes, in that the Extended-Life Brigade is severely regulated because of the nature of the personnel, I mean because they will live for several generations of ordinary people."

"That may well be, Mr. Governor, but neither the Bishop nor I in our respective roles gave prior approval of such a search. Nor do we intend to do so retrospectively."

"Your Honor, what can you say to this?"

"They are perfectly in their rights, Mr. Governor. I should not have signed that warrant, which is valid only in areas under the jurisdiction of the Mars Government. The reservations are specifically excluded from our jurisdiction, unless Earth Government intervenes on our behalf. I find it hard to believe that they will do so in the present case. On the other hand, I find it hard to believe that it is strictly for religious purposes that the Bishop and the Mayor wish to suppress this evidence. Is there not some other purpose? Economic or political, perhaps?"

The Bishop, silently listening up to this time, spoke in deliberate tones in his extraordinarily deep and rich voice. "Are you suggesting, Sir, hypocrisy on our part?"

The Chief Justice glared at him, silently. Then, his face lit up slightly, as though he had just thought of an expedient. Lose the battle, win the war. Reveal everything we've learned, get the people stirred up enough to force Earth Government to intercede on our side.

Ms. Dreyfus, watching him closely, chose this moment to reach into her briefcase. "You might be interested in reading this document, Your Honor." She handed copies of an official Earth Government writ to the two officials. The writ contained this paragraph:

In view of the gravity of the present situation, in light of the signal service that Captain Christina Vasa and the late Dr. Stanley Narb have given to the Earth Federation, bearing in mind the delicacy of the operation directed on Mars, in Canaan,

139

and noting that the Reservation's civil and religious authorities granted on 5 September 2701 express authorization of the establishment in the reservation of a laboratory linked to Ares for the above-named purpose, the Chief Council of the Federation orders that this case be closed at once, with no publicity at all except to indicate that the charges have been dropped because of a defective warrant. The Chief Council further orders that all mention of these charges be forever removed from the records of the aforementioned Captain Vasa and Dr. Narb, along with those of the latter's associates, Dr. Det Stisreg and Dr. Numamba Stisreg.

"Why didn't you show this to us first?" asked the Chief Justice, clearly angry.

"We wanted to plead our case on its legal merits, and that's what we did. It's obvious you would not bring this case to trial under the circumstances. Still, a press leak here, a bit of information passed on there, and you might get the population stirred up against the Canaan Reservation, and maybe against Captain Vasa. Before that happened, we had to make sure that you'd seen this document."

The Governor, looking very discomfited, pressed a button on his jacket. He called for the Minister of State and the Minister of Justice. When they arrived, he showed them the writ and ordered them to execute at once the orders contained within it. Christina was freed within the hour.

———

"Namumba and Det must have powerful friends on Ares," said an exultant Judith Dreyfus. "And Christina must have powerful protectors in Space Fleet. I had expected that we'd win the case because the warrant was illegal, but the Council made it very clear that this whole matter is to be kept top secret. That's how I interpret the explicit order to clear the records. Usually that requires another bit of legal maneuvering."

Christina was glowing with relief and joy. "How did the proceedings go? I mean, what was the tone?"

"The Mayor was magnificent in the way he took charge of the discussion. There was a moment when I knew we'd won, when the Chief Justice suddenly realized that he had made a major blunder. He tried to cover it up by accusing the Mayor and the Bishop of hypocrisy." The young lawyer then repeated almost word for word the scene in the Governor's office.

"We owe a great deal to those two men. But we owe even more to you, Judith. And frankly, Det and Numamba and I are worried for your future career here. You've made powerful enemies."

"Don't worry about me. There's a rumor that Space Fleet is looking for a high-level civilian lawyer on Earth. I suspect that you've pulled some strings for me, Christina, now that I think of it. Thank you very much."

"Strings or no strings, you deserve a big promotion."

"Det and I would like you to come visit us in Canaan, Judith. You'll be able to meet some of the people whose interests you defended so well, get to see our little operation, and most importantly, get yourself ready for that Earth gravity."

"Earth gravity? What do you mean?"

"When you visit our Earth-gravity Center, you'll understand."

"I'll take you up on your offer, Numamba. But now it's time to celebrate! I brought along some of my staff, the Bishop and the Mayor will make an appearance, and a delegation from a certain space craft and a certain space station has come to join us. The party will be in the best hotel in Eris."

141

WORMHOLE

"Commodore, we appear to have reached the wormhole," said Kwali, breaking the silence that had descended on the control room. "It is right where we were told it would be, within a hundredth of a parsec from an Earth perspective. And it's not going through a black hole. Too bad they can't know we've made it here."

"Do we have a visual, Commander?"

"Not a visual, but we're where Colombina indicates we should be to enter it. She is trying to work out a program to make the sixth dimension visible to us."

"Is there some other way to sense it?"

"Maybe April can answer that, Commodore."

"Lieutenant, have our sensors located the wormhole?"

"Yes, Commodore. They can't send us a visual, although using Colombina's hyperspace converter, we can get a faint picture of a kind of gap in space, roughly circular, that seems to be moving about slightly. I don't know what it will look like on the large screen, where it will lose some of its definition, but I will put it up for you."

"A gap in space. This is a first for me, and I've been at it for almost 300 years! Heavens! Look at that!"

Even Mujama gasped. "It looks menacing, Commodore. I think I'd rather spend the extra couple of years our journey would take through hyperspace than have to go through that. On the other hand, being on the first spacecraft to go through a wormhole is pretty exciting."

Colombina's soft voice broke in. "I believe I can now give you a sharper image, Christina. I've never been directly confronted with the sixth dimension before. It does not seem to conform totally to predictions."

"Ah, that image is much clearer. Still, I have the impression that the resolution is not very high."

"That is correct, Christina. The entrance is just about two kilometers in diameter, but the irregular swaying patterns of the gap would make entry difficult. As you see, the gateway moves in an arc that suddenly is broken by short bursts of horizontal or vertical lunges."

"See if you can find a pattern in its motion, Colombina. Maybe some of those old formulae you have for chaotic systems would work. April, Lieutenant, have you found any trace of rational life in or around the gateway to the wormhole?"

"Our sensors have not found anything at all, Commodore. There is plenty of noise, lots of energy, but it seems random and not directed."

"Keep trying. If there's an intelligence somehow connected to the wormhole–guarding it on this end or using it for its own purposes–it would behoove us to contact it and ask permission to enter."

Martin arched his eyebrows at this suggestion.

"Commander, suppose we're dealing with a civilization that's a thousand years more advanced than we are, or that has higher capacity brains, or is bellicose. We could be vaporized in a second. As our security officer, you must be ready to react to any such danger. On the other hand, an alien civilization might use it for the same purpose we're using it: rapid transgalactic transportation."

"A kind of subway in the sky, Commodore?"

"Oh, let's say something more like an express to Venus. There may be intelligent forces in this area that are used to travel intergalactically. They might want to bypass this smallish galaxy of ours to get to where the big kids play."

"Christina," Colombina said, "I have worked out an equation which will allow us to enter the wormhole safely. Unfortunately, I don't know what's inside, or what it might look like to humans. Our astrophysicists on Earth inferred that it is transversible, that it runs in a roughly direct line right through the galactic core, and that it extends a bit more than half a radius length to each side of the center of the galaxy. If their calculations are correct, this would bring us to about the middle of the other spiral arm."

All eyes turned towards Christina. "If?" she asked.

"As you know, Christina, their calculations are based on relatively sparse data and rely on several unproven suppositions. Nevertheless, if what they calculate is correct to within 10%, we will end up near where they believe we will go, and in real time of less than an hour."

Even Kwali, with all his faith in Home Command, gagged in disbelief. "They told us we wouldn't believe how fast we'd go through the wormhole, and they're right. I would have guessed at least a day," he added, recovering some of his sense of humor.

"Commander, " Christina said to Martin, "alert the entire ship. The crew are to be prepared for anything, but they must also be secured in their places and at their stations. Let them know as much as necessary about our present situation. And make sure all the crew will be ready for anything. Even the worst."

"At once, Commodore."

Turning to Mujama, she ordered her have the entire medical staff in position for possible heavy casualties, then added, "We don't know what dangers lie ahead. We don't even know if our ship will be able to maintain its gravitational rotations."

"I'll go at once to the infirmary, Commodore, and I'll make sure that the first aid stations are fully staffed."

She then addressed Susanna. "Commander, set a course to station us directly in front of the gateway. As soon as everyone is ready, we'll go through."

"I'm setting the coordinates and I'm using both Colombina's calculations and the more traditional ones, Commodore."

"Good. Commander," she said to Kwali, "the entire staff of engineers and mechanics must be ready for any eventuality. We don't know what kinds of exotic matter will be waiting for us there, so we'll have to keep close tabs on the ship. Constellation was built for any known eventuality, but of course its builders knew nothing about this sixth dimension. If we lose our gravity, or if part of the ship is broken, whatever happens, we've got to minimize the loss of life. That has to be our top priority."

"It will be quite a learning experience, Commodore. I'll get my crew on red alert. Should we put up a shield? It would drain some or even most of our reserves, but it might give us protection against whatever is in there."

"Yes, take care of that right away, then come back up on deck."

145

"Lieutenant, she said, returning to April, "we might have to pilot through manually, so we'll be counting on you to keep the visual sensors functioning."

"The sensors are ready for use, Commodore."

"Good. We have about an hour to reach the gateway and to make all our preparations. Once we're in position and prepared for entry, we'll take a shortcut through this wormhole and past thousands of black holes."

Her human staff in place, Christina spoke to her non-human crew member.

"Colombina, since you don't know what the inside of the wormhole might look like, what kind of calculations can you do that would allow us to navigate through it? We need to have a plan, some idea of what we're up against."

"I can make an assumption that the difference between hyperspace, or the five dimensions we now know, and the sixth is similar to the difference between the four dimensions and the fifth. This could provide us with a working definition of the space as we're going through it. There is a major problem, though."

"What's that?"

"You brought up the matter of chaos. As you know, chaos theory posits that any error in calculation, or any small difference in the input we provide, increases enormously with each iteration of output becoming input."

"And?"

"And we don't have all the data we need for accurate measures. Therefore, we can anticipate that any unexpected effect will become perhaps exponentially greater as we progress through the hole, or more precisely, through the tunnel."

"What you're saying is that our trip might become totally unpredictable, and that we might be at the mercy of chance to come out alive and in one piece?"

"I was not literally saying that, Christina, but your inference matches mine. There is great risk in this venture."

"How does your probability program look at this? What are the chances that we will survive?"

"Let me check the data... The odds are 2 for to 3 against."

"That's not good enough. Try factoring in the unpredictable reactions of a human mind and of human actions. We might do better with something other than a pure logic machine guiding us. No offense intended."

"I am incapable of being offended, Christina. Let me add the human factor, based on my observations of this crew on this flight so far... I have two answers: 51 for to 49 against if humans use my services sparingly, and 55 for to 45 against if they make use of my services as they do in most emergency situations."

"So if you navigate without human intervention, our chances are worse than if we go on manual, but with significant input. It's counter-intuitive, but it proves that logic sometimes isn't enough."

"It calculates that way, although it sounds erroneous."

"In either of those three scenarios, the situation looks pretty grim. I'd much rather have our odds closer to 100%. When my people all return, I'll tell them that we'll go on manual control with full input from your calculations. Whatever happens, make sure you have a couple of copies of the data generated on this flight through the transversible wormhole. I'm sure our assumptions will be proven at least partly inaccurate, and I'm also sure that we'll make mistakes in our guesses and probably in our manipulation of the controls."

"I'll set up a second back-up system while waiting for further orders."

———

The loudspeakers could be heard in every workroom. All eyes were fixed on the visuscreens, all ears were attentive to the commanding officer's voice.

"This is Commodore Vasa speaking. We're about to undertake a mission that no person has ever experienced before, passing through the center of the galaxy via a transversible wormhole. As you can see on the visuals, the gateway is there, it's just where it was predicted to be. There's no reason to doubt that it will let us out exactly where our astrophysicists believe. But we really can't predict what the next hour or so will be like.

We will be moving into another dimension of hyperspace, one that none of us here on the bridge can imagine, and one that Colombina is totally unfamiliar with. She gives us odds of 11 to 9 to reach the exit gateway safely. Your section leaders have briefed you on your duties. Consider our passage not only as hazardous duty but also as a red alert. Each of us must do what we're called on to do; anything less than that could lead to disaster. I'd like to add that we don't know if the gravitational field will be affected by this, so make sure you're all properly tethered. When the countdown reaches zero, we will move toward the portal."

Colombina's count began, this time at 50. 29, 28, 27...10, 9, 8... 3, 2, 1, 0.

The great ship sped forward, hitting the gateway right in the middle. They were in the wormhole!

—

"Commodore, the sensors have picked up what looks like several identical meteorites. They appear to be coming at us and at the same time to be following us and surrounding us."

"Lieutenant, get us split visuals, the big scene and our immediate area. And Commander, get ready to manoeuvre by hand."

"It looks weird, Commodore. Something seems to be reaching into the area just ahead of us," replied a puzzled Susanna.

"Good job of avoiding that! But they keep coming! It's like a family of cloned meteorites! Keep your eyes attached to the tunnel. We seem to be starting to spin."

"Christina," said Colombina, "the gravity level has fallen to 90% and seems to be going down slowly."

Christina signalled Kwali. "What's going on?"

"Can't say, Commodore, it looks like we're leaking gravity!"

"Leaking gravity?"

"I can't think of another way to express it. It's like a slow decompression."

"Commander, there's a roadblock ahead!" Susanna tried to

manoeuvre around a huge meteor that seemed to come at them almost at the speed of light, when suddenly it disappeared! At the same time it reappeared from the wall of the tunnel, and it crashed into Constellation. A second crash followed: the same meteor? It knocked out some of the sensors.

April shouted, "We've lost the life detectors, Commodore! And it's dark at four o'clock!"

Another smash. An immense noise. Christina felt herself ripped out of her safety belt and thrown across her work area, then snapped back. Did she lose consciousness for a moment? She did not know, but she noticed that the bridge crew had all been knocked out of their safety belts, too, and that the bridge was in disorder. Martin was checking the rest of the crew.

"Security A-2, come in!"

No answer.

"Security A-2, are you there?"

"Security A-2 here, Commander. This is Ensign Mgamba. Please send help at once. We have two fires in the room, gaping holes in the interior walls, cracks in the ceiling. Several persons are injured. We have called for emergency medics."

"Mgamba, evacuate all the injured at once. Extinguish the fires, then have the team leave the area. Evacuate all ajacent rooms. Seal off that portion of Decks 7 and 8 where monitors show heavy damage. Do this at once!"

"We have heard the orders, and we are following them already, sir. Mgamba signing off."

The situation was grave in other sectors, but Kwali's alarm was evident when he scanned his support system measures.

"Commodore! Gravity has fallen so much that in some rooms the crew is beginning to float."

Spirals of formless blobs, maybe some exotic matter, swirled past Constellation. Some seemed to be clinging to the side of the craft. It was not clear if it was a life form or not, if it could eat away the alloy of Constellation's exterior. But then it disappeared, only to show up in the engine rooms, where Kwali had gone to help his staff make repairs on damaged conduits. Then it disappeared again!

Christina surveyed the damage as she knew it. She feared the worst for the crew. At moments of extreme tension, she tended to drop the formal address required by Space Fleet protocol. She barked out orders over the increasing din of the control room.

"Martin, have everyone get prepared to use auxiliary life-support systems. Kwali, try to get the back-up system ready for instant use. Watch out, Susanna! A meteor!"

Too late! the meteor hit Constellation head on, knocking it off course.

"Damage report, Kwali! As soon as possible!"

"We're working on that, Commodore. The main system just kicked out, maybe it was hit by whatever that was. We got the back-up online just in time."

"Susanna, make sure we can fly straight. You might have to compensate to starboard after that hit."

"That tactic seems to be working, Commodore. If only I can keep avoiding these things. They loom up at you, veer off unexpectedly, show up somewhere else, hit you from nowhere! What are they, some kind of quantum meteors?"

"Commodore, the sensors are picking up a light source that seems to be permanently surrounding us. It's going to overwhelm us! It's like trapped photons! They'll kill our sensors."

"Quick, drop the level of intensity of the light sensors. What's that in front of us? Watch out! It looks like a huge rock! We've gone right through it!"

It was amazing: a boulder growing in size as it came out of the tunnel wall! The great craft went through it as though it were a cloud of vapor! But no, the rock, huge indeed, came down directly on the upper roof of the craft and exploded with a huge noise. The exterior walls of Constellation were shattered at the point of impact, sector R, levels 15 and 16. The force shields had become ineffective.

"Kwali, any word on damage?"

"The earlier damage is severe. Martin is moving the crew to safer areas, away from the periphery of the craft. We are evacuating all the exterior rooms, just in case. There is significant damage to the exterior and to about 15% of the interior. Surely it's twice that, with the latest explosion! We are putting out fires, cutting cable links, evacuating whole sectors."

"And the medical report?"

It was mixed, at best. "Heavy casualties as far as numbers are concerned, but there are no deaths and no life-threatening injuries to report so far, Commodore."

"Thank you, Mujama. I suspect you'll be busy for a while."

"Colombina, try to make sense of what is happening."

A thundering crash prevented Christina from saying anything more. A boulder seemed to fly past them and go through the wall without tearing it, but at the same time from another direction it tore a hole in the wall before coming to rest at April's feet. A smoldering fire was about to break out. The fire prevention system was not functioning. Martin raced for the extinguisher and contained the fire.

"We've lost all but two visual sensors, Commodore."

"Susanna, do you think you can keep on avoiding whatever comes your way?"

"I can't avoid what I can't see, Commodore. But I do see another of those blobs."

"Get prepared to switch controls back to Colombina. Meanwhile, if you can't avoid them, try heading straight towards them!"

" Colombina, have you been able to figure out what's going wrong? This looks to me like some of the things we saw when we first encountered hyperspace a few centuries ago."

"I am constantly updating the program as new data is being fed in, but I have not been able to calculate a safer way to fly. The information you have given me does not help because I do not have data on those events."

"Try feeding irregular, chaotic and random moves, but always going forward. A strange attractor mode!"

"That seems irrational, Commodore. It would be better if we..."

Another direct hit. More damage. Engineering could not possibly get to this while they're working on other serious damage. I have to make a quick decision: to save lives, or to risk further damage to the ship. But if the ship blows apart, no lives will be saved. No time for hesitation, to be or not to be!

"Seal off all the external compartments, Kwali! And

Colombina, don't reason with me: do as I say!"

"It will take me some time to set things up, Commodore. Three minutes, perhaps."

At about this time, Kwali realized that what they were seeing was a series of "windows" to the sixth dimension, which moved randomly about, sometimes presenting the "outside," other times showing the "inside," and other times views from other points of perspective. And always, they seemed to come back to where they started, except the crew of Constellation knew that they were advancing at incalculable speeds through the tunnel. Escher? Picasso? Artists always seem to be ahead of science. It was like a surrealist movie, or a horror dream, or like walking in hyperspace. This is what Christina had wanted to get across to Colombina. Kwali reported his thoughts and ideas to Christina, who had Colombina add that to her calculations, which added a couple of long minutes to the time before her program would be complete. At last the moment came.

"Calculations complete, Christina."

"Good. Execute the program!"

Colombina took control of the ship, or rather it flew itself following the new course she had laid down.

Suddenly, they saw what looked like ordinary space, just up ahead! Was it a mirage, like much of what they'd been experiencing? Or was it real, like those meteor holes and the fires and the injuries and the untold damage they'd encountered so far?

"Real space up ahead, Christina. We should reach it in a minute. At the most."

"I hope you're right, Colombina. I don't know how much more Constellation can take."

Again, time seemed to stop in its tracks. Thirty seconds went by as slowly as an hour. Another ten seconds. In all this time Constellation kept hurtling forward, lurching unpredictably, glancing off the wall of the tunnel, striking, or rather sliding by, an occasional meteor. Finally, delivery! Christina looked at the clock. "They said it would take less than an hour; it took us 57 minutes. I hope we'll never have to repeat that again."

Once out of the wormhole, the full gravitational field

recovered to full strength. The process of regravitation had already begun, but under the circumstances, no one had noticed. And no one was admiring the heavens in this part of the galaxy, stars that no human eyes had ever seen before. April, though, shivered as she focused the two remaining sensors back at the site of their disastrous journey.

"Look, Commodore, the wormhole gateway looks friendly. Look at how gracefully it's swaying! If I didn't know better, I'd think it was inviting us to come back in."

Christina spoke to her computer. "Colombina, use a portion of your calculating power to analyze what we went through. If we know what went right, and why, we should be able to avoid that kind of danger on the way back."

"I do not understand why your irrational command worked. If I can solve that problem I might be able to give us a better picture of how to cope with the sixth dimension, and not just for the trip back."

"Sometimes we humans have intuitive responses that even the best of our computers can't have. Logic, no matter how powerful, sometimes can't deal with the unknown. Or maybe I was just lucky."

"Luck does not compute, Christina. But neither did your instructions."

———

Mujama reported that, by some extraordinary stroke of luck, there were no deaths. There was, however, almost no personnel not wounded. Most had suffered bruises; there were a few broken bones, some damage to organs. No life-threatening injuries were reported. Within two weeks everyone was able to function normally, or as normally as possible, given the circumstances.

The technical crews first set about to restore the main life-support system, then to assess damage to the various subordinate computers that, along with Colombina, made the giant spaceship work. It seemed that kilometers of cables had been damaged or destroyed, ventilators blocked, secondary computers broken, some destroyed. Fortunately, the engine room and the colliders were untouched. However, some of the spare parts, stored in a room with an blown-out exterior wall in Sector R, Level 15, were lost to space. Christina shuddered at the sudden reminder of her near-death experience on Aphrodite.

The security and maintenance crews went to work immediately to do the first priority repairs. Constellation had some self-repair capacity, but the damage was far too extensive for automatic repairs to do the complete job, or even a quarter of it. Once the internal structures were stabilized, beams replaced, temporary walls installed, Martin looked at his next task. By contrast with what remained to be done, this had been a cakewalk. "Just a few rivets to put in place," he joked.

The sensors were another problem altogether. Constellation could not dare venture farther until most of them were restored to at least basic functionality. But that could not be done until the very heavy damage inflicted on the ship's exterior could be repaired. Three gaping holes, and much smoothing out of dented alloy. This repair became the chief occupation of those who were sound of limb, the highest priority. It would require that most dreaded of long-term repair jobs, those that take place in the weightlessness of outer space. Space walks look exciting to those who don't have to do them; they are frightening to those who are asked to put their lives on the line to face the near absolute zero world of space virtually alone. Kwali and his team of engineers and mechanics joined forces with Martin and his double crew of security forces and maintenance. Kwali and Martin worked out plans to require the minimum amount of time outside, so as to reduce the risks of this type of work. And to encourage their workers to face the perils of heavy construction in outer space, they were themselves among the first to go out to assess the damage and to begin gradually rebuilding this huge ship.

Real heroics are sometimes found in the unglamorous acts of everyday life.

CONTACT!

"Klor, our first images from Unias have come in! Our scientists were right! We have visual proof that there **is** another planet out there! Just where they said it would be– 180^0 away from us, on the same orbital plane, hidden behind Chromos! Proof!"

"By Oarnn, you're right, Noyl! And look at it! It has an atmosphere! It's blue, like Damos! It probably has life on it! How big is it?"

"We'll have to wait a bit for more images and data, but offhand I'd say it looks to be about the size of Damos."

"Just like Ecnelav predicted!"

"Don't you think we ought to call in the boss? She's staked her reputation on the existence of Unias. Where is she when we want her? No, wait, here she comes. Ecnelav! Ecnelav! Proof! Unias exists! See what it looks like! The Unias probe has found it!"

"It's a blue planet! It's so beautiful! And look, it seems to have two small moons. Can we get a close-up of Unias, then the moons? Has the small land probe been launched?"

"Yes, everything's going along as planned."

"Break out the wine! It's time to celebrate! And call up the press corps!"

"There seems to be a kind of cloud cover, a bit of lightning, can't see through... ah! a clearing in the clouds. Is that water? A land mass? Do we have a habitable planet on the other side of the sun?"

"It's a great day for the Kolok!"

———

"Damn! That's the fourth dead end here. Four stars about the age of our sun, each with several planets, but not a sign of intelligent life yet. Colombina, do you have any suggestions?"

"Christina, I have located another possible system in our vicinity, about a half light-year from here. We should be able to

155

get there in about two hours."

"Details?"

"It's a medium white star with what appears to be four or maybe five planets. The one farthest out looks huge, bigger than Jupiter and Saturn combined. We're still too far away to get clearer details."

"Set a course for it, and mark it on our grid."

"Yes, Christina!"

Addressing Martin, Christina said, "Commander, when we get within range, let's have some full visuals. I'd like to stop just far enough away to capture an image of this system; we flubbed it the last time."

"Yes, Commodore!"

"Lieutenant," she said to April, "are the sensors repaired yet? We want to make sure that we'll be able to send a party down there, if one of those planets looks viable."

"This time everything's in order, Commodore. The heat sensors, the atmosphere sensors are functioning. We've finally been able to get the life sensors up–for the first time since we got through that worm-hole."

Christina and her crew were ready for anything. Or were they? They were still not really recovered from the worm-hole experience, what with the damage to Constellation II, the unexpected powerful x-ray radiation and the photon storm as they approached their first target star, then the rain of comets. And then the frustration of the four solar systems. Two of them lifeless. At their second stop, there was some sign of very primitive life, something resembling algae, on the third planet; and on the second planet at their next try, there was a dead world that seemed to have had a civilization at one time. It looked like the planet had died of a kind of greenhouse effect. It'll take millennia at least for life to begin again there. Didn't those people realize that the planet was dying? Did they try to get off it? Maybe they weren't advanced enough, although there were signs, under the dust of who can tell how many centuries, of a technological life. Earth could have gone that route, but fortunately our leaders finally showed some common sense.

Common sense: what we're doing seems so logical, and yet

it's not working. Here on the other spiral arm of the galaxy, things should be like they are where Earth is, but it's somehow different. It's a bit denser than we had expected. Heck, not a bit, twice as dense, twice as many stars here on almost the same spot as Earth is, near the end of its arm. Among these thousands of stars, we have so far located only five, including the one Colombina just found, that resemble the Sun, stars about 4,500,000,000 to 5,000,000,000 years old, and with planets. You'd think at least one of these systems would be crawling with life.

We haven't encountered intelligent life in the galaxy, yet, anywhere. Habitable planets, like Mesnos and a few others, but no sign of a current technological civilization with a human-like intelligence. There's got to be a race of highly-evolved beings alive and flourishing right now, somewhere! Colombina keeps telling us what the odds are of intelligent life elsewhere in the galaxy. It all sounds so possible, but we've come up empty-handed so many times.

Christina reflected on how she had gotten to rely on Colombina. That computer had a real personality, she was, she was... she was almost human, that what she was. No other way to put it. And the crew, what a great bunch! A space walk to repair the extensive damage in the middle of nowhere. Interior damage caused by fires after the comets hit us. No one panicked, they all did their jobs. Just as they did when we were in the wormhole and when we finally got out. The training continues as though we were on Earth. We're preparing for... what? What's out there? Suppose we do find intelligent beings? Will they be hostile to aliens? It's hard to think of yourself as an alien, but you have to put yourself in the other person's skin. Wonder what their skin will be like? It seems we can't get these ideas out of our minds, it's all we talk about at mealtime. That and the shape of Constellation.

Kwali broke into her thoughts with the announcement that he had at last figured out what had happened in the wormhole. He had then checked his ideas out with Colombina, who corroborated his calculations.

"What happened, Commodore, was this: we were trying to

157

see the sixth dimension as if we were in our own four dimensions, or through the perspective of the fifth dimension. Those meteors that seemed to go right through Constellation or that dissipated into fog were actually in the sixth dimension, and were not "real" to us in our world. A few coincidences of four-dimensional boulders hitting us at the same approximate time that we encountered the sixth-dimensional stones made it seem as if they were the same things. Colombina has a better handle on this now, and should be able to help steer us back without problems."

"What about the photon shower?"

"That was in fact a single beam of light caught in a loop near the end of the tunnel. We don't know why it happened there instead of just outside, which would make more sense (at least that's what happens outside of black holes). And by the way, we also don't know what caused the other photon shower we ran into later."

"I'm glad to learn it was all outside and not in our collective psyche. That would have been terrible to contemplate."

Christina, perhaps buoyed by the almost-finished major repairs, and by this assurance of her basic sanity, decided to drop the formalities for a moment. "Martin, while the rest of us slip off for lunch at the local commissary, you and Kwali keep an eye on things, ok? We should be back in an hour. We'll have some of the best take-out stuff sent up to you."

"Indian?"

"A surprise."

Actually, she wasn't sure what there would be, it would be a surprise for her, too. But she was sure of one thing: the cooks were really terrific. And Christina made sure that everyone got the same treatment, that there was no special stuff only for the senior staff.

"And Martin, let me know instantly if there's any news. I'll have a small viewer with me. Let everyone know where we're heading. See you soon!"

"Aye, aye, Cap'n!" said Martin, who had somehow managed to slip a black patch over one eye and get a kind of hook up his sleeve.

"Squawk!" chimed in Kwali, trying to imitate a parrot.

"Very funny, guys. Keep it up and who knows, our security officer might have you walk the plank. No, wait, Martin **IS** the security officer." What pirates! Oh, well, at least they haven't lost their sense of humor. They kind of remind me of Sven.

———

In the middle of a surprisingly small Control Central, where a dozen or so scientists and technicians were jubilantly celebrating their great breakthrough, about 20 computer screens displayed spectacular views of a planet on the other side of the sun. Long suspected by astro-physicists and mathematicians, and assertively predicted by Ecnelav Enohr, the existence of this planet, about the size of Damos, was nevertheless treated as mere science fiction fantasy by much of the public, and as a danger to religion by the devotees of Schad, the mystical religious group that preached a veneration for the literal interpretation of the sacred scriptures, especially the Book of Oarnn. In Oarnn's cosmology, Damos was the center of the world, of all of creation, and all of creation was designed for the benefit of the Kolok, the undisputed rulers of Damos, the species at the top of the food chain.

In the midst of much confusion, a distinguished woman was talking into a camera.

"This is Otnas Omer, with a fast-breaking news story from the Catta Space Center. The Unias probe has just discovered the planet, apparently about the size of Damos, just where Dr. Ecnelav Enohr had predicted such a planet would be. The scene here is organized pandemonium. Everyone is celebrating. High Commissioner Ylro is in contact by satellite distance vision. The first images are now being shown around the globe, and in every part of the world sets are tuned in, as people want to get their first glimpse of this unknown world. What a day for the Kolok people! Just a few years ago we saw our first close images of what Dr. Enohr renamed Tertia Major and Tertia Minor. And now this! Then Damosians set foot on the moon! What a decade!

"Dr. Enohr, Dr. Enohr! Could we have a word with you,

Ma'am?"

"Yes, of course, Otnas. We're all so thrilled here, we've not only proven that Unias exists, look at that image coming on: an atmosphere! an ocean! a continent! We've sent down a land probe to see if there's life there, plants, animals. This is exciting beyond words. First Tertia Major and Tertia Minor, both with an atmosphere, both with life; now this!"

"What do you think this will do for the Kolok people? Will we be able to..."

Otnas's voice was drowned out by the cries coming up from the small crowd gathering at the site. They had just seen the first pictures taken on the surface of Unias–the land probe had alighted on what looked like a glade, with some sort of grass. A group of strange spherical objects, apparently life forms of some sort, came up near the probe. They seemed to be trying to eat it!

"By Oarnn! What is that?"

"It looks something like a plant," replied Klor. "Look at them! They're able to move very fast by rolling up or down hills. There must be a hundred of them around the probe! I wonder what they sound like."

At just this moment, the Unias probe, circling far out from the planet, went behind the sun. What a time for the transmission to end! They would not have new images for ten hours!

"Otnas, in an hour we'll have processed some more pictures, and we'll have had a little time to sort through and process the pictures we have, and to analyze what we've seen. Then we'll be able to give you a better idea of what we think this is. Excuse me now; I've got to get to work!"

"You heard Dr. Enohr. We'll be back to you in about an hour. This is Otnas Omer reporting. Back to Studio Central."

———

"Omigod, look at that! Kwali, make sure everyone can see this extraordinary solar system."

Extraordinary it was. Blocking out the light of the sun allowed five planets to be seen very clearly. Two of them had the same orbit, but were at 180^0 of each other. They appeared to be

160

about 130,000,000 km out from the sun, or on an orbit equivalent to halfway between Earth and Venus. Two more planets, smaller than the first two but apparently identical twins, were in orbit at about 200,000,000 km, or equivalent to halfway between Earth and Mars. These planets seemed to be serving as satellites to each other. Much farther out was the fifth planet, a gaseous giant appearing to be a failed star with several times the mass of Jupiter. They could see no asteroid belt, or any other planet. Nothing but clear space between these three orbits.

Kwali made a brief announcement, and had the images put on the screens. What an awesome sight! Everyone raised a cheer, and then the hubbub began. Basically, they all were sure that this time they'd hit paydirt. "There just has to be life there! This solar system looks too perfect for another false alarm!"

Christina called her staff together in the briefing room just off the control room. It was a small room, with a conference table, a visuviewer, a computer, some office supplies. And a real window looking out on a truly spectacular sight.

"I think these opposite planets are just about the right distance from their sun to support life. At least one of them. If these don't work–or for that matter, even if they do–we should take a look at the other two that are orbiting each other while they orbit the sun. I guess I should be more cautious. After all, I thought we'd found what we were after the last four times!"

"Commodore, why not start with the planets farther out? They might not have so much heat to deal with."

"Susanna, you have it all wrong," said Martin. If there's life there at all, it will surely have taken root on that first orbit. Look, it's about half the distance from Earth to Venus, according to what Colombina told us. If there's water on one of those planets, there's sure to be life. And I bet that if there's life on one of those planets, there's bound to be life on the other one, too. I think the Commodore's right. Let's start from the inside and work out."

Mujama, who seldom spoke, agreed with Martin. "To tell you the truth, given the distances these first four planets are from their sun, they might **all** support life. At least they have a chance to support life. Heck, Mars does, now, it's even warm enough to live on somewhat comfortably. So does Venus, where it's now

cool enough to support life comfort ably. Sure, it's only because we gave Nature a boost, with the Ares and Aphrodite projects, but still, I'd say, let's explore all four planets, starting with that one over there on the left."

"Why the one on the left?"

She replied, in her laconic manner, "Because you have to choose one, and I'm left-handed."

"I'm not sure that Mujama's reason for her choice of the one on the left makes sense, but I suppose it's no more arbitrary than any other choice. And I agree with her that it will be more logical to start with the inner planets, because they have a better chance of being what we're looking for. If there are no objections, let's get our teams ready. Martin, you'll lead the landing party."

"You're not going this time, Commodore?"

"No, I'll take Planet Two, or One-B."

"Commodore," said Mujama, "I really think that we should try to find a sign of life before we alight. We have the resources, with a great Communications Officer in Kwali and a something-else computer in Colombina. I secretly asked Kwali to have Colombina start scanning the solar system for radio waves. The fact is, they have found some that can only add up to intelligence."

"Why didn't you say so before? This is the most exciting thing that's happened on the trip!"

"Unless you think that almost blowing apart in the worm hole was dull, that is," interrupted Susanna, slyly.

"Be serious, Susanna; this is the purpose of our mission, to find intelligent life, and to make contact with the aliens. Mujama, what has been found?"

"There's a small emission coming from the planet on the left, which is why I suggested that one. The one on the right has a huge series of emissions. It's clearly the planet that these people inhabit. I thought it might be a good idea to see what they're doing on the other one, because there probably won't be too many of them there, in case they're dangerous. Meanwhile, we can try to figure out their lingo."

"Alright, since it's time for secrets, Colombina and I have

been working on a translation program for a whole bunch of time, about two centuries, and we think we have what is needed. The first working model just got me to understand and to speak the dialect of the Ancient-Day Primitivists on Mars, not too hard a job. If this much bigger model does its job, we might all speak whatever these folks speak!"

"What does this thing look like? How is it used?" Kwali asked.

"It looks something like a hearing aid. It sends a beam to a tiny computer that can be worn as a kind of belt ornament. This device, without any further help, can do what the thing I used in Canaan did. In this case, though, we'll have to run it through Colombina's translation program."

Martin could barely contain his excitement at the thought of speaking with aliens. "I can't wait until we're close enough to hear them, and to find out what they're saying."

———

The probe turned its cameras, unexpectedly, upwards, further above the surface. It was programmed to do this in case some interesting object appeared–a moon, a meteorite, something of the sort. But at a distance of about 500 km away, it revealed a shocking sight.

"Ecnelav, look at this strange image. If I didn't know better, I'd swear it was a space ship! It looks just like what I thought these things would look like."

"Let's see if we can get a better picture of it. By Oarnn! It's huge! It looks big enough for a small village! Quick! get hold of the High Commissioner!"

On the screen there was a picture of a disk-like structure, slowly rotating, and apparently examining the small probe. Ecnelav could make out what seemed to her to be cameras, and also some small sensors, some kind of devices that were able to discern what the probe was, and what it was doing.

"Don't let these pictures get out to the public until we get official clearance. We don't want to cause panic among the people. Let them see what our little land probe is doing, now that it's gotten free of those spherical things."

"Oh, no! This is worse!"

"What do you mean? What are you talking about?"

"Take a look for yourself: somebody's there! Is Unias inhabited by an intelligent alien species? Or is that what the creatures in the space ship look like?"

They all gathered around the large screen. A leader was there with a small party. They held a few of the spheres in their gloved hands, they were petting them and talking to them while coming near the land probe. They appeared not to be as tall as the Kolok, but were like us, bipedal. They soon located the camera, and appeared to be talking into it. Damn! We had not loaded sound on the probe, because of cost overruns and various other problems.

"What are they saying?"

"We'll have to turn on the sound."

"Sound? What sound?"

"I had an extra 100,000 flen to spend, and packed in a sound transmitter. Since we weren't officially authorized to have sound, I was going to surprise you all with the sounds of Unias. In fact, I already have a recording of the whirring chirps of the spheres, and of the wind. Let's listen to these aliens."

Martin was speaking. "... of the people of Earth, we wish to let you know that we are here on a scientific mission, and that we come in peace. If you have a language synthesizer like mine, perhaps you can understand me. But since we know where the land probe and the main ship are sending their messages, we will soon come in peace to meet you."

"I can make out a rhythm to what that alien was saying, but the words make no sense."

"Ecnelav! What's happening there?"

"I can't believe it! They've disappeared in thin air! They must have come and gone in transmat beams. More science fiction! Gar! Get the High Commissioner here at once!"

———

"Contact!" cried Christina. "Intelligent life, certainly coming

164

from this planet's orbit-mate! And this seems to be a planet that we Earth people could live on. As soon as we get word from the bio lab, let's do what we can to keep these spheres alive so that we can present them to the people we'll soon meet. I sure hope they're friendly types!"

"Well, Commodore, so far the spheres seem to be friendly enough. We found some lichen-like substance that they seem to delight in. We've got them and their food supplies isolated in the alien area of the bio lab, so as not to contaminate them. Let's hope they live through the trip to Planet 2."

"A pretty sophisticated land probe, Martin? It seemed stationary to me. And I must say that the control vehicle looked a bit primitive, like the things sent to the Moon and to the other planets back in the 20th and 21st centuries."

"With all due respect, Susanna, let's not forget that our technology in those days was pretty sophisticated, or at least sophisticated enough to begin exploration of outer space as well as of the solar system. All we've done is continue to build on their discoveries and their technologies. They moved so fast in just four or five centuries. Have we gone as fast since, say 2500?"

Kwali opined, "I understand what you're driving at, but without belittling that bygone era, compared to what we have, this civilization seems to be close to the beginning of its technological phase. I bet they didn't harness electricity until 100 years ago. On the other hand, they are far enough advanced that they'll be able to understand us, and we should be able to understand them. I wonder what they look like."

"Little green monsters, probably," quipped Martin, "with antennas coming out of their heads and googly eyes."

"While you guys have been chatting, Colombina has prodded our somewhat reluctant radio to listen for signals from Planet 2. Our sensors have transmitted the sounds to our translation matrix, which is beginning to make some sense of it. Listen to this."

"...alien life forms that seem to be somewhat shorter than us, with two legs and two arms like us, a kind of fur on their heads instead of scales, and appendages on either side of their head.

165

Their skin is various shades of brown. They ... [an undeciphered portion of the message, a mixture of sibilants and plosives separated by vowels] ... craft is immense, large enough to carry perhaps 1000 people, and is perhaps ten stories high, or more. It dwarfs our probe. ... [Static makes the rest untranslatable]."

"Colombina, does our translator know enough of this language to allow us to communicate with these people?"

"Yes, Christina, we've actually been able to decipher quite a bit of their language, which seems to be called Kolok. But you will need an adapter so they can attach the ear piece somewhere."

"What do you mean?"

"You heard their description of humans as having appendages on either side of the head. It probably means that they don't recognize ears."

"Of course! I should have guessed. Still, they must have an otic or auditory membrane of some sort that allows them to hear. After all, if they're speaking that means someone can hear them."

"Mujama, would you remind us of what we know about these people?"

"Yes, Commodore. They're tall, have two arms and two legs, scales on their head instead of hair, ..."

"They must be lizards or reptiles!" exclaimed Susanna. "I focused on their not knowing a word for *hair*, using *fur* instead. If they're lizards or reptiles, that would explain their lack of ears. I wonder if they're warm-blooded or cold-blooded, if their young hatch or are born live, if they have hands with opposable thumbs. I'm sorry, Mujama, I got carried away."

"They're intelligent and literate, they really don't know much about their own solar system (I infer this from their having to prove that this planet exists, judging from some of their statements about what they're calling Unias)."

"We also know that their home planet is called Damos, that they are Damosians and also Kolok."

"How do you figure that, Kwali?" asked Mujama.

"The same way we learned all that other stuff: I listened to the translator."

"Damos," repeated Christina, "Damosians, Kolok. I suppose

their name for themselves is Kolok, just as we call ourselves humans. And the other planet is called Unias. Let's ask the translator if this is the way the word is said in Kolok, or if it's been transposed into a Latinate form for our benefit."

"And while we're at it, do they have a name for their sun?"

"It is called Chromos."

"Now we must find a place to land. How are we doing on that score, Kwali?"

"Commodore, I think I've identified their capital city and the chief government buildings. There's a large statue out front, in a kind of courtyard. Right now it seems not quite deserted, but at least when you materialize you won't be in a crowd."

"As we've agreed, and following our mission statement, we'll go down with a small group, three senior staff from Control, seven non-commissioned staff from security, support, and engineering. We'll bring along the spheres as an offering. We should have a dozen headsets and one speaker. I've strapped on a translator homing device that works two ways. Kwali, you, April and Susanna will stay here. Also as we've agreed, Martin and Mujama will come with me. You've selected your assistants?"

"Yes, Commodore."

"Christina," said Susanna, "be careful."

Christina usually insisted that in the Control Room people refer to her by title, but she let this slip by, understanding that Susanna was speaking to her as a friend more than as an officer.

"Don't worry. We won't do anything that Kwali wouldn't do."

———

"Their craft is hovering overhead, High Commissioner Ylro. It's very high up, beyond unaided eyesight, but our telescopes have it in full view."

"What do you think they are planning, Neac? As Chief of Security for the Planetary Government, what plans have you made in case they are hostile?"

"We do not believe they are hostile, sir. Dr. Enohr, who is here now, says that they have tried to communicate with us, unsuccessfully so far. And in any case, we have not been able to detect any other craft. I would suggest that this is a scientific mission, probably exploring the galaxy. It is obvious that they are a technologically advanced society, much more advanced than we are. If they were hostile, they would certainly have taken action against us by now. I would stake my reputation and my career on their being peaceful."

"I don't ask for such sacrifices, Neac. Let's wait and see what they have in mind. Meanwhile, what preparations have been made for their arrival?"

"We do not know where the aliens will land their craft, or rather their shuttle. Furthermore, we did not see a shuttle or any similar craft in the images we have of Unias, and so we can only speculate on how or where they might choose to land. We have nevertheless sent Deputy High Commissioner Amil to Bobol; we believe the landing strip there will be long enough for any shuttle the aliens send down. A small greeting party is accompanying her, along with the official band. We hope to show them by outward signs that we bear no hostility to them, but that we welcome them to our capital city and our planet."

"Are the highways cleared of vehicles?"

"We have done better: the rapid train has been sent to Bobol, and the tracks are being secured to protect the people who might press too close."

"When they come here to Ihled, we must greet them most warmly. A state reception of the highest order is imperative. We need our wisest counselors and teachers to be present, and some representatives of the people."

"This has been done, and in addition I have ordered the finest of our linguists to study their language when they arrive, so as to allow us to begin to communicate with the aliens as quickly as possible."

"So far, I am told that we know they have come from a great distance, from a planet called Irrt or Ert, from somewhere beyond the solar system. This worries me, Neac."

"Why, High Commissioner? It is an exciting moment for Damos, coming as it does in this period of unprecedented advances in the world of science. An unhoped-for but often dreamed-of encounter with the unknown from beyond the stars."

"It is the devotees of Schad who worry me, Neac. Their belief in the literal truth of the *Book of Oarnn*, their interpreation of certain passages in such a way as to equate life beyond Damos as the domain of Evil, their sense that the universe exists for the benefit of the Kolok, these tenets coupled with a fanaticism that is dangerous might incite them to do violence to our visitors. We must take steps to protect these people from the Schadites. We should not show this dark side of Damosian culture."

"I understand, High Commissioner, and indeed we are offering all the protection we can. Only authorized personnel will come into contact with them."

———

The small group assembled in the Transmat Room. Christina decided that they should all appear at the same time in the large courtyard facing the Capitol, rather than in the small numbers that the individual booths would permit. Ten people entered the small alcove the crew had nicknamed "The Den," and when they were all in place, Christina nodded. Ju-Sen checked her coordinates once more, made sure that she could locate ten homing devices, then nodding in assent, she pressed the large green button. The party seemed to be covered in a shimmering veil of snow, then it disappeared. This time, though, it seemed much more portentous than ever before. They would meet intelligent aliens!

Ju-Sen checked her charts. They had arrived safely! She sent the agreed-on message to the Control Room and to the entire ship. Kwali and Susanna heaved a sigh of relief, then April focused the lenses as closely as possible on the scene below. It was no fun being in the control room rather than down on the surface, but they could at least follow some of the action.

———

The strange tingling sensation that accompanied distance matter transportation, so familiar to this veteran group, seemed

169

somehow more intense that day. Then they landed, hundreds of kilometers below, at precisely the point Ju-sen had selected. Once their nerves had calmed a bit–a matter of two or three seconds that felt like hour–they formed a line that advanced towards the imposing figures at the bottom of the steps. They walked silently and slowly, looking at the powerful architectural splendor of the Capitol and the surrounding edifices. They paused at the monumental statue of what appeared to be a hero or a god. Then they resumed their pathway to the tall people awaiting them.

"Neac, they materialized from nowhere," whispered the awe-stricken High Commissioner. "Are they gods?"

"Ylro, this must be how they transport themselves from their spaceship. They are paying respect to the statue of Oarnn."

"Have the band strike up a lively fanfare when they reach the flower-bed. I shall then advance and greet them."

The familiar music, stirring and welcoming, announced the visit of important state visitors. Ylro moved forward, bowed, then raised his arms in greeting. "Welcome, strangers, to Damos. May your stay among us be long, and your hearts warm as long as you remain here. May our peoples be friends forever."

Christina and her group stopped. Christina bowed, lifted her right arm in a gesture of friendship, and spoke, thanks to the translator, in flawless Kolok. "We come in peace and friendship from across the immensity of time and space of our common galaxy. We wish you long life and warm affections, and we offer you, as a pledge of our intentions, these first living beings we found on your sister planet of Unias, near your land probe."

The first contact: a miracle of peace, mutual respect, and friendship.

———

"Schad and Oarnn will not tolerate these emissaries of Evil. We must drive them from our world, for the salvation of the Kolok people, for the future of Damosian life! We must arrange a meeting of Schadite leaders to deal with this crisis."

So spoke Ogatrac.

DAMOS

The interminable receiving lines ended at last. Fortunately the little group brought the small translator, which allowed people to exchange a few words (providing only one person spoke at a time) as they grasped left elbows with right hands, the Damosian equivalent of a handshake.

At the head table sat High Commissioner Ylro and the Deputy High Commissioner Amil, flown back from Bobol for the event. Chief of Security Neac and Director Enohr flanked them. Christina, Martin, and Mujama sat opposite them. Each of these dignitaries had a headset connected by radio to the translater, which made real conversation possible.

The other members of the party were seated at smaller tables of four or five persons with a variety of notables. For the sergeants and the technicians it was a particularly great treat: normally only officers received the kind of treatment they were offered. But they had spent two long and full years together on this expedition, and had shared in the triumphs and failures of the flight. All those disappointments, all those planets with no intelligent life! In particular, to have come across dead civilizations, one that seems to have annihilated itself in war, another that had choked itself with the destruction of its natural resources! And the wormhole experience! They were also grateful to their leaders, who put so much faith in them and who never failed to treat them with dignity. Maybe that can explain, at least in part, why so many of the ordinary crew members on Constellation spent a good portion of their leisure time in the pursuit of skills and knowledge. "We're getting to be scientists in our own right," as Sergeant Torquato put it.

Many notables were present, mayors, governors, scientists like Klor and Noyl and Gar from the Catta Space Center. Only eight of the people seated with the sergeants had headsets. Christina noted that many more of these would be needed for future contacts. In the meanwhile, the speaker was set at one table, in hopes that the guests there could communicate. Instead, a veritable Babel ensued, as English and Kolok were constantly being translated, and the translations retranslated back into the original, with some funny distortions.

"I've noticed that all of you have fur on top of your heads, except Sergeant Torquato, whose head is smooth like ours" became, after retranslation, "I've taken account of the fact that you have rich pile atop your craniums, except Sergeant Torquato, whose skull is debonair like ours." It was clear that Colombina and the Commodore would have to work on their little program. It was finally decided that just one person should speak at a time, and that they would use the delayed translation button. Not as funny as the speaker, but it made real dialog at least imaginable.

The large room glittered with the bright lights from crystal chandeliers, tall pier mirrors, the highly polished floor over which the serving staff seemed to glide. The ten Earthlings did not recognize any of the food, except that there was a delicious meat course that reminded them of ostrich, and curious orange-colored vegetables that looked something like lima beans but were unusually sweet. A bright red wine with a delicate and fruity taste accompanied the main dish.

Bit by bit the conversations all tended to turn to details of the technologies employed by the transgalactic visitors, which fascinated the Kolok: the translating devices, teleportation, the huge spaceship, the now-fully functional sensing devices were among the most popular. Accounts, even summary, of the space travelers' adventures and experiences in alien worlds, the wormhole transverse, their training and occupations. And the Earth dwellers discovered that the Damosians were on the verge of space exploration themselves.

Their first space exploit had been the visit to the Damosian moon, which was found to have a light atmosphere and primitive life forms that had evolved to a kind of algae. Then an unmanned spaceship had been sent on a photographic fly-by of the twin planets Tertia Major and Tertia Minor, on both of which evidence of life had been discovered; Damosians were dreaming of exploring these worlds, with the expectation of discovering new life forms. After that, of course, came the discovery of Unias and its biota made possible by the new landing device

172

designed by Dr. Enohr's associates, Klor Emor and Noyl Zerof, first deployed on the very day that Constellation arrived on the scene.

The Damosians already had ambitious plans for manned expeditions to all three of the neighboring planets, probably within a decade. And in the meanwhile, the robot ship that had flown past the twin planets was soon to reach the giant gaseous outer planet, Oarnn, named after the great god worshipped by most Kolok; several important experiments were to be conducted.

Martin, in particular, was amazed at the energy and drive of the hosts, just as the entire party was when they learned that this little solar system was teeming with life: life on the four rock planets and one moon!

Just before dessert, High Commissioner Ylro lifted his glass in a toast to the honored guests. His wishes for their life and safety, and for an extended stay among the Damosians, were cheered by all present. He offered to have the entire crew shown around the planet, with no restrictions. "All 500 of us?" asked Christina. "If you were twice that many," he replied, "our planet would be open to you."

Christina rose, and offered to have Damosians, in small groups, visit Constellation for as long as the Earth people remained in stationary orbit. "You'll have to decide who will be eligible," she said, "because we can't take you on by the millions. And because we want to visit and explore your solar system, we would be honored to do so in a series of joint expeditions. I propose first a voyage to Unias, lasting for perhaps several months. We might even decide to establish a joint scientific station there. Then a second voyage, this time to Tertia Major and Minor, where two groups can explore the planets simultaneously. Thanks to teleportation and the speed of our ship, expedition leaders will be able to get to both planets."

When she had made her suggestion, a rumble arose in the room, and the tumblers rocked on their not-quite-flat bottoms as an earthquake-like movement shook the hall. The Kolok were giving her their strongest cheer, the Tremor of Damos.

Naturally, details of the expeditions and the visits would take time to work out, but within days, the crew had all had their first direct encounter with an intelligent alien species in its own habitat, and the chief Damosian dignitaries had set foot in an alien spacecraft for the first time. Some people were even becoming friends.

———

The somber face of Ogatrac seemed to be darkening during these first euphoric weeks. He and other ministers of the Schadite sect were following events as closely as possible; some had even ventured to join the lottery for tickets to board Constellation, and had won. The Schadite leaders devoured every news item, sent spies to bars and public places to see what effect the space travelers were having on the Kolok, watched the evening news on digitvision, monitored the reception the leaders and the people of Damos were giving to these aliens, who were the very face of evil. Furrowing his forehead, he withdrew into dark musings.

We must find a way to train our women and men as rapidly as possible. The aliens have captured the imagination of the entire planet. It is not possible that they have traversed an entire galaxy for the reasons their leader gave. Scientific interest, indeed. Looking for intelligent life beyond the stars. Desire to know if they are alone in the universe.

We must discover what evil they intend to visit upon the Kolok people. Their mask of friendliness must be penetrated. We must drive them away. Schad has warned us, Oarnn has spoken explicitly against such bearers of evil coming from beyond the moon. The world will not be safe until they leave. But if they leave, they will surely return, perhaps with an invading army. Better to find ways of detaining them here. Their people will assume they were lost in space. Yet, how do you detain them, when they have a ship as large as a village, and implements of mass destruction that our people cannot even imagine? In this era of bonhommie, how can we turn the will of the people against them? How can we show our people that they are being led into grave transgressions of Oarnn's sacred laws?

I must find a way to call the Schadite leaders together to plan strategies for our deliverance. This will take time. This will take some political maneuvering, some incisive words, the right psychology. I must think carefully, plan carefully, be prepared in advance. Do I dare consider violence? Violence is prohibited by Oarnn's law; and Oarnn's law has united the Kolok into a single people that has not known the ravages of war for over one thousand years. Is there another way? Moral persuasion? Passive resistance? Do we have time? Already we have fewer people at our religious services, and we are hearing blasphemous speech in the mouths even of our children. Already the official church leaders have bent the meaning of the words of Oarnn to make it seem as though the aliens are embodiments of good, not evil itself, as Oarnn has called them. We must rid our lives of this evil influence.

I must think carefully, plan carefully, be prepared in advance. Plan for what? Be prepared for what? This is what my thoughts must turn to. First thoughts, then deeds. Oarnn will be served by the servants of Schad.

———

On a tall bluff overlooking a vast plain through which meandered several streams and a large river, Christina and Han Lee were examining spectacular rock formations that glowed in various colors like the Grand Canyon of North America. One could see the evidence of at least a billion years of geological activity, from seismological faults and mammoth movements of planetary crust to centuries, millenia really, of inland seas and fossil life forms; from underground limestone caverns with stalactites and stalagmites to layers of granite and marble. A lot like Earth in many respects, the same geological basis manifested somewhat differently because of variants such as movement of the crust, the size of the tectonic plates, the effects of the weathering caused by rainstorms.

"Damos has never experienced what you describe, Han," explained Tsepadub; "no ice ages, ever. We have had, while our ancestors roamed the world, periods of planetary drought and planetary flooding, great earthquakes and tsunamis, but never ice. Maybe it's because we're closer to our sun than Earth is to its, or because Damos tilts an almost imperceptible 5^0 on its axis, which means that we have climate belts rather than what you call seasons. And, compared to what you describe as your planets' elliptical orbits, our planets have orbits closer to circles."

"Where did the Kolok people come from, Tsesadub?" asked Christina. "I mean, we humans evolved from great apes, bipedal mammals that gradually developed large brains, opposable thumbs, and an intelligence that no other creature on Earth had ever seen."

"On Damos, Commodore, mammals are looked on with disdain. They are little things that eat our grains, spread disease, smell bad. But they do seem to be about as smart as some of our lizards. The Kolok evolved from four-digit warm-blooded lizards that had developed large brains, like your apes. All our warm-blooded lizards have larger brains than their cold-blooded relatives and have four digits. We believe that this symmetry is somehow connected with our mathematical way of confronting nature. And, as you know, we have opposable thumbs like you. A million or so years ago, when the first clearly Kolok-like creatures evolved, they were already ovovivaporous like us. This is a second characteristic that sets us off from other reptiles. There is a huge fossil record that you would perhaps like to see when we return to Ilhed."

"We would love to do so. We've all been fascinated to see that your biota is in many ways similar to ours in general, although the evolutionary processes have produced very different species from ours. For example, the mahlils seem to fill the same niche as our birds, but they are not feathered, and it's clear they're flying reptiles of some sort. Some of the ocean creatures look like our fish, but others don't. You have crustaceans and gastropods and amphibians and other animals that have similar but not identical counterparts on Earth. You have trees and flowers and herbs and grasses, as we do, but they are quite different from ours. Nature is amazing in its variety and also in its sameness. When we first arrived on Paracelsus, the life

176

forms on land were unlike anything we had ever seen: little scurrying vertebrates no bigger than insects. Some vegetation, but no trees or other wooded plants. Mesnos had been closer to Earth-like in its life-forms, but there were no one-to-one match-ups. Damos seems to us like an Earth that somehow evolved differently. It's a strange feeling."

"You perhaps do not have venomous serpents and even venomous plants. Many of ours are deadly. In some areas, people are routinely vaccinated against snake-bites."

A rumble seemed to come from the ground above them. Christina suddenly had an image of the rockslide on Paracelsus and its almost-fatal consequences to her. She paled visibly.

"Commodore," said Han Lee, "maybe we should seek some shelter until this passes."

"Ah, you heard the thunder before I did," said Tsepadub cheerily, not knowing the cause of Christina's nausea. "It is the afternoon shower. It should start in about five minutes. Let's go watch the rainfall from inside that cave over there. I see the others are on their way there already. We'd better hurry: the rains here are very heavy, although they last only a half hour or so. And they come like clockwork in this area. We call them Old Faithful."

"I see the mahlils have flown back to their nests. A few more meters and we'll be there. Then I'll tell you what made me grow pale a moment ago."

———

Atraps seemed particularly eager to join the group of people visiting Constellation. They were taken up into the craft in groups of 20, teleported 10 at a time in a two-minute interval. Atraps was assigned a place in the first group.

They were not the first people to visit Constellation. The major scientists and engineers, the national politicians had gone first. Now tours were arranged for ordinary citizens on the basis of a lottery. These tours alternated with tours offered to second-level politicians and academics. Special visits were arranged for authors, artists, musicians, school and university students. While everyone was fascinated by the craft, the students seemed particularly attracted to the Constellation crew, to the concept of space travel, to the thought of crossing the galaxy. This had Ogatrac and other high-placed members of the Schadite clergy very concerned. Atraps was sent to gather intelligence.

"Is our first group ready?" asked Sergeant Torquato. "OK, come this way. I'd like you to establish three lines in a quincunctal formation." The group arranged themselves appropriately. High levels of excitement (and, truth to tell, anxiety) could easily be sensed. Atraps felt his blood flowing stronger, his heart beating faster. I'm not used to this feeling. I must control myself, I must not show my concern. My job is to observe, question, touch, discover. And report. Directly to the great Ogatrac! Be calm. Concentrate. What is Torquato saying? I missed the first part.

"...a disintegration of the particles that make up your being. They will be instantly reproduced on board ship by the computer. Nothing to worry about. You've already seen a thousand people come back from one of these visits, all of them in good health. You'll feel a tingling sensation, then some brief disorientation when you're reconstituted. We here on the ground will see a kind of white glimmer, and then you'll disappear. If you're worried about this, now's the time to drop out."

Drop out? I've been waiting for a month to be here! I must record my sensa...

At this point, Torquato gave a signal to Ju-Sen, up on the huge craft that was invisible from this distance. Atraps felt the tingle, then the disorientation, then he blinked and found himself in the alien ship. The ship was filled with a soothing light that came from some unknown source. Four or five aliens greeted them, led by the one called Susanna, who identified herself as the pilot and navigator of Constellation.

"You're in a utility area of the ship, a working place that our technicians and engineers call home. This room is used only for teleportation. Lieutenant Ju-Sen is our operator. Someone else will be leading the second group in a couple of minutes."

The first little group was led to a corridor, then to an elevator. "We're on level seven here. I'd like to let you see what my quarters look like. Then we'll visit various parts of the ship: the bridge, the medical center, the library, the biological laboratory, the engine room, whatever you'd like to see in the two hours we'll be together. Some of the people will be working; they'll let you know if they can't be interrupted. Otherwise, feel free to ask whatever questions you'd like."

"Commander," asked Atraps as they emerged from the elevator, "what kind of training have you had on Earth? It must be difficult learning to be a pilot of this kind of craft."

"Actually, we have some six years of training and education at the university level; the last two years are internships in our choice of three specializations, and at least one full year in the field we hope to enter. I had a two-year specialist training. I didn't get to pilot a Constellation-class ship until I had flown about 15 years on smaller craft. I've been a pilot on Constellation for 25 years."

The group gasped. "You must be over 60 years old, but you look so young. Like the Commodore. So many of your people look older than she does: their skin has wrinkled, their hair has changed color." Atraps's implied question was on everyone's mind. Normally a Damosian would not ask such a question, but Atraps was a man on a mission.

"Some of us on board have had our genes altered so that we are frozen in age, and have had our lives extended by about 200 years. I underwent this operation when I was 26, a short time after my internships had ended. The Commodore was 28."

At this point, the group noticed that the corridor they were taking had a view of the outside in several large windows placed at 30-meter gaps. They saw their planet below them; they were not so high up that they could not see cities and geographical features. Above and beyond, they saw the sky with an almost unthinkable clarity. Everywhere they went, they saw crew members working on maintenance, or exercising, or carrying on their various duties. They continued their walk, amazed at the vastness of the spaceship. Finally they came to Susanna's quarters.

"As one of the senior officers, I have a somewhat larger personal area than the technicians and the non-commisioned officers," she explained before they went in. "They have just one large room instead of the two that I have."

"The rooms are beautiful," exclaimed Atraps. "Still, I don't understand how you can have an exterior window when your room faces inward. We can see Damos from here!"

"That's actually a kind of illusion. It's really what you just saw outside, but it's a hologram of that scene projected on the wall. I have a large number of holograms to choose from. Keeps us from getting claustrophobic."

The outer room was a large workroom-study-living room, filled with books and scientific instruments and a small nook for meals near a computer terminal. There were musical instruments, a cello attracting the attention of several visitors. There was also a device to play recorded music. The inner chamber was smaller but comfortably furnished, with a bed, chairs, another study table with a computer terminal. A private bathroom completed the little apartment.

After seeing the bridge, speaking with Colombina ("You can actually talk to that computer, and she answers you!"), looking at charts and maps of the galaxy that the Earth people had generated, the group made the rounds of the medical center and the other points that Susanna had suggested. At Atraps's suggestion, the group ended its visit with a tour of the engineering facilities, the engine room, the antimatter colliders, the communications center. Everyone had relaxed enough to ask questions of their hosts, and Atraps tried to commit everything he saw to memory.

"You did not show us a place of worship," he said as they were approaching the elevator that would take them to Level Seven. "Do you have no god?"

"Many on board are believers and attend regular religious services in chapels set aside for them. Some of our crew members are ordained priests and ministers of their religion. There are many crew members who prefer to spend some time in meditation or in study."

"Not everyone is a believer?"

"No. Many of us are not."

Ogatrac will be pleased to hear this. Their god seems to be

their quest for knowledge, and not the source of knowledge and the creator of divine design. Their attitude proves that these people are evil. They are proud of their accomplishments, of their travels, of the work they have done. Do they wish to suborn us in some way? Maybe their plan is to wean us away from the devotions we offer to Oarnn and Schad. I will have much to tell Ogatrac.

THE PACT OF TERROR

Ogatrac arose, approached the dais, and looked out at his fellow Schadite leaders. He was an imposing figure, over two meters tall–taller even than tall women–with a presence that made you notice him and dark eyes that seemed to burrow within your soul. His deep and mellifluous voice carried great distances, always clearly and distinctly articulated. The classical syntax of his well-wrought phrases (first the direct object and its modifiers, then the indirect object phrase, the subject phrase, and finally the verb, perfectly chosen and occasionally expressed in archaic forms of past tenses) impressed even those who disagreed with his ideas. He was a natural leader, spellbinding when he had to be, able to make his peers believe that it was they who were giving him ideas when actually Ogatrac had implanted the ideas in the minds of his hearers.

What would he suggest tonight? Everyone agreed that something had to be done about these intruders, who had spent fully half a year on Damos, and were about to set off in their spaceship, with a party of Damosian scientists, to explore Unias. There was also talk of a joint expedition to the twin planets of Tertia Minor and Tertia Major before the aliens crossed the galaxy once more and returned to their planet, Earth. Maybe some Damosians would fly there with them! The gathering of some 200 of the greatest Schadite priestesses, priests, and scholars quieted down. Everyone sensed that Ogatrac's message would somehow change the world, that Damos would never again be the same. The Earth people had already changed Damosian civilization forever; now the Damosians must alter the course of their history themselves.

Ogatrac looked out at the assembled elders of the Schadite movement. He felt their anticipation, he sensed his power over them, he knew that what he would say would constitute a break from millennial customs and behaviors. He was not sure, not yet, that they would come to agree with him, that he could arouse in them the emotions needed to chart a new and dangerous course, that they could see the necessity to seize the moment and inspire dread and hatred of the aliens among the Damosians. The dais was bare. He spoke, as usual, without a text, even without notes. He noted that the cameras were already running. If he was successful, the press and the government would have much to fear! He wished to strike terror in their hearts.

At last, he spoke. No witty introduction, no "we are gathered together here," no scene-setting anecdote. In some sense, what he did was preach a sermon, a sermon unlike the rational sermons Damosians were accustomed to.

The *Book of Oarnn* states clearly, my fellow Damosians, my fellow Schadites, "From beyond the sun come the forces of Evil, from beyond the sun come they. Evil dwells beyond the moon, in the dark firmament dwells she."

We have seen the aliens, this embodiment of Evil! Oh day of wrath for our poor planet! Oh, day of wrath for Damos! Their heads, covered with fur like that of the beasts that we eat at table! The aural appendages that make them so terrifying! Their skin, not a soft green like ours, but displeasing shades of brown– the very color of Evil!

We have seen the aliens, who have come from the land of Evil to tread the hallowed soil of Damos! We have seen the aliens appear and disappear in shrouds of ice! And we all know the prophesy: "You will know Evil when you sense its presence, for it comes in ice and steals the warmth of the land! You will know Evil when you hear its voice, for it speaks in strange tongues! You will know Evil when you smell it, for its odors are as of the beasts of the fields! You will know Evil when you see it, for its skin will be the color of the soil and the sand and the bark of the ingrot tree! But you will know Evil when it comes, for the people will embrace it!" So wrote Schad in the *Book of Oarnn*.

We have seen the aliens, and they are Evil.

Evil must be destroyed!

Their spaceship, in which our civil leaders have been, which many of our of our citizens have visited, to which indeed some

184

of our fellow Schadites have been seduced, hides above the clouds. These emissaries of Evil, we have grown accustomed to them! My fellow Schadites, we have become accustomed to Evil itself! Its very presence disturbs us no more. If you do not believe that these aliens are Evil itself, consider how they eschew the thought of teleological purpose in Oarnn's plan for the Kolok. Schad writes, in the great Book:

And Oarnn spake unto me, and he said: "I have made you from the reeds of the fields, with reason to think. I have made you a world over which you are to extend your dominion. I have made you a sun to give its warmth to you. I have made you a firmament, so that you might enjoy its beauty. Behold all that surrounds you, all the creatures of the sea, all beings that soar in the heavens above you, all the things you see about you that walk or crawl on the face of Damos; I have made all this for you. From all eternity have I created them, and for you have I created them, that you might know my glory.

In our schools and in the halls of government, we hear blasphemy! "The *Book of Oarnn* is a book of poetry, a book written by ignorant people in days before people knew how the Kolok evolved from the rapid-running lizards of many eons ago." They say again, "There is no discernible purpose in the world, and none in life. Life evolved by random unions of atoms, and we evolved not as inevitable beings created with all of creation by Oarnn, but as perhaps accidental growths, mere accumulations of genetic material, no more worthy than the others!" And they say again, "Perhaps the universe is a monstrous entity, begun inexplicably in a great burst of undirected energy at a time so distant in the past that we can scarcely imagine it. Perhaps we are all monsters, all the trees and the reeds, the soil we stand on and the water we drink, the air we breathe and the food we eat." Can we tolerate such blasphemies any longer? Can we tolerate such blasphemy in the presence of the aliens? Will not Evil incarnate spawn yet more evil in our midst?

Evil must be destroyed!

These emissaries of Evil, these excretions of Evil, agree with the sacrilegious words of so many of our leaders. Using the prestige of their technology, the aliens have drawn our youth, our teachers, our scientists, our industrialists, our workers, into the ways of error. In six short months our temples have become deserted, the word of Oarnn is ignored, the writings of Schad are treated not as sacred texts but as the ravings of a mad poet.

The future of Damos is in danger. The darkness predicted in the great Book will soon fall upon us unless we act.

Evil must be destroyed!

I see, my fellow Schadites, that many of you wonder what we can do. We must dedicate ourselves to serve Oarnn and to obey the dictates of Schad, even if this means that we must rise and stand fast against these aliens, these ministers of Evil, even if this means that the moral death and destruction they have brought to Damos be matched by the physical death and destruction of those who would fall in their thrall, even if this means that the wise teachings of Schad, who has made us live in harmony despite our disagreements, who has made us see that wisdom comes not from the emotions but from our divine faculty of reason, not from the heart but from the mind, even if his teachings, say I to you, be set aside in order to better protect the integrity and to honor the sanctity of those very teachings.

For Evil must be destroyed!

The aliens must be destroyed, and their allies and friends among the Kolok, these poisoned souls who would lead us to perdition. In this we must forbear tolerance. For as Schad has written, "We must praise Good with Good, but we must fight Evil with Evil." It is not enough to excoriate those who oppose truth and justice, it is not enough to drive off the emissaries of Evil, it is not enough to turn the minds of our people back to the words of our holy Founder, nay, it is not enough to reindoctrinate them in the way of Oarnn.

Evil must be destroyed!

In the Annex to the great Book, Schad says:

And how will my people know you, o Oarnn? For never have I dared to look upon your face, never will I dare to look upon your face. By what sign will the Kolok know Oarnn? And he said unto me, "You will know me by the Truth, for I am Truth." And I said, "But I know not Truth, I know but my truth and my neighbor's truth, and her truth is not mine." And he answered, in his voice of thunder, "I am Truth, there is no Truth but me, no Truth but mine! Those who wish to know me must seek Truth in the writings I have inspired in you. I am Truth and Truth is me. Those who know not me know not Truth; those who know not Truth know not me." I saw that we must seek Truth not in the ways and the words of the Kolok but in the ways and the words of Oarnn.

We know, my fellow Schadites, where Truth can be found; our leaders, blinded by the aliens' false truths, have forgotten the ways of Oarnn, despise the very words of Oarnn. There is no truth but Oarnn! Those who deny Oarnn deny Truth! Those who embrace the aliens embrace Evil!

And Evil must be destroyed!

In times of peril, we must find the courage to act with decision, knowing full well that in our brief lifetimes, the mere moments that our 150 years are compared to the many eons of the life of the universe (for does not Oarnn tell us that the universe exists from the beginning of eternity?), we will not see the end of the kingdom of Evil. But we must begin the long journey to salvation, we must bring our people back to the footsteps of Schad.

Evil must be destroyed! We must destroy Evil!

Schad and Oarnn will not tolerate these emissaries of Evil. We must drive them from our world, for the salvation of the Kolok people, for the future of Damosian life!

To do this, we must form mighty hosts with the weapons of terror that control the criminals who would rob and kill us. We must begin by destroying all contact with the aliens who walk amongst us with the face of Evil. We must kill the aliens and all those who wish to befriend and defend them.

We do not yet have the power to overcome our enemy, so we must seek another means. There is but one other means: dread, terror!

We must dedicate ourselves to the destruction of the forces of Evil, wherever they can be seen: in our cities, in our academies, in our market places, on our airfields, in our trains, in our sports arenas, on our farms, in our fisheries! We must spread the Terror of Oarnn! The Dread of Schad must reign!

Evil must be destroyed!

We must pledge our finances to this holy task, our minds, our hearts, our lives, our souls.

I know that some of you might be thinking how different this is from the behavior of Damosians, a people whose culture is based on the cultivation of reason. How can we justify the use of force, the stirring of long-suppressed emotions, the violation of the commandment to respect life? I answer that a sailing ship has need of sails to capture the wind as well as of a rudder to steer it. Without the rudder, the ship has no direction, but I say to you that without a sail the ship cannot move forward. Our mind is the rudder which will direct us; our heart is the sail that will enable us to move.

We must always remember that Evil must be destroyed!

I propose to you, then, Sisters and Brothers of Schad, mystical Daughters and Sons of Oarnn, a great Pact of Terror, a Pact that will in the end restore the great beliefs of our past and make them live in the future. A Pact that will necessitate the sacrifice of innocent lives for the greater good, for the future of Damos and the Kolok! I propose that starting today we establish semi-autonomous Tactical Units to spread out over the entire planet and to begin to spread Terror in the world. May the very name Schadite be looked on with Dread, as the Scourge of Oarnn! May a Leadership Council be formed to direct the Tactical Units of the Schad ites. May its first task be to study means of procuring arms and equipment necessary for our holy war.

Evil must be destroyed! Look around you: you will see the collective face of the Destroyer!

The audience, despite the strange feeling of emotion and hatred that Ogatrac had stirred in them, sat for long minutes in silence. Finally Nilreb the Head Bishop arose, went to the podium, and addressed Ogatrac and the assembly.

"We have heard your thoughts, Ogatrac, and you speak clearly. You describe the aliens as emissaries of Evil, and you call on us to destroy them. You wish us to go further still; you wish us to begin a period of Terror in the name of Oarnn and of Schad. You give us no option that does not violate a law of Oarnn or a principle of Schad. You know that not everyone can agree with you. And yet if we do nothing, perhaps we will call down the wrath of Oarnn upon us.

"I do not know what others wish to do. I propose, however, that we do indeed enter into a Pact against the presence of these aliens. I propose that we authorize those who would follow you to do so. I propose further that the Holy Fellowship of Schad tolerate Tactical Units which you and your group will establish, and that we preach against the invasion of Evil in our lives."

The assembly heard other speakers, and in the end agreed to adopt the strategy of Nilreb.

Approximately one quarter of the assembly, women as well as men, scholars as well as clergy, became the Leadership Council of the Schadite Tactical Units dedicated to spreading the Terror of Oarnn throughout the land. The STU had been born.

READY TO GO

Dr. Ecnelav Enohr, the Director of the Astrophysics and Aerospace Institute, and its Space Center at Catta, perhaps the most respected scientist in all of Damos, was as giddy as a child. Yes, she had been beamed up to Constellation before, but she had never yet traveled in it. Today, accompanied by her associates, Dr. Klor Emor and Dr. Noyl Zerof, and a large number other Damosians from life scientists to geologists, she was to fly off to Damos's twin planet, Unias, hidden behind Chromos from the beginning of time. While the party was being led to their quarters, and while the countdown for the takeoff had yet to begin, Ecnelav and Christina found a moment to be alone in Christina's quarters.

"Ecnelav, you're brimming with excitement, I can see it in your face and in your eyes! I know you've got a thousand questions to ask about Constellation and perhaps about Colombina, and I have a thousand things to show you, but we don't have a lot of time right now. We will have a lot more leisure during the flight and later on. I think we have about an hour before the countdown begins. If you don't mind some interruptions, I can help satisfy some of your curiosity. Let me guess: besides Colombina and Constellation, you're wondering about the dangers of space travel, right?"

"Yes, Christina, all those things are on my mind, but I have a more pressing matter to discuss. I am by training an astronomer and a physicist. One of the principles of astrophysics on Damos has always been the impossibility to travel faster than the speed of light. And yet, from what I've heard you and your crew say, you routinely break this fundamental law of physics. Do you travel illegally, or is the law at fault?"

"It may seem strange to you at first, but suppose I told you that even though we get places faster than light can get there, we never actually travel faster than light? And there's no mystery to it: what we do is warp the fabric of space-time and advance in little jumps that cover vast distances. It only *appears* that we're breaking the laws of physics, but really, we'll never get a ticket for speeding."

"Warp the fabric of space-time? Are you feeding me science fiction? You know, some of our theorists, like Lotsirb, have speculated about somehow warping space, but very few of us have taken them too seriously, especially those of us who have to apply science in the everyday realities of our jobs. It's always sounded like science fiction to us. If it's real science, how do you do it? What's your trick?"

"There's no trick to it, there's no magic in our science, and it's not fiction, either. What we do, when we seem to go faster than light, is move into the fifth dimension, beyond space and time."

"The fifth dimension? I thought there were only four, the three in space, plus time or duration. It's true that Lotsirb and many of her fellow theorists talk of as many as ten dimensions. It's unimaginable."

"Sure it's imaginable. Look at it this way. You Kolok can see things that are beyond human vision, because we can't see into the infra-red, but you can. We can see the infra-red only via pictures taken by instruments that can read it, and after they're interpreted into the colors that we can see."

"Well, that's true. And we Kolok can't hear all of the higher notes on the musical scale that you humans can hear distinctly. So I get your point: just because our brains can't process a fifth dimension is no argument against its existing."

"Commodore, please excuse the intrusion." Susanna was speaking.

"Yes, Commander. Is there a problem?"

"There is a major storm on Chromos, which has cast off a considerable amount of plasma in a wide arc. Our projected path goes right through this plasma, which Colombina judges to be very dangerous for the life support systems on board. I am seeking authorization to reprogram our itinerary."

"Permission granted. Let me know when the new projectory is established, and how this might affect our travel time."

"Thank you, Commodore. Colombina is preparing several alternatives as we speak. I should be able to report back to you shortly."

"Encelav, where were we? Oh, yes, the fifth dimension. Once there, we send out powerful signals, or force beams, that crumple up a local area of the continuum, somewhat like you'd crumple up a table cloth. The stronger the beams we send out, the greater amount of the 'table cloth' we can drag towards us. We move by jumping over the warp at very high speed, about 95% the speed of light; then we release the warp so that the 'table cloth' spreads out evenly again, moving us forward a huge distance, although we ourselves have only traveled a fragment of that distance; the 'table cloth' dragged us along the rest of the way. Then we begin the process all over again. It sounds easy the way I'm telling it, but scientists of our world spent decades in research and our navigational staff has spent years learning how to do this."

"By Oarnn! And to think that the hyperfast jet planes that are the ultimate in travel on Damos take almost a day to circle the globe, and our spacecraft have not yet sent anyone to another planet. And we've never taken the idea of a fifth dimension seriously. Lotsirb would feel avenged if she could hear you now! Our technology must seem primitive to you!"

"We've been at it a lot longer than you, don't forget, about 800 years longer! If after all that time we didn't have some technological advances over you, it would be astonishing! But you've got all the elements in place: a sound scientific background, a unified planetary government, a society that wants to enter the space age as rapidly as possible, all the natural and intellectual and political and economic resources you need. You also have one advantage over us that we didn't have in 2020 our era: we could only hope that there was intelligent life out there, and you know there is."

"I certainly hope that our civilizations will be able to cooperate with one another. I'm not sure what we can offer you in exchange for all the knowledge we hope to be able to absorb: eight hundred years of knowledge doesn't come easily!"

"Once our peoples formally establish relations, I'm confident that the exchange will not be one-sided. For one thing, we've still not mastered the non-violent ethic you have on Damos, we still think of doing things competitively rather than cooperatively, we still think almost exclusively in terms of winning and losing. It's true you've not seen that side of us with the great crew I have on board Constellation, but you'll have to take my word for it when I say that we here are not your typical Earth people."

"I hope some day to meet Earth people on Earth. Until then, I'll take your word for it, even though what we've seen is not at all like you're describing it. I have another question for you, now that I know that you're law-abiding travelers. What kind of power source do you have? The amount of energy required to warp space must be enormous. You must have almost a limitless supply!"

"Limitless may be putting it a bit too strongly. Still, we do have a tremendous energy source."

"Commodore, the new course has been set. The disturbance has caused plasma to explode into the atmosphere of Chromos at the poles, but there is no danger lurking at its equator. We've set a course to the starboard side of the sun. This will add just over four hours to the trip at our projected speed."

"Thank you, Commander. Anything else I should know now?"

"Nothing for the moment, Commodore."

"Signing off."

"Christina, I've noticed that down on Damos your staff usually speaks to you by your name, but here on board you seem to go by your title. It's curious."

"Actually, on board or on the ground I am called by my title when we're functioning formally as a crew. Sometimes I address them by their titles. For example, at state dinners, I call Susanna Lieutenant and she calls me Commodore, while at the racquet court it's Susanna and Christina. Up here, off-duty, it's informal. We do spend years together on a mission, you know, and so it's not surprising if we get to be friends. On the bridge it's somewhat more formal. This protocol reminds us all of our particular and relative responsibilities, when necessary. But now I've forgotten what we were talking about."

"We were talking about energy use when you go at warp speeds."

194

"Right. We also use as little of it as we can get away with. For instance, instead of warping a relatively large sector of space, we try to create a path of warped space: my analogy of the table cloth breaks down here, because with the table cloth you warp the whole thing in length and in width. We limit the field that's warped. The action of limiting the field takes about half the energy of crumpling the whole thing, which in effect gives us double the apparent speed that the same burst of energy would provide otherwise. Maybe it's more like creating a fold in paper, or falling over the cusp of a hidden chasm, except that it's all controlled, all planned."

"I like your table cloth analogy better. But doesn't this warping action disturb the entire universe? It could cause cataclysms, maybe destroying entire galaxies or at least solar systems."

"Fortunately, for reasons I don't fully understand, these manipulations take place only relative to Constellation. There's no danger to other worlds."

"OK, back to my original question: what is your energy source?"

"Constellation's engines are run by the same kinds of colliding devices we used to remove the tops of countless mountains over four hundred years ago, when Earth was threatened by a new Ice Age. It's an antimatter collider. You know the tremendous energy created when you bombard matter with antimatter: the trick was to learn how to harness this energy. Before we topped the mountains, we had learned how to store this newly-created energy for use in our space stations as well as on our space ships. In theory, we should be able to find a new fuel supply everywhere something breaks into the void of space, something like a star with a planetary system, or rogue asteroids or comets, which we could pick up while we're traveling; again in theory, we could store these relatively little bits of matter and antimatter in isolated storage areas."

"You seem to be saying that the theory and the facts are not in agreement. And I can see why: in theory, you could use, say, iron or calcium and their antimatter components for fuel. The problem is breaking off individual electrons and protons, which is not really feasible except with highly radioactive materials. So you can't use any chunk of rock you happen to see on your flight. You need uranium or some other radioactive mineral."

"Exactly. And we replenished our supply outside the wormhole, while we were doing the necessary repairs. We're fully stocked now. Now, to continue with our fuel needs: the collisions of this material provide so much energy that a little fuel goes a very long way—literally. Of course, the higher warp factors require exponentially increasing quantities of fuel, which is one very real limit on our speed. Another limit is the strength of the material used to construct the craft. Not to mention the constant, although slight, drain of fuel caused by simply keeping Constellation livable and lit up, maintaining a good gravity level on board, operating the colliders, and doing the other things that make these long flights feasible. And tolerable."

"Didn't you tell us a few months ago that it took you three years to cross the galaxy?"

"At maximum warp factor, that would have been the case. We saved about a year thanks to the wormhole. In fact, probably more than a year, because I don't think we would have dared to traverse the galaxy at the central core or bulge. Too many black holes there, too much danger. Going around it might have added a year to the trip, making it four in all. The flight took us about two years, but the part in the middle, in the wormhole, was terrifying. I'm sure we'll do better on the way back. The problem was with the sixth dimension, which is where the wormhole exists."

"The sixth dimension! I haven't even gotten used to the fifth yet!"

"We have learned how to cope with the fifth dimension (our brains, like yours, are made to visualize three dimensions and our mind can easily deal with the fourth dimension), but the fifth dimension is beyond our basic concepts of the space we live in. What we try to do is convert the fifth dimension to four-dimensional logic. We can visualize it in a way, thanks to Colombina's careful calculations and her presentation of data. But the sixth dimension caught us by surprise. We tried to manoeuvre in it as though it were the fifth. The combination of the two extra dimensions brought about phenomena that we misinterpreted; some of it was like illusions, some of it real. By now, though, thanks to some clever thinking by Kwali, Colombina has had time to sort out the data she collected on our first swing through, has seen where we made mistakes, and can help us fly more safely, or at least with more assurance, through the wormhole. Along with a big dose of human imagination and daring, I think we'll make it through smoothly when it's time to go home."

"But that won't be for at least two or three years, right?"

"Yes, we'll explore Unias with you, and also Tertia Major and Tertia Minor. We're all excited about that. All the more so in that we never expected to be so well received by an alien civilization: we feared encountering a society even more aggressive than our own, rendered very dangerous by virtue of their being a millennium ahead of us in technology. But in truth we all wondered if we'd survive the wormhole experience, let alone meet with new intelligent species."

"Survive! Was it that bad? People have made allusions to that experience, even starting at the first state dinner when you materialized, but no one has ever really described it and its effects, either physical or psychological. It must have been traumatic."

"Traumatic is a good word for it. It was terrifying, even if it lasted less than an hour! The effects stayed with all of us for a long time. We had extensive damage to the interior and the exterior of the craft that took a long time to repair. Of course, we couldn't travel safely until the exterior was fully repaired; but the interior needed lots of patching up and reconstruction. Even hovering up here the work continued, and has finally been successfully completed. We're as good as new now."

"Good. I thought for a moment that you were trying to frighten me into thinking that Constellation was about to fall apart."

"Scare you, Ecnelav? No, I'm just letting you know well in advance that your team may be in for more than they bargained for in terms of adventurous living. And the risk of boredom."

"Boredom and adventure together?"

"Commodore and Professor Enohr, this is Commander Kwali. We have just received very distressing news from Damos. It appears that a terrorist organization has been formed, and has bombed a Police Commissary in Bobol."

"By Oarnn! Terrorism on Damos? Who could possibly have created such a group? Have there been any casualties?"

"A group of fundamentalist commandos, the Schadite Tactical Units, formed by a preacher named Ogatrac, has claimed responsibility for the bombing. Preliminary reports indicate that five officers have been killed and scores wounded. A large store of weapons has been stolen. This has just happened moments ago. We have no further information at this moment."

Both Christina and Ecnelav had gasped at this unexpected news. Ecnelav was deeply distressed; she could not hide her initial reactions. Christina's mind was working with great rapidity, trying to see what she and her crew could do.

"Commander, get in touch with Security Chief Neac in Ihled. Ask him if we should postpone our flight, or if there is some way we can help out. I suspect that this group is really after us. I've lived through this kind of thing before, with the Militia. I wouldn't be surprised if this is the same sort of organization."

"I will get right on this, Commodore."

Ecnelav seemed to have made up her mind to return to Damos at this moment of crisis. "It will be emotionally difficult to postpone this trip, difficult because we're all so excited about it. And yet we must help in some way, do whatever we can. I find it hard to believe that a group of people could even conceive of doing something like this. It's so completely against our culture, our way of living, or even our way of thinking."

"I must admit that when Kwali mentioned this I was stunned. I love your people's gentle and cooperative but vigorous patterns of life and thought. I wonder if we shouldn't postpone this trip. Your security forces might need the kind of help we can provide; it could save you years—decades even—of grief and murder. On the other hand, it may be that the best thing for us to do is carry out our mission. We'll do whatever your government tells us to do. What is this Schadite group? I know of the *Book of Oarnn* and the devotion to Schad, but I don't know anything at all about these Schadite Tactical Units."

"There is a group of fundamentalist believers who are opposed to any advance in science. It may be that your very presence here is threatening to them because your existence can invalidate their interpretations of the scriptures. But until now they've never been aggressive."

"No more than the other Damosians?"

"No more than the rest of us. I'm very worried. Our civilization has not encountered this kind of activity for over five or ten centuries. I'm not sure we know how to deal with it."

Christina looked at her friend, who appeared to be distracted and concerned. She tried to smile, then said, in a comforting way, "Well, let's get back to space travel. It might take your mind off this problem for a few minutes."

"A good idea. I hope it works."

"We were talking about boredom on board. A three-year journey is a long time. In many respects Constellation flies itself; we're there mostly as observers, and in case of emergencies."

"You will have to tell me about the wormhole adventure, Christina."

"I'll tell you what: when we're on our way around Chromos, we'll all, all the flight deck staff, we'll all relate what happened. Each of us experienced the passage through the wormhole differently, and maybe you Damosians will want to ask us, and for that matter, the other crew members, about different aspects of our experiences."

"In any case, we knew before getting on board that there's no guarantee we would come back alive. You made that very clear."

"When we've made preliminary investigations of your solar system, we would like to be able to take a delegation of Kolok across the galaxy, to see how we live on Earth, Mars, Venus, Mesnos and Paracelsus, not to mention the five space stations we maintain. But it can be a dangerous trip, not the least because of that wormhole. It's not traveling within your solar system that should worry you."

"We understand that a trans-galactic voyage will be even more dangerous than a solar-system voyage. I've often wondered, since meeting you, how your people are affected by a voyage like this. If I understand correctly, when you return to Earth you'll have been gone about ten years."

"We'll all be affected in different ways, but there are two very different kinds of reactions our space voyagers have. About half the crew are ELBers like me. We remain to all appearances, and in all bodily functions, as we were when our genes were altered: same age, same physical state. I think we'll all return to Earth pretty much as we were when we left it. But the other half of the crew will age more or less normally: when they get home they'll look and feel ten years older than they were when we left. It will be harder on them than on us, not only because in fact everyone they know will have aged, and so will they, but also because unlike them, we ELBers don't have family to go back to. Still, for all of us, there will be ten years of news to catch up on with the people we know, many of whom might have died in our absence. Not to mention news of the world, or of our worlds (our crew comes from four planets!) and our local areas. I'll have people to visit on Earth and my best friends on Mars. You can come with..."

"Commodore, I have established contact with Security Chief Neac. I'll open up your visucapsule."

"Commodore Vasa, Director Enohr, you are familiar with the main part of the tragic events. We have captured two of the terrorists. So far, they refuse to speak. About half of the stolen weapons have been recovered, but it appears that the rest of the STU has escaped. We are currently attempting to track them down."

"Chief, have there been any further casualties?"

"No, Director. Five deaths, and several wounded, but none in a life-threatening way."

"Is there something we can do to help? I could dispatch a security squad with some of our latest equipment, and perhaps a medical team, which could put the latest medical advances at your disposal."

"And perhaps all of us Damosians should postpone the mission to Unias."

"No, Director, that is what the terrorists want. You must

continue on your journey as planned. You will be able to keep in contact with us, I understand. And Commodore, I will be happy to accept your gracious offer."

"Within the hour you'll have two crews on the ground, with full equipment."

"We appreciate your generosity more than I can express right now. I must leave you to organize our pursuit. Kluuk spar, Ecnelav!"

Colombina chose to leave the traditional "bon voyage!" untranslated.

Christina contacted her right-hand man, Kwali, immediately. "Commander, get the two teams you heard us talk about readied as soon as possible, maybe ten members in each crew, as many as twenty. Try to find volunteers; many of our crew have good friends on Damos, and might want to work with them, even if it means missing out on Unias this time around. You might offer them incentives, like a guarantee that they'll be among the first on Tertia Minor or Tertia Major."

"I will see to that at once, Commodore, and let you know when we're ready. Will you want to address the volunteers?"

"Yes, I will. Signing off."

"Our medical equipment is in truth a marvel. You might not believe it to look at them, but some of the crew have had extensive reconstructive surgery, and have been restored to a state that is at least as good as normal. I was almost killed twice, and was made whole again. Brrr! The memory of those struggles both freezes me and inflames me. I hope these Tactical Units will not be as vicious as the Militia was. It took us literally hundreds of years to stamp them out!"

"Fortunately, we won't have to cover as much space as you: five planets in three solar systems, and all those space stations! If we're lucky, our police can track them down quickly. We've only got one planet to cover."

"We'll make sure that some of our best tracking devices go with the security force. Without them, I don't think we could have flushed out the Militia on Mesnos."

"What kinds of injuries did you have that were so dangerous?"

"The worst, and the most terrifying, was the severed spinal cord when a boulder slammed into me on Paracelsus. I needed to have several organs rehabilitated, bones repaired, and nerve cells regenerated. If the operation had failed, I would probably be paralyzed, or more likely dead, today. But as you see, if I hadn't told you about it, you'd never know."

"We've just begun to experiment on frogs with techniques for regenerating nerve cells. So far it's been a success. In the long run we hope to be able to use frog nerves to link severed nerve cords in Kolok. Some religious groups are opposed to the research, though. Hmm. The Schadites are among them, now that I think of it."

"The parallels with Earth society are just..."

As Christina was speaking a voice broke out of a speaker. "Commodore, everyone is settled, the crews are waiting to be teleported, and the countdown can begin whenever you're ready."

"We're on our way, Commander. We'll be at the Den as soon as we can get there. I want to speak with each individual volunteer personally."

"I would appreciate the opportunity to see them all myself, and offer them thanks on the part of the scientific group on board and all Damosians. They are brave and selfless people. What is this Den you spoke about, Christina?"

"I'll tell you about that en route. Come on, Ecnelav, this way!"

EN ROUTE

Martin had volunteered to lead the Security squad, and chose Ensign Mgamba and Sergeant Torquato to be his chief aides. Another dozen Security personnel would accompany them. Their mission was to assist Security Chief Neac on Damos with technical advice, materials, and (if necessary) training. They would beam down an array of equipment (personnel tracers, weaponry, radio transmitters, and the like). In case of necessity, Constellation would not be far away: a satellite would be set up in stationary orbit around Unias for communications. This team had had considerable experience in dealing with criminals on the Five Planets. Martin had been a major force in cleaning out the Militia near the end of their reign of terrorism.

The Medical crew, which Christina had judged would also be needed, beamed down much important equipment, from drugs to operating materials, enough to set up a sort of field hospital. The silent electric generators, the solar cells used for operating some of the fanciest gear (and the storage batteries slim enough to fit in a backpack) were a source of amazement to the Damosians. Mujama, as Chief Surgeon and Chief Medical Officer, volunteered her services, and was backed up by two physicians and seven nurses and orderlies. They had an immediate task to try to save the lives and limbs of several people wounded in the attacks. A problem would be the structural differences in the skeletons and organs of the Kolok and humans; without full and immediate use of the resources of Colombina, there would be a good deal more guess-work than usual.

"I've always known this crew had more than its share of heroes. Even if I had never experienced it before we passed through the terror of the Wormhole, you all displayed the kind of courage and devotion to duty that makes Space Fleet the exceptional organization that it is. For the first time ever, you have volunteered to help out our friends of a different species, aliens in an alien land, at the risk of your lives. You can count on my support, and that of all of us on Constellation. If you need our help, do not hesitate to call on us. There are people who are more than willing to replace you or to augment your efforts if necessary. We'll be back in six months unless you need our presence earlier. Dr. Enohr and her party were ready to cancel this scientific expedition; but the Damosian government wisely refused to yield to the blackmail of the terrorists. Good luck to you! We'll see you soon!"

Shortly after this brief address, the two squads were teleported to Damos. Moments later, in the tense bridge, the countdown began. What would happen to these brave people? I know them all too well to believe that they will hold back for even a moment in the face of danger. If these STU people are anything like the Militia in their organization and their ruthlessness, we'll return to a dangerous situation.

———

"Commander, are the coordinates set? Are we ready to go?"

"Yes, Commodore," replied Susanna, "we should be there within an hour."

"An hour!" gasped a startled Ecnelav. "260,000,000 kilometers in an hour!"

"Well, you wanted to get there fast, but you asked me not to go as fast as light, which would have gotten us there in about a quarter of an hour, if I calculate right."

"Just under 16 minutes, Christina; if we were able to go directly to Unias right through Chromos, it would take us approximately 14.4444 minutes to arrive," said the serious voice of Colombina. "But we must skirt around the star, adding approximately 1.3847 minutes to our projected time, or a total of approximately 15.8291 minutes. Light travels at approximately 300,000 kilometers a second, or..."

Christina interrupted her in mid-sentence. "Yes, yes, I know, Colombina, but we must continue our count-down now. Commander, if you're ready, take us approximately to Unias. And after all, let's go at the speed of light!"

Susanna made a final check of coordinates, received input from Kwali on the status of the engines, and from April, who was acting as co-navigator, then touched the area of her computer screen designated for warp speed starts. The familiar hum of the engines reaching the designated capacity, then the rapid movement towards their destination. They were now truly on the road to Unias.

"Lieutenant, put the exterior sights on screen. I'm sure that Dr. Enohr will want to see Damos receding in the distance, Chromos burst into view, then Unias!"

April immediately activated the main screen in three parts, showing precisely the planet rapidly growing smaller, the sun growing in size and intensity to their right, and space deep into the solar system beyond: Unias would not be in sight for about 10 minutes. Ecnelav was overwhelmed with emotion as she saw this. She asked if it would be possible for her colleagues Klor Emor and Noyl Zerof to come see this sight.

"We thought you might like to share this moment with them so we made sure they'd be able to join you here. Ah! they've arrived."

"Klor! Noyl! Look, our homeland disappearing to a point, Chromos growing huge, and soon we'll see Unias!"

Actually, everyone in the bridge was sharing similar emotions, and the rest of the crew and the geological and biological parties as well.

"Can you believe we'll be in orbit over Unias in just about 12 minutes?"

Colombina decided not to be precise this time. For one thing, as soon as she announced a time it would be obsolete; for another, she thought she had sensed a bit of annoyance in Christina just before. It's so hard to understand human temperament. What's wrong with being a little bit more exact than a whole number or a fragment of an hour?

"Commodore, if I didn't see the screens, I would not believe we're even moving. But we must be going a good 75,000 kilometers a second, or about a quarter the speed of light. It's amazing."

Colombina could not resist giving her seal of approval on Ior's rapid calculation. "That is correct, Associate Director, we are moving at approximately .25 the speed of light."

"Thank you, Colombina. Dr. Emor, our crew has managed to put this ship together after a truly jarring episode that you have surely heard about more times than you can stand. I did promise Ecnelav that we would give you our impressions of passing through the Wormhole, but I forgot we'd have no time en route. Maybe over dinner after a hard day's work? In any case, what you noticed is correct: you can't sense any motion when the screen's not on. A faint rumble of the engines, or a buzzing of the service lines, and that's all. Imagine going for a year like that? Or two years? Or even more, if we go at lower speeds, as our early space flights did. If we couldn't look out and see what's going on, it would be truly monotonous. Thank heavens we have a chance to get out and explore the occasional life-supporting planet we've come across."

"Some of our theorists believe the galaxy must be fairly crawling with life-supporting planets."

"In a way they're right, but most of the life that we've encountered is at an early stage of evolution, or the atmosphere has not right for our lungs. We've actually come across very few Earth-like planets, and as you know only one with intelligent life forms."

"Commodore, we can now begin to see Unias, on the lower left-hand picture. I'll put a pointer on it. As you can see, it's getting bigger as we speak."

"Thank you, Lieutenant. Sorry to break this up, but we have to get to our work stations. This has been the fastest flight from one habitable planet to another that I can remember. It will have taken us only approximately 15.8291 minutes to arrive. Commander, prepare the ship for stationary orbit at the habitual altitude, near the planetary probe."

"I've set the coordinates for the orbit, Commodore. Now we just have to wait until we arrive."

"Arrival is set for 1.2976 minutes at the sound." A kind of gong went off.

Colombina has a weird sense of humor. I wonder where she got that from. Has Kwali been up to something? I'll have to check that out.

"Chief, it might be better if we did not interrogate the terrorists, because it's pretty obvious that without our presence there would not have been a cause for terrorism."

"Commander, what you say is true, but your presence might astonish the terrorists enough to pry at least some information from them. They've not even given us their names."

"Well, it's worth a try. Why don't we have them come in here. You can start the interrogation, and I'll emerge from the shadows, perhaps holding a weapon—which I will not use."

"Guard, send in the prisoners."

"You, whom we are calling A, be seated, there; B, take a seat beside her."

"You won't get anything out of us. We know you torture your prisoners, but we won't give in."

"So, A, you were caught fleeing the scene of a heinous crime in which you killed a number of people. Did you hope to kill some Earth people? You failed; but you did manage to kill some police personnel, perhaps your own neighbors, wounded several others. Why did you do it? For a few weapons? As a political statement? As a religious statement?"

B's eyes twitched slightly at this last suggestion. Martin took this as an opportunity to emerge from behind a screen. Both terrorists gasped. A whispered, "Oga..." and bit her tongue. B was visibly disturbed. Martin pulled out his weapon, still not saying a word. B shouted, "You'll never stop the STU!"

The interrogation went on for almost an hour. At the end of the time, the prisoners had decided to remain absolutely silent, until Ylro uncovered a digitscreen which played a disk of the wounded. "Look at this, B; see anyone you know?"

In his shock, B blurted out, "Mago!" A immediately said, "Stop swearing! You must not take the name of the great priest in vain!"

"Mago, eh? What temple does he preach in?"

Silence. Blank expressions.

"High Commissioner Ylro, maybe a month on prison food and in solitary confinement will make these two come to their senses."

"A good idea. Guard, put these two in opposite corners of Cell Block 3 in Hell's Portal. No privileges, no visitors. One hour daily for exercise and showers."

"Yes, Commissioner."

The two prisoners gone, Ylro said, "At least they've confirmed that they're agents of the STU, the Schadite Tactical Unit. It's a fanatical religious sect believing in a strictly literal interpretation of sacred texts; but the texts exist only in imperfect copies, and in translation from a long-dead language. Still, they've never been violent before."

"Christina, I mean Commodore Vasa, believes that they have become active because somehow we are triggering a reaction in them. In any case, we had very few reactions in a full hour: Oga, an eye twitch when you spoke of religion, and the name of one of the wounded police officers, Mago. The accusation of cursing was clearly a cover-up, calling him a priest. We should look into Oga."

"I'll work on that. Meanwhile, we need a plan to find out where they're from, who they are."

"Chief, we have a substance that can be mixed in with food and that will stay inside a person for at least a month. It's not toxic, at least to humans, but it does allow us to use a personnel tracer."

"Are you suggesting that we release them on some grounds? Maybe have a lawyer prove that they are being held illegally?"

"No, that might make them suspicious. They'll have some time every day to be together. Suppose we make it possible for them to plan and to execute an escape. Make it realistic: some risks, we shoot at them, maybe even wound one of them. Then our tracer does its job."

"It sounds as though you've used this before."

"There was a similar group on Earth, and eventually on the other planets and the space stations, that went on a 400-year rampage. This is what did the trick for us in the end. You have only one planet to worry about, and you might save yourselves decades of destruction and death. If it works."

"I like your idea. I'll get my people working on arranging

things as soon as possible. Maybe in a week our prisoners will make their getaway."

"One caution: the guards must not know anything of these plans. Unless they're superb actors, they'll subconsciously give everything away. A word, a gesture, a smile..."

"Of course. This will not be the first unspontaneous escape from Hell's Portal."

———

"Your skills and your equipment worked wonders, Mujama. Mago's recovery, in such a short time, is a miracle."

"We have no miracles, Iborian, only solid science and medical practices. Mago's hand was found and preserved in time, and your frog's nerves were perfect. Fortunately, there are enough structural similarities between us that our technologies could function properly. If we worked miracles, we would have brought those dead officers back to life. We have lived with terrorists; they are a disturbing breed."

"We must learn some of your techniques and learn to make some of the equipment you have shown us. Perhaps we could begin to manufacture this kind of equipment. Maybe you and your staff could instruct our medical faculty. Think of all the lives that could be saved, people made whole again!"

"I'm sure the Commodore will approve that plan. We'll ask her permission when we speak to her tomorrow. For now, I'm exhausted, as are all my crew. We would appreciate a good night's sleep. We must visit the wounded tomorrow morning."

"We, too, need our rest. Let me personally show you to your quarters."

———

"Before we teleport to the surface, let's make sure our transmitter satellite is in position to send both sound and pictures to Damos. We have to keep in close touch during these first days, and perhaps abort the mission if things deteriorate there. Lieutenant, is everything in order?"

"Yes, Commodore. The satellite is far enough away to transmit directly to Damos without interference from Chromos. It is also close enough for direct transmissions from the surface of Unias, or indirectly, via Constellation."

"Our initial party of 50 will look for a suitable spot for an encampment, perhaps the place where the land probe settled and we found our cute spheres. If we can find such a spot, the full set-up party of 200 will be on ground. With luck, we can establish a base camp-laboratory within a week. By the end of that week, everyone on board will have spent at least a day or two on the surface of this planet. Lieutenant, I'd like you to begin charting probes of the planet for seismic activity."

A take-charge leader, one who has thought of so many things, and who acts in consequence of those thoughts. We Kolok are planners, we are logical to an extreme, but we tend to delay acting. Maybe the presence of humans will accelerate the pursuit of the terrorists, while helping us to reason a bit less and to act a bit more on intuition. On the other hand, I hope our scientific study of the biota and geology of the Unias will not be moved along too rapidly, too impulsively.

"All the gear for the initial party is ready to be teleported down, Commodore."

"Good, Lieutenant. The first squad, which will include me, has assembled here."

Ju-Sen knew her routine perfectly. Still, you could never tell: the slightest miscalculation could be fatal. She verified her coordinates, then beamed down the gear. Then came the first group. Christina pointed to the radio transmitter she was carrying. Ju-Sen nodded, and pushed the switch.

In a moment they were down. "This is a good landing spot. We'll move out of the way as soon as I can get this exuberant bunch of people to calm down a little. I never realized that the Kolok, who seem so dominated by their intellects, could be so carried away by emotions."

Eventually, four more waves of personnel emerged from the electronic shower. The sun was shining directly overhead in a dazzling display of light. It was very warm, over 35^0, and humid. Much like Damos, in fact, much like Earth and especially Venus.

April made her first transmission to Damos, testing the radio signal and then the digitscreen (Kwali had worked out a method of converting the visuscreen transmissions to the Damosian standard). Until the crew below decided where to establish camp, they were not taking pictures. But April realized, hearing the jubilation from below, that she had been wrong in judging the Kolok incapable of strong emotions. She had argued against sending pictures to Damos. But the Damosian party thought it would be important to show people back on Damos that they had indeed arrived. The first pictures came up, a shot of the Kolok team, then the humans, then the grove of fern-trees, the grassy glade. The wind made a rustling sound in the leaves of these huge trees. From the top of the hill where the spheres had first been spotted, they saw that the location was ideal: a waterfall coming from the side of the hill created a lake; a river valley stretched off to the horizon over open plains and woody groves. It looked like paradise.

Now it was time to get to work. Quonset huts and hemispheric structures were beamed down. As Christina had promised, everyone was able to get down to the surface and help establish what they could only consider as the first interspecies home base that the galaxy had ever known.

—

"Now's our chance, Lero. Let's head for the tunnel."

"Heads down; let's not be seen. You go first, Sagev. And we'd better not talk until we're really away from here."

Stay out of sight. Crawl just a few more meters. Lift up the debris. OK. Now we'll have to dig the rest of the way. Hope there'll be enough air. What's that noise?

"Sagev, a siren. Our escape has been noted. Let me relieve you with the digging."

"Time to start angling up. It's stifling in here. I don't dare go back and open up the hatch, though."

"Why don't you pile up the dirt behind us, make them think it's just an abandoned escape route, in case they find our trail? They might have some bulas after our scent."

211

"Good thinking. I'll get to that while you're pushing on ahead."

Ah! I've hit the surface. Got to be careful. I'll dig a clump of grass out, to use as a door if we have to stay here until it gets dark. Let me take a look. Yes, the prison wall's behind us. Sirens. Guards are out. Get back down. A little hole for light and air.

"We're out, Lero, but so are they. We've got to keep quiet. Maybe even take a nap: we'll need all the energy we can get when we leave."

———

"High Commissioner, they have dug under the east wall. They must be waiting for night to fall. We should let them get out and cross the square, then fire at them, missing, and sound the alarm again. They'll have enough time to get away, perhaps lost in the crowd, especially since they were never issued prison uniforms. Your technicians can follow their movements and see where they go."

"I'm sure they'll go to a temple run by the Holy Fellowship of Schad, but they might have a stopping-off place first."

"Have you located this mysterious Oga?"

"Yes. One of the leading priests of the Schadite movement is named Ogatrac. His temple is located on the seaside not far from Bobol. We have some agents alerted there. But there's a problem."

"What's that?"

"Ogatrac has not conducted services or preached in his temple for the past five weeks. His assistants claim they don't know where he has gone. They claim he's gone somewhere to do missionary work."

"Some missionary. Most of them at least try to do some good. This one seems to want to blow up people."

"It gets worse. We've found that in many police posts arms and ammunition are missing. In some cases supply authorities sympathetic to the Schadites are implicated. A few are in prison, awaiting interrogation. In other cases, there have been burglaries, often held in broad daylight. I fear there'll be another series of attacks soon. The Schadite Tactical Units seem to be well organized, and they're rapidly becoming dangerously armed. More bombings are probably their next step. It's hard to anticipate where they'll strike: it's a big planet."

"It's getting dark out. Let's call off the search, then get over to where our burrowing animals have set up their lair. We should find out who their supporters and sympathisers are."

"I'll have the back-up team ready to strike about two hours after they leave their way-stations. They'll know we're on their trail, so they shouldn't be too suspicious."

"High Commissioner, do you usually get this involved in a case? I thought you'd be a political type."

"Well, my job has its share of politics. But I'm a detective by training, and I always have a firm hand in important cases. This is without question the most important one we've ever had. It could have transgalactic consequences!"

CLOSED IN

Damn! The door closed. And it's locked. We're in one of the interior courts of the new but as yet unoccupied government office building we had entered, looking for the STU. What's going on here? Did they somehow lead us into a trap? Did they let us think they were out here, only to pen us in? Pitch black. Cloud cover. No stars, no moon. Street light doesn't penetrate here. My night vision goggles let me see three identical walls; this one almost certainly looks just like them. A door in the middle of the ground floor, flanked by four pairs of windows to each side. The ground floor high, about four meters. The first floor, also four meters; floor-to-ceiling windows, leading out to small balconies. Probably all locked. Above that, four more floors, each about three meters high. Smaller windows. Probably unlocked.

The architecture of these government buildings is identical. Same height, same number of floors, same width. From above, a square divided into four identical courtyards, separated by walls each containing a central corridor and offices facing to one side or the other (on the perimeter, one set of offices faces the outside; the other sets of offices face the courtyards). At every exterior corner, an elevator; at the beginning of every part of the central cross, a staircase; in the middle, more elevators. Decorations on the exterior walls: geometric patterns; on the courtyard walls, a subtle difference in the brickwork.

All the doors and ground floor windows are surely locked. I think they're going to wait for morning to appear, then they'll rush out to kill us. Or execute us, as they'll say. Trophies for their followers, a lesson for people who collaborate with us.

Wonder what's happened to the Damosians who were with us? Mago, Notlink, the others. Good people. Have they found a place to hide? Have they been captured? What will happen to them if they're captured? I've got to find a way out of here. We have to save them, but we have to save ourselves first.

"Ensign Mgamba, Seso, come here. ...Seso!"

"I can hardly hear you, Commodore. You're speaking in a

very low voice."

"Shh! Don't speak above a whisper. I don't want the STU to be able to know exactly where we are, but really I think they feel they've got us trapped here. Are we all here? Torquato?"

"Yes, Gino's here, so are Marcia and Mireille. They're over on the other side, around the corner, trying to see if any of the windows have any give."

"Get them back here quick. If the STU are just inside, there might be some mischief."

"No need to go after them, Commodore; here they come."

"Now that the pentad is all in one place, listen. They've got us closed in. We have to find a way out. I'm going to try climbing up to the second floor right here. I think the windows that high will be unsecured. If I can open the window, you'll see me go in. Don't do a thing until I reappear: I'll have to check the door to the corridor, and the door to the room on the left."

"How do you know there's a corresponding room on the left? We've never seen this place before."

"I've been in five or six of these buildings; they're clones of each other. And I don't make mistakes about this kind of thing, once I get the pattern. Now, when I reappear, if everything looks ok, I'll make a call like a gongong. When you hear that, climb up one at a time after me. No noise. Ensign, you come up last. Torquato, MacFloe, then Merteuil will precede you in that order. Got it?"

"Yes, Commodore."

Good footholds here next to the door. Bit by bit, not a sound. Good. Up to the balcony level, first floor. Careful. Look to see if danger is lurking. Grips and footholds a bit smaller here. Will Seso be able to manage this? He has big feet, thick boots. Oops, almost slipped. Got to be more careful. Windows open in. Have to force this one a bit. Ugh! hope they didn't hear that inside. Probably not: I guess they're on the ground floor. Still, can't be too careful. Slide over, ease up and in. Thank heaven for these night vision goggles.

There's the door to the other office. It's unlocked. Door to the corridor, near the staircase. No one in view. I'll check the staircase. All clear. Ah, a rope next to the fire extinguisher.

Creep back in, give the gongong call.

Good. Here comes Gino. I've secured the rope. Lower it down to him. "Shh! Get in and don't move." Gongong for Marcia. Now it's Mireille's turn. OK, now for Seso. Damn! Shh! "Stay there a full minute. Don't move." They heard something when he slipped. A door partly open directly across. A head, scanning, or trying to scan. Let's hope the STU haven't discovered any of these goggles. Door's closed. "Keep still and immobile for another minute." Don't want them to rush out and find us here. I don't think they've had any real training, but maybe someone has an instinct for this sort of thing. Ah, the door's opening up again. Head out, listening. Going back in. Safe for a moment. "OK, come on up."

Pull up the rope. Dangerous part now: we split up in two groups, reconnoiter. We all have our standard assignments, we've been over this sort of thing a hundred times in our Ranger training on board. Mireille with me, through the other room and out to the corridor, then left; Seso leading Marcia and Gino, directly to the corridor, then right. "We meet at the other staircase. Set weapons to top-level stun."

"Commodore, you left the window open. Should I close it?"

"No, Marcia. We won't be here when they see it. With luck, we'll be directly above them, on this level. OK, let's go."

———

"Neac, how much further to Olso? If we can judge from past performances, the STU will strike at daybreak. I don't know where exactly Commodore Vasa, Colonel Notlink and their party are."

"We should be there in less than a half hour, Martin. Your tracking device puts them in the new government building, right in the center of town. When we arrive, we'll have cars and soldiers set up on every street two blocks from the building. The commando forces will be moving in on foot from the periphery."

"Your penchant for exact geometric symmetry should help us here. Unfortunately, Ogatrac will surely not be right in the thick of things. He seems very good at getting other people to do his bidding."

"Good leadership principle, you know: delegate. If it weren't for the gravity of the present situation, with your leader and my deputy hoping to capture an important group that has taken over this disused office building, we wouldn't be here either. Does the Commodore frequently go out in the field and do this commando-type work?"

"She can delegate everything but this kind of activity. We couldn't keep her away from it if we tried. The Militia knew who she was, and they tried to capture and execute her several times. They almost succeeded once or twice, too. That was back in the days when her rank seemed to be better suited to this kind of activity. But it's in her blood, and she's a marvel at it. Still, I have a bad feeling about this time. I think the STU is not only getting to know how to conduct themselves in this kind of situation, but they're also able to procure more and better equipment. And as you know, I am an operative, too. I intend to lead the human party."

"Let's hope our equipment is better than theirs and that our people can escape without casualties. I see the city looming up ahead. We're closing in on them."

———

"Mago, we've lost contact with the Earth people."

"Yes, I know, but the Commodore is amazingly resourceful, Agir. I'm sure she'll find a way out. Our task is to find Lero and Sagev, who are somewhere in the building, probably on the ground floor. My guess is that they're in the northwest quadrant, on the courtyard side."

"Why there?"

"The courtyard, because light will not be visible from the street. They'll probably post a guard on the street side, though. The ground floor, because if necessary they can escape from there; they'd be easily trapped if they were up higher."

"And why the northwest?"

"That's where the main road out of town is located. If they had a getaway car, it would be most likely there. That's why I had you 'doctor' every car in the street in that area."

"Well, what now?"

"Colonel Notlink, Siriso, Latan, and Algnab should have reached the north staircase. We'll climb down the northwest elevator shaft to the ground floor. With luck, we should be able to emerge undetected and meet them near the suspected hideaway. Now, no more talkng unless it's absolutely necessary. You know what we have to do."

The door opened as planned. The car seems to be about three stories up. Good. Agir made it to the ladder. Quite a reach to get that door closed. Amazing how much strength I have in this reattached hand, probably more than I had before it was blown off. Down to the second floor now. Two to go. Wish I had some rope. These night vision goggles are a great invention. Good. Agir remembered to dip a bit below. I'll try to reach the door. Oops! Hope no none heard that. Keep quiet for a bit. No sound outside the door. Uh, oh, the elevator's coming down! Quick! we'll drop down a full story! Hope it stops at ground level. No, it's still coming. Thank Oarnn! It stopped at the first basement. Voices. Can't hear what they're saying. We'd better get out of here. This hook should do the trick. Good.

"Agir, let's go quick!"

To the north staircase. Wait! Shots! Someone's hit! More shots from another staircase!

———

"Sagev! Why did you do that? Now they know where we are!"

"They've known that all along! We think we have them trapped, but they have us trapped. You heard that noise in the courtyard, Lero, then some noise in the elevator shaft, then the three people in the staircase. I hope one of the ones we got was that Vasa. Hope she's dead."

"From the glimpse I got of those people, you shot at Damosians. Maybe you got my cousin, Mago, the traitor. That would be worth it. Into this office. It connects to another one, over there. A storeroom with a trapdoor leading to the basement. We'll be safe there for a few minutes till we figure out where to

219

go from here. Maybe Atraps will guess where we are."

A familiar voice answered, "Or maybe Mago will."

"Mago! where are you?"

"Drawing a bead on you, cuz. Fancy you dropping in to have a chat with me. Drop your weapons, both of you."

"How did you know...?"

"I said drop them. I mean now!"

"OK, I'll drop mine, but not before I kill you, you traitor! Take that! Aaaarh! I'm hit! They've got us surrounded!"

"If you know what's good for you, Sagev, you'll drop your gun now, before it's too late."

"OK, traitor, you've got me."

"No, they don't! Take that, Sagev! Now to finish myself off!"

"Mago, he killed her! then himself!"

"We'd better get out of here fast before they close in on us. We don't know how many of them there are, but they're shooting to kill!"

———

"Siriso, can you hear me? Siriso!"

"Latan. My arm. It's numb."

"You've been shot. I've managed to stop your blood from flowing. We have to get you off this landing. Can you move? Siriso, can you move? Damn! She's unconscious."

"The poor thing is unconscious. You'll be unconscious, too, Latan. Permanently unconscious. Like Algnab. Say your prayers, if you evil-lovers know what praying is. You're history now."

"Oriac! Algnab's your uncle. How can you be so cruel? Have you no respect for your relatives, for the dead and the wounded?"

"Respect? Respect for the evil-lovers of Damos, the enemies of Schad? I'll show you the respect I have. Here you are Siriso: I'll deliver you from your pain. Ah, ha ha ha ha!"

A bullet aimed at the wounded Siriso struck Latan in the chest. She had flung herself over the body of her wounded companion.

"A hero! Bravo, Latan! Now it's really your turn. Ready?"

Latan, bleeding abundantly, could not answer. A shot rang out, striking Oriac. It was Mago! Oriac fell, holding on to her right arm, sobbing convulsively, screaming in pain.

Without a word, Mago and Agir removed the weapon from Oriac's hand, picked up the other weapons, and went out the door to the first room they found open. But what they saw was not designed to make them feel better. Atraps, with a half-dozen others, had Christina, Mireille, and Seso in chains. Colonel Notlink, his head wrapped in a bandage, was tied to a chair. The others were dead or wounded, in the corridors, like Latan, Sisiro and Algnab. They turned around: more STUers. They were caught! They dropped their weapons.

"We heard some shots outside, Mago. Anyone we know? Ha ha ha ha!"

Atraps's demonic laughter sent a chill down Mago's spine. Agir, on her first mission, was terrified, but somehow was managing to hide her emotions.

"Actually, just a few corpses. Sisiro shot at us, thinking we were cowardly terrorists."

"One more snide remark like that and you're history, Mago. In fact, there's no reason you're not history right now. And get over there. You'll have the supreme pleasure of seeing Notlink and Vasa die with a bullet in their brains. Too bad. The Government could have used people like that a bit longer."

"Why don't you just kill us and get it over with?"

"Because I want to see each and every one of you squirm as we kill the evil from beyond the moon and the allies of evil, Notlink. Let's see, suppose we start by rank? Rank has its privilege. Ha ha ha ha! Is a Colonel higher in rank than a Commodore?"

"No, I'll be first to go."

"Christina! No!"

"Shut up, sergeant. You'll be the last to go. Hope you enjoy seeing blood spurting out of bodies and people writhing in agony."

"You're beastly! How can you do this? Kill us, if you hate us so much, but spare your own people, at least."

"Oh, aren't we being noble? Princess Christina, the gentle soul who saved the lives of repulsive enemies of Schad and traitors to Oarnn. Your minutes are numbered, Commodore. Get down on your knees."

"Well, it's been a pleasant 320 or so years. I've crossed the galaxy and discovered intelligent life far away. Thank goodness some of you are like Agir, Mago, and Colonel Notlink, sensitive and kind people trying to keep the rule of law on their planet. Ugh!"

An angry Atraps kicked Christina in the face. Blood began to drip from her mouth. Because her hands were tied behind her back, she stanched the flow of bood by rubbing it onto her shoulders.

"Enough! No more preaching for you! Snaelro, put your pistol five centimeters from her right temple. Heh, heh! Take a quick look at the blood, the impure blood dripping from the corners of her mouth. Now get ready to..."

Blam! In a flash, or more precisely, in ten flashes, Atraps and his cohorts were hit by deadly red bolts. All of them fell to the floor, lifeless.

"I told the High Commissioner we were closing in on them. Didn't mean to come in at the last second. Are all of you all right?"

"Martin! You're a lifesaver! How's everyone else?"

"Some of the people are wounded, one or two seriously. Some are dead. And I see we have to take care of you and the Colonel."

"Lieutenant Mago saved a couple of our people. But so many have died!" Agir said, as she began to cry. "They shot their own relatives in cold blood, at point-blank range. I didn't think the Kolok could be so cruel and heartless."

"There's something about religious fanaticism that brings out the worst in people," said Christina, trying to comfort her. "How many people killed in the name of their gods?"

"We've seen it on Earth and the other planets. Otherwise sane people do terrible things to each other. Our job then and now is to face it, this insane evil, and contain it."

"Contain it? How do you do that, Martin?" asked Neac, who

entered at just this point.

"Contain it. A great idea, Martin!" shouted Christina, suddenly exuberant. "Contain it! Close in on them, then close them in!"

———

All the wounded survived. Among the STU personnel in the building, everyone died except Oriac. Sisiro, Latan and Notlink among the Damosians, and Christina and Mgamba among the humans were wounded. Algnab had been killed by Oriac; Gino Torquato and Marcia MacFloe were killed in action, the first human deaths in this struggle. Their ashes were brought on board Constellation to be presented to their families.

"I don't know what trials lie before us, Chief," mused Christina at the burial services for the fallen Kolok, "but I do know that those people will be avenged, all five of them, and all the victims of the terrorist bombings. But we must not act in anger. We must keep calm, plan carefully. Martin suggested the broad outlines of a strategy. Let's get our staffs together to see how we can make it work."

———

"Look at these headlines in the newspapers! Every day more senseless murders!

Five allies killed, four wounded in Olso government building. Fourteen STU members killed, one wounded now in prison.

Bomb explodes in crowded mall; 40 feared dead, hundreds injured.

School explosion rocks small town. Teachers, children all dead, 250 in all.

Every day a new atrocity. What force have we unleashed? How can we atone for the sins of our coreligionists?"

"Nilreb, you must not feel guilt for the crimes of Ogatrac and his followers."

"My dear Madstop, we **are** responsible, or more exactly, **I** am responsible. Do you remember that day when I proposed that we not only tolerate the formation of the STU, but also actively support them? The Schadite Tactical Units! We allowed the sacred name of Schad to be associated with murder! It was I who made the proposal. It is I who must accept blame for all that has transpired and for all that will transpire."

"I cannot agree with you; we are all guilty, all of us who voted in favor of your motion, which seemed to be a decent compromise at the time. Who could have imagined how far Ogatrac would want to carry his anger?"

"He has chosen to respond to my call for a truce by insulting all who would agree with me. Read this arrogant answer."

"Nilreb, he wants to continue the violence, to carry it in what he is calling apostate Schadite temples!"

"Madstop, my friend, as High Bishop of the Schadite sect, I have written a letter to be sent to all the temples, all the congregations. As you will see, I ask them all to support a truce, and to try to find a solution to this crisis that has shaken Kolok society. I have reason to believe that the government will accept our offer. But what if Ogatrac remains adamant? Do we continue to support his cause with money, prayers, and words?"

"What alternatives do we have? We pledged our lives to this struggle?"

"We pledged *our* lives, but not those of our people, even if they agreed with us. The humans perhaps deserve no better than what they have received. And yet they continue to struggle alongside our own brave fighters. What are we to make of them? Perhaps we have misread the words of Schad. Perhaps they are not evil incarnate. I think we have one alternative: exile. There are parts of the planet that could support life, but that have been set aside as preserves. Perhaps we could arrange to withdraw there with our followers, and start anew. But we cannot do anything until we acknowledge our guilt. Could we persuade the government to let us live, cordonned off, perhaps among the ruins of Ksnim and its area."

"Our people and our leaders must ponder your words, Linreb. We can only pray that the madness of Ogatrac will isolate him from ever more Schadites, and make the STU an abomination among us. Ogatrac is closing himself in, within himself, closing himself off from his advisors and his friends. And yet we cannot ignore the fact that he has fired up the imaginations of thousands."

"My friend, I must let you in on a secret: I am going to speak with High Commissioner Ylro tomorrow, in Olso. We are both going incognito. Only you know this from me; only Deputy High Commissioner Amil knows it from him. Pray for us, and wish us well."

"What a risk you are taking! What if somehow someone knows of this meeting? What would ensue?"

"What a risk we would take if we were too timid to seek a remedy for the evil that is abroad in the land! an evil for which we must bear the responsibility! My friend, if we, if something should befall us, you must carry on."

"If something should befall you? I see by your visage what you mean. Nilreb, you can count on me."

———

"Tomorrow at noon, Wocsom? At the Triumph Restaurant in Olso?"

"Yes, Ogatrac. I have wired the High Bishop's office for sound, and have heard his conversation with Bishop Madstop. They want to seek a compromise, perhaps go into exile."

"Exile? They'll get exile. Permanent exile. I myself shall set the explosives. Tell no one. You will hear from me tomorrow night, on the usual channel."

"Ogatrac, will we be able to bring our people out of the enclosure in which they find themselves?"

"Wocsom, I will lead my people out of captivity. We will prevail! And we will be free!"

225

WAR ON DAMOS

"This is Otnas Omer in Ihled with an extraordinary story of horror and pain and a living death–and rejuvenation. Among the images you will see and the sounds you will hear are many just made available for this documentary program.

"Our story begins on Unias when we saw for the first time the unparalleled beauty of the long-hidden and exotic sister planet of Damos, Unias. Who could forget those adorable spheres? And who could forget this first view of an unknown people from the other side of the Galaxy? But at that time we could not decipher the words of the party's leader, Commander Martin Duval. Now we can. Listen:

... of the people of Earth, we wish to let you know that we are here on a scientific mission, and that we come in peace. If you have a language synthesizer like mine, perhaps you can understand me. But since we know where the land probe and the main ship are sending their messages, we will soon come in peace to meet you.

And who can forget the words of Commodore Christina Vasa, as she led a small group to meet High Commissioner Ylro, Chief of Security Neac, and other officials:

We come in peace and friendship from across the immensity of time and space of our common galaxy. We wish you long life and warm affections, and we offer you, as a pledge of our intentions, these first living beings we found on your sister planet of Unias, near your land probe.

"Here on Damos, most people responded warmly to these messages of peace and friendship. But there were some for whom these aliens seemed to pose a threat: the Holy Brotherhood of Schad. For most Damosians, these past several years have been full of excitement and joy; but these religious zealots have striven to make it a time of war. Their terrorism is our subject, their vehicle the Schadite Tactical Units set up by Bishop Ogatrac, which within six months began to plan its campaign of terrorism.

"We have recently come into possession of a powerful speech delivered two years ago by Bishop Ogatrac. We will play his speech for you now, in its entirety, exactly as he himself had it taped. You will see how his interpretation of the sacred scriptures saw the visitors from Earth as incarnations of evil. We will then present an edited version of the debate that followed, including the startling agreement by which the leaders of the sect agreed to what was termed a compromise fashioned by High Bishop Nilreb. The Pact of Terror engaged the sect as corporate sponsors of a holy war: fully 25% of the high clergy present became members of the Leadership Council of the Schadite Tactical Units. The STU were born that day."

———

"Since that fateful day, we have seen all too many scenes like the ones about to be shown on your screens. We must warn you that there is much graphic violence in them, and much bloodshed. You will see much more of what you see now: bridges and houses blown up, children murdered in playgrounds and schools, shopping centers and open-air markets burned out by incendiary bombs. In town after town, in city after city, even in sparsely-populated areas, and in several cases on isolated farms, what is believed to be a relatively small group of STU terrorists went on a rampage, wreaking havoc, almost with impunity, for the better part of a year, once the campaign of terror began.

"In the beginning, the attacks seemed to have two objects: first, to capture arms and munitions with which to carry on the attacks that we have become so accostomed to, and second, to inspire terror so as to incite the people to riot. The first aim was an immense success for five or six months, as these pictures taken in Eekuawlim attest to; since then, with increased security, fewer and fewer attacks have succeeded, and no weapons have been seized for the past six months: a perfect parabolic curve. It

228

is believed, however, that the STU has been manufacturing car bombs to carry out its plan of mass murder, reserving its handguns and rifles for aiming at individuals.

"The second goal, to inspire terror, also succeeded wildly at first, and for a longer period of time. It is only in recent months that a program of progressive containment has proven effective. At first, the primary targets of the attacks were people, such as those shown here, who seemed to favor relations with the Earth people. Many Damosians were tortured and killed in this effort. Once again, we must warn you that some of the scenes on your screens will be perhaps too graphic; we are showing them to reveal the horror of the actions taken. Men and women strangled after unthinkable tortures: their tongues cut out, their eyes burned out, their fingers and toes cut off one by one, then their hands and feet, and if they were still alive, their limbs. In one of the cruelist ironies of this war on decency, dozens of STUs actually filmed the proceedings. The scenes you have been witnessing, again for the first time, are official STU training films.

"If you will pardon my dropping whatever objectivity this series of disgusting acts allows me to have, I must add that such acts, unthinkable for over 1000 years, at one point almost made me ashamed to be a Kolok. Fortunately, most people have been revulsed by what they have learned, and a large number of STU defections have occurred, while general public support for their activities has been declining precipitously as the truth is becoming better known. Many of the followers of Ogatrac, the Schadite leader, are right now being interrogated; others have given much valuable information, which has helped to drive the STUs into retreat. They now find themselves in a small area, closed in. But after these initial orgies of torture, their successes were increasingly violent and heartless.

"Soon the STUs began to target public figures. Not just the officers guarding supplies and arms, as at first, but government officials at every level, and ordinary citizens. The only strand uniting these people was that they had had kind words to say about our guests from the planet Earth, had taken part in meals, festivities, celebrations, expeditions, and the like, with them.

Mayors of cities large and small, members of regional councils and provincial governments, principals of elementary schools, even leaders of community organizations and workers in every walk of life: no one was spared. Finally, the STUs hit not only main-stream congregations but also Schadite temples deemed not sufficiently supportive or not aggressive enough in their weekly denunciations of the supposed enemy.

"The STUs' violence has resulted in the deaths of well over 50,000 people thoughout the planet. The number of wounded is over twenty times that. Their wrath and madness have known no bounds.

"Look at this bombed-out temple in Ksnim. It was destroyed during a regular service; over 800 people lost their lives; few were saved. These sights have horrified you before, fire bombings of temples and sacred shrines, innocent victims. By a curious coincidence, the organization's leaders have been forced into hiding in the mountains behind Ksnim, which was for reasons as yet unknown the hardest hit of our cities attacked by the STU. Every day the terrorists can see their handiwork below them. We're circling and zooming in on the worst-hit of the schools... the playgrounds... the factories... the temples... the stores... the office buildings... the amusement parks... the government buildings... and countless private residences that have been destroyed by car bombs, incendiary bombs, and other explosive devices. All survivors have been evacuated. Govenment forces have closed in on them. The mountains have been sealed off. Ever since several of the terrorists emerged apparently to surrender, with their arms raised, but then opened up fire on the police, all terrorist not waving a flag of surrender have been shot on sight as they emerged from their encampments.

"Meanwhile, the Earth people have joined forces with the Damosians in exploration sallies to Unias and to the twin planets of Tertia Major and Tertia Minor. We will be reporting on the discoveries made in these extraordinary lands in a documentary to be shown at a later date. But already the public is familiar with the indescribable beauty of Unias, its incredible huge animals the size of which we had never seen, its other animals, including vast colonies of flying amphibians (truly strange creatures equally at home on land, in the air, and in the water), which you now see on your screen; the great flowering trees and the tiniest wooded plants ever seen in our part of the galaxy—and our Earth scientists claim that all these wonders are totally unknown in their lands.

"We are also familiar with the strange world of the twin planets. Both have polar ice caps, abundant water, hot equatorial forests, and fauna very different from what we have on Damos and what we have seen on Unias. All the animal life seems to be relatively small, about the size of pet animals or smaller. Here's a darling, snuggly reptile. In the deep oceans swim fish and other creatures unimaginable for their beauty and grace. There is strong seismic activity on both planets, which seems to be a factor in the creation and maintenance of the atmosphere. Tertia Major is exceptionally dense: its gravitational pull is nearly 90% that of Damos, although its diameter is just three-quarters ours. Again, we will have full reports on the wonders of our planetary neighbors within the next few weeks.

"But we must now leave these verdant vistas to return to the subject of our documentary, 'The STU: the dark side of the Kolok.' Prepare your mind for yet more scenes of brutality and bloodshed, and for the as yet untold tale of forced drug addiction and mind-robbing terror.

"Who can forget the capture of Dlawso, who under the guise of a friendly visit to the great ship Constellation, was caught just as he was to enter the teleportation area with gunpowder? A goodwill tour of the craft, just days prior to departure for the Tertias almost ended in disaster. And this was not all. One or two terrorists actually made it on board before being detected in the unfortunately necessary second searches carried on kilometers above us, in the sky. Here is a pair caught by a surveillance camera trying to blast a hole in the exterior wall of the craft; only swift work by the Damosian guards on board, who were racing towards them because they recognized them as terrorists sought for having blown up bridges, averted catastrophe.

"While we were preparing this story, we learned, in an exclusive interview, of one of the most repulsive of the STU's tactics. We have been able to corroborate these stories by speaking to the victims themselves. It was at first thought that the incidents of addiction to DOP among the humans were caused by experimentation, a desire to try out something new. Their Kolok friends were suspected of procuring the drug for them.

"Schadites somehow managed to deliver high doses of DOP to Earth people and their Kolok friends in various parts of the planet, and even on Constellation while it was on its mission to Unias. The spaceship's water purification chamber had been broken into, and several kilograms of DOP were dumped in the central filtration vat.

"We all know only too well why this is a banned drug. It is so highly addictive that a single dose usually causes apparently incurable addictions in susceptible people, and even the most resistant fall under its spell after only five or six doses.

"Because of differences in brain structure, it affects humans more acutely than Kolok, but both have similar symptoms: extreme pleasure in everything, friendly to all when high; a high that lasts for hours, in some cases for days; but when need for more arises, humans become aggressive and violent, Kolok submissive and impassive; in both cases, portions of the brain are gradually eaten away.

"Here is some file footage of addicts during their initial periods of euphoria. Here we see them unable to act, easy prey for thieves and drug suppliers. What they don't know is that entire centers of cranial activity gradually cease to exist. They lose their memory, then control of their muscles, finally their lives. Over 6000 victims, many of them young people, die from this horrible addiction every year.

"On board Constellation, and on the ground in Unias, many Kolok and scores of humans were poisoned by the DOP before the source was discovered and the drug neutralized (for on these ships everything is recycled). The result was predictable; the ship's medical facilities were strained to capacity, and the aggressivity of the humans required many of them to be restrained. Upon consultation with Damosian officials, it was decided to cut the expedition short and to return to Damos.

"I promised you a story about rejuvenation. Here it is. The

Kolok and the humans on the surface were teleported to the spaceship, to be rushed to hospitals on Damos, where new treatments were being tested. But on reaching the "Den" or teleporting room, they were found to be cured! No more symptoms, neither the intense euphoria nor the subsequent impassivity or extreme aggressiveness. For reasons not fully understood, the teleportation process somehow prevented the further progress of the drug's destructive path. However, brain damage was not reversed in transit, so that the damage already wrought has been irreversible. Two of the most severely injured victims are currently undergoing experimental operations to rebuild part of the brain cells, using frog nerves and magnetic therapy, with equipment manufactured in Bobol. We will have an interview with Dr. Iborian, who is pioneering this procedure, as soon as she is available for an on-screen interview.

"The Earth people experienced identical relief. They are now undergoing similar treatment under the supervision of Dr. Mujama. Plans are underway to expose all other victims of the drug to teleportation. A miracle cure might have been fortuitously found for this devastating addiction.

"What about the perpetrators of the crime? They are currently in solitary confinement in Hell's Portal. They have adamantly refused to say where they procured this drug, how they were able to carry it on board, and why they chose to use it at the time they did."

———

The program was abruptly interrupted at this point. Dab Retsnum came on camera, and said tersely:

"I have just been told that there is an important new development in the ongoing battle against the STU. We interrupt our planned broadcast to bring you Sinng Stoarn in Olso."

"This is Sinng Stoarn in Olso. I am standing outside the ruins of the upscale Triumph Restaurant in this city, where it is now 2 p.m. About an hour ago a car illegally parked outside the restaurant exploded, detonating a powerful bomb. Officials

233

contained the ensuing fire rapidly, but few survivors could be found. The detonation in the car caused a secondary detonation of a bomb placed in a lavatory near the rear of the building, leaving little place for people to find cover.

"A stretcher is passing before me as I speak. By Oarrn! I would swear that this man is High Bishop Nilreb of the Holy Brotherhood of Schad! ...Excuse me, excuse me, Medic, do you know who this victim is?"

"Please step aside, Ma'am. We have to rush this person to the hospital. He's one of the few still alive."

"Another stretcher. This looks like High Commissioner Ylro! ...Medic, is the High Commissioner alive?"

"I don't know anything about the High Commissioner, Lady. This person is severely hurt. Let us get by, please!"

"I have covered news events with both of these men so many times that I can recognize them as easily as my own image. Why would they have come to this city? The usual entourage of official cars is absent. Were they meeting each other here? What is going on?"

"Sinng, we have a call for you on the phone. The caller claims to be Bishop Ogatrac."

"It must be a hoax. Hello. This is Sinng Stoarn speaking."

"Sinng Stoarn. This is Ogatrac. I have an important message for you and your public."

"Your voice sounds like Bishop Ogatrac's, but he is said to be with his followers in the hills above Ksnim."

"I was there two days ago, but the governement can't hold me. Listen. I don't want to spend much time with you. I do want to let you know that I personally set off the two explosives you spoke of. My objective was to kill High Commissioner Ylro and the treacherous High Bishop, Nilreb. They were meeting in secret and incognito to find a way to stop the STU. Let this be a lesson to all who wish to defy the STU! Your days will be numbered."

"You may have succeeded in killing them, although they are still alive. But officials put the death toll at 300 so far, all of them innocent bystanders. There are as many as 150 people injured, many of them passers-by in the street. How can you justify that?"

, "I don't need to justify my activities to you. Those people are meaningless in the long-range strategy we have developed. The individuals must be sacrificed to the greater good of Oarrn's one true religion, the Holy Fellowship of Schad!"

"But Bishop Ogatrac, if it is indeed Ogatrac I am speaking to, and if it is indeed the High Commissioner and the High Bishop that I saw, what could they possibly... He hung up. We have reporters dispatched to the University of Olso Medical Center, where the ambulances were heading. And now, back to the studios."

———

"Neac, our tracers put Ogatrac in the vicinity of the port. That's two hours from here. Can we get the local Police on the case?"

"Martin, my friend, as soon as we saw where Ogatrac was calling from, they were dispatched. We must thank Sinng Stoarn for keeping him on the phone long enough so that we could zero in on him."

"It seems that all such criminals want to tempt the Police, give them a chance to catch them."

"If you permit it, I would like to get Christina in our party. Please get your people rounded up within 15 minutes. We'll leave from here."

"Neac, it will be our pleasure to join you."

———

"Why are you getting a plane ready, despite the bad weather?"

"Christina, Commodore Vasa, we must get to Olso by the quickest means possible. Under the circumstances, this is as fast as our transport will take us."

"Why not beam up to Constellation, zip to a spot above Olso, and teleport down?"

"Neac, she's right! We could be there in minutes rather than

235

hours."

"Let's get all these agents on board at once. Ju-Sen, be prepared for a series of people coming on board!"

———

They think they can catch me, do they? I've given them the slip. Shouldn't have spoken so long with that reporter. Probably shouldn't have spoken at all. They appear to have been able to trace my call, despite my scrambling mechanism. Where exactly am I? Near the marina. Good. I can get on a speedboat and get out of here fast. Go north to Ublask, where there's a hidden cove, take refuge in the bombed-out temple until the storm is past. That Sinng Stoarn woman wants to know how I justify killing innocent civilians. Hah! None of them is innocent. They're either with us, or against us. They believe in Oarrn, or they're infidels. If they're infidels, they don't deserve to live.

Hmm. Police here. I see a boat moored out in the water, maybe 100 meters out. If I slip in quietly here and swim out, gently, making as little noise and as few ripples as possible, I'll be able to get on board unnoticed. Ah, a ladder going down. Good. Into the water now. Light shining up ahead. I'll get close to it, then swim underwater. Good thing I've kept in good form.

Damn tetrapods, get away! Calm yourself, Ogatrac, they don't hurt, they just try to nip you. Don't let them make you give yourself away. Ow! It got me on the neck. Got it; I'll crush you to death, you damn pest! Ha, ha! Good to get some air in the old lungs. Underwater again for a few meters. OK, just a short distance to go. What do I hear? Arrgh! Bitten on the arm! Oh, no, it's not a tetrapod! It must be a sea serpent. Hope it's not a ruasacsip. It is! More than one. Got to make it to the boat! My arm! it's paralyzed! They're biting my other arm, my legs, my neck! AAARRRGH!

———

"Did you hear something, Oogar?"
"Yeah, sounded like someone screaming way out there."

236

"How can there be anyone out there? The marina's been closed for an hour."

"Notuom, look! There's someone thrashing around there. He or she is being attacked by one or more ruasacsips! Quick! Call up the Chief, tell her we're on our way to help a victim. We'll need an ambulance. While you're calling, I'll get a boat ready."

———

Pain is terrible. I can't resist them any more. I don't have any feeling in my limbs, but I seem to be able to control them enough to float. What are they doing just hovering in the water around me? Why don't they finish me off? I'm drifting towards the boat. If I get there, will I be able to get on? Oh, the pain. My head is aching, my body is chilled! Are they afraid to swallow their own poison? A meter away. Maybe I can somehow force myself up. No! Get away! Those fangs. At my throat! Can't get up! Schad, I'm coming to meet you and Oarrn! What do I see? All those bloody people! No, just phantasmagora. Pain. AAAARGH! Can't... keep... up... any...

———

"Shoot that snake! Grab that person!"

"We're too late, Notuom. He's dead."

"Wonder who it is and why he's here?"

"I don't know that, but I do know that there's a hungry bunch of ruasacsips swimming around here. Let's rev up the engine and get to shore!"

"I've got him under wraps. His body is all stiff from the poison of those things. Another minute or two and they'd have eaten every ounce of flesh on him."

———

"Christina, Martin, we've found Ogatrac. Dead."

"Are you sure it's him?"

"Even in death his hatred can be seen. The guards fished

him out of the bay. He should have known that with stormy weather the ruasacsips come into shallow water around here."

"With luck, the death of this charismatic leader will make the rest of the STU throw down their arms."

"I wonder what Nilreb wanted to speak to the High Commissioner about?"

"We might never know, Christina. With both of them dead, it might be impossible to ascertain."

"Don't you think they would have let someone into their confidence? Those are not people who act without consultation. Even if it's a major secret affair like this, someone should know. Someone **must** know."

"Well, I have to make my report to Deputy High Commissioner Amil. She will be sworn in shortly. Let's ask her to hold off the swearing-in ceremony until I can get back."

———

"Chief Neac, I found High Bishop Nilreb's secretary on the floor when I came in to tell him of Ogatrac's death. A self-inflicted wound. He had some disks in his hand. I played one. It was a recording of a secret meeting I had had with the High Bishop. Your agents had been bugging us for months! The action your forces took were unconscionable. I shall protest to the courts."

"Bugged? We didn't bug him. We had no reason to suspect him of anything. But my agents did find something you should hear, Bishop Madstop, before you go to court. Listen to this."

"Tomorrow at noon, Wocsom? At the Triumph Restau rant in Olso?"

"Yes, Ogatrac. I have wired the High Bishop's office for sound, and have heard his conversation with Bishop Madstop. They want to seek a compromise, perhaps go into exile."

"Exile? They'll get exile. Permanent exile."

"Wocsom! Ogatrac!"

"Yes. Your trusted secretary was an undercover agent for

the STU. If I were you, I'd rather consider starting to speak in earnest with High Commissioner Amil. She, too, was in on the mission. If it were left to me, all these people and their supporters would be rounded up and dumped in the sea. She probably has other ideas."

"Exile?"

"I would guess permanent exile, but not in Ogatrac's sense. Know any far-off isolated places?"

"I must contact the STU leaders and the Holy Brotherhood leaders. Could you arrange for a meeting next week?"

———

"You know, Neac, I've been thinking about that exile idea. They could be left around Ksnim, couldn't they?"

"Keeping them there would require major security efforts for decades, Martin. I'm not sure there's a place on Damos that would be safe. And the cost!"

"What about a place off Damos?"

"What do you mean, Christina?"

"My guess is that Amil is looking to the stars. Actually, I know she is. I planted the idea in her mind."

"You mean Unias?"

"No, Martin. We've already agreed in principle to enter into a joint exploration of that planet, to survey it thoroughly geologically and to catalog its biota. No, that's out. But there are two other planets."

"Tertia Minor and Tertia Major!"

"I get it! Especially Tertia Major, which has a gravitational field almost as strong as Damos. People could live comfortably there near the equator and up in the mid latitudes."

"Yes, Martin. The idea came to me because we had offered such a refuge to the Militia. Do you remember?"

"Of course! Paracelsus!"

"Their response was to blow up a port on Mars. The result was their extermination. I think the STU are more reasonable, in their way. I think that with the High Chief of Security promising a life of Hell's Portal type prisons, in solitary confinement, they might look on Tertia Major as a place of refuge rather than as a place of exile."

"We could let them name it whatever they want, maybe something after Schad."

"It would make sense to draw up a kind of charter granting them autonomous government on one of the continents, under the control of Damos. In a couple of decades, once your party has returned from Earth, you can have your own space-age ships to establish contact with them. The other Damosians can set up colonies on the other continents. You'd be able to keep an eye on them that way, and also begin a long-range exploration and discovery of the life on the planet, its geography, the whole works. It could also serve as a platform for examining Minor."

"Christina, what a great solution, if they accept it!"

"But Neac, they'll reject such an idea for two reasons: first, the idea was thought up by humans; second, they oppose space travel."

"Yes, Martin, but consider this: they don't have to know it was Christina's idea. And Nilreb seemed to have been toying with the idea that perhaps the writings of Schad have been misinterpreted. With the Hell's Portal persuasion, maybe our friend High Bishop Madstop will see that his predecessor was right. This may seem like the honorable way out. They'll have their land, their dignity. They'll be left alone. And instead of the punishment they deserve, and that by now they must know they deserve, they'll have a safe refuge. But the costs will be, if you'll pardon the pun, astronomical."

"Not so much in the long run, when you consider the cost of building and maintaining prisons for so many people."

"Martin, you're right. Christina, a brilliant idea. When we meet tomorrow, I'm sure Amil will start to feel out Madstop. And I'm sure that under the circumstances we can get the plan underway. There's only one problem. Transportation."

"People? Materials? Neac, as you know, we're planning on returning to Earth in six months. Constellation is able to handle this kind of mission. All we need is the highest level of security, and we know we can count on you for that."

"Christina, Neac probably doesn't recognize the great

influence the Kolok have exercised on us Earth people. Like you, Neac, I have an instinct to do away with these brutes. Maybe that goes with our kind of job, but I think that most of my crew members would have felt like me before we met you. Christina didn't need conversion to your way of thinking: she was already there. You're making the rest of us better, more human."

Christina smiled. "No, Martin: they're Kolokizing us."

THE LONG TRAIL BACK

"Christina, I've been thinking that Martin's decision to lead the team of Earth people on Unias had more to it that he or you have told me. Nothing suspicious. Rather, something more personal."

"Do you think we had a lover's spat, Ecnelav?"

"No, it's not that. A spat, or even a quarrel, would be unlikely to have a person of his obvious stature and importance volunteer to lead what might well be a dull ten-year assignment. I mean, it's exciting to see the new animals and plants and other life forms; it's exciting to travel around in a totally new and different environment; it's exciting to see and to swim in new oceans, lakes and rivers. But the job is really, like so much of science, full of dull routine. Basically, the Joint Exploration Team will record in images, sounds, and even odors the flora an fauna of Unias, will catalogue species and phyla and the like, will file reports, analyze specimens, establish habitats. This is the work of more or less contemplative types of people, people who've been trained in methods of investigation that are not like a Security Officer's. Martin's been trained for action, he's had a life of 330 years or so full of action. This is not up his alley."

"Well, he's done a lot of studying, especially over the last 100 years or so, and he's developed a taste for something new and exciting. In fact, he knows more about certain aspects of biology, like comparative anatomy, than anyone alive on Earth. You make that branch of study sound boring."

"I know what I'm talking about: I've spent a good 50 years learning and practicing my profession. And while I'm excited about what I do, a lot of people would find that a lot of my work is really pretty dull."

"OK, suppose I accept your premise that being a scientist is not all glamor, and that much of the day-to-day work is routine, dull even. Even so, spending three or more years on board a spaceship, even one like Constellation, can hardly be called exciting. You've been with us for a month now; you see what we do: a routine of staying fit and trim, a routine of developing and maintaining our skills, a routine of study and recreation. We see the same 500 or so people every day, eat the same food, live in the same place. Sure, Constellation is a big craft, but it's sort of like being walled in a village. We have a prison island on Paracelsus, a prison without walls. But the prisoners can't escape because of the vicious jellyfish-like creatures in the sea around them, jellyfish that seem to have a collective if not an individual intelligence. Prison consists in being there for life. Their lives are comfortable, but the thought of never being able to go somewhere else is their real punishment. In the end, space travel can seem like that, except for two things: it's not forever, and from time to time you actually get out. When you get out, there's always the chance of excitement, be it danger, or a novel world, or finally meeting up with a race of people we can communicate with."

"Be all that as it may, I still think there's more to Martin's story than he has told me or that you've been willing to let me in on."

"The truth is, you've already put your finger on the reason, Ecnelav."

"You've had a lover's quarrel, and he's too stubborn to come on board and take orders from you?"

"No, there's been no quarrel, and as you've noticed we tend to function here in Constellation as much as possible by consensus. Usually it's only in emergency situations, or when there is no clear consensus that I have to make a decision that's binding. The same procedure works all up and down the chain of command. Next guess!"

"He's got some romantic notion about becoming a great discoverer of new life forms, which will assure him a place in some mythical Hall of Fame, or maybe earn him an honorary degree from a famous university?"

"No, actually it would be hard to find someone as competent as he is, and so modest about his accomplishments. This romantic notion you're talking about might have played a small part in some of the other crew members' decision to explore Unias as part of the JET, but as you know most of them are already technical and scientific people. Try again."

"Hmm. Third guess. Back on Damos, this is the last one. But frankly I'm stumped. I refuse to believe he's decided to stay on Unias just for the sake of adding to his store of knowledge, or to that of our worlds. Our worlds! What a great thought!"

"Do you remember that great view of the entire solar system? There was Chromos, surrounded by three orbits containing five planets! And our sensors indicated that four of them might support life! What a thrilling scene it was! We had never seen anything quite like it: the density of the spiral arm as background, a perfect sun just the right age, and those planets in a array we had never encountered. And radio signals that indicated that at last we had found what we were looking for: an intelligent race of people.

"We were concerned that you might be hostile to us. We wondered what you might look like, what level of technological development you had reached, what the conditions of life on the four inner planets might be. We debated where to start looking. We decided to check out Unias because we noted many more intelligent messages coming from Damos, and we wanted to ease in to your culture, learn the language (or have Colombina learn it), before we tried to make direct contact. And then, when we thought the time was ripe, we teleported down. What a great experience!"

"On Damos, we captured your entry on disk! We had had no idea that teleportation was feasible, and when we saw it we realized that you somehow managed to make use of quantum mechanics to do it. What a great scientific discovery! We, too, feared that you might be hostile, and for us the consequences would have been worse, because of your obvious technological superiority. We wondered where you came from, what you were doing on Unias and then high up above Damos. We had seen you on Unias, not very clearly but enough to suggest to us that you were probably mammalian. I can't tell you how delirious we were to find you so wonderful!"

"You know, it might be fascinating for you to see our three solar systems from up above. While naturally I think the Earth's is the most interesting and beautiful of the three, Mesnos has a double sun, and Paracelsus has a solar system that's almost isolated: there are no nearby stars. Extraordinary!"

"If I understand you right, I've still got a two or three years of anticipation and study ahead of me before I can actually get there. The charts I've seen are fascinating, and I don't know which one will be the most exciting to see in person. But we were speaking about Martin. I have to get back to my last guess. Can you give me a clue or a hint?"

"A clue? A hint? Let's see. Hmmm. What happens to the image on your screen when you get out of the program?"

"Why, it goes away, it disappears, it dies out. The program's over, the screen becomes blank. ...Christina, you're crying!"

"Ecnelav, when I think of Martin now, I... I..."

"I'm sorry I raised this issue, I've upset you so much."

And Christina began to sob convulsively and to weep uncontrollably for a long five minutes, unable to talk. Ecnelav had never seen this side of her friend, and it frightened her. What did she say that could upset Christina so much?

"I think I'll be all right now. I'm sorry for that outburst, but thinking too seriously about Martin... Grieving is supposed to do you a lot of good."

"Grieving?"

"Yes, Ecnelav, grieving for his loss."

"His loss? Do you mean that he intends to die on Unias?"

"Yes. He'll be dead before we reach the wormhole."

"How do you know? Do Earth people have such predictable ends? Can you all tell with precision how long you'll live? I can see how that can be disconcerting when you reach your allotted time."

"Not all humans, just we ELBers can tell. We're frozen at our age until the end; when we die, we age by about a year every three days until death comes. Martin became an ELBer at the age of 30; he had lived his 200 or so years of extended life and almost all of his natural life, which is in the 125-150 year range for us. He tried to hide from most people what was happening, but I knew: I'd seen the process begin with a great many people. He told me that he has no family at all on Earth (none of us does, for that matter. We're all orphans, but he doesn't even have distant relatives that he could find a trace of); and he also said that he'd like to spend his last months doing something constructive for our two cultures. The people who have joined him, all ELBers, are all the family he has, along with us here on board and a few back in our part of the galaxy. They will help him finish his life with dignity, and in conformity to his wishes, they will scatter his ashes on Unias."

"Oh, Christina, how sad you must be!"

"When I was very young, I used to think that heroism consisted of bold and brave actions and decisions. I still think that. But I have added so many other characteristics to it, from doing your job well every day to accepting courageously the blows that life sends. Martin's life fits every part of my definition."

———

"Ecnelav, I've often wondered why the state of astrophysics is so far behind the other branches of science on Damos."

"What do you mean, Kwali?"

"Your medical expertise is almost at the level we've attained. In some ways your knowledge of biology, especially marine biology, beats us out flat. You have done wonders in chemistry, biochemistry, high-energy and particulate physics, a whole parade of advances far beyond your knowledge of the galaxy and the universe. I don't get it."

"Yes," added Christina, "and your Stratoskipper uses the same basic technology we still use for long-distance transportation on Earth and the other planets."

"Gosh, how can I answer these questions, or really, that question, in a few words, Christina?"

"Will a nice tall and cool drink help?" queried Kwali.

"It would make it refreshingly possible. I especially like that green concoction I had the other day."

"Ah, the little green drink. One for you, too, Christina?"

"Yes. And hurry!"

"Don't let her start without me. I'm all ears."

"By Oarnn! That's a funny expression for us. Without ears, we don't really have a way of expressing that image. Hmm. This lounge is nice. I've noticed that it's not limited to people of a certain rank. Is that the usual way you humans operate?"

"I wish it was! In some ways, especially in the military, we remain very class conscious. I've received permission to have mixed lounges for these long trips, just as centuries ago I received permission to experiment with small self-contained units to combat the Militia, units in which we all had a say. Of course, there's a chain of command, a hierarchy, but I wanted to make sure that everyone could take over in an emergency, even at the lowest ranks. And I've always thought that the best way to do that was for everyone to be able to talk to everyone else, without the rigmarole of rank and order. It still works for us, and the idea has finally taken hold in Space Fleet. Only took 300 years; but what's 300 years compared to eternity?"

"Ha, what an idea. But really, we've been moving in that direction, too. It started, of course, in the civilian sector, such as my lab. We work together as teams rather than as units with a rigid hierarchy. And it's been a success! We wouldn't have discovered Unias otherwise: one of the lab assistants came up with an algorithm that made our computer calculations possible, a bright young woman with a great future."

Kwali sauntered up and asked, "Ah, have I missed anything?"

"No, I was just filling Ecnelav in on your background, letting her know how to push your buttons."

"Push his buttons? I don't know what his buttons are, but I don't want to push them!"

"Aha! The Commodore caught in a web of her own making. So, you weren't talking about me, and probably weren't getting into the subject of our interest, either."

"Now, the short answer to your question is, the Schadites. For the long answer, if you want it, I'll have to tell a story."

"It won't take more that two or three years, will it?"

"No, Kwali, just an hour or so."

"Let's go! We're all ears!"

———

Clu Catta, after whom our Space Center was named, was an

astronomer and mathematician who lived some 400 years ago. Along with a friend, the lensmaker Elleroc Gninroc, Catta had developed pretty powerful telescopes, when you consider the state of the art of that time. Basically, Catta and Gninroc rapidly moved from single lens telescopes to the much more complicated type utilizing mirrors. Of course they worked out details, and they developed a glass so pure, that they reached a magnification level of 100x. Eventually, they found a way to enhance the light, so that it was brighter leaving the telescope than entering it. Gninroc even discovered that they could fix an image on silver-treated paper, which effectively led to a primitive photography.

With Gninroc's lenses (already responsible for long-distance viewing that made traveling on the oceans less hazardous), Catta began to survey the stars and the constellations that are part of our folklore. He began to realize, in comparing their then-current shapes and positions with the shapes and positions of the old tales, that over time the constellations no longer looked exactly as the ancient Kolok had depicted them, and occurred at different times of the year than the old tales indicated. He suspected that they were not all fixed in place, as traditional teachings would have it. He suspected that maybe the stars that seem to be on the same plane might be separated by unimaginable distances.

Catta developed several new forms of mathematics, in particular calculus, which he applied to his research. He soon taught that the stars were held in place by what he called the "attractive force"–an idea that revolutionized astronomy.

He then looked at the star we call Oarnn, and another star called Sehtah. For many decades some astronomers considered these heavenly bodies to be not stars at all, but planets of Chromos, our sun; thanks to new calculations made possible by his discovery of calculus, Catta proved them right. He also perceived several satellites orbiting Oarnn, and soon discovered that Sehtah was actually two planets revolving around each other while revolving around the sun, and noticed that they exercised a small but measurable–and calculable–influence on our tides. He also noted that one of the planets was a little smaller than the other. He kept these discoveries to himself for several years

249

while working out a map of our solar system and while trying to explain the gravitational forces that kept the planets in motion.

All his calculations, no matter where he started, led to just one conclusion: Chromos had a hidden planet, a counterpart to Damos! This led him to realize that Sehtah, although occupying the second orbit around the sun, was actually the third planet, or rather the third and fourth. He renamed this pair, in his notes, making use of the ancient language of the Kolok, the Larger Third and the Smaller Third, or in your terms, Tertia Major and Tertia Minor.

Meanwhile, fearful of losing his records in a conflagration, he had taken to copying his journals and calculations, sometimes by hand, sometimes using the photographic system Gninroc had developed. Indeed, he always made a second copy of the telescopic views (that is, he always took a second picture). These copies he put in a dry cave that he visited weekly, near the site of the present Space Center. The originals he kept in his study.

Catta had become well-known as a teacher and researcher, and was sought after by countless people curious to learn more about our world, and by those looking for some economic advantage to be gathered from his knowledge. Gninroc, thanks to his fabled lenses (and to this day they are marvels of perfection), had become quite rich. Traders in particular were interested in them. Naturalists were able to see animals in their natural habitat from a distance. And the biologist Eiruc had him turn a small but powerful telescope upside down, and invented the microscope, which opened up another world. What an epoch to live in! What a sense of adventure! What an explosion of knowledge!

Once his calculations proved to be accurate, Catta decided to publish them, albeit privately, in a treatise known as *The Universal Attractive Force*. It was a sensation! It was soon published by a respected academic press. The greatest doubters found the arguments irresistible. All that was needed to seal the point was to spot the missing planet, which Catta named, again in the ancient language of the Kolok, Unias, meaning the First. He speculated that the universe was immeasurably large, and that beyond our star, beyond the stars we could see, there must be other stars. Many of these stars would have worlds comparable

250

to ours, and perhaps people like us. Naturally, he put a copy of the manuscript of this book, and two printed copies of it, in his secret cave.

One day, returning home from his weekly trip, he was arrested as he entered the city. His friend Gninroc was already in prison.

You must know that in those days the religion of Schad was the state religion. Some literal interpreters of the *Book of Oarnn* saw in Catta's work, abetted by the technical skills of Gnigroc, a blasphemous cosmology that denied the truth of the word of the great prophet. You have heard these words before: Ogatrac made use of the same charges against those who befriended you that the Church Elders of Catta's time used against him in his trial, and cited the same texts. Because Catta had thought of finding beauty beyond our little world, and goodness there, they cited this passage against him:

From beyond the sun come the forces of Evil, from beyond the sun come they. Evil dwells beyond the moon, in the dark firmament dwells she.

When he tried to defend himself by saying that they were misreading and misapplying the scripture, they asked him how he would know Oarnn if he saw him. Of course he had no ready answer. Their own reply to their question was simply another quotation:

By what sign will the Kolok know Oarnn? And he said unto me, "You will know me by the Truth, for I am Truth." And I said, "But I know not Truth, I know but my truth and my neighbor's truth, and her truth is not mine." And he answered, in his voice of thunder, "I am Truth, there is no Truth but me, no Truth but mine! Those who wish to know me must seek Truth in the writings I have inspired in you. I am Truth and Truth is me. Those who know not me know not Truth; those who know not Truth know not me." I saw that we must seek Truth not in the ways and the words of the Kolok but in the ways and the words of Oarnn.

251

His crimes were clear: he had sought knowledge and truth outside the teachings of Oarnn as recorded by Schad. He was reaching beyond the bounds to which knowledge was to be limited. And because Catta had lent his support to new theories that suggested that the Kolok might have evolved from lower animals, a third crime was added: heresy.

And Oarnn spake unto me, and he said: "I have made you from the reeds of the fields, with reason to think. I have made you a world over which you are to extend your dominion. I have made you a sun to give its warmth to you. I have made you a firmament, so that you might enjoy its beauty. Behold all that surrounds you, all the creatures of the sea, all beings that soar in the heavens above you, all the things you see about you that walk or crawl on the face of Damos; I have made all this for you. From all eternity have I created them, and for you have I created them, that you might know my glory."

Catta had no right to legal assistance, no time to prepare for the trial. It took place on the day he was arrested, and the penalty was severe: solitary exile to an uninhabited volcanic island. Gninroc fared little better: he was stripped of his wealth and all rights and titles to his inventions; he was forbidden to continue working in the field he had pioneered; and he was exiled to a wasteland. Neither man survived for more than a year.

But while the telescope continued to exist, the Kolok were forbidden to use it to survey the heavens. Every copy of Catta's books and articles were destroyed, his house and all its documents were burned down before his eyes. Everything seemed lost. We had to start all over again.

Other sciences prospered over the centuries, but it was not until the iron grip of the Schadite Church was broken that we could once again turn the telescope to the skies and develop ever stronger ones. But we had lost 300 years in astronomical studies! It would have been worse if a child had not taken refuge in Catta's Cave to escape a surprisingly strong rainstorm 100 years ago. By chance she had a flashlight with her, and looked around the cave. She was surprised to see it had a real door off behind a little turning. Behind the door was the warehouse of Catta's research! My mother's discovery made my work possible.

A center for astronomical research was established near there, thanks to the efforts of my grandparents, and eventually I became director. The day that you landed on Unias, we had just received physical proof of its existence, thus vindicating the great astronomer's life work.

Thanks to you, we've been able to accelerate our learning. There's so much to learn! So little time before I die!

HALLUCINATIONS

"Lieutenant, what do our sensors report?"

April responded, "Commodore, the temperature currently ranges from 25° to 35°, depending on whether it's the sunny or dark side of the planet. Atmosphere is 95% of Earth density. Good mixture of nitrogen and oxygen, with some CO_2, possibly indicating organic life. There seems to have been some recent seismic activity. Surface water covers much of the planet. There are no radio waves or other indications of intelligent life."

"Too bad about that, but otherwise, it sounds like we can give it a whirl. I'm sure the crew would like to take a little working vacation down there. Even though we came through the Wormhole without incident this time, we've spent a good two years without leaving Constellation. Does my bridge staff agree?"

Hearing only cries of joy, Christina had Kwali notify the crew of the decision that had been made. The Kolok were almost beside themselves in anticipation of setting foot for the first time on a planet in a distant part of the galaxy. The plan, as usual, was to rotate personnel on the planet for initial stays of two days, until everyone had had an opportunity to have a brief holiday. Then, leaving only a skeleton crew of 50 on board, most of the almost 500 people traveling on Constellation (473 humans and 25 Kolok) would begin to explore the new planet. The standard procedure called for a preliminary survey that might take three months to complete; at the commanding officer's discretion, a longer stay would be permissible if the planet seemed like a good candidate for possible future colonization.

——

Captain's Log, 6 March 2860

I touched down on this planet, which we've named Stepladder, with a party of 50 (45 humans, 5 Kolok). Stepladder, or at least the coastal portion of the continent we are on and the ocean, has a rich plant life both in the water and on the ground. There is a kind of kelp in the water, which is not as saline as Earth oceans, but no other life forms that we could see without a microscope. On land there are moss and lichens. Again, we could not discern non-microscopic animal life. We will send unmanned surface and submarine craft out to do a preliminary search of the nearby ocean, and have already launched two robot aircraft, one to survey the continent we are on, the other to examine the planet as a whole.

The personnel are very happy to be able to walk around on this planet. The air is breathable, the temperature quite acceptable both to us and to our Kolok guests. We have located several sources of potable fresh water that has passed all the standard tests for purity.

Once all the Constellation crew and passengers have had two or three days of relatively free time on the surface, we will begin our formal exploration of the planet. By that time, the unmanned sea and aircraft should have given us an idea of the most interesting places to investigate. It might be that other parts of the planet are more–or less–developed than our bivouac area.

———

Captain's Log, 6 April 2860

We have begun our investigations on the north shore of a large continent in the southern hemisphere, just about a thousand kilometers from the equator. At first glance, this area looks similar to our original site. We have yet to find evidence of even primitive animal life, such as trilobites or sea-worms.

Exploration parties have been established. Lieutenant Han Lee, assisted by Dr. Tsepa Dub, is leading the geological party. Lieutenant Commander Strother Pulver, assisted by Dr. Siol Saats, is leading the biological party. Ensign Amadou Mgamba is in charge of Security. I am leading the surveying party, accompanied by Dr. Ecnelav Enohr. The leaders of these parties will file reports, as required by ordinary operating procedures.

Captain's Log, 20 April 2860

Today I aborted our mission on Stepladder for two reasons, of which the less important is that the state of development of this planet is a good three billion years from reaching the current state of Earth in terms of evolutionary development. We spent a week trying to discover the source of the unusually high levels of oxygen and nitrogen in the atmosphere, since it is clear that the relatively sparse microbial life forms are not capable of producing these elements. We had to abandon our search when we all returned in some haste to Constellation. This leads me to the second reason for aborting the mission.

At first, early in the morning three days ago, a half dozen members of the surveying team came down, unexpectedly, with high fevers; we teleported them up to Constellation's sick bay, putting them in the care of the Chief Medical Officer, Commander Mujama. By noon, another twenty or so people had become ill. I checked with the other expeditions, which reported similar findings. Their ill personnel were also teleported to Constellation.

I called a temporary halt to the expeditions, ordering the groups to meet at the point at which we had gone our separate ways. The leaders were instructed to teleport to Constellation anybody who became ill, pending our meeting, which took place yesterday evening. I was alarmed at what I learned: each expedition had been obliged to send about 25% of its personnel back to Constellation. Commander Mujama reported that her facilities were overcrowded, and that she had pressed anyone healthy enough into helping her care for the sick. Furthermore, while she had been able to control the fevers, there were alarming symptoms developing in almost all the patients, the most frightening of all being hallucinations that all seemed in some ways similar.

We decided by consensus to return to Constellation and to abort the mission. It seemed evident that the fever and other symptoms were caused by some alien microscopic creature, probably a virus or a bacterium. As a precaution, we had Colombina check the air in Constellation for such microbes, and we made sure that we would all be decontaminated — our clothing and our bodies would be thoroughly cleansed. This had, of course, been done with the infected crew members now in sick bay.

———

Captain's Log, 25 April 2860

What follows is an account of the fever and hallucinations suffered by Ensign Amadou Mgamba written in his own words, followed by further reports and discoveries.

I feel terribly warm, hot even, in my body. I have been perspiring for what seems like days. My head is aflame, my eyes ache. But the worst is what I hear, or think I hear, when I drift off to something resembling sleep. The voices come back, terrifyingly persistent. They speak in a marching cadence, repeating threatening phrases that are never completed:

"You are our prisoner you will tell us everything you know about... You are our prisoner you will tell us everything you know about..."

It's persistent. It seems to last for hours. They speak in a flat monotone. I have the sense that I'm losing my mind. I'm afraid to try to sleep, because it always comes back.

These voices, I hear them, but I don't see who's speaking. I think that's what makes it so terrifying, I can't see them.

Reports from all the subjects are similar; only the content or the medium differs. Some people report hearing snatches of menacing music, for some accompanied by unintelligible words; other people are beset with voices or machines that present terrifying technological situations (a machine that threatens to kill its owner, for instance, or an intelligent planet that uses technology to capture passing humans); still others (mostly ELBers) are suffering delusions of being accused of having committed unspecified heinous crimes in the distant past. These hallucinations are, for all the patients, the worst part of the

258

disease. The specific subject matter of each person's hallucinations is closely related to his or her professional orientation or personal life.

We believe that the strange cadence of the dreams might be related to the hum of activity in the sick bay itself: the very machines that are keeping our patients alive seem to be at the root of the hallucinations. Perhaps, too, the hum of Constellation's engines might be for some the source of the background march-like cadence. It is worth noting that all these hallucinations are non-pictorial.

The cause of the hallucinatory fever appears to be a virus that attacks the central nervous system, entering the brain from the spinal cord. This might have implications for any injection developed in the future. No permanent damage to the brain has been noted in any patient. We have not yet discovered this virus, however.

———

Captain's Log, 27 April 2860

Every crew member has been hit by this strange illness. Some have recovered, others have passed the crisis point, but about 350, including Commander Mujama and her entire staff, are still very ill. Oddly, I have not been touched by this disease; neither have the Kolok, who have been helping care for the sick.

With the aid of Lieutenant Commander Strother Pulver and Dr. Siol Saats, I have been able to develop a protocol for investigating the cause of this disease. For one experiment we have obtained blood samples from all of the Kolok, from myself, and from all the recovered humans. For the second experiment, we have obtained blood samples from 50 of the ill, in various stages of this disease.

We found three distinct types of antibodies in the healthy and recovered persons: one for the humans, a quite different one for the Kolok, and a third one for me. We had expected that the Kolok and the humans would have different antibodies, but did not anticipate a separate kind unique to me. We will be investigating this strange situation. The antibodies led us to the virus-like creature responsible for the disease, which we are trying to neutralize.

We tried to see if the Kolok's antibody, which is obviously robust, since it attacked the virus directly and prevented disease, could be used in human subjects. Test-tube experiments indicated that this antibody would be rejected by host humans. We also tried a second line of inquiry, believing that a safe alternative might be a serum containing an enhanced version of the human antibody. Colombina was able to produce this, which we have injected into fifteen consenting subjects. We expect to have some results in a day or two. A third experiment was to use my antibody in some subjects, if laboratory tests indicated it would be safe. The tests being positive, fifteen more consenting subjects were chosen. Again, we will have to await results, which should come in within a day or two.

Despite high fevers, often in excess of $40°$, we have suffered no casualties. Some patients, however, have been extremely slow to recover, and the symptoms described in the log entry of 25 April have not abated in these persons.

———

Captain's Log, 29 April 2860

All the test subjects injected with serum containing human antibodies are recovering; the five injected directly in the spine made a more rapid recovery, 24 hours vs. 36 hours for the others, who received the serum in their veins. Results for those injected with serum containing my antibodies produced almost identical results. We are now proceeding to treat every remaining patient with serum as soon as it is produced.

In a conversation with Dr. Ecnelav Enohr, I believe I discovered the reason why my antibodies are different from those of the other humans. I record here the relevant portions of that conversation.

"Ecnelav, I continue to be disturbed by the fact that my antibodies are so different from all the other humans'. It doesn't make sense to me. I mean, it can't be because I'm an ELBer, since about half the crew have had their lives extended."

"Christina, is there something in your life's history that might explain this? I don't mean anything to do with extended life; I mean something else."

"Hmm. Something else. I've surely been to more places than anyone on board. Not only the colonized planets and the space stations, but all those planets I've been to, throughout my career, that we have catalogued, a bit like Stepladder. Maybe I picked up something there."

"If you did, it doesn't show in your blood, which seems like everyone else's, except for the antibody."

"Are you on to something, or is this just a line of inquiry, a way to stimulate my thinking, or my memory?"

"Well, it's a bit of both. I'm trying to stimulate your thinking and your memory, and also my own. It seems to me that among all the adventures you have had, there must be something connected with aliens."

"There are the Kolok, but I don's see the connection."

"That's not what I had in mind. I recollect that somewhere you had a terrible accident that left you paralyzed. Somehow you got over that, because here you are, hale and hearty, ready to live another 360 years or more, to all appearances."

"You're right about an accident. On Paracelsus I was hit by scads of rocks that tore my body apart. Every organ, so it seemed, had to be rebuilt. My bones, so many of them were broken. The worst was my spinal cord, which was severed in two locations."

"That's it, that's what made your reaction so different from the other humans': the reconstruction of your spinal cord."

"What do you mean? A little bit of frog nerves and... and nerves from a little scurrying thing. An alien presence in my body, persisting for all this time, well over a century! Ecnelav, you've got it! Somehow, it was that creature's cells that must have produced the antibody before my human cells could do the job. And they must have worked fast, very fast, because I never had the slightest symptom."

"Just like us. None of us had any symptoms, either."

"Ah, you're a genius, Ecnelav! You've solved what for me was a serious problem. I was beginning to think I was something of a freak. But you've found a perfectly logical explanation for my curious situation. Paracelsus! Little scurrier, I owe you a second debt of gratitude. You helped me get whole again, and you prevented me from suffering like my shipmates. Thank you, thank you."

———

Captain's Log, 12 May 2860

Every member of the crew has recovered. We are conducting, under Commander Kwali's direction, a thorough cleansing of every area of the ship before we proceed. So far it appears that on the first sweep we had managed to eradicate any trace of the virus. Or perhaps it could not exist outside of a living organism.

An interesting discovery concerning the way the virus works also helps solve another problem. The virus somehow manages to render certain compounds associated with neurotransmitters unstable. Some of the neurotransmitter molecules break down, and in the process release oxygen atoms. This explains simultaneously the mechanism that allowed the hallucinations to take place and how the planet could have the high level of oxygen that we encountered. In turn, this suggests that some sort of animal-type life must exist on Stepladder, life forms that we were unable to discover, unless the organisms simply attacked various amino acids that abound on the planet.

We must make sure that every person on board is up to maximum physical capacity before we continue on our way home. To this end I have been personally observing every person's physical training, and have ordered special meals to build up resistance to further exposure to diseases.

———

Captain's Log, 6 June 2860

The following conversation, involving Commander Kwali, Dr. Enohr and me, was recorded in the conference room of the Bridge yesterday.

"Commodore, given the direction we have taken, I note that we will pass within a few light years of Paracelsus. Would it be untoward to suggest that we make a slight deviation in our course and alight there? We could give our guests a first-hand view (or first-eye view) of a colony planet, perhaps including a stop at Christina's Rock and another on Prison Island. It's been a long time since you have been back there; and I'm curious to see my home planet again, as are the score of Paracelsans on board. We all imagine it is a quite different place from what it was when we were last there, even if it's only a question of 20 years or so."

"Oh, Christina, what a wonderful idea Kwali has! I think I can speak for all my people when I say we'd love to get this first-eye view of an Earth colony planet. And we'd be sure it is not contaminated by that Stepladder virus. The things you've told us about the natural life and the geology there sound fascinating. And, frankly, the boredom of space travel that you warned us about has set in. We're ready for some adventure!"

"Have you two gotten together on this? I can see by the expression on your faces that you have. Actually, I have already checked this out with our entire navigational staff and with Colombina. Given our original orders, we can spare some time on Paracelsus, somewhere between five and ten weeks, and still reach Earth within the projected time span. That would give us plenty of time to renew acquaintances, visit new spots and old ones, and if possible include excursions for those who want them to Prison Island and the place that you're calling Christina's Rock, Commander."

"Hey, I didn't make up the name. It's an officially designated parkland now. According to Colombina, the site is no longer barren and arid as it was when your accident occurred some 140 years ago, Commodore. There and elsewhere on the planet there are trees, even groves of trees, grassy dells, rivulets. I guarantee that you won't be reminded, at least not in the same way, about your experiences there in the past."

"I suppose it's no surprise that you know more about your own planet than I do. Well, I'm all for the idea. But first, I'll have to call a meeting of the senior staff to get their input. We do have obligations to Earth Government, and we must make sure that our guests are properly introduced to life on the home planet. But I must admit that introducing them to our civilization as it has been adapted on Paracelsus is an intriguing idea. If the staff approves of this plan, we'll make the slight deviation required."

This morning, the senior staff approved of our going to Paracelsus for a period of six to eight weeks. Our course has been altered accordingly.

NUMAMBA'S GAMBLE

"Det, Stanley's death has made me think a lot about our future here in Canaan. What do you think?"

"Hmmm. Yes."

"Dr. Stisreg, put down that book and listen to me. I have to talk to you."

"What? Oh. I'm sorry, Numamba. I'm reading a great old story from over a thousand years ago, written in the French of that era. *Jacques le Fataliste*, by a guy named Diderot. Have you ever read it? I think I finally learned how to handle that ancient language. It's about whether or not we have free will, or if everything we do is predetermined for us. OK, the book's down. What's up?"

"Will you ever stop making puns? Listen, Stanley's assassination has affected me greatly, even now, more than 50 years after the fact."

"Yes, I know. It's affected me terribly, too. He was like a father to me, like the one I never knew. Did I ever tell you how we met?"

"Never directly. There were always allusions to some dark secret in the past. Something you never wanted me to know. I've been waiting for hundreds of years to find out something about that part of your life. Your pre-existence, so to speak."

"OK, time for a confession. He picked me up, literally, from the gutter of a street in Sandstone, on Mesnos. I was a rambunctious teenager, in revolt against society. I had gotten my hands on drugs, had begun stealing to pay for them, and would have slipped into a life of crime except for him. When he came upon me, the scene could not have been appetizing. I was unconscious and beaten, robbed. I was lying in the street, with puffed up lips and black eyes. Blood here and there. He picked me up, took me in, put me through detoxification, got me to be clean and honest. He gave me something to live for, Numamba, dreams to dream, an intoxication not with sardon but with the quest for knowledge. Knowledge and service. He made it possible for me to appreciate you. My life was all about me until he took me out of a nightmare.

"Then he made sure I got a proper education. He trusted me: no one had done that since my parents had died in a terrible accident and I was left to my own devices, in a strange land, at the age of 15. He made sure I got a good education at a university on Earth, the University of Dar es Salam. That was before he became a fugitive himself, on some trumped-up charges."

"Trumped up?"

"OK, not trumped up. He had extended his life and mine illegally. But you know that part of the story."

"My story is similar, but more roundabout. I've never told you all the facts about it. I entered Stanley's life via that friend of Christina's, Boris Smirnoff. When he bumped into me in a bar on Earth, in Brazzaville, I was in the same state as you were. But I was a girl, and I was suspicious of any man who came near me. I didn't trust him. How could I? You know the terrible life I had led up to then. Poverty. Abandonment. Drugs. Prostitution. I couldn't trust any man, and I couldn't trust any woman either. But I was in no condition to argue with this guy who told me he had a friend on Mars who would help me. Somehow I believed him. Maybe it was the adventure of coming to Mars."

"Or maybe you had burned out your brain so much that you'd believe anything."

"Be quiet or I'll bop you one. Boris (or Alexander Romanov, as he called himself then) brought me to Mars and introduced me to Stanley. You had just recently left for university life on Earth, so we didn't meet for a few years. I could feel my suspicions rising again. Isolated house. Middle-aged man, teenaged girl. I was a bit scared, especially when I learned he was growing herbs to use as drugs; I thought he used his herbs to make sardon. I wanted to get clean. I wanted to become what I could be, as Boris told me Stanley would make it possible for me to do.

"Still, there was something about him that let me lower my guard, a part of Stanley that few people have ever known. You and me and Christina. I don't think anyone else ever knew the real Stanley Narb. When I learned he was 'Dr. Narb,' and not just some old guy coming on to me, and when he offered me the

266

chance to live a better life, I moved in with him. And he made me understand that not all men are vicious bastards. He made it possible for me to appreciate you. And he had me clean up my act."

"You're right. I was away at university then. He told me that a girl about my age was living in the house, and assured me that I'd like her. Was he ever right!"

"I felt the same way. Eventually we found out what his secret experiments were all about. You must have learned something about his mysterious experiments from your friends at the university. I found out accidentally, stumbling across some of his notebooks when I was packing to go to university. You had been sworn to secrecy. At first, I was mad at you for not telling me anything about that. And he wasn't able to extend my life for years, until we were able to move here to Canaan."

"You'll never know how much I wanted to be able to tell someone!"

"Well, I ended up admiring you for being able to keep as quiet as a clam, and learned how important it is to do that at times. Even after we were able to have his trial invalidated, we really had to keep a secret of his past, our pasts, the nature of the set-up here."

"We were his second and third experiments with the 500-year extension, the only ones who never had the 200-year treatment first. He was of course his own first subject for the 500-year extension, and Christina his fourth. And there have been no others. But we've added a few recruits to the ELB."

"Speaking of the ELB, have you noticed that there are almost no new members?"

"Numamba, I heard on one of the channels that there is talk of disbanding the ELB. No need for us any more, what with the latest craft in the fleet, and with a new quantum-drive ship in the planning stages."

"Quantum drive? Get rid of the ELB, or let it die a natural death? You've got to be kidding!"

"No, actually, when you think of it, the two ideas fit together. Suppose a quantum-drive spaceship gets beyond the drawing board. People could zip around the galaxy in seconds—

or rather in no time at all! The power demands would be enormous, and the technical demands might be even greater, but who would have thought that the matter-transport teleportation system would be replaced by a quantum teleportation system?"

"I guess you could say it's a first step to a quantum-drive spaceship. But quantum teleportation is still effective only at relatively close range, a few kilometers, I think."

"Not *effective*, Numamba, but *safe* and *proven* up to a few kilometers, maybe 20. I know that the Constellation mission is experimenting with inert objects at distances of up to 100 kilometers initially, more if they're repeatedly successful at that range. When Christina comes back, she'll fill us in."

"But suppose she doesn't come back, and suppose something happens to you, or to me. Eventually, you know we'll be alone, after the last of the ELBers dies, if you're right that Earth Government will phase out the process."

"Well, yes, but that's in the order of things. We'd have a strange stature, until that terrible last year, a stature of being immortal. Until then, even if it's just you or just me among the ten or twelve billion people scattered around our little corner of the galaxy, we'll be happy, I think, in our state. And then, who knows? With luck we can go on longer."

"You make it sound so romantic. You make me want to become immortal, or quasi-immortal."

"Hey, it's just a dream, Numamba."

"Dream or no dream, it sounds just terrific! Numamba the Immortal. Just imagine the kind of conversations I could engage in. 'How old are you, Dr. Stisreg?' 'Oh, let's see, next month will be my 1,200th birthday. Do you want to celebrate with me?' What a joy to contemplate!"

"My dear wife, has your mind taken a vacation? This is the real world, down here, see?"

"My dear husband, with another 500 years, I could make it easily to 1,150, and who says there can't be more!"

"You can't be serious, Numamba. All our experiments in that line have failed. Two operations seem to be all that any creature can take. In fact, one operation, if the first one is for the longest term. No creature has ever survived the operation after the longest extension, the equivalent of 500 years in human terms, no creature has been able to live through such an extension. There seems to be a natural limit to extended life."

"You're not sounding like our adoptive father. He would push things to the limit, and beyond. Wake up, Det! Be bold! Be creative!"

"Numamba, your eyes have that glow in them that spells the end of discussion. You're going to want to do this. I refuse to go along with you on this unless within a couple of years we can come up with an experimental animal who lives through it. Even a worm! I don't want to run the risk of losing you to some half-thought-out experiment."

"OK, you're on. One success, and it'll be my turn."

"I don't like it. This can only spell trouble. But I'll do my best to help you with your experiments. And I promise that I'll do whatever I can to make them work. Some of our herbs have recently increased the rate of success of ordinary extended life with our grasshoppers, that have been resistant to the process. Maybe if this is injected into the blood or the tissue of other creatures..."

"Oh, Det, I knew I could count on you, even if you are overly cautious! When do we start? Tomorrow?"

"Hey, first we have to draw up our plan, map out all our variables, line up the most likely subjects, try to maximize the potential of success. We'll have to re-examine the data from the centuries of experiments we've already completed so as to avoid duplicating any errors we might find and to see if there was a step or two in the process that might have improved chances of success. If that's what you mean by tomorrow, no problem. But it might take a good year for tomorrow to get here."

"After that, we'll see where our new experiments will take us. I'm thrilled by the prospect of starting."

"Numamba, Numamba, don't forget that we're still working on important matters concerning life on Mars. Creating a more Earth-like gravitational field. Bringing the tectonics to the point where more heat is generated in the core of Mars, and where gasses are emitted to make the atmosphere somewhat denser and warmer. Perhaps steadying the planet's swaying and wobbling, to make the seasons more predictable and more regular. We've made progress in these fields, but we have to do more. That's our primary job."

"Sure, along with training more and more herbalists so that eventually the Reservation can get along without us on this score. The ADPs seem finally to have taken to the idea of experimental herb farms for medicine and also for food and flavorings. But we have plenty of spare time, even with all that. I'm so excited! I'm determined to get this to work this time around."

"All right, all right, we have of our own free will decided to start tomorrow, as redefined. Now I want to exercise my free will again to go back to my deterministic friend and his story."

"Oof! another pun. If I had any free will I'd want to bop you one."

Extracts from Numamba's Telelog Entries from 2860

1 March

Almost a year gone by since we began working on a second maximum extended life. Det has been keeping his word: he's been doing his best not only with setting up some of the experiments, but also in working on herbs to deliver natural chemicals to the animals' bodies. We've come up short, though. 700 worms in two species, all dead in hours. The grasshoppers, one of our best hopes, all 2,000 of them, dead in 3 to 24 hours. Our 75 laboratory mice and our 18 field mice, all dead inside of a week. There's some hope, though: three of our salamanders have lived beyond a week, the longest stretch so far. Not a good percentage, it's true: we tried out 105 of them. But what's this? All of them used a combination of extracts from basil, tarragon, and oregano, mixed in with St. John's Wort and a few other garden herbs. They're still being fed that. And look at them scamper around! I've never seen them so active!

Hmm, we've been using a lot of those herbs these past two months. Maybe I should give it a try. Det won't like it, though. I promised not to do anything rash, not until our results are demonstratedly sound and replicated. Still Numamba the rebellious teenager? Yes, but who am I rebelling against? Det? No. I'm really rebelling against that Numamba I've become, the one who doesn't want to take chances, who doesn't want anything to happen to her. I need to show her that I am still an adventurous person, willing to take risks. I know that Stanley would agree with Det on this matter. Don't rush into things!

But can I wait? No, this is my one and only chance for a while. If this works, we'll perhaps have found a more natural way to live a life that's unnaturally long. Nice paradox. I'll compromise and wait until tomorrow morning. I'll still have enough time, before Det comes back from his business on Venus, to recover from the procedure. A month to see if everything has worked, and if not, another month for the second procedure to run its course. I remember Stanley saying that he had had 100% success the second try. Of course, that was with the shorter-term procedure, and the first time around only. With him and Christina as the only persons to have undergone a double procedure, he had a 100% success rate. If I succeed, I'll have a 100% success rate with a double-maximum procedure.

If.

Think positively, Numamba. When. When I succeed. And I will succeed with myself just as I've succeeded with these three salamanders. At seven tomorrow morning, it all begins. Then we'll wait and see.

1 May

The pain is horrible. Is that what our subject animals had to live through? The thought of their suffering is terrible. No more experiments on them. Just on me. Too bad the first attempt didn't take. Ouch! Oooh! My head! My back! From right inside my spine! Aah! went away. Breathe deep, Numamba.

The month has gone by. I'm ready for my second try. Tissue samples taken from all over. Worked on the appropriate gene.

The little salamanders are still scampering about. Looks promising. Now to get on with the injection. Maybe the first time I didn't do it absolutely right. Maybe I should have made sure I hit the nerve. It did sting, but it didn't hurt in the same way it did when I had my first procedure, without which I wouldn't be alive to do this one.

Serum tested out strong. OK. A bit of calm now. Remember to get it well within the nerve. Maybe I should inject at a somewhat more oblique angle. That's it, it might have been the angle. Not enough of the serum got into the nerve. Make sure you don't shake; hold steady. That's better. Nothing to be nervous about. Squeeze down, now. Ow! OK. It's done. Now to wait and see.

8 May

Two of the salamanders died overnight. Only one left. They lived for just over six weeks. Doesn't bode well for me. Maybe I rushed a bit too much. No, that can't be: a week after the second try, I still feel fine. That pain has gone. I feel strangely keyed up, hardly able to contain myself. I don't seem to need more than 3 or 4 hours of sleep. My log looks odd since the second injection last week. Improved health. Skin tone looks good. Eyes are clear. Intellectual abilities really heightened. Made a breakthrough on two fronts: the wobble and the atmosphere. The results are already noticeable with the wobble, which has really calmed down a lot; and there are clear signs that the atmosphere is getting a bit denser, less like Earth at 3000 meters, more like what it is at 2500 meters. That might be coming from something else, though. Perhaps gases spread from the increased seismic activity we've been noticing. But I think it's from the new formulation I've worked out. I've put a long summary on Det's computer. I won't say a word to him about it. Let him discover the phenomenon and the notations on his own. It'll be funny to see his face when he realizes I got on my own what the two of us have been working on for 25 years!

15 May

The third salamander died, a week after the other two. Odd. I see in my notes that they were all unusually active after the operation until just a few hours before their death. Running around, catching insects, climbing, jumping with extraordinaty energy. This behavior went on for days, even weeks. Suddenly, the cameras caught them stopping almost in mid-step. They began to mope around, as if tired. They seemed to spend a lot of time sleeping. They moved very slowly, as if dragging themselves around. No appetite. Breathing seemed to become difficult. Then they spun around a few times, and stopped in their tracks. They were dead.

Can that be what will happen to me, translated to human terms? I wonder if my heightened acuteness and—let's face it—my hyperactivity are in some way related to what happened to them. I have never felt quite like this before; even in my worst days, before Boris rescued me, when I was high on drugs, it was different.

This has me worried.

If there is a parallel, it will be clear that I made a terrible mistake. An irreversible one. Instead of living longer, I'll die sooner. Was it worth it?

29 May

This last week has been hell. I feel as though my bones are turning into gelatin, or more likely, cartilage. My muscle tone is down. Can't do my daily routine. I'm spending more time resting, sleeping. Can't seem to get my work done. Haven't had the curiosity or the energy to check out results on the wobble and the atmospheric density problems. My pulse has slowed down. My heartbeat is a little irregular. A slight blueish hue has discolored the skin near my eyes. I have been increasing doses of the herbal drink. Things are bad. I've got to write a letter to Det to tell him about this. No, the logs tell it all, the written ones and the telelogs, like this one.

I'm sure now that my gamble has not paid off. I can only hope to hold out a couple of weeks. Maybe Det knows a trick or two that I don't. Det, I wish you were here. I need you now. Come on home.

A dull headache. I'll let Hélène know what to do with the shop and sleep a bit.

6 June

Det should be home in a couple of days. I hope I'll live long enough to see him one more ti...

RETURN TO PARACELSUS

"Ecnelav, you'll hardly believe the information Colombina just passed on to me about Paracelsus."

"I've become so accustomed to the amazing since we began our journey to Earth, Christina, or really ever since we first saw your party appear and disappear on Unias, that I'm almost at the point of believing anything at all. But try me out this time: maybe I won't believe you."

"Colombina, will you please repeat, for Ecnelav's benefit, what you just told me about Paracelsus?"

"Yes, Christina. Paracelsus, within less than 150 years, has become a very habitable planet, with a climate akin to that on Damos or Venus, and with an abundant growth of plant life. It was virtually a desert when Christina and her party visited it in 2720. They set in motion processes that have led to frequent rainfall throughout the planet; they have planted Earth plants that have prospered, and that in some cases have pollinated or been pollinated by native plants; the Earth animal life forms they left behind have found their niches alongside the native life forms; this world has changed character radically.

"In addition, Prison Island's population of hard-core Militia cadre has dwindled from 1,067 persons to about 40. The last persons sentenced to exile there left Mesnos in 2802. At that time the youngest prisoner was 35 years old, and if still alive she is 94; the oldest on the island was at that time already over 100, and he is now presumed dead. We cannot be much more accurate than this, since the prisoners are reluctant to communicate with Earth Government.

"The population of Paracelsus has grown to over ten million, who live in the two large cities and the numerous large farms in the only inhabited continent, called New Asia. About 10,000 settlers arrive on a regular schedule every year, to begin a new life on the land-grant farms or in the cities, where there is a great need for workers of all sorts."

"Thank you very much, Colombina. I'm going to turn off my computer now, so I'll say good-bye."

"Colombina signing off."

"The growth of that planet seems phenomenal, Christina, especially since it is so far from Earth."

"That's true, but we do have considerable experience by now, since we colonized three other planets before Paracelsus. I have to admit being amazed by how fast cities went up on Mesnos, and I assume that the technologies and the techniques that made rapid growth possible there have been updated and applied to Paracelsus. And we have quite a fleet of Constellation-class spacecraft now, which makes transporting colonists possible."

"There was something that Colombina said that makes me wonder a bit. Earth people live to be 125 to 150 years of age. It appears that most of the prisoners would be over 100, given that the youngest one is 94, and that the island was already populated when she arrived."

"Well? I don't get your point, Ecnelav."

"If people are 100 years of age, and have reached about 75% or 80% of maximum life expectancy, how vigorous are they? I mean, ordinary people, not you ELBers."

"Mujama's just about 100 years old. She's in sort of late middle age, perhaps the beginning of elder status. But it must be the same on Damos: people live to be 150 or so there, so figure what it's like for you if you were a few years older than us."

"I hadn't thought of it that way, but what you say is logical, Christina."

"I take that as a high compliment, coming from a Kolok. Now, are you and your group ready to visit Paracelsus? There'll be some formal government parties, and visits throughout the planet."

"When will we arrive? We're all getting really excited, especially since we're sure that Paracelsus won't have the deadly virus we encountered on Stepladder. We'll be ready for officialdom, and we'll be thrilled to see what the place looks like. Hmm. Will we be able to visit the Prison Island? And what about the place where your accident occurred?"

"About Christina's Rock, or whatever it's called now, if the place is still maintained, no problem; actually, I'd like to make a pilgrimage there myself. But as far as the prison is concerned, we'll have to yield to whatever the local Paracelsus government allows. Makes me shiver just to think about it, though: the Militia has always been so full of hatred and anger, much of it directed towards me, because my groups were charged with eradicating them. A lot of the people on Prison Island are there because I had them sent there. They might well want to injure or even kill me if I go there. Still, 59 years have gone by since the last ones arrived. Maybe they've changed for the better."

"So we'll see about that when we land. If we're given permission to visit the island, you would probably be wise not to accompany us."

"It would be interesting to see what kind of self-government they devised over the years, and what they have become. I think I'll join you if permission is granted. But of course we'll have to teleport down first."

"And when will that take place?"

"I'll tell you what. I'm due on the Bridge in about ten minutes. Why not come with me? Maybe they have information that they've gotten from Colombina or from other sources."

"Oh, sounds like a great idea!"

————

"Commodore Christina Vasa here, aboard Constellation."

"Lieutenant Hue Sangok responding from New Edo."

"I have a crew of 473 and 25 visitors from a distant planet, Damos, across the galaxy..."

"[Gulp!]"

"We seek permission to enter into and to maintain a fixed orbit above New Edo, and to teleport down."

"Yes, sir. I have to check with Captain Marlowe first."

"Is Captain Marlowe's first name Mariko?"

"Yes, sir."

"Lieutenant Hue, can you put Captain Mariko Marlowe on the visuscreen? I would like to speak with her. Please contact me in fifteen minutes. Commodore Vasa out."

"Hey, did you hear that?" gasped Hue to the entire command crew that had gathered about his visuscreen. "That was Christina Vasa herself! And did you see that tall bald person next to her? That must be one of the inhabitants of that planet, Damos. They found an intelligent alien civilization! There **IS** intelligent life out there! Across the galaxy!"

The near pandemonium of the command room brought Captain Marlowe out of her office. She was a short but athletic woman whose apparent youth seemed to belie her rank. A sure sign that she was an ELBer. As commander of the military unit on Paracelsus, she wielded considerable power, and worked with the Central Government as well as with the various city and town Police Departments.

"What's going on out here? Did somebody have a baby?"

"No, sir, but..." The din of ten people trying to explain what had happened to cause the uproar made communication impossible. Finally, Hue was able to calm people down. He said, "It would be best if you saw it for yourself on the visuscreen, sir."

"Christina!" shouted Mariko, recognizing her old friend. "And what we can assume to be intelligent aliens!"

"Yes, sir, both of those things have gotten us excited! Commodore Vasa is a legend to us, and she's succeeded in this spectacular quest. We never thought we'd ever get to see her or to meet her, and as far as meeting aliens is concerned...!"

"Your excitement is not misplaced. But we have to get things done. Put me through to the Governor on his hot line. I must speak with him at once. Then we'll have to contact Commodore Vasa on Constellation. What are you waiting for, Sangok? Get hold of the Governor now!"

———

Governor Sven Svenson IV, a middle-aged descendant of Christina's school chum from long ago, was a tall, blue-eyed, blond man whose almost perpetual smile and generally cheerful demeanor hid a serious mind and a strong personality. He was a remarkably successful administrator on this planet, whose millions of inhabitants were virtually all rugged individualists. Somehow, he had managed to instill in the planetary conscience a sense of working for the common weal while building the kind of life that is possible only in remote corners of human populations. Perhaps his wife was partly responsible for his success. Ilse Jorgensen seemed to be equally comfortable with miners and ranchers, farmers and factory workers, government officials and intellectuals, the wealthy and the less well off (there was no poverty in this land of opportunity for everyone), old settlers and new arrivals, individualists and communitarians. Tall, blue-eyed and blonde like her husband, Ilse was a handsome woman in early middle age. She traveled tirelessly, meeting many of the Paracelsans in their homes, bringing cheer, advice, aid, and messages of hope to all her compatriots.

It was an extraordinary coincidence that one of Christina's friends from the time of her later trips to Mesnos to complete the campaign against the Militia, Mariko Marlowe, had just recently been named commander of the military unit on Paracelsus, shortly after the Svensons arrived. Sven had for years wanted to meet the legendary Christina Vasa, friend of his equally-legendary ancestor, who had become if not President of the Earth Government, a long-time Senator and cabinet minister. And so a look of disbelief crossed his face when Mariko announced that Christina was about to teleport down, accompanied by a delegation from Constellation and a delegation of aliens from a distant planet.

"Is this another of your practical jokes, Mariko? The last I heard, Christina was sent across the galaxy; nobody has seen her for a good ten years. She probably died in an accident at a wormhole or in some unfriendly planet."

"Sven, this is no joke. I've just spoken with her, seen her on a visuscreen. Come over here, with Ilse, just as soon as you can. We're planning an informal welcoming celebration, prior to a more formal gathering later."

"We'll be over with a group from the government offices. In an hour."

"For our part, we'll turn out as many people as we can, and we'll ask Christina to teleport down almost everybody except a minimal crew that will remain on board the spacecraft."

———

The teleportations continued for a good stretch of time. Finally, all who would be coming down on the first round – everyone but the unlucky few who were needed on board –had materialized on the surface. They formed an imposing group, over 450 of them, in a kind of meadow or open field located within a park in the center of New Edo, the capital city of Paracelsus. They looked about them. The trees were tall and green against the deep blue sky. Flowers–Earth flowers– appeared to be in blossom everywhere. Insects and scurriers rushed here and there across the grass, while birds flew individually or in flocks overhead. The day was calm and warm.

Beyond the verdant stretches of the park and the delicious aromas that wafted to the travel-weary wanderers from all the life they saw and heard around them rose the tall buildings, the elevated roadways, the glistening hallmarks of 29th-century Earth culture. New Edo was an ultra-modern, but distinctly human, city, its exuberant, Baroque-like asymmetry so different from the meticulously logical and mathematically constructed buildings and public spaces that could be found all over Damos. Both beautiful in different ways, both powerful and exciting, once the esthetic keys were found. The Kolok had been intellectually prepared for what they were to see, they had viewed countless images on the three-dimensional visuscreens, but they were unprepared for the rapturous effect of the first live experience of this aspect of Earth civilization.

But they had little time to discuss that, for coming forward to meet them was a large party consisting of the Governor and his wife, the Commander of the planetary military presence, the President and other officers of the fledgling university, and their entourages, dignitaries and ordinary people alike.

Governor Sven Svenson made the first address, inviting the humans and their Kolok guests to Paracelsus, expressing delight that the inhabitants of this small colony should be the first humans to welcome an alien race to their soil, and ending with a personal note in which he revealed to Christina his direct desendance from her old friend from so long ago.

Christina, taken by surprise by this news, thanked the Governor for his welcome and hoped to have the occasion to reminisce with him about her friend Sven. She then introduced Ambassador Ecnelav Enohr, who said a few words on her own in English, then switched on the translation machine. She presented the Governor with a pair of dog-like lizards that were the most common house pets on Damos.

Captain Mariko Marlowe advanced, greeting Christina personally, and then welcomed her and all the people on Constellation to New Edo, and had a reception set up for the entire group, which numbered about 800. It was a perfect situation for people to get to know one another and to renew old acquaintances. The Paracelsans had thousands of questions concerning the current expedition of Constellation, and were in awe over the tall and gracious people of Damos.

Arrangements were made for everyone to spend the night with the Edoans, and to attend a major and more formal celebration the following day.

———

"Mariko, how wonderful to see you here, with your promotion, and with such delightful colleagues."

"Delightful, and superb. I was so excited when I saw you on the visuscreen. That's one of the down parts of being in the ELB: all too often we make friends we might never meet again, even though we live to a ripe old age!"

"And I can't tell you how hard it was to hold my enthusiasm when I learned that you were the C.O. here. It was not in our directive to make a side trip to Paracelsus on the way home. We were expected to head straight for Earth if we encountered intelligent life elsewhere. But the Damosians and the crew wanted to come here. We have about 20 Paracelsans on board, you know."

"Commodore, we are thrilled that you decided to come. In my family you're something of a legend, you know. The pranks that you and my ancestor played on one another are almost mythical."

"And," added Ilse, "probably exaggerated beyond belief. Commodore, did you really ever lock Sven in a closet containing only a virtual ski machine?"

"Well, that one is true. He had sneaked into the gym one day, and hid when I came in to go 'skiing'. He teased me mercilessly about my falling down so often! One day, I secretly moved the machine into a very small room, fixed its setting at such a level that he'd be constantly falling, and also secretly hooked up a means of recording the scene. I figured that after a while, when he realized that he'd not get out soon, he'd pass the time of day by using the machine. He fell for my explanation of why the machine had been moved (I said it was because I wanted to be able to practice without being observed), and then he went in. He was there for hours! I still have that disk, and if you're interested, I'll get it for you. It's a scream!"

"Oh, we'd love to see it, Commodore!"

"Please call me Christina. I feel more comfortable to be called by my name in informal circumstances."

"Very well, Christina it will be, and Sven and Ilse, too. We've heard several allusions to experiences you and Mariko had on Mesnos back around 2800, when we were little children. Now that you're both here together, would you be willing to share a reminiscence or two with us? Since you knew Sven until his death, there's not much we can add; but when your story is told we'll do what we can to fill in whatever gaps you have."

"It's a deal. I was, at that time, a Captain, and Mariko was a Lieutenant Commander."

"You mean you've only been promoted a grade or two in all that time? That's terrible!"

"When we joined the ELB we were told that promotions would come slowly, and that we'd have to be patient. I am impatient for a promotion for one of my staff, though, who replaced Martin as Chief of Security but is still an Ensign. Any chance the Commanding Officer would consider promoting Ensign Amadou Mgamba to a permanent rank of Lieutenant junior grade and to a temporary rank of Lieutenant senior grade?

I am not authorized to promote my crew, but I am permitted to make such requests."

"If the Captain of Constellation makes a formal request, it will be honored."

"And we'll be honored by your story."

———

"Mariko, where's the rest of our team?"

"I'm not sure, Christina. Blinko and Tamara have been captured by the Militia."

"More fodder for the wolks and the stots."

"You really think they've killed them?"

"They say proudly that they have no jails, and that they take no prisoners. You saw what happened to Ali Akbar's squad."

"Yes, it was horrible. Severed limbs, decapitated corpses which were then left to to wolks and the stots. Nothing left but sun-whitened bones."

"They're even crueller than they were when Boris blew up the underground settlement."

"They're certainly more desperate. If we can wipe out these guys, Christina, we should have them all. It'll be all over!"

"Don't celebrate yet. First, we haven't wiped them out here. And second, there are–or were–a few stragglers left on Mars. Maybe our forces have eliminated them there."

"I don't like this situation we're in, Christina. The méki bush doesn't provide much cover."

"I have a feeling of déjà vu, or déjà entendu, as though I've had this conversation before. With Boris. Actually, it's more that I know this place. I've been here before; I recognize that small building there. About 200 meters behind it, and partly down an incline, is a low garage-like structure; on the right side of that is a hidden entrance to the basement of that smaller structure. If it seems worth while, and there haven't been any changes around here, we could find our way in from there. It would be better to alert the other units about our whereabouts, but without our communicators there's no way to do that."

"How do you think Martin's squad is doing?"

"We haven't heard or seen very much, no shouts of battle, no indication of laser beams, no fires begun by the weapons, so it's hard to tell. Mariko, duck quick!"

A trio of Militia. That small building must be their headquarters; maybe Blinko and Tamara are being held there. There can't be more than 20 Militia left, maybe 25 tops. Mariko and I would have no chance against them if they confronted us *en masse*. And stunning these three would only let them know for sure we're in the vicinity. We'll have to lie low and think, and plan. If Martin's squad–two quintads–came here by chance, we'd have a shot at it. Otherwise...

"Let's move over towards the woods. We need time to work out a plan."

"You're the boss. But to be honest, I don't have the foggiest notion where we are, and how to get back to where our units split up."

"That's my department, Mariko. I never forget such things."

Got to do this quietly; check around for anything that might make noise. First to get under that other méki. We'll be exposed for about ten seconds. Choose time carefully. No one in sight. "OK, low to the ground, and head for the méki!" Made it. Stay here for a minute or so without stirring. Still no one in sight. There's a hollow just behind us that should offer protection. Best to back down into it, so as to keep an eye on their HQ. Can't see anyone behind us. Easy does it. Good. We're in what seems to be safe grounds.

"From here we can get back to our rendez-vous site, Point X, by going off to the right and doing some twisting and turning. It might be risky with the sunlight on us."

"I don't think I'll ever get used to these two suns."

"The distant one, right now, seems to rise about the same time the other one sets. It acts sort of like bright moonlight."

"Where do we go if we take off to the left?"

"That will lead us to that low garage-like building I mentioned. That could be risky, too, not only because of the light but also because the Militia might be using it. Maybe our best bet is to stay here until it's relatively dark, and either go back to Point X, or straight behind us into the woods. On the other hand, what if they have Blinko and Tamara there?"

"We could try that hidden entrance you mentioned. Their lives might depend on it. If they're there."

———

"Ah! there's the hidden trap-door. Let me put a few drops of oil on it before we try to open it. Rusty as it is, it'll probably squeak."

"And the squeaky door gets the oil."

"Down we go, super quietly." Let's see. Seven steps forward, take the right-hand passage to the end, turn left. Up the stairs and... Damn! There's a wall there, near where the door should be! Did I make a mistake? I don't think so. But to be sure we'll have to get back to where we were and go straight instead of turning right. Did I hear a noise just then? Is there someone behind us? We'll freeze for a moment or two. OK, no further sounds, must have been some small animal. We're back to the fork. We'll go right and then...

"Not so fast, Vasa. We've got you cornered. No tricks if you expect to live."

"Noslohcin! The Butcher of Sandstone! What are our chances of living if we don't try any tricks? Now that you're the Deacon, have you become even more heartless and devious?"

"Shut up, Vasa. We have the two of you in our hands; there's no way out. Throw down your guns."

Mariko knows what to do in this kind of case: she really knows the training manual. She removes the power pack from her gun, and slips it into a kind of timed flare. I do the same with mine. I stall for time while we're doing this. I notice Mariko putting her flare on a sort of shelf behind us, out of sight of the Militia. Then I ask, "What would happen if we aimed them at you and your gang?"

"You'd murder one or two of us, then you'd be killed instantly."

"Murder! You who brag about the 1000 victims you've handled all by yourself?"

"Quit stalling. Throw those guns down."

"I guess we'll have to do what you ask for. Here they are."

"Tie them up, Stoddard. Do a good job. I don't know about her comrade, but Vasa's a slippery thing. Be careful."

"Ow, not so hard!"

"Shut up. We'll go out now and on to HQ. We have a couple of your friends there. Well treated. At least thy're still alive."

"You bastard! You've probably tortured them to a point near death!" I drop my flare while talking and pretending to try to free myself. We're pushed and shoved and hit across the back on the way to the Militia HQ.

"Put them in Room 2, tied to a chair. Then come back here to prepare their friends."

"Prepare their friends! Ha! ha! ha! Deacon, you know how to tickle me!"

———

"Nokio, have you seen the Captain? Her squad was supposed to meet us here at Point X about now."

"No, Commander. But I did find a few traces. I think they've found the Militia somewhere near here. We could try following those traces, but it might be hard, with the sun setting."

"I think all that's left of Earth Federation troops on the ground are the ten of us and whoever the Captain has left. Her squad was decimated, judging by the blanched bones and bloody uniforms we saw back there. Damn wolks! Damn stots!"

"Unless that was Ali Akbar's squad. I didn't have any way to identify the victims. What should we do, Commander?"

"We'll have to try to find her and her squad. The smaller sun should provide us with enough light to see. Lead the way, Nokio."

———

"You've beaten them and drugged them."

"At least they're feeling no pain, Vasa. Sardon will do that to you."

"Is that how you've 'prepared' them for us to see? Drugged

so that when they come to they'll feel euphoric, even though their bodies are bloodied and they have countless broken bones?"

"It's fun watching our prisoners see their wounds and giggling about it. It makes the final beating all the more fun. You need some diversion, a bit of comic relief, in a war like this. But now let's get down to business. How many troops do you have, Vasa?"

"You're looking at them."

"What a liar! You've got to do better than that! Or would you rather have me start burning your friend Tamara? I've got a torch prepared for her, and a fire in the fireplace."

"OK. Just about everyone else who came with us has been killed by your assassins, or is hunting you down on Pacifica."

"On Pacifica! Why would we go there? It's a wildlife preserve, without any of your ilk in sight."

"Our Intelligence seemed to point to Pacifica. We came here more or less on a lark. I guess our Personnel Tracking Devices need more work."

"Personnel Tracking Devices, eh? You believers in technology should read the Bible instead of high-tech manuals."

"Fortunately, I adjusted mine enough so that it indicated your presence within five kilometers of here. You see, we follow your DNA."

"Christina! Don't tell them any more. They're going to torture Tamara and Blinko to death anyway, in our sight, before we suffer the same fate."

"What a perceptive comrade you have, Vasa. Marlowe, eh? I think we'll just... What's that?"

Stoddard rushed in, shouting, "Deacon! An explosion! The hangar's on fire!"

"What? Get the ammo we have there, Stoddard. Hurry!

"We tried, Deacon, but the flames and the smoke were too much. We lost a pentad in there, too."

"Quick! Get everyone outside. We've got to salvage whatever we can. Lock the door on these two!"

"Good going, Mariko. Your flare did its job. Now let's undo these ropes. There! We'll get out through the window. And by the way, I gave him some more or less public information. But I didn't tell them Martin's here, too, if his group has avoided annihilation."

"I noticed you also didn't tell them that the main body is due back from Pacifica at Point X in about an hour."

We pick up some branches and strip off the leaves so that in the dark they might be mistaken for weapons. Then we sneak up behind the Militia group, but stay back at the HQ building. We have to survey the scene and fix on a plan of action. About a dozen of them, looking at the fire consuming their warehouse of pretty primitive weaponry. Suddenly, a familiar voice can be heard as Martin's squad appears out of the darkness.

"The jig's up, Deacon. Your life of crime is at an end. We have you and your twelve apostles surrounded."

"Martin! That damn liar Vasa told me that everyone was dead or on Pacifica."

"Move together, lads and lassies, into a circle. Try to escape and you'll atone forever for your sins."

Stoddard rushed towards Martin, handgun drawn. A red bolt stopped him in his tracks.

"Don't say you weren't warned."

Two Militia persons suddenly appeared behind the squad.

"You're lucky we didn't send you to Hell, Martin. Drop your..."

Mariko leaped forward, striking him in the middle of his back with a powerful kick. As he fell, his weapon discharged, striking a third Militia person emerging from the shadows. Mariko fell upon her victim, disarmed him and applied a karate blow to his neck. He was out. In the distraction of the moment, the Deacon saw a chance to escape. But as he began to flee, his jaw was met by Christina's right fist, which dislodged a couple of teeth. He staggered back, then rushed her, swinging wildly and shouting, "I'll get you, you non-believing killer!" Christina side-stepped, caught up with him as he swung around.

"Here's for one of your 1000 innocent victims, Butcher!" A blow to the solar plexus rendered him unconscious.

"You forgot me!" shouted the other armed Militia person. "And I'll get you!" But as he spoke, Christina's flare went off just in front of him. He was set ablaze by the force of the flare. His death was instantaneous.

Their leader captured, their situation hopeless, the Militia personnel all surrendered. Except for two, who chose suicide as a way out–a fiery death in the burning hangar. The rest were ankle-cuffed, three by three, and marched to Point X, which they reached just after the Constellation crew returned.

Martin and Christina led their drugged comrades along the path just as soon as they were able to walk.

———

"What a story! My ancestor would have been proud of your success in ridding Mesnos of the Militia. And for that matter, the rest of our planets."

"Christina, I'd love to take you to see Christina's Rock. I think Mariko has not had a chance to go there. Tomorrow we'll have various ceremonies officially welcoming the Constellation crew, the heroine of Paracelsus, and of course the Kolok people who are accomanying you. How about the day after that?"

"That sounds just wonderful, Ilse. Even though I'm shuddering a bit at the very thought of going there. You don't get over such a traumatic experience in only a century or so! And that's one of the places the Kolok want to go to."

"We'll work out the details tomorrow. Now how about some port wine? It's my last bottle, straight from Earth. I've been saving it for just such an occasion as this."

"It will be just what the doctor ordered, Sven."

PRISON ISLAND

"I see you're watching the news on the visuscreen, Deacon. I believe our turnkeys have provided us with them just to remind us that we're not free."

"I can't believe my eyes! Is that the viper, Christina Vasa, who condemned the 15 of us left alive here, to this perpetual prison? Take a good look, Adews."

"Yes, Deacon. Oh, that's Vasa, all right! Let me get my hands on her!"

"Be reasonable, Adews. We're all getting on in years, and she's still a damnable 28 years old. She'll fry in Hell for violating the laws of Nature and of God."

"Not to mention killing or causing the death of so many of God's servants."

"Oh, my God in Heaven! What monsters does she have with her?"

"They're hairless, tall, earless, greenish!"

"And she seems to be talking with them! They must have some sort of intelligence!"

"Do you think she's toying with us, Deacon? Maybe those creatures are just humans in costume."

"She doesn't fool around. She has no sense of humor. She's found intelligent aliens."

"Deacon, intelligent non-human life in the universe?"

"Yes, I know what you're thinking, Adews. Could it be that our interpretation of the sacred texts has been wrong?"

"Maybe what they found is a bevy of demons."

"Well, that could be. Call the others to the chapel so we can talk things over. We're facing a crisis in our beliefs if these things are what they seem to be."

"And if I know Vasa, she'll bring them here to torment us. We'll have to be prepared for a visit."

"I have some reservations about this trip, Ecnelav. I'm not

so much worried about my own safety, although the Militia targeted me specially for many years. And there can't be too many of them left. Still, they could be armed, and they are certainly dangerous."

"But your laser guns should keep them at bay. And we're interested in seeing this curious prison, where everyone is apparently free. Our STUs must be in a similar state."

"My real concern is for your safety and that of the other Damosians who would be coming with us. The thought of there being non-human intelligent life in the universe is anathema to the Militia; in a sense, that's why they were formed. They thought our climate-changing activities were sacrilegious, and that our building space stations, planning to colonize Venus and Mars, beginning to explore our corner of the galaxy were contrary to the law of their God. One look at you will fill them with hatred. They will try to harm or kill you."

"I understand, Christina; we've often discussed the Militia and the STU. But how dangerous can they be? After all, you have the weaponry to dissuade them from acting."

"I see that you'd be really disappointed if we didn't go there. So let's see: you've picked five people to accompany you: Tsepa Dub, Siol Saats, Kram Ned, Amil Urep, and Onapac Mot. I'll have our newly-promoted Security Officer, Lieutenant Amadou Mbamba, pick a squad of two pentads for protection. We'll also make sure that if our communicators fail us, more troops will come down."

"With preparations like that, we'll certainly feel safe."

"I only hope you'll **be** as safe as you'll feel."

———

"My friends, here near the end of our lives we have come to a crossroads. Adews and I saw, on the visuscreen, Chris tina Vasa (*Vasa! The Militia-killer!*) materializing in the company of what seemed to be intelligent aliens (*My God in Heaven!*). Judging from their appearance, they seem to be lizards rather than mammals (*Thinking Lizards!*) . They're tall, greenish, hairless, earless. Adews suspects that they might be demons

(That's it! They're devils!). But to tell you the truth, I think that Vasa has found, somewhere, intelligent creatures. And I must confess that my faith is shaken by this. Shaken but still firm. I believe that Vasa will bring these devils here to torment us. Devils or mortals, they appear to refute what we've believed all our lives, and what our founders believed over 450 years ago when the Militia was begun."

"Deacon, may I say a word?"

"Certainly, Ycnan. We might be prisoners, but we're free in spirit."

"Except for me, we're all over 100 years old, and at 94 I can scarcely be considered a child. We have about 25 or 30 years left to live. One by one we'll disappear, and right now there are only 15 of us left. We'll soon be needing assistance just to be able to grow what we need to eat; it's hard enough now to produce enough food for the little community that has survived. Maybe this is a time to ask for help. I'm sure that our tormentors will be able to see our needs. We could ask Vasa to intercede on our behalf. *(Ask Vasa? Never!)*"

"Vasa! Help us! Ha! She put us here, and smiled with insane pleasure when we were put on board a spaceship, in chains. No, she's our sworn enemy. Trebor, you seem to want to speak."

"Yes, Deacon, I do. We all have good reason to hate and to distrust Vasa. Without her, our movement might have succeeded. She's responsible for the death and imprisonment of countless brothers and sisters. And yet, maybe we can use her to enable us to get off this island, once and for all."

"Trebor, what folly! We've been told about the giant jellyfish, and the tide has brought back the rafts of our colleagues who tried to sail to the undeveloped continent we saw when we were brought here. But never a living person, never even a trace of their clothing came in with the tide."

"Yes, Ycnan, what you say is right. But remember that we're talking about rafts, and we're talking about people who had only crude weapons, bows and arrows, spears, knives."

"What's your point, Trebor?"

"My point is this, Deacon: we can get weapons from Vasa and her party, when they come–we know they'll come, and soon.

We can get a good boat from her, too."

"Do you think that out of the kindness of her heart she's going to supply us with the means to escape?"

"Not out of the kindness of her heart, but suppose we can make her give us these things."

"What? Have you lost your senses, man? A well-trained squad of well-armed fighters? Look around at us, Trebor. We might have been able to fight them 25 or 30 years ago. But not now. Be reasonable."

"Adews, I am being reasonable. They must have a vulnerable spot: we'll have to look for it, we'll have to find it. If we succeed, we'll have our ticket to freedom."

"Or at least escape. I agree with your idea in principle, Trebor, but let's sleep on it tonight. Maybe one or more of us will have come up with an insight that will point to their weakness. Once we find that—and everyone has a weak spot—we'll have to work on a plan of action. Let's meet after breakfast tomorrow."

"Hear, hear, Deacon!"

"After breakfast, Deacon!"

"Somebody will have a plan, a good plan, I'm sure."

"An idea is already starting to take form in my mind."

————

"Each of us has a communicator, and Lieutenant Mgamba's squad and I are armed with laser handguns and rifles. I think it best for our guests, who are all civilians, to be unarmed. But you will have to remain alert, ready to deal with crafty and desperate people."

"We understand what you're saying, Christina. And although we're scientists and politicians who have not faced combat, we think we know that danger might be lurking there. But this is a once-in-a-lifetime opportunity for us to observe and eventually to report on the behavior of hardened criminals in a free environment, a prison that they control."

"Commodore, this is Lieutenant April Leira. Captain Marlowe has just beamed aboard. She would like to speak with you and your party."

"Send her right in, Lieutenant."

"It's obvious I can't dissuade you. But whatever you do, Ecnelav, don't trust them for a second. Now, we're not sure how many of them there are; I would guess about twenty. Most of them must be 100-120 years old. But that doesn't mean they're not dangerous. They might have some weapons, certainly at least knives and spears and clubs. We must all stay on our toes. Ah! Captain Marlowe."

"Commodore, unless you have strong objections, I would like to accompany you. I will not go as a member of a military squad, but since I am at least technically in charge of the prison, I would like to see this island and these prisoners myself, from up close."

"Captain, you are most welcome to join us. But you must go armed, at least with a handgun. Lieutenant Mgamba has arranged to provide each of the military personnel with a weapon. As you know from personal experience, these are not people to be trifled with."

"Yes, we have to take them seriously. They will surely try to kill us if they get the chance. And I have my own weapon."

"If no one has any further questions, let's beam down. First the two pentads, then the Damosians, then Captain Marlowe and me. Is everything ready, Commander Kwambe?"

"Everything is set, Commodore."

"I wish you could join us, Kwali, I mean Commander, but you are in charge here."

"We'll be monitoring the site, Commodore. Incidentally, we have found evidence of only 15 living persons on the island, if our personnel tracking devices are functioning properly."

"Fifteen! Well, at least we outnumber them!"

———

"No need to come here armed, Vasa. We have no weapons, and as you can see, we're almost 60 years older than we were when you sent us here."

"One thing I've learned in dealing with the Militia, Deacon, is that we can never be too careful."

"Oh, you flatter a group of aging men and women. But no matter. I assume you've come here to show these loathsome creatures, these emissaries of the devil, our humble quarters, and to torment us. Did you scrape these green monsters from some corner of Hell?"

"Deacon, some of us want to be more cordial with the Commodore and her guests."

"You're right, Ycnan. I'll control my tongue."

"Where do we start the tour, Deacon?"

"I hope you don't mind the slow pace we have. Adews and Trebor are a bit lame, and most of us have some ailment or other. Living in this damp climate doesn't help. The village is about a kilometer to the west, just beyond the cemetery where thousands of our comrades are buried. We'll pass by many unoccupied houses that once were needed, when our village had over 1000 people. Since you deprived us of the ability to propagate our species, in defiance of the biblical command to our first parents, our population has withered away as one by one our friends have died."

"Noslohcin, your guilt is enormous, you and the rest of the Militia. In any case, it was not I, nor any of the members of Space Fleet, who made the decision to render you all sterile. That directive came from Earth Government. We were carrying out our orders."

"Criminal orders, and you participated in a crime. But enough of that: it's water under the bridge; we'll never be able to turn back the current and retrieve those years we have lost here. And we'll never be able to bring back to life those who lie buried here."

"The cemetery is built in a beautiful place, and it is well maintained. One can see a lovely bay from here, and the ocean beyond."

"What? You speak our language?"

"Deacon, on the planet Damos in the solar system centered by a sun called Chromos, across the galaxy, Dr. Ecnelav Enohr is Director of the Catta Space Center. Damos is an Earth-sized planet with a similar climate. The Damosians are Kolok in the same sense that Earth people are human. Dr. Enohr is also the

296

Damosian Ambassador to Earth. She and her party of scientists and politicians have asked to see this prison. They want to know how we treat our prisoners, and what life in this kind of exile is like. Dr. Enohr has learned to speak English, as you have observed."

"Yes, Deacon, as Commodore Vasa has explained, we're interested in this special kind of prison. We imagine that ordinary prisons are places where the prisoners are deprived of freedom. This seems to be a new concept. An exile that can be humane."

"All right, Enohr, you'll have your wish. You see we have a little farm near here, where we raise vegetables and some animals for meat and milk. It was once much larger, extending far down to the south, where all you can see now is open prairie. And as far as the cemetery is concerned, we respect our dead. We are very religious people."

"We have learned something about the human religions from the crew of Constellation. We are astonished at the extraordinary variety of beliefs. On Damos, we too are religious, but we have only one principal religion, along with a few dissident sects."

"If you're really religious, maybe we could interest you in visiting the chapel. We have some old Bibles there, along with various religious vestments and objects we use in our services, many of them dating back several hundreds of years. Adews and Trebor will be glad to show you around."

"We'd love to accompany you. Tsepa Dub and I are elders in the First Church of Oarnn in Catta."

"Do you mind if I join you?"

"Marlowe, when's the last time you've seen the inside of a church? You wouldn't know what to do there."

"Adews," the Deacon interceded, "let her go with you. She might be an infidel who only wants to admire the old Bible and other devotional objects we possess, or she might have decided to go because she believes that we wish to harm the Damosians. Let her go."

"Grrr. I don't like it, but I'll take her with us. I'm only doing it because you're asking, Deacon. This way, everyone."

297

"We'll join up with you in an hour or so, Adews. Vasa, perhaps your soldiers and the remaining aliens would like to see our food processing area. We do everything by hand, like the people in our Mother Church, in Canaan. I think you're familiar with them. Rumor has it that you go there to visit some infidels while pretending to be interested in the work of the ADP."

"Rumor has it partly right, Noslohcin. I go there to visit my friends, some of whom are ADPs. I admire their way of life, in a way, although I must admit that I've never fully understood their beliefs and the reason they've resisted even the good aspects of post-industrial technology. I suppose they think that once you begin to allow things like electricity or visuscreens into your life, the temptation to take in more is irresistible."

"What makes you go back there? Do you laugh at their primitivism? Do you preach atheism to them?"

"It might be hard for you to believe, Noslohcin, but I respect their ways, and I've tried to learn from them. I find their way of life very calming, very tranquil. I can enjoy it in small doses, but frankly, I prefer the kinds of things modern technologies allow us to do, on a day-to-day basis."

"OK, in we go, honored guests. We can start with the water mill. I'll open up the sluice gate for you, so it can grind up some grain. It makes a lot of noise. Don't say you weren't warned."

———

"This Bible comes to us, in a direct way, from one of the founders of the Church of the Ancient-Day Primitivists, to which we adhere. One of his descendants, our first Deacon, was the founder of our movement, the Militia, which was dedicated to fighting evil and to spreading the word of God."

"It must be very old, Adews."

"It dates from 2262. Hmmm. That makes it exactly 600 years old now. We should have a little festival to celebrate. In here you'll see a beautiful side chapel, with extraordinary stonework. You'll have to get up close to the altar to see the detail."

"These paving stones are unusually large. Was this once

used as a burial place?"

"You're very observant, Dub. But it'll be *your* burial crypt! Ha ha ha ha ha!"

While Adews was saying these words, Trebor released a mechanism that made the large stone fall four meters down to a sand platform below. Ecnelav, Tsepa, and Mariko fell with a shout into a tiny cell. The two Militiamen turned upside down a large table that served as an altar, and enclosed their captives. Then they released a poisonous gas through a small hole in the wall. In minutes, the three visitors were overcome by the fumes and lay unconscious.

"They should be out now, Adews. Let's get these masks on and climb down to retrieve their communicators and their weapons. Then we'll tie them up, hoist them up here with the pulley we set up yesterday, and march them to the Deacon's little show-and-tell party. Ha ha ha ha ha!"

"I hope our trick works. I've got an idea. We'll put Marlowe in the middle, tie her left leg to Enohr's right leg and her right leg to Tsepa's left leg. It'll be a scream to see them walking, because she's so much shorter than these aliens. Ha ha ha ha ha!"

———

"Let me turn off the mill. You get the idea. We have a few hundred kilos of grain stored above, much of it as flour. I can show you our vegetable canning operation, if you'd like."

"Will it be as noisy as this?"

"Not quite, but no matter: you don't have any ears, so you can't be hurt. Oh, I'm sorry, I promised Ycnan to be polite."

The door opened at this point. The three captives entered, followed by Adews and Trebor, who was wielding Mariko's handgun.

"I understand we have an Ambassador here. If you value her life, drop your weapons, now."

One of a Pentad's members went for her weapon. A red bolt ended her life.

"Anyone else want to join your Maker? Drop all those weapons, now, then back up to the wall. If not, this one goes

299

first. Next it'll be shorty in the middle."

"Drop your weapons," ordered Christina, who set an example by placing her handgun on the floor. "These people have nothing to lose. They'll kill us all, one by one, even if it means they'll die, too."

"Always thinking, Vasa? Now we want your communicators. Everyone's except Vasa's."

The communicators were dropped, and one by one the "honored guests" were searched, bound, and made to sit on the ground. All the communicators were destroyed, except Christina's.

"OK, Vasa, call up to your cronies, and have them send down one of your surface boats. Tell them you'd like to take some of your party fishing."

"You must be mad, Noslohcin. Do you really think you'll escape by sea? Those jellyfish will get you once you're just three kilometers out. You might get away from us, but there's no escaping them."

"Good sermon, Vasa, but keep it to yourself. Do as I say, or your green friend there gets killed."

"Don't listen to him, Christina! Do what you have to do to save everyone else's life."

A club fell on her head. She slumped over.

"You swine, Deacon! I see you haven't lost your touch."

"Do as I say, or she'll be a martyr."

"Commander Kwambe, this is Commodore Vasa. We'd like to take some of the Damosians on a little fishing trip in a cove nearby. Would you send down a Wavehopper, fully equipped?"

"A fishing party! And we thought you were working, Commodore!"

"They say that fishing is hard work. Set the craft down in the little harbor."

"I'll make sure this is done. It will take about 10 minutes."

"Thanks a million, Commander. Commodore Vasa signing off."

Kwali looked puzzled at this brief conversation, and let Susanna and April know of the strange way Christina spoke. A crisp, really military manner of speech they were unfamiliar with, coming from her. Still, they obeyed their orders. April had suggested that they slip a few commandos in the craft, just to be on the safe side, but the others rejected her suggestion.

———

"All right, Vasa, now drop your communicator on the ground, and stomp on it. Good. Now you won't be able to contact your friends."

"You're mad, you'll never get away with this!"

"Your conversation's getting repetitious and boring, Vasa. Shut up."

Out on the shore, Wavehopper materialized. Seeing this, the Deacon ordered, "Kill them all."

The weapons all seemed to fire at once. Only Ycnan protested, and Trebor aimed Mariko's handgun at her, and fired on a nod from the Deacon.

"Let's get going. Now we're only 14 strong. We can kill those jellies with these guns. To the Northland!"

———

"Commodore, this is Kwali! Are you there? Damn! Still no answer."

"Kwali, let's face it, they're in grave danger. Let's get down there with a couple of squads. It'll almost empty out Constellation, but we do have this back-up plan if we lose communication."

"You're right, Susanna. We'll round up whoever we can. I'll summon everyone to the teleport room. Make sure everyone is armed. April, you'll be in charge here. Let's go!"

———

"Everyone's alive except for this woman and Martina.

Somehow they killed Martina and one of their own, but just stunned the others. I don't get it."

"Maybe Christina or Mgamba can explain what happened when they come to. Meanwhile, let's get our people up to Constellation, and find a spot in the cemetery to dig a grave for this woman, whoever she is. We'll get Martina's body on board for a full service."

"Kwali, shouldn't we go after the Deacon and Wavehopper?"

"They won't get far. The jellies will eat them all. Look, Mgamba's stirring. They're all regaining consciousness! So fast! What's going on? Mgamba, can you hear me?"

"Hear you? Kwali? What happened?"

"That's what we'd like to know."

"See if we can get them to sit up. Christina, what's up?"

"Ooh, my head! What's up? They shot us, thought they'd kill us all, but we're alive."

"All but Martina and this woman."

"Martina and Ycnan? Ycnan didn't agree with the idea of killing us all. Martina tried to shoot the thug who had a weapon."

"Yes, they left you all for dead."

"Well, they didn't know that Mgamba had doctored all our weapons. We didn't want to take any chances, and to be sure we didn't accidentally kill someone in a potential scuffle, he froze the weapons at the lowest level of the stun control."

"That explains why you're alive. But what about Martina and this Ycnan?"

"I don't know."

"I do," offered Mariko. "They were both shot with my personal weapon, which they must have set at kill. Mgamba had not touched it."

"The jellyfish will get the Wavehopper gang, and they killed one of their own," offered Susanna. "There are no prisoners left on Prisoner's Island."

"Kwali, April here. We've located Wavehopper, or what's left of it, about three kilometers north of the island. There are no survivors."

"Kwali here. We've lost Martina, but everyone else is safe

and alive. We'll get outside in a few minutes so that we can be beamed up."

"We'll be waiting for your signal. April out."

Christina thought for a moment, smiled slightly, and said, "Suicide, or the nearest thing to it, and murder. What an ironic way for the Militia to come to an end. There are no Militia left anywhere. That long chapter can be closed."

BACK ON MARS

"I regret to inform you that Bishop Chi has died. His death came suddenly just two months ago. We have yet to name a replacement for him."

"Dead! Mr. Mayor, I am shocked. When I last saw him, about ten years ago, he seemed so animated, so full of the vigor of life."

"That's true, Commodore, but he was already much older than he appeared. When you last saw him, he was over 100 years of age."

"I will always cherish his friendship and his wise counsel. Indeed, I came down here alone to seek his advice on what might be a delicate matter for your people, from a religious point of view."

"Hmm. From a religious point of view. Would you care for some more tea, Commodore?"

"Yes, thank you. And please call me Christina. I know you well enough to think of you as a friend."

"Thank you, Christina. My Christian name, as you know, is Mihály. I would be honored if you called me by that name. As far as the religious matter is concerned, perhaps I can be of some assistance, Christina. While I am not a theologian, I do fully understand the tenets of our faith, and I do represent the Ancient Day Primitivists here in Canaan, if only from the secular point of view."

"Well, I'll be blunt about my message, because I know you don't like things sugar-coated, and unless some traveler has discussed the matter with you, what I have to say will be news to you. Our most recent mission took us an incredible distance, literally to the other side of the galaxy. There we finally found what we have been looking for for such a long time: a civilization of intelligent beings."

"Incredible! I assume these are humans, like us?"

"Actually, Mihály, they are not. They appear to have evolved from a warm-blooded lizard-like creature. Like us, they are bipedal, have opposable thumbs, and are capable of reasoning. Their reasoning, in fact, is more central to their lives than ours is to our lives; on the other hand, they are much less emotional, much less impulsive than we are."

"What do they look like? Can they speak?"

"They are taller than we are, hairless, and are without external ears (but they can hear very well). The women are taller than the men. In outline and from a certain distance, they look much like us, but up close these differences are very apparent. They do speak; their official language is called Kolok. Most of those traveling with us have learned enough English to converse with us, and we have learned enough Kolok to converse with them; but we rely on translation machines in important situations, to make sure that we will all be fully understood."

"What is their planet like, Christina? Is it like Mars?"

"Actually, Damos is similar to Earth in size and mass, and has a climate that's like ours. Good, breathable air. Warm and moist. Perfect place for cold-blooded animal life. Insects, amphibians, lizards, some that fly and look like birds. Small mammals have evolved, something like platypuses and voles. Flowers, trees, grains. You would like it. We've got some good friends on Damos."

"Are the Damosians the descendants of those cold-blooded lizards, or of warm-blooded mammals?"

"The Damosians evolved from lizards. They are warm-blooded, though, with large brains. Ovoviviparous. A lot like us, in a way. Skin has a vaguely pale green look–a bit like my eyes. Hmm... Their eyes close from the sides instead of from the top, like ours. Technology has rapidly reached the point where it is about where it was on Earth 400 or 450 years ago, about when I was born, or just before."

"Do they have a religion?"

"Yes, they do. They call their God Oarnn. If you meet them, you can find out much more than I could ever help to tell you. There are two church elders in the party, one of whom is the Ambassador. She is also an astronomer."

"God surely works his will in mysterious ways. What you say about these people does not appear to be incompatible with a certain understanding of the Scriptures. We will have to re-examine the Sacred writings to see how to present these people to our citizens. Can you give me a week or two to consult with our theologians and with our civilian leaders? We would not like to cause riots by having these people suddenly appear in our streets. Without a proper presentation, some might take them to be manifestations of the Devil."

"I understand, and I appreciate the broad-minded approach you are taking."

"We are not like the Militia, those misguided souls who thought they were carrying out the will of God in their murderous attacks on the ELB and the Earth Government. And we have learned to trust and to respect you, personally, Christina, even though your belief system is so different from ours. You have been a frequent visitor to Canaan since long before any of those still living were even born."

"My many trips to Canaan have helped me learn much about your religion. I can respect your beliefs, even if I can't share them in conscience. There is something about your way of life that restores my equanimity of spirit. I will always cherish the time I have spent among you."

"Shall we say two weeks, then?"

"Two weeks it will be. I would like to see Det and Numamba now."

"I'm afraid I am ever the bearer of bad news. Dr. Numamba Stisreg died about two years ago. Were you not informed of this on Earth?"

"Numamba dead also! I was told nothing about it."

"Perhaps you should go to The Mansion and help console your friend. He has never quite recovered from the shock of discovering his wife dead when he returned from an extended trip to Venus."

"I shall do so immediately. And I'll return here in two weeks. But, Mihály, maybe you'd like to meet some of the Damosians before you speak to your officials and your people? First-hand knowledge is irreplaceable."

"I am not sure, Christina, that it would be permissible for me to make use of your transporter. And it might not be a good idea to send the people here."

"What about The Mansion?"

"That sounds like a good idea. How about the day after tomorrow, around noon. This would give you some time to speak with Dr. Stisreg and grieve with him."

"A good plan. We'll meet in two days."

———

"A bit more wine, Christina?"

"I'd appreciate it, Det. I still am in shock over Numamba's untimely death. I've read and listened to her diaries, as you asked me to do, but I can't understand what drove her to carry out such an experiment on herself."

"You can imagine my shock when I found her here, wasted away. She must have died just an hour or two before I returned. I would have given my teeth to hear her voice again, not on a machine, but coming from her."

"The truth is that I can't imagine your shock, Det. Not in any meaningful way. I've had similar blows in my life, with Boris and just recently with Martin, for instance. But it's not the same thing. You and Numamba had a commitment far greater than any I've ever dared undertake."

"You mean, our long marriage? Yes, that really sealed our fate. We shared everything, our research, our friendship with Stanley and you, our experimental farm, the business end of this pharmacy, everything. In the time of stupendous energy that preceded her rapid decline, she had managed to solve some of the major problems that we had been encountering for 25 years, the wobble of the planet and the density of its atmosphere. What a mind she had! In a week or two, Numamba effectively completed the mission that Stanley (and of course, the Earth Government) had given us. It might be time for me to move on to other challenges. But for the life of me, I can't find any that tickle my fancy. Any ideas?"

"Ideas? You know I always have ideas. Can't live without them! The trouble is, none of them springs to my mind as something that might interest you as a new and exciting career. Now that it seems the ELB will come to an end, your career as

308

Stanley's successor has also ended. And you and Numamba have completed every task that would require talents like yours: from here on, it's something of a holding action, as I understand it."

"You're right on both scores. Still, my talents, as you call them, are surely needed somewhere. I think I need to get away from here, for at least some time."

"Well, as a civilian member of the ELB, you can fly with us in this solar system without asking permission. And of course you could go with us beyond that if the authorities have no objections. In about two years we'll head back to Damos. And, while I'm waiting to introduce our Damosians to the Canaanites, why don't you spend some time aboard Constellation with them, and later visit some other parts of Mars? They'd love to see the sights, and you could travel with us."

"That sounds like a great idea. I'll have Hélène take over the operation for a week or so. That should be enough time to let me clear my head a bit, and get away from morbid thoughts."

"Oh, we'll have to be here at noon the day after tomorrow. The Mayor will be here. I thought it would be a good idea for him to meet some of the Damosians then, in secret. Can you arrange to have Hélène go off to the pharmacy on the Town Square at that time?"

"By chance, that's a day when we're closed. We can have the run of the house all to ourselves."

"Good. I'll let the crew know you're coming, when you're ready. And I have a surprise for you: the quantum teleportation system is now authorized for people. No more dismanteling of the cells, no snowy shimmer, no split-second of disorientation: the operator presses the button, and voilà! you're at your destination!"

"Quantum teleportation! What a great advancement! I can't wait to use it. I'll close up things as fast as possible. I should be ready within a half hour."

———

"I've been thinking, Madame President, of recommending that you ask Commodore Vasa to serve as our Ambassador to

Damos. She knows the people, she even can speak their language, she has bonds with them that they forged during their battle against the STU, and in exploration of the other nearby planets, not to mention their having shared with her the experience of everyday life."

"I like your idea, Mátyás, but frankly I don't see her willing to take on that kind of responsibility. She would not want what is essentially a political and sedentary job. What I would prefer doing, if Space Fleet Headquarters agrees, is this. I would recommend they promote her to Rear Admiral (with the understanding that she would continue to be Captain of Constellation and later of the new craft we have on the drawing board), and give her the opportunity to travel to Damos as part of her continuing missions of exploration. I think Headquarters will agree with this plan. Already they have accepted her proposal to promote her entire crew by two ranks for the ordinary personnel and one rank for the ELB personnel."

"You are right, as always, Madame President. She will have the personal recognition she deserves, and the crew certainly has proven its collective and individual mettle, judging from all the reports we have read and seen, and from the debriefing interviews we have held. And the culmination of centuries of dreams has come about: we have discovered alien intelligent beings, have established contact with them, and have become their friends and allies."

"Tomorrow we sign the pact of friendship officially. Ambassador Enohr has proven to be an honest and forthright person, as Commodore Vasa has represented her as being. All 25 of the Damosians have been a delight to get to know."

"Interestingly, although we have the technological edge on them, they have a lot to offer us in their methodologies and their unique experiences. I think, Madame President, that our artists, our writers, our musicians, will participate in this exchange just as fully as any scientist or politician."

"In the meanwhile, suppose we appointed Admiral Vasa as a plenipotentiary Minister of Galactic Affairs or some such thing. In such a position she would have to keep moving, which she would like, and we would have a person authorized to act promptly on behalf of Earth Government. Not for everything, of course, but we can write in the limits needed. That type of job is something she could handle as part of her appointment as Rear Admiral. It would be an additional title and additional responsibilities for her, which I am confident she will be able to discharge admirably."

"A splendid idea! I'll get in touch with Space Fleet Headquarters right away, and then I'll call the Cabinet together to speak about this proposed appointment. With luck, we won't have to create an entirely new Department or Ministry, together with a huge bureaucracy, to bring this to fruition."

"No need to worry about that: with the Minister away for periods of 10 years or so at a time, there would be no need for a bureaucracy."

"I see that sparkle in your eyes, Madame President. It tells me that you think bureaucracies do not necessarily depend on need. Or on the presence of their leader."

"Sometimes they seem to exist only to exalt egos."

"I'll report back when I've completed these tasks."

"Thank you, Mátyás. I'll be waiting to hear from you."

———

"...And it is with the greatest personal pleasure that I commission you to the permanent rank of Rear Admiral in Space Fleet, with express duties to be Captain of Constellation and, when it is completed some decades hence, of the first of the new generation of space ships which we are currently planning to build. Would you please step forward, Admiral, to receive the epaulets and the insignia that are the outward signs of this high rank."

In the presence of what seemed to be the entire Headquarters staff, from Fleet Admiral Jiang to the newest recruit, and of the crew of Constellation, who had all just been installed in their new ranks, as well as numerous friends from her many years of service and the delegation from Damos, Christina stepped forward. Old Admiral Jiang smiled as he attached the epaulets to Christina's uniform, and handed her a gilt box with the other signs of her new rank, and a scroll affirming her new rank. The band broke into a fanfare, and all present cheered loudly.

Before Christina could utter the few words she had been planning on saying, Admiral Jiang raised his hand for silence, and then stated that the President wished to make an announcement.

President Ionnanides moved to the center of the stage, resplendent in the white robes of her high office.

"Meeting in closed session, the Earth Senate has unanimously endorsed your nomination to be Minister of Galactic Affairs. Your duties in this post will be consonant with your new rank. I hereby give you the orders naming you to this post, bearing my signature and the Seal of Earth Government. Welcome to the ranks of the politicians, Madame Minister!"

The President's eyes had that teasing twinkle in them, all the more so in that Christina was taken completely by surprise by this latest honor and responsibility. Again the band played a fanfare, which gave her time to phrase a double message of gratitude for the high honors that had just been bestowed on her.

———

"We are prepared, Christina, to meet your guests from outer space. Our people are eager to meet these creatures of God, who by their very presence betoken the great power and wisdom of the Creator. It is our hope that, like you, they will visit with us often, and become cherished friends."

"Mihály, I'm so happy about this news. You have seen how kind and intelligent and gentle the Damosians are. After the opening ceremonies, I will leave them in your hands for a week, which should give them enough time to appreciate at least some of what draws me constantly to Canaan."

"By a strange coincidence, or perhaps by a decree of Divine Providence, the appearance of the Damosians will take place on the very day we celebrate our Founding Day. We will incorporate their arrival in our midst into the service."

"This is an extraordinary honor, Mihály."

312

"This is an extraordinary occasion, Christina. And there will be yet another service following that, at the High Church in the Town Square. We have chosen a new Bishop, a man you know well: the Reverend Doctor Jeremiah Hormuz."

"A triple play! And a wonderful choice from my point of view, a man who believes intensely in his ministry, and like so many of the Bishops I have had the pleasure of knowing, someone not rigidly doctrinaire. If he were doctrinaire, he would never have befriended someone like me!"

"His investiture will take place, as I said, in the High Church. The Church Council has authorized me to invite you to the ceremony–exceptionally, because normally only the faithful are permitted to attend such a ceremony, and the high officials of Mars Government."

"I am deeply honored by this kind gesture, and I shall be there. How should I be dressed for the occasion?"

"Why, in your Admiral's dress uniform! We wouldn't have it any other way!"

———

"Well, here you are together again! What on Mars do you talk about all the time?"

"Christina, don't scold us. Remember that Ecnelav and I are both astrophysicists. Well, she is by profession, and I am by dilletantism."

"Det is being very modest. The work he's accomplished here on Mars, the skills he's developed over the years, the knowledge he's gained by his work on problems with the space stations and the three habitable planets in your solar system, not to mention the time he spent on Mesnos, if all that doesn't qualify him as an astrophysicist, what does?"

"I think I'm more of an astroengineer than an astrophysicist. But, no matter. What do we talk about? A small space station, or at least a satellite relay station, in the Damos and Unias orbit, halfway between the two planets..."

"That would be 183,847,760 kilometers from each planet..."

"meaning that a signal from one planet could be relayed

regularly from Damos to Unias or back without interference. The problem is that the signal would have to be sent 367,695,520 kilometers, more or less, to be received."

"And, at the speed of light, it would take a lot of time to reach its destination. It's bad enough when we send signals from Earth to Venus or Mars; conversation is not possible."

"That's over 20 minutes each way, more than 40 minutes for a question and response."

"Det thinks there are three things we can do: once the station or satellite is in place, we would have to accept the fact that communication (while infinitely faster than what we have now),..."

"You scientists! You don't mean 'infinitely' literally, do you?"

"Oh, Christina, stop joking. We're being serious..."

"For once, I see."

"OK, for once. We'd just have to accept the fact that communication would take a long time. Even from the space station to Damos would require 10 minutes each way."

"Yes, but while we were working under those conditions, we would be able to do two things: study the galaxy and the extra-galactic objects from a place with no atmospheric interference, and work on ways to send messages more rapidly."

"Det has come up with two ideas, which our government will gladly sponsor, I'm sure: applying the principles of warp drive to stationary objects (planet and space station), and trying to see if it's possible to somehow package the electrical messages sent into quanta."

"Into quanta! Why, if you succeed in that, we could apply the principles to the new space ship being designed right now."

"Christina, both of these methods could be of use for the Earth Government, too. With an adaptation of warp drive, imagine how much easier and faster it would be to communicate with Mesnos and Paracelsus, Mars and Venus, Damos and Unias and the Tertia Twins! Certainly faster than we can manage now. And if the quantum signal works, communication would be instantaneous."

"Actually, Christina, thanks to the quantum teleportation,

we've already made a step in that direction. This idea is feasible."

"Amazing stuff! So you've actually been working all this time! Seriously, I think the Earth Government would be interested in sponsoring this research, too."

"Christina, we've already made a major presentation to them. We're waiting for a decision."

"What exactly are you proposing?"

"Let me answer, Det. We're proposing that Earth Government send back with Constellation the basic technology for a small station–maybe even a complete tiny laboratory that could be utilized while the space station was being assembled–so that work could begin virtually immediately. The value of this to Damos is obvious. But Earth would acquire a knowledge of the galaxy that would be impossible otherwise; and the technology developed in the course of this project's life would also be shared by our two civilizations."

"How come the Minister of Galactic Affairs has been kept in the dark about this project? She might be upset, you know. You'd be walking on her toes."

"We wanted to surprise you, and we asked Earth Government officials to keep it as secret as the law allows."

"Which, in this kind of matter, is totally secret," mused Christina. "When do you expect to have an answer?"

Kwali popped his head in the room at this moment, and announced that the Secretary of Space Programs was on his way to Mars, and should arrive in an hour or so.

"When you bring the Secretary in, stay with us, Kwali. If he's coming himself, he's likely to be bringing good news, news that I'm sure will excite you."

———

"And so, in short, Ambassador Enohr and Dr. Stisreg's proposal has the complete support of the Department, and in fact as we are speaking work is beginning on a small station that can be transported in Constellation. Plans for a larger station, much smaller than the huge stations we have here but about half the size of Constellation, including all technical details, will be given to the Ambassador and to the Director of Galactic

315

Research. Oh, damn, I wasn't supposed to leak out this title, which will be Dr. Stisreg's."

"Det, how great!" shouted Christina, Ecnelav and Kwali at the same time.

"I've let the cat out of the bag, but don't let anyone else know about this. Dr. Stisreg will receive an invitation to present his case once again, along with Dr. Enohr, at which time the surprise announcement will be made."

"Our lips are sealed concerning the great news about Det's appointment, Mr. Secretary. When may I share the news about the project with my crew?"

"Oh, we have prepared a public announcement of this project, Madam Minister, which will be released publicly on all our planets. We are hoping that you will agree to read it."

"I'll be happy to make that my first official act."

"It's a day of firsts! This will be the first planned act of intragalactic cooperation that we've ever done. Of course, we know about the cooperative efforts taking place on Unias right now and that had taken place on Damos. But we're entering into a new era, one in which we show our mutual trust in concrete ways. Naturally, we're counting on the Ambassador's and the Minister's ability to persuade the Damosians to join in."

"You can count on Christina and me to do just that. Actually, it will be a soft sell. This is a wonderful opportunity for us."

"Just think, if you succeed in the quantum aspect of the project, we might someday be able to travel intantaneously across the galaxy, and even beyond! I hope I live long enough to see that day arrive."

"We'll do our best to make that possible, Mr. Secretary."

"Dr. Stisreg, you should receive your invitation by tomorrow. But please, when the President and the Scientific Council and the Cabinet offer you this post, please act surprised."

"You can count on that."

"Each of you is permitted to bring five guests into the chamber, which is really a fairly small room. But Ambassador, make sure all of your people are on hand; we can arrange to have them see the ceremony on a huge visuscreen. We're planning a great gala: formal ceremonial announcements, state dinner, a three-day party. And Admiral, Space Fleet will make all the arrangements for your staff and crew. We expect that Constellation will be completely ready to go by the end of the month. It will be only a question of the time it takes to construct the station and prepare the various documents I've spoken about, and for our Damosian friends to complete their visits here. Part of your orders will include a stopover on Mesnos, as you know."

"We are stupefied by the swift response, Mr. Secretary, and thrilled by the possibilities that are opening up to us. Thank you very much for your part in the process, which I'm sure has been great."

"The presentation and the plan and the presenters themselves were all you needed, Dr. Stisreg. But I appreciate your feelings. Now I must be off. I have to visit Ares, various sites around the planet, then return to Earth to help prepare the ceremonies. I'll see you in about two weeks."

"And we understand that mum's the word."

EPILOGUE: THE QUANTUM GALAXY

"Prepare the fractal chart, Lieutenant."

"Already done, sir. I've set the coordinates at the spot on the Eastern Arm that you indicated, in the vicinity of Chromos."

"You have a quizzical look on your face, Lieutenant."

"Well, I've seen Damosians from a distance, and I know that we have a good number of them on board. But I've never really learned anything about their solar system and their planet, or the other life forms that have evolved there."

"Colombina has prepared a program, with a selection of visuclips of the fauna and flora of the planets Damos and Unias. You'll be able to examine them at your leisure later. But honestly, I thought everybody at Space Academy learned about Damos as thoroughly as they learn about Mesnos and Paracelsus. Where were you during those sessions, Lieutenant Laplante?"

"I must have been playing hooky those days, or more likely went to the lab to work more on the math I needed to pass my navigator's exam," he replied, a hint of a blush in his cheeks.

Christina looked at him, shook her head, and muttered something to the effect that there's more to life than crunching numbers. Then, abruptly, she added, "We'll get back to that later, Lieutenant. Captain, are all members of the crew aboard?"

"Yes, sir, all accounted for."

"What about the passengers?"

"The passengers are also all aboard, and eager to take off."

"Begin the final count-down, Captain. Lieutenant, how close will we be to Chromos?"

"If everything works properly, sir, about half a light year."

"IF... Do you have any reason to doubt?"

"Just natural caution. This is, after all, only the second time a ship like Argos has ever gone any distance greater than 10 or 20 light years. And I wasn't the navigator on the first trip."

"Is the warp drive ready for use when we reach our destination, Captain?"

"As warm as your morning coffee."

Christina Vasa had been in the service a long time. She had

been a crew member on the first warp-drive ship, the Constellation, back in the twenty-sixth century. Did the same job that Kwali was doing now. She'd known him for over two lifespans, that is, ordinary lifespans. She knew, and he knew, that his life would not last much longer; it could not be extended longer, as hers had been back around 2800, on Mars. In fact, extended lifespans and the Extended Life Brigade itself had become obsolete with the new drive, as Det had suspected long ago. Back then, when she was freshly promoted to the rank of Commander,... well, it seemed so long ago, those 375 years. Heck, it **was** a long time ago. Three full lifespans. So many things had happened over the centuries, and she felt sure that the next several hundred years would present new challenges. What new technologies would replace this latest, this magnificent achievement of human ingenuity, this quantum-drive space craft she commanded? No time to think about that now. Count-down is almost over.

"Three...two...one... Displace!" said the friendly and familiar voice of Colombina, the powerful computer that sometimes seemed to be the Admiral's alter ego. Christina had made sure that Colombina was upgraded and moved to Argos from Constellation II a year ago. Colombina now knew everything she could know about this ship. She loved it, reveled in it.

Lieutenant Laplante looked at Christina, an air of puzzlement in his face. Despite the execution of her command, he hadn't noticed any movement at all. Did something go wrong? It was with some hesitation that he said, "According to my monitor, we've arrived, sir; right on the button."

"Let's take a look at the stars. Oh, look up there! Great job of navigating, Jacques!" Christina bubbled with joy. "We're on the Eastern Arm! Look, there's the constellation Giniew the Hunter!" The flight deck was elated. No more worm-holes from here on out! How could anything be easier than this? It's like driving down the street in your air-car! But this isn't a street, and this isn't an air-car. It's transgalactic travel and this is a space ship the size of a small town. And this isn't a pleasure cruise: the business of space travel is serious, and there is, as always, a lot

320

to do.

Lieutenant Jacques Laplante was proud of his knowledge of computers and of his navigational skills. Still, he had had only one previous run in a quantum-drive ship before, a relatively brief hop across the galactic dust, to the fringes of the central sphere. It all seemed so easy to the casual observer–or it would have seemed easy if there had been a casual observer on the deck. It was much more complex and tricky to set up than the warp drive, and God knows that's complicated enough! It took him the better part of a month to get his coordinates right. You have to set up separate coordinates for Argos itself, and for large pieces of equipment, and for other inorganic matter, and for living beings, and so on. It takes a lot of planning and a lot of checking. A single error could be disastrous.

Jacques was comparing the position of Argos in the real world and its projected position on his fractal chart. Perfect coincidence. He was positively beaming. It worked!

"Colombina, have you saved all the data? I'd hate to have to do all this over from scratch on the next flight out from Earth."

"Yes, Jacques," hummed Colombina, who addressed everyone by their first name. "Don't worry; I've charted the return to Earth from this point, too."

"You think of everything. Thank you, you're a doll!"

"While I am not a toy, I believe you mean that as a compliment, and I accept it as such."

The flight deck crew smiled at Colombina's literal-mindedness. Then Christina turned to her old friend Kwali and said, "Captain, do you think the crew and the passengers would like to see the dense and quite alien sky of the Eastern Arm before we proceed to our first destination?"

"Yes, sir. Do you want to make the announcement?"

"No, Kwali, you deserve that honor." It is true that Kwali was a great colleague and a great friend. And a damn hard worker, who knew every detail of his job, and kept learning more. He'd turned down the command of Constellation II in order to continue working with Christina. Space Fleet promoted him to the rank of Captain, with the understanding that he would be Christina's deputy as long as he chose to fly with her, and get his own ship to command any time he wanted it.

Christina trusted him implicitly, and respected his talents, his insights, his skill in delicate personnel matters. He had grown so much over the past 100 or so years!

"Attention, all passengers and crew. This is Captain Kwali Kwambe speaking. I know it may be hard to believe, but we have displaced across the galaxy to the Eastern Arm. Have a look at star systems you've never even imagined before! What beauty! How I wish, at times like this, that I were a poet!" His voice trailed off, as it usually did when he was deeply moved. Christina smiled at him. What an old softy!

One look at the open windows and the monitors, and a huge cheer went up throughout the craft. Argos was filled with happy noises!

"I often wonder what the Militia, or for that matter the STU, would think if they could see the spirit of cooperation that unites our two peoples," said Kwali, quietly. "And what would your friends, the Ancient-Day Primitivists, think if they could see this sky?"

"There were times I really thought the Militia would take over the Earth!" she whispered in reply. "And how close I came to dying, more than once, because of them, in encounters and battles with them, even in court cases! Boris, you can smile now, if there is a you out there somewhere and if you can see what's happening here! And Martin, you saved me twice from death, once at the hands of the Militia, and then at the hands of the STU. I wish I could share this moment with you. And Stanley, my mentor, my old friend, you would be here today were it not for a coward's action on that fatal day."

Then she brushed away a tear and said in her more official voice, "Captain, we'd better announce that we'll begin the warp-drive portion of our voyage now, so everyone will get prepared. Please let Damos and Unias know where we are, and tell the Damosians we'll be on the mother planet in about three months, after we accomplish our missions on Tertia Minor and Unias. And tell President Mbwani on Unias that we expect to see him in about two weeks. Ask him to let Dr. Stisreg, our Director of Galactic Research, know that thanks to the ground-breaking work that he and our much-regretted friend, Dr. Ecnelav Enohr, accomplished a few decades ago, we have been able to traverse the galaxy faster than the blink of an eye."

"Yes, sir. I'll take care of all those details as soon as the initial shock of warp speed is over."

"Warp drive ready, sir."

Jacques hardly needed to tell her. Even in this giant ship, the faint rumble of the great warp drives could be... well, *sensed*, not exactly heard, not exactly felt.

"On to Tertia Minor, Lieutenant."

ABOUT THE AUTHOR

Brooklyn-born author Theodore Braun holds a Ph.D. in Romance Languages and Literatures from the University of California at Berkeley. He is currently a professor of French and Comparative Literature at the University of Delaware, where he teaches a course on Literature, Science, and Technology. His research interests include the author Voltaire (author of a science-fiction novela, *Micromégas*, 1752) and chaos theory. He has been interested in astronomy and evolutionary biology for virtually all his life. *Six Suns, Ten Planets, One Woman* combines his vocation and his avocation, his deep love of literature and his keen interest in science, his experience in research and his creative imagination.

Braun lives in Newark, Delaware with his wife. He is grateful to have a daughter as interested in science and fiction as he is, and whose critiques have proven to be invaluable.